THE WEATHERMAN

A Novel by

BULL MARQUETTE

BRAVE NEW GENRE, INC.

Fresno, CA

BRAVE NEW GENRE, INC.
Publishers of Books, Music & Films
6535 N Palm Ave. #101
Fresno, CA 93704
www.bravenewgenre.com

The Weatherman
© 2010 by Marshall Patrick Smith

Library of Congress Control Number: 2010928108

Marquette, Bull
The Weatherman/Bull Marquette
ISBN 978-0-9820474-3-9

1. Thriller—Fiction 2. Paranormal—Fiction
3. Time Travel—Fiction 4. Tornados—Fiction
5. Weather—Fiction

For Sheilah

Also by Bull Marquette:
THE FIFTH PLANE, *a novel*

GOT 8 IF YOU WANT 'EM,
The first short story collection by Bull Marquette

Available through bookstores or online through
www.bravenewgenre.com.

Print-On-Demand, first release: August 2010

The Cuban Missile Crisis was a hoax…

Sironia, Texas
October, 1962

Chapter 1
Andrea Wiggins

The Cuban Missile Crisis was a hoax.

Young people today might not understand what the big deal was – that skirmish in the Atlantic Ocean in the autumn of 1962 doesn't even rate a full chapter in modern history books that spend more time on famous people's sexual persuasions than they do talking about the most frightening few weeks of the Cold War, a war that lasted fifty years.

For two or three weeks that October, just as the weather was starting to turn in Central Texas, we, and everyone in America, and also in Russia for that matter, lived under the threat of immediate nuclear war.

Sure, we went about our daily lives, but the pressure was building. We could hear it in the voices of the news guys on the radio, and the worried looks those same trusted heralds wore when we saw them on that still-new invention, the television screen. It was the only talk at cocktail parties, though Andrea never let me go to cocktail parties.

Hell, the whole world was terrified, because nuclear radiation doesn't go away so quickly. If Russia and America let go with every nuke they had, it would put enough plutonium up into the air to kill people in all the other countries, too.

The threat was tangible to us – just the winter before, we had been warned to quit making snow ice cream – though Sironia got snow only once or twice a year – because American and French nuclear bomb tests in the Pacific were filling the` upper atmosphere with radiation. It would be like that movie, *On the Beach*, which came out a couple of years before – the world's population dies, except Australia, and them, too, after a few months.

Scary photos on TV showed Soviet missiles being hoisted into position in Cuba, only ten minutes away (as the crow rockets) from our nation's capital. Everyone knew what that meant. We were going to have to attack Cuba, and wipe those missiles out. And even if we did, it was likely the hot-headed Russians who commanded the weapons would have time to shoot off at least one of their monsters. This was it. The fabled, feared nuclear war was finally going to happen.

All we could do was wait, and hope that our young president, who had once commanded a Navy crew in World War II, wasn't about to let our nation suffer the same fate that his PT boat had endured – it was sunk.

The Texas summer ended with a couple of weak cool fronts, then came back with a vengeance, and hot air in October hurts worse than the July variety. When the Crisis first began, I couldn't really focus on the scary details, since I was in my last weeks of the patrolman's course in the Sironia Police Academy. I was also engaged to Andrea Wiggins, who had a talent for ignoring world events entirely, because, by God, she was going to fashion the perfect wedding, because her future in the Hedonia Club – indeed both of our futures in the mid-sized, serene city of Sironia, Texas – depended on it.

So, my days were filled with memorizing laws and citation forms and handgun varieties, and my nights were busy chauffeuring Andrea around town, looking at wedding dresses and place settings and knick-knacks she wanted to put in our register at Cox's Department Store.

"You're a stupid man, George Blair," Andrea said often, in her shrill way. "You quit Daddy right when a housing boom was getting started. How in Hades can I make it in society and you with just a policeman's salary?" She posed that question on a daily basis.

My desire to become a cop broke the Eleventh Commandment, in her mind. I had quit working for her father just the previous spring. He was an asshole, and overcharged on his projects, and shorted the materials on the houses he built whenever he could get away with it. It's a wonder that the homes in Ridgeview Acres, out by the lake, didn't fall down in the first windstorm. Yet, we were still engaged.

Then came that day – when the Missile Crisis became a real crisis for me. This was before I found out the whole thing was a charade.

That afternoon, we were on our way to my Police Academy graduation. I remember her waving that cheap Japanese fan in her parent's hot, humid Lincoln whose air conditioner barely made a dent in the sizzling Indian Summer afternoon. I was driving, as always.

"Andrea, I'm smart. You've always said so. I'll get promoted soon enough. We'll live a good life, take trips down to Corpus Christi, save our money and do all the good things you always planned for us," I assured her.

"Corpus Christi's a white trash dump," she said, crossed her arms and huddled against her side of the car. "Just because that dirty old marshal always told you to go to police school. Your father's dead, George, and Marshal Tup-ne-pup ain't no substitute. He's a washed-up old pipe-smoking lush, like every policeman or fireman gets to be before they die. You want to wind up like that? Oh, Lordy, am I doomed to do penance for your daddy dying in a car wreck when you were six?"

"Leave my father out of it, Andrea--"

"George, you may be quick to learn stuff, but you can't add. I don't want to be poor until I'm forty-five. And darn it to Hades if we're gonna live off my parents."

She always talked like that – like a storm puffing out huge clouds of pressure. I didn't like it, but I'd never really had any other girlfriend, and I guess I thought all women operated that way. I figured that was the way most guys who were about to get married felt – the same way a plump bass or crappie feels when it's in the process of being reeled in.

"I told you all summer." She started up again. "Take your pay, then throw in a raise for making sergeant, then lieutenant, then detective. How old are you by then?" She folded the fan and slapped my arm with it, her voice rising to a screech. "It won't be enough to buy a shack on Lasker Avenue until we're in our thirties, Blair."

"Shush," I said, and turned up the radio. An anxious reporter was talking about Cuba, nuclear missiles, imminent war.

"Just listen to that," I said, ignoring her bloated, red cheeks and trying to hold my own temper. "I may not even be a policeman this time next month. If war breaks out, they'll be drafting every able-bodied man."

"And I'll just bet you'd go, wouldn't you?" She sneered. "You don't even have the sense that Rusty Carter has."

"Who's Rusty Carter — you mean that plumber that came to your house last month?"

"He says there's ways out of a draft. Says they ain't going to haul him off to some *Cari-been* island to fight."

My stomach churned. "Now, how could he say that? Nobody knew about missiles in Cuba a month ago, did they? You been talking to him on the phone?"

Andrea ignored the question, and squinted her eyes slyly, the way she did when she had made a decision. I braced for the worst. "Army, Schmarmy. I'll tell you what you're going to do, George Blair – don't hit that car! Jeeminy, you scratch Daddy's wax finish and your first twelve paychecks will go straight to him. Never mind. You go ahead and have your little celebration today. Tomorrow morning, you're getting up early, and you're going to take a letter into that Marshal Tup-tuppence –"

"Marshal Tudberry?"

"Exactly right." She scooted across the bench seat and dug the fan in, right below my armpit. "If you're gonna ruin your life because of that dirty old man, then the least he can do is to throw you a bone, if he's so high and mighty." She poised her fan for the *coup de gras*. "You're going to write Marshal Turnbull a request to be hired as his deputy."

"His name is *Tudberry*, for the thousandth time, and I would have to be a cop on the beat for ten years, a minimum of five, even to be considered for a federal job."

"That shows you have no grasp of business concepts, Blair." She huffed, and scooted back to her own side of the car. "What good is knowing somebody if you can't use a little influence? Grow up. You're gonna get ahead in life, if I have to drag you kicking and screaming."

My head was swimming, as it always did when Andrea threw one of her fits. I remember turning off of River Bridge, and following the winding road along the Brazos, until the Police gym came into view. She had our lives planned out – completely – but my idea of a comfortable retirement many years from now was different than whatever she had in her master-blueprint.

There was no way I could tell her about the fishing cabin on Lake Whitney, the one I dreamed of – or the winter hunting trips to South Texas – both ideas I had also inherited from Marshal Tudberry. At that moment, driving that borrowed Lincoln, and facing either nuclear annihilation or a life with Andrea, that fishing cabin sounded better than ever.

Bleachers had been set up on one side of the parking lot that we used for a parade ground and shooting course. Out in the middle, my classmates looked like cops, clad in newly pressed uniforms, kibitzing around with their families. Some even looked older at first glance, as if their new career had already claimed them. A few were married already. Others, like me, were spoken for. In the years ahead, some of these fresh faces would likely die in the line of duty, shot by a burglar, maybe, or wind up in a deadly wreck with a drunk driver. Or maybe we would all be climbing onto a troop ship in Florida a couple of months from now. The autumn air sizzled with possibilities, but who could know what the future held? Only Andrea, it seemed.

"It's too danged hot. My hair's frizzing up," she complained as we stepped onto the pavement. But she pasted a smile on her face, like the budding socialite she was, and, arm-in-arm, as the Sironia High Marching Band started tuning up, we waded through the crowd of milling cadets, and into the future.

I took a deep breath. I was embarking on a new career. That was the only way I could explain the pregnant, steamy apprehension that muddled my mind. How was I to know that the frantic voices on the radio were worried about something unreal? How could I know that the real future was somehow already set in place – and that I, George Blair, was the one who had set that future into motion?

Andrea Wiggins was the love of my life – up to that point. I could not have imagined that there, on the hot pavement of an Indian Summer afternoon, Andrea the imp, the blowhard, the harpy, the soft idealist, the child in a ferocious woman's body was beginning her swan-song-act in my life. Her last real scenes. And she would play it like the virtuoso that she was.

The Cuban Missile Crisis was a hoax.

It is left to me to reveal that truth for the record. Because, after these many decades of hiding from the FBI, the CIA, the whole U.S. government, my days on this Earth are dwindling down to just a few. And if I don't tell what really happened, then no one else will.

I know the reader's logical objection: it could never be a hoax unless the United States and the U.S.S.R. acted in collusion to fabricate the most horrifying little play of their own – the stuff of conspiracy theories, right?

But that's exactly what happened.

Two things I have learned over all these years:

The first: some secrets CAN be kept. Some conspiracies sustain, even when thousands, maybe even millions of players are involved.

The second undeniable fact: Life was slow and easy for me up until that afternoon. Then time sped up, and nothing was ever the same again …

Chapter 2
Victor

Perhaps Andrea was right. Marshal Homer Tudberry is
the one who got me into this mess. As I stood there in my crisp
cotton-wool police uniform, sweating like a pig in the Texas
sun, wondering if we might glance up to see sleek, dangerous
projectiles coursing through the scattered clouds, I had no
hope that my fiancé would forget her demand that I write the
old lawman a letter. Once she created a new hoop for me to
jump through, she held it up until I jumped.

To hell with her theory, I wanted to yell out loud. No
one could replace my father. Not even my grandfather, whose
main contribution to my upbringing was love, and his eternal
dictum: that hard work was all that counts in life.

Chief Lafferty droned on and on through his bullhorn,
the cadets sweated, a cheer went up, and I threw my hat in the
air with the rest of them. It took a good five minutes,
grappling in a melee of new, naïve cops, before I found the hat
with my name in it. By the time I escaped to the fringe of the
crowd, Andrea was standing with her mother and father.

"George, you do look smart in a uniform." Mrs.
Wiggins was always a dear, meek little woman. She leaned up
and kissed my cheek. "Charles won me over in an army

uniform, didn't you, Charlie? That's the last time I ever saw him so neat and clean." She laughed.

Mr. Wiggins only looked more wry and sullen than ever. "That's a wonder, after all the horse manure I shoveled at VMI." He extended his hand. "No hard feelings, George. I just wish you were still with us. This missile crisis is a gold mine. We got twelve more orders for bomb shelters this week alone."

"Thank you, sir," I said. "I didn't realize the company built bomb shelters."

"Oh, hell, we never did. But we do now."

"It don't matter," Andrea said, jerking on my lapel, straightening my tie and slapping at dirt on my service coat that I couldn't see. "Daddy can build anything. That's what he was going to teach you if you had stuck around, George. But this is as good a time as any to tell Daddy how you're going to get ahead by calling the U.S. Marshal tomorrow."

"Andrea--"

Billy Freedman and Dirk Polk crowded up behind her, arm-in-arm. It was a good bet the both of them had killed a six-pack before the ceremony.

"Hey, George," Dirk yelled over the noise of the milling crowd. "You gonna meet us over at Perkins' house later?" To my horror, he pantomimed turning a bottle upside down and emptying it into his mouth.

"Well, --" I started to fake an answer, but he had blown it.

"He most certainly is not," Andrea bellowed. She wrapped her arm around me. "My man's spending his last night of freedom going to dinner with his new family. He's getting up early, going to work on time, and he'll sail past you boys and be the biggest lawman in Central Texas."

"Andrea--" I tried to shoot them a look. "Perkins' place, eh? I guess I'll be too busy. Maybe some other time--"

"Nonsense," Billy yelled, acting like he was cocking and shooting a rifle into the sky. "Get drunk today. They launch the missiles tomorrow."

They both started guffawing, and thank God they had the sense to head the other way. Mr. Wiggins was choking down his own laughter, but Andrea was up in my ear. "You're not going over there, George. You're a family man, now."

Then she smiled, and put one arm through mine, and the other around her father's waist. "Come on. Daddy. Where we gonna eat?"

There is a God, I guess, because a full meal seemed to tame my fiancé's suspicions, and she let me leave their house at eight, saying something about getting her hair done early the next morning. I got to my apartment, and made a few phone calls. It seems the party at Perkins' had played out – but before I knew it, six of my fellow rookies were lounging on my couch and kitchen chairs, rifling through my record collection and filling the coffee table with dead soldiers – empty beer bottles.

"Well, hell, I guess we gotta get up and actually go to work," Hank Pierce said as the conversation started to lag.

"Oh, quit moaning." Billy scolded him. "Driving a beat, even walking one ain't nowhere as bad as hitting those books. I've read more books in these last six weeks than I did through all of high school."

Hank sneered. "Hell, you only finished half of high school, Fish."

"Won't be walking any beats, sounds like," Dirk said glumly. That brought a few tired ears to attention.

"What's that?" I said.

Dirk shrugged. "Chief says we may be put into riot training right off. If them Russkies don't take those nukes out of Cuba, the government's on the lookout for people going crazy in the streets."

"Hell, Kennedy's dumb, but he ain't that dumb," one of the others said.

Hank scowled. "And what the hell's riot training? We gonna have to stand downtown and knock our own cousins over the head?"

"You know," Pulver said, standing up and drawing a diagram with his hands in the air, "if they launch a missile from Cuba, it can hit Florida in five minutes, Washington D.C. in fifteen, and Texas in twenty."

"Who gives a damn? We'll just shoot back," Billy said.

"Yeah, we'll shoot back, but we'll be dead."

Hank made an ugly noise, and opened my front door with such a sudden movement that we all stood up. I jumped when the phone rang in the very next instant.

They razzed me in unison. I think it was Billy who cried out, "Holy shit, it's your future ball and chain."

"Ahoy, Mama's callin'," someone else said, and they stopped at the door while I shook my fist at them.

"Damn it, boys, I gotta answer, so shut up." They were already filing out the door. But not fast enough. "Hello?" I said.

Of course it was she. "Lucky for you that you answered, Blair. Something told me you went back out to carouse with those low-lifes."

"Andrea, it's late."

"Blair, are you slurring your words?"

"Andrea, you woke me up," I lied.

"He's sleep-walking," Dirk cried out. The remaining clowns doubled over, laughing. I motioned frantically, waving them the hell out, but I started giggling, too, in spite of myself.

"Blair, who is that? Who's there with you?"

"Nobody," I insisted. "I have the TV on too loud."

"Well, what the heck is on at this time of night? Jack Paar?"

"Yes," I said. "I'm watching Jack Paar."

Pierce's face acquired a stricken look.

"Paar just quit," Billy whispered.

"No." I scrambled. "Not him. That new guy on the Tonight Show."

Now they were falling all over themselves, falling back, banging the door, and I buried the receiver in my stomach, but I could still hear her voice.

"My God, Blair, shut the dang TV off and put your letter in an envelope."

The door slammed behind them. Loud, my brain too jostled to track. "What letter?"

I could hear her exhale. The way she did before she let someone have it. "Don't tell me you didn't write the letter before you nodded off, George. You know darn well what letter. I'm trying to help, or would you rather have some little floozy who lets everything go, like white trash, and you'd never get anywhere? Not anywhere, George. What does it take to teach you that you have to call in your favors sooner or later?"

"What favors, Andrea? I never did the marshal a favor. If anything, he did me favors, at least for Grandpa. He even donated for my summer camp that year--"

"Blair. My first wedding shower is one month away. I am not going to sit there getting expensive presents and then have somebody like Missy Baird smart off in the middle of it and ask me 'Didn't I see George walking a beat on Lamar Avenue?' By gosh, I'll be a laughing stock."

Silence. The mixture of beer and Andrea's shrill voice had paralyzed my brain.

"And that's *not* going to happen, now, is it George? I'm calling back in twenty minutes. You better have your pajamas on and you better have that letter written, because you're going to read it to me." The line cut off with a ringing echo.

I couldn't move. The empty bottles stood before me, a miniature city of brown, spent skyscrapers on the coffee table. I reminded myself how good and personable Andrea had been back in high school when we first started dating. How much mother liked her, so much so that my mom's dying wish was that I take care of Andrea for the rest of my life.

"She needs you, George," Mom had whispered through her pain, looking at me with those clear blue eyes.

I picked up beer bottles, composing that stupid letter in my head, with no thought of rebellion, or concept of getting Andrea out of my life, even that many years after I took that vow. But a knock came on my door at that moment, so loud, it almost lifted me out of my skin.

"Hey, guys, keep it down --" I was really fed up with them now, but when I opened the door, it wasn't my cadet comrades, but a gray-haired Mexican man, dressed up in full Old Mexico regalia – sombrero, multi-colored poncho, crisp shirt and bolo tie. He looked almost clownish, and my first instinct was to slam the door on in his face, but he held out something to me – a sealed envelope.

"What is this?" I said, putting an edge in my voice.

The *caballero* was all smiles. *"Buenos Noches, Señor,"* he said. "You are Mister George Blair?"

"Yes, but it's late. I don't want to buy anything--"

He removed his huge hat revealing a full shock of salt-and-pepper, not just gray, well-combed and greased, and held the sombrero in front of himself. "My name is Victor, Señor. I can't believe it. You are really Mr. George Blair. I have seen pictures – *pardon --*," He actually giggled, and shoved the letter into my hand. "A message for you. *Muy importante.*"

My heart was pounding, but the smiling man seemed harmless enough. I ripped the letter from the envelope, but he started reciting the message before I could even look at the words.

"A message from Marshal Tudberry, Seňor. He wants you at his office first thing in the morning. Six a.m. And please use the back stairs. He does not wish for you to be seen by any of the deputies. *Comprende*?"

I looked at him. Then read the whole page again for myself. It looked real enough, on official stationary, with some sort of embossed seal down by the marshal's signature.

"Sir, it is an honor to finally meet you." His hand came forward, and shook mine. I didn't know what that meant, and didn't care, for the truth was finally dawning on me. I read it again.

"My god--" My voice started as a whisper, but there could be no mistaking what this was. "Mister – Victor, or whatever your name is – did Andrea put you up to this?" I asked, and looked up again.

Victor was gone.

I finished stuffing all evidence of a party into the trash barrel, and sat down beside the phone. When Andrea called, I would play dumb, I resolved. Give her some rope, and see if she hung herself. If she had already contacted the marshal, it would mark a new milestone of interference – even for her. If she was that determined to run every little part of my life, I might just have to break this whole engagement off, even if Mom didn't approve from her heavenly perch.

That was the first time I ever met Victor. Whenever I recall that night, I wish I had been more attentive, more polite –Victor was the great pillar around which the crazy events of that October were built, you see. But all that will come out as I tell the story. In the moment, I could only think of how I might make Andrea pay for being such a busybody.

Chapter 3
Homer Tudberry

It was a first, but Andrea didn't call me back at the threatened time. I didn't realize that lapse until I jolted awake, hanging half-off the couch at five-ten in the morning. That proved her guilt, I groggily concluded. She had gotten to the marshal before I did, and there was no telling what sort of hogwash she had subjected him to. Why else would he send that bodacious old Mexican man as a midnight messenger?

I felt emasculated. But there were only thirty minutes left to clean up and get to his office, so I waited until I was in the car before I started plotting my revenge. As I did, the diabolical nature of the way she had controlled me for the last six to seven years began to dawn on me.

Nevertheless, I played the part. My knees knocked as I climbed the back stairs of the old Federal building. The door that bore the marshal's name stood wide open, and when I crossed the creaky wooden floor of his outer office, I could easily see through to where his bulky form reclined back in a chair, feet propped up, face hidden behind the sports section of the paper.

"You know, George," he began, though the paper never moved, and he couldn't possibly have seen me yet, "for the first time in my life, Sironia State's football team is ranked first in the nation. Their aerial attack is dynamite."

"Yes, sir."

He folded the paper, laid his coffee mug down, and fixed me with a somber look. "It's a crying shame it all has to go to hell."

I chuckled. "Don't be pessimistic, Marshal. Aren't they playing Ole Miss this weekend?"

"That's right." He stared at the ceiling, finishing his thought in a sort of sigh, "But you can't catch passes in the pouring rain..."

"It's supposed to rain this weekend?"

A look, sly and dark. I had never seen him that way before. "The forecast says clear and sunny." A deep breath. "But only a fool takes a weather forecast to the bank."

I caught myself squirming. He would expect my sales pitch now. The reasons to hire me, and all that stuff that Andrea had probably already saturated him with. Hell, she might even have told him tales of her father's limitless bank account – a myth I had uncovered during my first week of doing his books. I determined to avoid the subject of Andrea altogether. I was a cop now, and I tried to sound worldly. "The way this Cuba thing is heating up, maybe nobody will be thinking about football this weekend, anyway."

He laughed, whatever spell had seized him was broken, and he squeaked back in his chair and lit a cigarette. "I can't believe it's little George Blair. Coffee?"

"I don't think I can handle more than one cup, and I've already had some instant."

"Good for you. Moderation. Coffee'll kill you. Just like these damned weeds."

I had composed a speech to thank him for all he had done over the years, but it lodged in my throat. I couldn't begin to guess how to play this – was I supposed to know that my girlfriend had set this up?

"I think it's interesting that you would bring up this crisis about the missiles, George." His eyes became slits, and the spell returned. "'Cause that's pretty much why I asked you up here--"

"Sir, if my fiancé--"

"Miss Wiggins, isn't it? Boy, does she seem like a handful. Ain't she?"

"Yes, sir. I mean, Sir?"

He sat forward. "How would you like to come to work for me, George?" he said. Flat out, just like that.

I gasped. The goal of every academy grunt was to survive long enough to get a shot at the highway patrol, the FBI, or the marshal's office, even – if your career wore diamond studs – the holy Texas Rangers. Here it was happening to me without a single day on the job. But he still hadn't answered whether she was behind it.

"That would be fantastic, sir. I can't think of a better way to do my duty and serve the people."

His eyebrows went up, and he puffed his cigarette and grinned. "I thought you would say that. I had you pegged, George, from when you were in diapers, believe it or not. I'll call Chief Lafferty and clear it all this weekend. I'll tell him I gave you a verbal test, you know, just for grins, but that you flunked it so badly, I felt duty-bound to recommend he rescind your passing grade at the academy."

All the air rushed out of my lungs – I blinked, waiting, hoping for the punch line – for him to finish whatever awful joke he was telling. It was the strangest mood I had ever witnessed – especially for this man whom my grandfather always respected – until the truth came to me in a terrible rush from my gut: Andrea had insulted him, enough to destroy a friendship that was almost as old as I was.

I tried to smile, but those old gray eyes of his seemed deadly serious.

"I don't understand. You want him to flunk me out of police school?" My lips were quivering. "Marshal, Andrea – I don't know if she called you – or what she might have said --"

His words boomed out in a storm of smoke. "Why you keep talkin' 'bout your girlfriend, Boy? The chance of a lifetime is beatin' down your door, and you can become part of history." His voice became something of a snarl as he leaned farther over the desk. "You afraid of your little precious thinking you flunked? Fine. I want her to think you flunked. She's a goddam megaphone, ain't she? I want everybody in this damned town to think you flunked. This is Sironia, George. Word gets around fast."

"But Marshal, why? If I'm washed out of the academy, how can you hire me at all?"

By reflex, maybe, I glanced at my watch. I was due at the central police station at seven-thirty. "Marshal, please tell me. Did my girlfriend Andrea ask you for any favors? Because I never told her to --"

Finally a smile, and his raised hand kept me from finishing. "Simmer down, son. You ain't let me do enough talkin' to sketch out the plan. A deputy marshal has to be able to listen. That's your stock in trade. And your other trade is acting, ain't it? Remember how I never missed one of your drama plays back in high school? You're a pretty damned fair actor, if you ask me."

"No," I said, and couldn't hold it any longer. "Dammit, Marshal, tell me what you're talking about. What does acting have to do with police work?"

Now he got up, and lugged his paunch around the desk, eyes all coyote-like. "A hell of a lot, George. You see, there's a big game afoot. A crime in the making. Maybe the biggest crime in history since the Savior was nailed to the cross."

He let that sink in for a moment, and brought his face close to mine. A cloud of coffee and cigarette smells came with it. "In about thirty minutes these old offices are going to wake up. All federal agents and employees. People I've worked with for years. And there's not a one of them I can trust. What do you think about that?"

When in doubt, swallow your ego and keep it simple. My grandfather told me that. Or maybe it was Tudberry. "Well if you can't trust them, Marshal, why don't you fire them?"

"Ha!" He laughed out loud. "Good answer, George. That's why I always liked you. Quick as a whip." He flicked his cigarette and leaned in again.

"There's a war on, George. With spies everywhere. Even in this building."

"What war? My God, did Cuba attack last night?"

He held up the front page of the Sironia Gazette. "They ain't gonna attack, George. This thing in Cuba is a fake. The real war is brewing right here in Sironia."

I fell back in my chair, and finally relief flooded my being. This was a joke.

"Wipe that smirk off your face, son," he pressed. "This is top secret stuff I'm telling you: A rebel nation is being born just west of here. It's called the Republic of Balcones, and agents of this new renegade country have infiltrated every government office in Texas. So I can't assign any of my own men to this important detail. I simply don't know who to trust.

"That's why I need you to be in disgrace, George. You are going to work for me, and no one will suspect it. You are going undercover to discover the identity of the leader of the Balcones nation."

I met his eyes, and my heart quit decelerating, and kicked into an even higher gear. "What are you saying,

Marshal? The newspapers are lying? The reporters on national TV are telling the American people lies about Cuba? And what's this new country? Really? A new country? Why?"

The old man had always been a well of patience. Not now. "Listen, Boy, I don't have time to explain everything to you. They should have taught you at the Academy that a good cop doesn't sweat the politics, whether it's graft and corruption or a husband and wife taking shots at each other. All you need to know is that news reporters are liars by trade, and that President Kennedy and Nikita Khruschev are working together – that's right – and have placed A-bombs in Cuba as a flanking movement, in case these crazy Balcones boys start launching missiles."

He stood up, and loomed over me. "You see, George, these Balcones rebels have nukes, too."

There was no way that any of this was true. America was the greatest nation in the history of the world, and nothing like what he was talking about could happen. I wanted to lecture him on checks and balances, and the brilliance of our constitution, but my tongue was dry in my mouth, and I was shaking.

He ambled back around the desk, and plopped into his chair. "All the files on you are innocent enough, George. That shoplifting caper your friends pulled in high school – we know you weren't mixed up in it, even though you were spotted in the same store that day. But we'll have to use that, too. I'm putting around that I was mistaken about you, that you're little better than a ne'er-do-well."

Tears welled up in my eyes. "But why, Marshal? Why?"

He was the old man I knew again, gray eyes tired, full of compassion. He might not be that far from crying, himself. "Because I'm sending you into the belly of the beast, George. I'll get you a job working for the only man who we know to be mixed up with the Balcones hierarchy. He's their money man, and you're going to use your acting skills to play dumb, play innocent, and get into this man's confidence. Do it right, and he will lead you to the man we're really after: Mr. Big. The head honcho of this whole rebellion."

As if on cue, a faraway door slammed. The deputies, G-men and secretaries were coming to work. My heart was in my throat, and I barely eked out a question without blubbering. "But if you know their money man, why can't you just arrest him and torture him until he tells you the identity of this – Mr. Big?"

He laughed. "That's my boy. Logical as always. Too bad it's more complicated than that. The money man for the Balcones revolution is none other than Emil Cadwallader."

"Cadwallader? That rich guy? Wait. He owns Channel Three, doesn't he? And the Bevo Packing House?"

"Just be glad I didn't get you a job bolting cows, Son. We could arrest him, but we'd never hold him – he owns a piece of every judge in Texas. And even if we could, they'd just get another money man. Tycoons throughout all the western states are already chipping in. It's the western divisions of the U.S. Army that Cadwallader's bought off, in the name of this invisible leader. Funny, but it seems like half of the American forces are stationed in Texas, so this was the right place to start a rebellion like this."

He reached into his desk, and extracted a torn piece of paper and a twenty dollar bill. He shoved both into my hands. "Use that money for phone change. Call me from a pay phone every night, and tell me how you're doing. There's also the name of the man you're supposed to report to. You know where the Channel Three studios are?"

"Out on the Temple highway?"

"Right. Your contact's name is on that paper. He's the only person we still have on the inside. We sent two others in before, but they disappeared. Cadwallader plays for keeps."

He stood up. I did, too.

"That oughta tell you how real this is, George. You gotta work hard. And smart. But most of all, it's got to be fast. You've heard the news reports. The only truth they contain is that things are heating up. The Russkies are pushing Kennedy, and so are all the Pentagon types. We've got days, not weeks. We don't find Mr. Big by then, Washington will have to start shooting before Balcones does. I don't want to see Texas become a nuclear playground, do you?"

"No – no, sir."

His hand came forward. "Your country – hell, the world – is counting on you. Now get outta here, and make me proud, boy. If you meet somebody on those back stairs, you don't make eye contact. Is that clear?"

"Yes, sir."

"Three o'clock this afternoon. Be at the station, ready for a job interview." He shoved me toward the door. "Don't forget you're in disgrace, George. Play the part. And that little girlfriend of yours can never know what you're really doing."

But she will *find out,* I wanted to say. This was Sironia.

I descended the stairs on automatic pilot, still mesmerized by the strange, omnipotent, desperate look in that old sage's eyes.

That odd Mexican man, Victor, had warned me to secrecy last night, so I had parked a full block away from the Federal Building. I walked, and looked at my watch.

In a few minutes, Chief Lafferty would be calling role in our central classroom, ready to hand out our first assignments. They would miss me, and make wisecracks, saying I was scared, or sleeping, or whatnot. Lafferty would be steamed, no doubt, and when he took the call from the marshal, and heard about my supposed stupidity, he would probably cuss, and say, "Good riddance."

It would be that quick. My new life – my bid to gain control – at least part of the time, and jump into a career out from under the thumb of Andrea's dad, one where I wouldn't die of boredom – all that was gone in the blink of an eye.

A parking ticket stuck out from the car's windshield wipers, an insult added to all the injury. The sky was overcast that morning – I remember well how I looked up, studying the clouds until the fog, or whatever spell the marshal had me under, cleared away in flash. This was, indeed a joke. Or madness.

For a moment I felt liberated. My fantasies about walking into police headquarters for my first assignment returned. There I would be, having coffee with my fellow new professionals, setting sail on a secure, challenging career. Then I heard a voice:

"That boy's got his tit in a wringer, for sure."

Another answered him, "Sarge is gonna have him thrown in the lockup, I tell you what."

Then laughter.

I turned to see two army soldiers, dressed up and sharp in their uniforms, passing behind me on the sidewalk. Nothing they could be doing in Sironia this early. They must be on leave, heading for breakfast in one of the downtown joints.

My breath caught in my throat. It wasn't that they were carrying weapons, for they weren't. But as they hustled by, laughing at the plight of some comrade of theirs, my gaze wandered across the street, where three more soldiers were walking the other direction, just as jolly. Ft. Hood was thirty miles away, and it was normal for troops on leave to visit Sironia, the biggest city in the area.

It was only seven in the morning, but I was already wrung out. Little memories bubbled up in my mind, trying to join the impossible conspiracy the marshal was claiming – I remembered wondering, during my cop training, why there seemed to be so many soldiers taking leave in Sironia in recent weeks. They could be seen on every street corner, at all hours, downtown or at the mall. Was this something I could ignore? Especially after all that bullshit the marshal laid on me?

Nope – I wasn't going to fall for it. If this wasn't some big joke, then maybe Ol' Tudberry had finally gone around the bend. I would report for duty, as scheduled. Get my assignment, work this morning, at least, and try to make sense of why this was happening. Hell, I might even have to seek counsel from Lafferty, himself.

My decision made itself: When I got to the police station, I didn't turn in. Didn't even slow down. A couple of puzzled cadets waved at me as I whizzed by. I kept going, all the way out to the Dallas Highway, and the Waffle Hut.

I ate like a man on death row – the way Andrea ate when she was mad at one of her girlfriends. All the while, I wondered if my loyalty to Tudberry was the reason I was there. Had he already betrayed me to the Chief? Was my name already being taken off the police roster?

What if it was all true? Did I have the moxy to be a spy, to work to stop a dangerous illegal revolution? Sexy notions, perhaps, to anyone else. But when I swallowed my sixth blueberry pancake, it fell into the same bottomless pit where the first five had disappeared.

I went back to my apartment and slept until two. At the appointed time, my car crunched onto the gravel of the Channel Three parking lot. I was unable to find the slip of paper with the man's name the marshal had told me to ask for. It was one of those days.

Chapter 4
Chris Ellis

I knew Chris Ellis only long enough to observe that he was the backbone of Channel Three. The tireless director, the guy who made all the electronics run, and the people. Cadwallader was rich, grumpy – Ebenezer Scrooge to Chris Ellis' Bob Cratchit.

But in the moment I stepped into the airy lobby of Emil Cadwallader's TV station, I had yet to meet the man, my knees were shaking, and I couldn't remember the name on that paper to save my life. "Mr. Sellars?" I made a feeble guess to the striking young lady behind the front desk.

The desk was placed on one side of that large room, opposite a cheap vinyl couch, and two rows of cloth chairs for people to wait in. On a wide credenza sat the largest television set I had ever seen. An afternoon CBS soap opera was playing, with the sound off.

"One moment, please," the girl said, and returned to the phone call I had obviously interrupted. She seemed put-out, and her disgusted look only intensified when the big TV flashed the symbol for a news bulletin. The familiar face of Douglas Edwards filled the screen. His lips moved, no sound, until his serious countenance was replaced by films of Soviet missiles being paraded in Red Square. My heart raced – were those the weapons they were installing in Cuba?

"I can't believe this is happening, anyway --" the pretty girl finished the call on a violent note, slammed the phone down, and looked up, blushing.

"What did you say?" She squinted at me.

"I think I'm supposed to ask for a Mr. Sellars."

"Not Chris Ellis?"

The bell rang in my head. "Yes. Sorry. That's the one." I hoped.

A scowl. "Is he expecting you?"

What was I supposed to say? She seemed to know he was -- "My name is George Blair, sent over by Mar--" My God, I almost said Tudberry's name. My undercover operation was practically over before it began.

"Chris?" She spoke into a bulky black intercom. "George Blair is here to see you, sent over by Mr. Mar."

A twangy male voice replied, un-intelligible. The receptionist rose, and led me down the short hall and through a door marked "studio." The airy, darkened room we entered was like a warehouse. Two huge TV cameras loomed in shadows, like futuristic robots. I recognized the news desk where Frank Watkins, the local legend sat. Off to the side were the weather maps – with no weather on them, just the outlines of the states. The jitters started in my toes, and the receptionist's lithe figure only amplified them. I was no spy, and no actor, so what would they have me do?

She took me through a control room of puzzled faces and the most amazing mass of cables and humming consoles one could imagine. No less than five TV sets adorned one wall, mounted above a picture window that overlooked the studio. An electric clock labeled "New York" ran an hour fast.

The girl waved me into a gloomy corner of steel girders and wires, then slinked away. A man's face emerged from behind a console, and I introduced myself.

"Thanks, Sharon," he called after her, then squinted at me. "Who's Mr. Mar?"

I whispered. "Nobody. Marshall Tudberry sent me."

"He told you to use the name Mr. Mar?"

I felt myself blush. "Forget it. I messed up."

He leaned back into his work, threading celluloid into a projection machine. Sandy hair and a sunburned complexion, as if he had been out punching cattle all day. "You know how to splice film?" His drawl was soft. Another cowboy trademark.

"No sir. I majored in journalism." I smelled burning rubber, likely a short somewhere in the mountains of wires.

"He talk to you about the announcer job?"

"What announcer job?"

"Kids show. The Zeebo Show."

My insides froze. The marshal's rattling on about my acting – I was supposed to be a cop – something wasn't making sense.

"But I thought Chuck Holiday was the emcee of the Zeebo show," I explained, as if he had forgotten that. Television had only come to Sironia six years before. Every TV personality was a huge celebrity in this little city.

"Tired of it." Chris flipped a switch and the projector clacked to life, its light too bright to stare into. "We gotta work fast, because Boss has had his army buddies paradin' through here pretty often, and they get nosy. Ever been on camera?"

The ice in my belly hardened into a glacier. "No, sir. You mean you want me to be on TV?"

He looked at me like I was the stupidest rube yet. "You gotta have a job here, for cover. What did you think you'd be doing?"

I swallowed. I had an inspiration. "But couldn't I gather more information in some behind-the-scenes job, instead of out where everyone can see me?"

"Don't matter," he said. "Not enough time, anyway, and my instructions are to put you on camera. That means we gotta screen-test you, to make it look honest."

"Whoa, there, Mr. Ellis," I said. My mind groped for a way out of this mess. "What do you mean you have instructions to put *me* on camera? Instructions from whom?"

He colored. "Never mind what I said. Just do as you're told. If anyone else asks, you worked at a station in Lake Charles for six months. Channel Thirteen. Station owner named McCallum. McCallum, understand? We have to get you past the old man."

His fingers winnowed into the insides of the projector, and he kept talking, as if I had asked for a tour of its inner workings. "The cameramen still use film sometimes. This photographs it onto magnetic tape. Easier to work with." He looked me over again. "How long you work for the government?"

His thick fingernails reminded me of my grandfather's, only not so yellowed with age. I decided not to lie. "Not that long."

"Well, come on. We'll set the cameras up."

My heartbeat skyrocketed. A screen test. That was what actors did. What the hell made Tudberry think I was such a hot actor? They were school plays, for chrissakes. I had wet the bed until I was five, and my old stage fright crawled out of the depths of my past. I had heard about TV cameras. When the red light switched on, you were out there helpless, for the whole world to see. What if my bladder lost control? What if my churning stomach decided to exit, through my mouth? I tried to stall.

"Is this stuff about Cadwallader, you know, this revolution stuff for real?" I asked. "What should I report to the marshal?"

Chris's finger shot to his lips. "Shut up. The boss bought an army amphibious troop carrier today. That's the only news. But don't bother reporting it to the marshal. It'll be on the nightly broadcast tonight."

My ears were ringing when he introduced me to Michael, the assistant director, and the others. Chris Ellis' dead-panned reply echoed over and over in my ears – it confirmed all the marshal's insane ravings, though what any army could need with an amphibious troop carrier in the middle of Texas was beyond me. If this were a joke, it was getting pretty elaborate.

Through the big picture window, the warehouse of lights and cameras came alive. Chris led me through the door. The floor was a minefield of cables to trip over, but I didn't need help doing that – and over toward the bleachers. I recognized this set – for the Zeebo the Clown Show.

Two Mexican boys appeared from nowhere. They were all smiles, and moved in quick, smooth motions. In unison, they set the huge cameras rolling across the floor, then one of them raised a big card – a picture of a smiling woman and a bottle of milk. They would start the camera on me, then switch to the picture, while I read the copy for the milk commercial off the teleprompter. The girl – her name was Gail – who operated this space-age machine came out of the control room and wiped the sweat off my face.

"Give it a try," Chris boomed over a loudspeaker, like the voice of God. The red light switched on, and I quaked like a leaf and read the cards in succession.

"Louder, dammit," God said.

Again. And again. Finally, it was over. Back in the control room, Zachary the soundman patted me on the back.

"Lake Charles, huh? I heard they pay more than minimum wage down there."

"Yeah," I said, reeling from a sort of drunken rush. Only this wasn't booze, but fear. "I guess so."

"Well, bend over." The soundman's smile was grim. "'Cause you're about to take it in the shorts."

Chris Ellis led me out through the convoluted room's back door and pulled a pinch of tobacco from a Redman pouch. "Good enough for government work, I guess." He started to chuckle, but the blood drained from his face while he poked the plug carefully into his cheek. After another moment of looking thoughtful, his eyes seemed to turn black, all business.

"Tell me the truth, son. You've never met Emil Cadwallader in your life?"

"No."

"The station owner."

"No, sir."

"And Marshal Tudberry is the only one who told you to come here? Scout's honor? You're not a double agent working for the army?"

The question, his whole manner, caught me flat-footed. He was peering into my eyes, looking for a lie. As if he were the last honest man, and I his only potential ally. That look was formidable – but I thought I saw fear, too. All I could do was shake my head. "I promise."

"Well, it's the beat of me," he said, using a finger to adjust the tobacco's position from outside his cheek. "I can't believe all this is finally happening, but if you're the one they've chosen--"

He shrugged, turned down the hall and spoke to me over his shoulder. "Come on. I'll introduce you to the man you're gonna have to kill."

Chapter 5
Russell Crump

The floor was a plane of cheap linoleum that stretched all the way down a long hallway whose end was lit up by the daylight blasting in from the lobby. But it might as well have been the walk down death row. Chris's cryptic comment made my legs freeze.

He was almost to the lobby before he realized I wasn't following him. He turned, and yelled, "Well, come on, boy. We got fish to fry." A pretty lady with hair piled high on top of her head barged past him, her arms laden with one of those electric typewriters that were so new and revolutionary in 1962.

After he helped her into an office, he stormed back down the hall, eyes flashing. "Well? You didn't think this would be a cakewalk, did you? When I tell you to move, move."

Somehow, I stumbled after him, figuring out how to tell him I wasn't above spying on my fellow Texans, but I drew the line at murder.

When we stepped into the lobby, Chris spoke under his breath. "The old man can go into rages, and if you do anything, stay out of the way of his bullwhip. Let me do the talking."

"Bullwhip?" This thing was getting physical, fast. If this Cadwallader guy attacked me, couldn't I just arrest him and be done with this whole thing? Chris paused, tucking in his shirttail before he knocked on the boss's door. It was right around the corner from the lobby, so I could still see the girl at the desk from where I stood. Perfect posture, she was on the phone again. "That receptionist is quite a looker, eh?" I said, feigning coolness under fire.

He shrugged. "Sharon? She's cute. The boss just keeps her around because she resembles his mother when she was young." He took a deep breath, looked at his watch, then up at me. A strange gaze in his eyes. "Damned if we ain't right on schedule," he said. "I can't hardly believe it."

His fist barely touched the ornately carved door, when it whipped open. A stout man – three hundred pounds crammed into a red banlon shirt and tan leather coat – stood there for a moment, staring – at me.

"This him?" the fat man said, and stepped into the hall. Why did everyone refer to me as if I had been expected? He drew a breath in through his teeth, and clamped his huge, fleshy paw around mine, and fixed me with those oyster eyes. But I looked past him, to the old, gray-haired specter who hovered just inside the doorway. Lanky, wearing a western shirt with snaps, a bolo tie, and a day's growth of gray whiskers. If I hadn't seen that craggy face in the papers before, I might have thought he was a bum just off an all-night drunk.

"George, this is the boss, Emil Cadwa--"

"Sure, sure," the old man interrupted. "Plenty of time for that later. Russell, you know what to do. Chris, get your tokus on in here."

Before I could resist, Russell barged past me, motioning that I follow even farther down that same hall, away from the lobby and daylight. The restroom doors were labeled in the corner, but when we reached them, he turned ninety degrees to the left, down yet another long hall.

"Where you work before?" he asked.

"Uh – Lake Charles. For a little while." I surprised myself by remembering.

"That so? They have nickel Dr. Peppers down in Louisiana?"

He bent over a horizontal coke machine, the kind where bottles hung from their tops along a metal rack. A neon sign burned in the gloomy recesses of the hall's far end – WXXK.

"Radio station," Russell said, watching my eyes. "Ever do any radio?" He inserted a coin. "Only machine left in Sironia that just costs a nickel. One of the benefits of working here."

Bottles scraped and clinked, and I cursed Homer Tudberry for sending me into this hell-hole with no preparation. An actor can't grasp a role unless he knows the character's needs, his history, and the marshal had given me only a name and a void. And a beer bust seemed like the only type of military coup this fat man could be involved in.

"Not much radio," I said, remembering that simple lies can stand more weight. I gulped at the drink, using the cold liquid to help me ignore his searching stare. Did he know why I was here? Was this the guy Chris thought I would have to kill? But no – I knew better than that—

"Don't mind Boss," he said, anticipating me again. "When you're as rich as he is, it's easy to get busy, and busy makes you gruff."

"Sure," I said. "I'm used to bosses."

"Oh, you are, are you?" He took a last strong drag on the cigarette in his hand, then dropped it to the linoleum and crushed it under a cowboy boot. My gaze lingered on the myriad burn marks that covered the floor, little brown galaxies concentrated in front of the machine. "Lake Charles – that means you must know Garner Hawks?"

"I worked for McCabe--" I said, and instantly knew that was the wrong name.

"McCabe?" A smile grew, almost too large. "You mean Archie McCallum?"

"Yeah. Sorry. Little nervous, I guess." I sucked at the cold drink, praying for deliverance.

"Hell, I'd be nervous, too, in your shoes." The smile disappeared. "But I was talking about Garner Hawks. Biggest drunk at the CBS convention every year. He's a goddam communist."

"Yeah." Now, it was time to wing it, I figured. "He's a real bastard. Never talked to him much, thank goodness. The newsroom was busy enough to let us go our separate ways."

"Well, he moved down to KXXR in Austin, you'll remember, and had them on strike. That won't go in Emil Cadwallader's shop. Word to the wise." A clumsy wink, and he lit up a new cigarette, and looked off into space. "Know who Douglas Edwards is?"

Testing me. This wasn't good. I threw my thumb over my shoulder. "He was on TV just a minute ago."

Nodding. "Yeah. This Cuba thing's heatin' up pretty good, ain't it?"

"I guess."

"How about Carter Beale? Know who he is?"

I wanted to scream. "Hmm. Name sounds familiar --" I started, but the fat man was in my face, eyes flaring, a sort of foam collecting on his lips.

"Come on, boy, stop the bullshit." His loud voice had transformed into a menacing whisper. A sick smile. "What are you doing here? You and Billy Dean? What the hell have you been cooking up for the last decade and a half?" He grabbed my shirt by the buttons. "Out with it, goddam it."

Red Alert. I pulled against that fat force, backed myself against the wall and hoped he wouldn't squish me. I couldn't imagine what he was accusing me of, but it was obvious he knew I was here as a spy.

He let go of me suddenly, and stuck his now empty bottle into one of the yellow crates stacked up next to the coke machine.

"So don't tell me." He tossed a curt nod toward the boss's office. "I won't raise a stink. Not yet. 'Cause I don't want to make him mad." Close again. Right in my face, and sweating. Whispering. "A nuclear war is about to start, and you and that clown have fooled a lot of people. But you don't fool me. Why don't you just high-tail it, and save yourself from being Billy Dean's roomie down in Huntsville for the rest of your days?" He pulled back one side of his leather coat, and patted a thirty-eight pistol that hung under his arm in a holster. "In the meantime, do anything to hurt that old man, and – well, you understand."

I was gasping. "Mr. Crump. I swear to God I don't know what you're talking about." The other men the marshal sent in here had disappeared, and now I was getting a glimpse of their probable fates. Chris Ellis didn't seem the squealing type, but something had leaked out. Or maybe the spies in the marshal's building had spotted me.

Russell Crump studied me for another long moment, then huffed, and veered away, headed back to Cadwallader's office. He made it halfway down the hall before I grabbed his arm and turned him around. Why was I so brave? I don't know, though there was some wild notion that if he intended to kill me, he would have done it back by the Dr. Pepper machine.

"Please stop, Mr. Crump," I blustered. "If you don't want me to work here, just say so. But you mentioned a nuclear war – tell me about that. It's all over TV, but what's the inside scoop?"

He recoiled, eyes wide, his face a mish-mash of feelings I couldn't read, but a loud *click* stopped him from answering. Chris Ellis stepped out into the hall only a few feet away. A hard glance at Russell, a cold one at me. "Boss is tied up. He'll see you tomorrow. We'll start your training at nine," he said.

"And don't be late, Mr. Know-nothing," the fat man said, and disappeared behind the heavy door. Before it closed entirely, a loud *crack* split the air, almost as loud as a gunshot. I jumped.

"Bullwhip," Chris said, with a wry smile. He motioned, and I followed him across the lobby, and through the doors, out into the sunlight. "What got you on Russell's bad side so fast?"

"You."

Maybe he saw how hard I was breathing. Maybe my face was boiling red. Something made Chris Ellis take a step back for the first time since I'd met him.

"You blabbed, Mr. Ellis. Or somebody did. He knows I've never been within a county from Lake Charles." I pointed. "I'll bet hell he's in there, telling the old man right now — "

"Just shut up for a minute," Chris said, glancing around nervously. "Crap. Did he say that he knew you were a spy? Did he say those words? Exactly?"

"No, but--"

"Damn it to hell." He slapped the side of his jeans. "Longstreet said he was getting suspicious, too." An embarrassed look, as if he had said too much. "That's the name of the last guy the Feds sent. They sent him out west on a story. Never came back."

I swallowed hard. "The marshal said there were two."

Leaning over the flower bed, he spat out the shreds of his tobacco, used a finger to rub the inside of his lips, then spat again. Out came the Red Man pouch, and the look in his eye almost had me convinced he was about to bolt. I resolved that if he ran, I would, too. A wave, and he led me to an old, beat-up pickup truck. The doors were unlocked, and he reached in to get another pouch of tobacco out of its glove compartment.

"The other guy, I never really met. They took him his first day on the job."

A shiver went through me. "Shit," I said.

"Damn it, figure this out. What did Russell say, word for word?"

I wiped sweat off my face, and tried to remember. The air was clean, and moving around, but the sun still had its sting. "Something about me working with someone. Billy — "

"Billy Dean?"

"Yeah, that had to be it."

Chris laughed aloud, and tossed the defunct tobacco pouch into the floor of his truck, already the resting place of beer cans and assorted crushed drink cups. "Oh, hell, why didn't you tell me at the start?"

"What's so funny?"

"Stupid Russell, that's what. He's paranoid."

"He is?"

"Hell, yes." Another rich laugh. "That poor fat slob is trying to get out of the little part he's been dealt to play – he'd rather sling his weight around – never mind. He's blowin' smoke. Billy Dean don't work with no one, except on TV. He's strictly a solo act, a strange bird if there ever was one. And Russell knows damn well."

I shared none of the relief that washed over the man's face.

"You know who he means, right? Billy Dean Brown. Our weatherman." A faraway look. "He's Zeebo, too."

"The clown?" I fumbled. This guy suddenly figured all was right with the world, while my heart was beating down my rib cage. Of course I knew the name, 'Billy Dean Brown.' There weren't that many TV celebrities in Sironia in those days. My head cleared a bit.

"I guess I've seen him do the weather," I said. "But I didn't remember he was the clown – damn it, Mr. Ellis, I tell you that fat guy knows something – he suspects me."

That distant look turned a couple of shades of something, then he met my eyes, and gave a weird little smile, and slapped my shoulder. "Everybody suspects something, son. These are crazy times, and you waltzing in here and reporting to work this afternoon – well, it just kinda kicks things up to a whole 'nother level."

He watched my mouth move, though I couldn't even form a question.

"Never mind, kid. You work here a little, you'll figure out what I'm talking about. That your car?"

When I nodded, he pushed me toward it. And now his smile was genuine, and not so eerie, and he yelled over his shoulder. "We'll start you in the studio at nine. Get here at eight, and you'll have time to settle in. Understand?"

"Yes, sir."

"Now go home and watch the Zeebo show. See how we do it from your own living room."

I opened my car door, but waited, as if some inner sense knew I should watch the man until he disappeared into the lobby. The hard-working type. Not someone who would sign onto some phony army revolt.

So I watched. I remember his sandy hair flecked with gray. His scuffed blue jeans and flannel short-sleeved shirt. Medium build, shorter than I, but with the air of one of those guys no one ever messed with back in high school.

He was strength. That was my impression, that first day. Chris Ellis held the building up by the foundation. The guys in the control room were the Keystone Cops, the Mexicans on the cameras were the innocent witnesses, Russell Crump was a self-important mountain of flab, and the girl – Sharon – at the front desk was a sort of goddess. The sort I had never even dreamed of having. She was the type of beauty that always went with men like Chris.

Then there was that specter in the boss's office. Cadwallader. He was the one I feared. But no sign of soldiers, or weapons, or blueprints of any rebellion. Those were the feelings – my first report to the marshal, from the phone in front of the Seven-Eleven, was mostly feelings.

"You're talkin' gobble-dy-gook," Tudberry said on the phone. "Nobody cares who you like or fear or respect. Start asking questions. Find out who Mr. Big is. Don't call me again 'til you got something the Washington boys can chew on."

"Yes, sir."

I drove home, and watched the Zeebo Show. It started about the time school kids were getting home. A lot of nonsense, really, this guy in full clown regalia, running around, tooting a kazoo at bleachers full of kids. Like the most famous clown, Clarabell, Zeebo never spoke – just used gestures and toots to challenge the young children to "stump" him by drawing squiggles on a big piece of paper – but they never could, because Zeebo followed them with his own stick of charcoal, and could always turn their messy lines into a respectable picture of something.

After the Zeebo Show came Dobie Gillis, then the evening news. Then I cleaned up and got into my car.

I'm sure I drove like a drunk, because I could focus only on the inevitable explosion that lay ahead. Chris had painted Russell Crump as a fat, powerless buffoon – but there was more to him than that, wasn't there? Something in his eyes when he was grilling me – something bad and strange. A gun under his arm.

But the fat man wasn't the explosion I feared. I was due over at Andrea's, for one of our two weekly family dinners, and when she found out I wasn't on the police force, there would be hell to pay.

Chapter 6
Dinner at Andrea's

"I been meanin' to ask you, George, what's each cop's quota for speedin' tickets?" Mr. Wiggins stared harshly as he dug out a small mountain of mashed potatoes for his plate. "I know the Chief of Police says there's no such thing, but he's a liar. I've watched cops for years. So be honest, George. They give you a limit, don't they? What is it? At least ten, twenty citations a month? A week?"

My mouth full, I fumbled the answer –

"Now, I won't rat on you," he insisted. "I know the whole damned hierarchy of city hall. They're just in it for the money. The hell with who's breakin' the law or not--"

"I – they haven't told us anything about any quotas, Mr. Wiggins. I don't think they do that – but maybe they do--"

"Damn right they do, the crooks."

"Now, Daddy, leave him alone and let him eat his roast." Andrea draped one arm over my shoulder. "George is a working man, now, and he'll need his strength. Come on, tell us, Honey. Did they put you in a cruiser? Please tell me you're not walking one of those downtown beats."

"Uh, no assignments, yet." The only thing I could think to say. I felt blood rush to my face.

"Well, you told me that was the main thing that would happen on the first morning." She huffed. "Never mind, Mr. Strong and Silent. Jeanette's cousin was in your class, too, remember? I'll ask her for the skinny, if you're not going to tell us."

I shivered. "Andrea, when something happens, I'll tell you. You know that." My God, anything I said was only digging me deeper into an impossible lie. "Tell me about the bomb shelters, Mr. Wiggins."

That pretty well saved the dinner. Once he started, he didn't stop, talking about trusses, and how we haven't really licked the water drainage problem underground, even after two thousand years of construction science. Et cetera.

Andrea only rolled her eyes, but she was steaming. After dinner, her mother took to bed with a blood sugar spell, and I sat down on the couch and girded myself for the third degree. My fiancé was psychic, and had her own spies all over town. I had never found a way to lie to her successfully. Tonight, maybe, I was safe. But that wouldn't last long.

She dimmed the lights and snuggled against me. "So, what's it really like at the station house?" she asked, using her sexy voice. "I know you were evading Daddy's questions, saving the best for me."

"Andrea, I can't really say any more," I managed to blurt out. "Some interesting things might be working out. Sort of like a surprise."

"Whatever you say." She kissed my cheek lightly, curling my hair with her fingers. "They're promoting you, aren't they, right out of school? Please tell me. I'll bet you go undercover, and spy on the mafia or something." Then, a big smile. "Oh, George, you did it, didn't you? You took that letter to the marshal? My gosh, my gosh, is it going to be a huge surprise, you darling man?"

Psychic, like I said. Stumbling too close to the truth, her whisper hot in my ear.

"You can tell me, George. Get used to it. We're not going to be one of those old married couples who live separate lives, hiding things from one another. I'm going to know everything you do. Otherwise, how can I help you do your job right?"

Then she laid a wet one on me, the type of kiss she dispensed only at Christmas and our yearly engagement anniversaries. My breathing sped up. She was sniffing around the truth, closing in like a bloodhound, and when that luxurious kiss ended, I would have to show at least a few of my cards. But I had no cards, so I panicked, and did the only thing I could think of that would stop her questions: I put my hand on her breast, outside her shirt.

"George Blair." She slapped my face and jerked me to my feet. "You're going home." She pointed to the door. "Having a big new career doesn't give you license. That's *after* the wedding, Mister."

I feigned disgust, and stormed out. Down deep, I knew it would be smarter just to come clean right then, but denial was consuming my brain, convincing me that I would fare better on Friday, during our weekly movie date. By then, I might have my first TV appearances under my belt, and my career change would be a *fait accompli*. By then, maybe I would have cooked up a new cover story that would save my hide.

It was folly, of course, but the marshal's reassurances had somehow renewed my faith. I wanted to plunge into my spying mission with the gas pedal all the way to the floor. By God, to hell with Russell Crump, and that old man with the bullwhip. I would find out the identity of Mr. Big, earn myself a place on the marshal's permanent staff. With any luck, my TV announcing career would be over before it started, and I would, by default, have the promotion that Andrea was insisting on.

But she caught me on the front porch, her eyes strange, her mood suddenly altered. "I'm sorry. It's your first day of a new life, George. Let's not fight. I'll get Momma's keys. You can take me by Dr. Kilgallen's. Linda says he's got a new girl friend. We might even cruise by Rusty Carter's."

Dr. Kilgallen was her gynecologist, her obsession. I could have nipped her childish reconnaissance missions past his house in the bud when they started, but he didn't strike me as a threat. Rusty, though, was a different matter.

"Andrea, you seem to know an awful lot about this random plumber. I thought you said he was ugly, in his thirties, but now you all of a sudden know where he lives. Tell me right now what's going on with him, or we aren't driving anywhere."

She pinched my cheek, her look a mix of innocence and aggression. "I like people, George. Especially if they're nice to me, and Rusty treated me like a lady. It's time you realize I can have any beau I want, and by hang, I will, if you don't come to your senses. We are destined to be a privileged couple, and I can make that happen, if you just shut up and listen to me."

"And I suppose if you dump me, a lowly policeman, this plumber is your ticket to the Hedonia Club?" The words came out before I could catch them.

"Stay right here, Mister."

She stomped into the living room, and returned quickly with her purse and her mother's keys. After a blinding rush, I was sitting behind the steering wheel of Ma Wiggins' huge Cadillac. "Don't be such a smarty pants," she said. "You owe me, George, for all this. Quittin' Daddy, a new job, and this prissy, nerve-wracking attitude you've got for yourself. This little trip can be your apology, so shut up and drive."

Chapter 7
Billy Dean Brown

In the decades since 1962, the movies have shown us graphic portrayals of federal drug agents working undercover – grungy warriors that grow their hair long, or get tattoos, or beards. Some even shoot heroin in the line of duty, but no matter how well a double agent like that gets on with his *paizans*, or henchmen or *hombres* or *homies*, he's still scared going to work every morning. I mean gut-wrenching, shivering scared, because he knows the least little slip-up on his part, or the squealing of some other law-dog who he doesn't even know could get him a bullet in the head, with no advance warning.

That was how I felt, going to work at Channel Three on that second morning. Chris knew I was a plant, and so did Russell Crump, or at least the fat man sensed it on some level. And no matter what the marshal said, Crump's pistol was real. This wasn't training, but for keeps.

Even if I could have forgotten that, the radio and TV announcers would have reminded me. All they could talk about was Cuba, and how nuclear war might be only days away. I had to stifle myself to stop from calling those network anchors, long-distance, to tell them the real threat was down here in Texas, not Cuba. But those big shot newsmen would never have believed it. Hell, I didn't even believe it.

I took a slot in the far end of the parking lot, just as a light rain started to fall. In the lobby, Sharon stared at me like I was the Creature from the Black Lagoon. I strolled, acting like I knew what I was doing. By the time I got to the control room, the butterflies in my belly were raging.

Both the studio and control room were bedlam – the opposite of what I had witnessed the day before. Michael was soloing – his first time, apparently – as director of Johnny's Farm Show, the noon show that anchored their daytime productions. When he saw me, his eyes glazed over, and my feeling of doom only multiplied.

Films of the Cuban president speaking at the U.N. – not Castro, one of his lackeys – blared from the network TVs overhead. Gail looked over from her teleprompter – nothing more than a tiny conveyor belt mounted beneath a bulky camera – and filled the void. "Chris wants us to give George a run-through for the Zeebo show," she said. "That OK with you, George?"

"Sure." I tried to stay cool.

"No time." Michael yelled, and turned to the soundman. "Zachary, where's the farm show intro?"

Zachary shrugged. "Chris put it somewhere."

"Well, idjit, I don't see Chris around here this morning, do you?" The soundman scrambled to an upright position, but Mike's eyes were still wild. "Where's Johnny, goddam it?"

Gail pinched his arm. "Quit cussing. He's at the Pancake House, like every morning."

"But the show's at twelve."

"That's hours from now." She rolled her eyes. "Michael, we can do a couple of quick shots for George, then you'll be back on schedule."

Mike's head sank to the director's console. "Can somebody call Chris?"

"He's hunting, Michael. You know this." Gail rubbed her temples.

"Hells bells, whaddya need him for?"

The new voice made me jump. A scrawny character in coveralls leaned against the closed studio door, and it took me a moment to realize I had seen his face every time I had watched the evening news. Billy Dean Brown, the weatherman, the only weatherman Channel Three had ever had in the six years since TV came to Sironia. He was also known – when in costume – as Zeebo the Clown.

Billy Dean had to be pushing forty, but his jet-black hair was greased like a teenager's. His dress shirt was freshly ironed, with its tails sticking unceremoniously out of either side of the coveralls. He held a cigarette in one hand. "Mikey bite off more than he can chew?" He laughed and pointed a finger at me. "This way, Mr. Announcer. I'll show you your marks."

Nervously, I shook his hand, and launched into my bogus history as we walked. Billy Dean sucked on his cigarette and nodded.

"Hey, come over here first," he said, and led me to the long desk where news, weather, and sports were broadcast every night. He tapped the glass that covered the map of Texas.

"Where's Brownsville?" he said.

I automatically pointed to the bottom of the map.

A sly look. If we have lived other lifetimes as animals, he might have been a coyote. "El Paso?"

I pointed. This was easy.

"Well, I'll be damned." Billy Dean chuckled. "A college boy who knows something practical. Think you could write the temperatures on this map in the afternoons? My hand's getting arthritis."

"Temperatures for the weather broadcast?"

"Naw, the sports." He guffawed, and Paco and Carlos, all the way across the studio, joined in.

Lights on the side set came to life. "We're ready, Senor Lake Charles," Carlos said. My stomach seized. Small tape crosses were scattered haphazardly around the floor, and while the cameramen rolled their heavy instruments, Billy Dean outlined my moves.

"Chuck stands over here for as long as possible before he goes over to interview the brats," he said. "But that old man shifts around like a robot. You oughta move as much as you want. Give these camera hombres some exercise."

"Yes, sir."

His instructions piled up in my brain, and my shirt was already sopping. The cameramen kept smiling, but it was obvious they didn't expect much out of me.

God's voice – Mike's this time, not as omnipotent as Chris's – boomed, scratchy and shrill over the control room speaker. "George, bleachers will be set up right where Johnny's desk is now. Face that way when you introduce the kids. Got it?"

I nodded, comprehending nothing.

God, again. "Go with the first commercial, then do your intro."

I tried to ad-lib an intro a dozen times, and it came home to me why undercover cops usually wind up getting shot. One can't possess the concentration to do two jobs at once without screwing them both up. That thought reminded me – why wait and ask all my questions of Cadwallader? Every one of the other workers here was bound to know something about the old man's revolution, if it really existed.

I don't know how long they had me out there, but one eternity stretched into two. Looking through the control room window, I started to sense that Michael was using all this practice for therapy. He could ignore the Farm Show as long as I was making an ass out of myself.

Billy Dean had disappeared in the hubbub, but now he came ambling back in, his hands dug into his coverall pockets. "It's hailing like a son of a gun out there. Anybody heard from Chris?" No reply. The weatherman sized me up. "Let's go upstairs. He's through," he yelled, and waved through the control room window.

I followed him, still shaking, down the halls and up a rickety metal stairway that led upstairs to the weather room. In my few years of working construction for Andrea's father, I had never seen such poor workmanship. Cadwallader was obviously a cheapskate, among his other virtues.

The weather room itself was a small cramped cubicle about the size of two large closets with walls of cheap wood paneling. Nothing like the sumptuous office I might have imagined. Half of the space was consumed by bulky consoles. An army-surplus-looking desk and a dilapidated secretary's chair dominated the other side. Billy Dean collapsed into that chair and flipped a switch. The teletype was pounding away, and a glance revealed it was printing out temperatures for the major cities in Texas.

"You're staring at the furniture," he said. I strained to hear him above the machine-gun pelting of the hailstones on the roof – more shoddy construction, obviously. "Well, these are my curse. I was surrounded by metal-frame shit like this in War Two, and I guess they'll follow me to the grave. Even that teletype--" He stopped, his face the picture of mischief. "I guess the digs in Lake Charles must have been nicer, eh?"

"Uh, not really," I said.

Another smile, and he put his feet up on the edge of the desk. "Ain't nothing to this job," he said. "I play the fool. You're the straight man. If you draw a blank, just make fun of me. The kids will laugh. You like kids?"

"Guess I have to." Andrea planned for us to have five.

"If we get a troublemaker, point him out during the commercial, and I'll shut him up. Clowns can be scary, too, you know." Another mischievous look, but icy. "Paco and Carlos will save your butt. Hell, they run the place, anyway."

"Where's your clown makeup?" I managed to ask.

He kicked the desk's bottom drawer, but my attention gravitated to the greenish glow of the screens behind him.

"That's the weather radar?"

"Damn," Billy Dean said. "Look at that." He fiddled with knobs, changing the intensity of the light splotches in the center of the screen.

"That storm's sitting right on top of us," I said, showing off what little I had learned from watching TV. It was at that moment that I realized I had always paid more attention to the weather segment of the nightly news. The flashing, then fading splotches of clouds and rain had me mesmerized.

"Where the heck did all this rain come from? The newspaper said it was supposed to be clear and hot."

"That's what the Weather Bureau says." He sneered, and motioned to the clacking teletype. "They print it, we have to recite it, but haven't you ever seen my forecasts? At the end, I always let the people know what's really going to happen." Maybe I remembered something like that, but before I could ask how he was supposed to know more than the weather bureau, he cut me off. "Hey, get out of here for a minute, Punk. I need to make a call."

The suddenly vicious mood swing left no room for protest. I paced outside the door, assuming he meant for me to wait there, but for how long? The cheap carpet that covered the floor had been laid without a pad, and the banging hailstones were playing the roof like a drum.

In all the noise, I didn't intend to eavesdrop, but Billy Dean's voice boomed through the thin wall. "Whaddya mean he's not back yet?"

A pause. It lengthened. The hailstones reduced his words to mumbling, and I was wasting time. I should start asking questions of the employees now. I decided to wander downstairs, but a loud *bang* split the air, and I had to grab onto the stair railing to keep from stumbling. Thunder? No. Billy Dean had only slammed the phone down. Hard.

I waited, collecting myself, once again cursing Homer Tudberry's name. I was supposed to find Mr. Big, but I doubted this mercurial nut in his little closet knew anything about anything. I tapped on the door, deciding to excuse myself to the restroom.

"What?"

"You OK in there?" I pushed until the door clanged against a support pole in the crowded space. Billy Dean was leaning back in his chair, relaxed again, drinking from a flask.

He offered it. "Old Crow?"

"No, thanks. What was that noise?"

His coyote eyes gazed far away. "Chris went hunting."

"So I heard. But in a hailstorm? Maybe he missed your forecast, too."

He didn't smile. "He was right down in the control room, directing when I was on the air. He didn't miss it."

So? None of that was my fault. I started out the door.

"You don't have to pretend with me," he blurted. I turned, and he measured me with a withering stare. He kept measuring, all the way through another sip of bourbon. "I know you never even been near Lake Charles."

I shuddered. Another proof that my cover was blown. Was there anyone at this station who didn't know I was a fraud? "I wasn't in there long," I said lamely.

A smirk turned into a calming look. "Never mind. Don't spread it around. You're a greenhorn in every way, I guess." The half-smile on his face evaporated into a hateful glare. "You're gonna have to think on your feet, boy. Mama ain't here to change your diaper, and I can't keep the train on the rails all by myself. Now get the hell out of here for a while. I gotta track Chris down."

He gestured toward the teletype. "Tear that report off and take it to Gail. Then draw the high temps on the map down there. Highs, not lows. Make 'em legible, understand?"

"Yes, sir."

Downstairs, Johnny's Farm Show was in full swing, red warning lights glaring, so I avoided the studio and went all the way around through the back of the control room. With an angry motion, Mike waved me down.

"Where the hell is Billy Dean?"

"In his office," I said. "He told me to draw the map."

He fumed. "Then hurry. We do the weather in the last segment. He ain't drinking, is he?"

I stopped in my tracks. My God – Clearly, the weatherman must be a lush – but was it my place to rat him out?

I just shrugged, and headed for the maps. My temperature numbers were clear, but I botched the clouds and the warm front with its sharp blue points and rounded red backs. It lay closer to Dallas than where it really was on the facsimile map.

To my relief, Billy Dean appeared the moment I finished. His coveralls had been replaced by a cheap-looking suit. He took a long look at the amateurish map, gave no criticism, but stepped in front of the cameras and started joking with Johnny Tate on camera, and he always did. He passed by me on the way out, after the Farm Show music quit playing.

"You find Chris?" I asked.

A glare was his only reply – harsh enough to sweat cotton. He stormed out, and I looked at my watch. Only three hours before the Zeebo Show started, and I could feel my bowels churning. This was insanity. Here I was, in the middle of a hornets' nest, and all the hornets seemed to know about my secret mission, but I knew nothing about them. Chris was my only contact, and he wasn't even here.

For a moment, I let myself dissolve into the fantasy that Chris was in an important meeting with the marshal, to jointly concoct a way to get me out of here.

When that dream evaporated, I decided to take the bull by the horns. I made a beeline for the lobby, and Cadwallader's office. The marshal and common sense be damned. My reconnaissance would start at the horse's mouth. But my fist was poised to knock on his door when nature intervened, and forced me to go straight to the bathroom, where the butterflies roiling in my belly demanded to be released.

Chapter 8
Zeebo's Last Show

I never made it to Cadwallader's door that afternoon. I took infinite trips to the john, between listening to instructions and warnings from first Mike, then Gail and finally Zachary the soundman.

"Whatever you do, don't curse on the air," Mike said. "You slip and say damn or hell, and you're fired. Anything beyond that – like a four-letter word that no one should ever say – and the old man will lose his broadcast license, and you'll probably wake up at the bottom of a well out near San Angelo."

"He knocks Mr. C off the air, he won't wake up at all," Zachary added.

"That's what I said, Dummy."

Right before four p.m., my belly demanded one more relief journey, and I wondered whether fear of the cameras would kill me before I could even start my mission here.

"Fresh meat for the grinder, eh?" The loud voice accosted me in the bathroom stall, just barely after I had finished my business. I hated that.

"What?" I said, as I walked to the sink to wash up.

A rotund guy with unkempt hair was using too many paper towels. His shirt-tails were hanging out, just as Billy

Dean's did, and his tie looked like it was washed and wrung, but never ironed. His nose went into the air. "I said, you must be the rookie. I'm Cuthbert Thompson, the only reporter with a valid journalism degree in this leaking ship. Don't tell me you've seen me on air. I'm hard to recognize. Slimmer on camera – the opposite of most people."

"Pleased to meet you." He waited until I had dried my hands before he shook one. We stepped out of the bathroom together.

"But surely you've read my byline in the Sironia Herald?" he asked. "I was their ace national news connection until I lost my mind and crossed over to this world of fluff and shallow reporting."

"The Herald?" Now his name did ring a bell, but I had to try one more lie. "Sorry, I've been working in Lake Charles for a while."

"Eight years I slammed a typewriter, my son--" He led the way back into the hall. "Eight, and I was being considered for the Dallas News' national desk – now, look at me."

I laughed, but a door slammed, and there stood Russell Crump at the lobby's edge, staring at us. Cuthbert seemed as repulsed as I was. "It's the Dauphin. Pretender to the throne," he whispered.

"Come see me later, Mr. Announcer." A wink. "I'm working the story of the century, and I need help. Don't say anything." He straightened up, and slapped my back. "Well, happy to meet a comrade in arms," he bellowed, obviously for Russell's benefit. "Take it from an old Shakespearean actor. There's something rotten in Denmark." Russell blocked the hallway.

"You're the only thing rotten around here, Thompson," he said with a snarl. "Don't go teaching the new help bad habits."

Too late. I felt a rush. I had my first source. This Cuthbert guy had caught the scent, and obviously had no allegiances to the station or any tin-pot revolution.

"Wouldn't dream of it, *mi lud*," the reporter replied to Crump, and escaped into the news room.

Russell's eyes narrowed. "Remember what I said about communists? Well, that boy is as close to one you can get without getting fired."

"Yes, sir." The studio door swung open before I could say more. Mike leaned out, waving frantically.

"George. Go get him," he cried.

"Get who?"

"Yeah, get who?" Russell echoed.

"Billy Dean. The kids are due any minute."

I ran, thankful for any excuse to get out of Russell's presence. The flimsy door of the weather room was locked, so I knocked.

"Stay out." Billy Dean's voice, but different. "I'm getting dressed." My God. He was drunk. "Chris ain't showed up, has he?"

"No, sir," I answered. "You need help in there?"

"Shit, no. Damn it to hell," he said.

I raced back to the control room, wishing I had never met Homer Tudberry. My stomach swelled with room for more butterflies, but I was certain there were none left to come out. A deep breath, and I addressed the control room for my first time. "I think he's been drinking."

A beat. Eyes wide.

"Lord, help us," Gail said.

Zachary sat straight up. "Did you actually see him take a drink?"

"I think so. Earlier."

Mike grabbed me by the shirt. "Why did you let him start drinking? We're all fired. Fired, do you hear? Zach, can we cut the feed to the boss's office?"

"No."

Back to me. Mike was desperate. "How bad is he?"

The lights in the studio came on, and Paco and Carlos started clapping while a line of school kids – nine, ten years old – paraded from the lobby door.

"They're here," Zach said.

"No."

Gail raised a finger. "It's too late. We just have to act like everything's normal. George, if the clown never shows up, you just introduce the cartoons, and interview the kids. The cards will tell you the next cartoon in the slot, like normal."

I panted. "But I don't know what normal is."

"No." Mike stared at the control panel like a chicken looking at a watch. I recognized the commercial playing over the New York feed. It was almost over. "George? Call Chris."

I pointed. "Aren't I supposed to be out there?"

"God help us." He moved levers, and Gail took my arm, and escorted me through the door, to my mark. A few youngsters stared, perhaps bewildered that I, not the famous Chuck Holiday, was holding the microphone.

"Tell me again, Gail, what do I do if the clown doesn't make it down here?"

A cheer erupted before she could answer. Zeebo himself was crossing the floor in long strides of his big, floppy shoes. Weaving, but upright – Billy Dean, in full regalia – white face, red mouth, cherry ball nose. He bowed and replied to the kids' yells with toots from a kazoo. A godsend. I had forgotten that the clown was famous for never speaking – he just squawked over his tooter.

I burped hot acid. When the camera's red light turned on, I would be expected to talk to thousands of people across Central Texas. Talk, and make sense, and act like I knew what I was doing. Zeebo was still making threatening gestures over the kids' heads – but they only laughed. Even my joy at finding Cuthbert had evaporated – because that red light was just aching to switch on, and what if Andrea were watching?

"Quiet, please." The voice of God.

The lights were too bright for me to look directly into the camera. Zeebo's circus theme music began, the cartoon logo flashed on the floor monitor, and I swallowed, scrambling to remind myself that this was temporary. My mind chased a few cute ad-libs I had concocted earlier – but now they refused to be caught. Maybe I should say something about Chuck Holiday retiring – but what? They hadn't told me anything. Carlos pushed the camera closer. This was going to happen. My heart ached, as if in its final thrusts – then the terrifying red light switched on.

Through the control room window, Zachary and Gail stared, their faces full of doubt. Everyone here knew about me, obviously, and no one thought I could do this. Mike shoved levers back and forth, then bent over and picked up a telephone.

I braced. Paco manned the camera over on the Zeebo side, and waved his fingers, counting down. "Five seconds," he said.

Still, I didn't look at the camera – something in the control room wasn't right. Mike hung up the phone, and God spoke again. "We're going straight to commercial," he said.

A stay of execution! Thirty seconds, or sixty, I wanted to ask, but couldn't. What the hell were they doing? I watched as Gail's head sank to the edge of her conveyor belt.

"*Que pasa?*" Paco asked his headset.

"*Zzeeeepp?*" Zeebo's kazoo echoed the question.

Paco blanched and put his hand over his headset mike, and even the kids' cheering fell quiet. "Chris is dead," he said. "Hunting accident. He's dead."

The circus music faded. Now the commercial. But no – that was my face staring out of the monitor. My eyes were wide, cheeks white as snow, washed out. I looked like a rabbit staring at a snake. The snake? All those people watching out in TV Land. I saw my Adam's apple bob with the huge swallow I forced. Thousands of people. Kids on couches, stretched out on living room floors. Their parents in rocking chairs, moms knitting, dads home early from work. My tongue – parched. Was I supposed to speak? Wouldn't somebody wave when it was time to start?

"Hello, boys and girls--" I uttered it into the mike, but, just as suddenly, my face disappeared, replaced by Zeebo's. The kazoo was twitching in his clown mouth, and he was shaking visibly.

He lunged. First I saw it happen with my own eyes – then I instinctively turned to the studio monitor. Zeebo was pulling the hapless cameraman onto the screen with him. Paco's headset went flying. Every other soul in the room went catatonic, and I imagined all the little kids of Central Texas freezing, too. The Zeebo Show was different this afternoon.

On screen, Paco's mouth fell open. Zeebo lifted him bodily off the floor and shook him like a rag doll. From the corner of my eye, I saw Mike waving violently in the control room. On the monitor, it was still Zeebo. He wasn't much taller than his prey, but the scrawny clown had strength. Paco's feet dangled above the cement floor, the kazoo dropped and clattered off the camera cables, Zeebo pushed his face close, and the clown's never-before-heard voice boomed across the studio:

"What the fuck do you mean, Chris is dead?"

Silence. Even God didn't answer. In that sound-proofed studio, you could have heard a mouse sneeze – until someone whimpered: the kids' teacher, sitting off to the side, out of the lights, her hands flat on each side of her face.

Another glance into the control room. Michael punching his console frantically.

A flash, and Zeebo and the petrified cameraman vanished from the monitor, replaced by film of Soviet missiles in a parade. Another punch, and that was my face staring out of the screen again – the rabbit, but the snake had already bit. For an instant, circus music returned. Then the monitor turned to snow.

Chapter 9
Emil Cadwallader

"Come this way. Get over here. Hurry, children, William. Ellen, form a line. Get in line!" The teacher's frantic voice echoed as an *Our Gang* episode brought the monitors back to life again. Studio lights switched off, throwing us all into a sizzling twilight. Carlos consoled Paco, but Zeebo had disappeared, and I found my way back into the control room.

Gail was sitting up straight now, using a tissue to catch the tears that streamed down her cheeks. She glanced at me, but there was no show of recognition. Zachary had his chair leaning back against the wall, his arm lying across his soundboard, and Michael stared into nothingness.

"What happened?" I said stupidly, but before anyone could tell me where to go and how to get there, the door behind me crashed open. Russell Crump, of course.

He stormed in, and put a finger right in my face. "You. Blair. Go upstairs. Get that son of a bitch and meet me in Boss's office. *Pronto*."

"Yes, sir."

Just as quickly, the chubby man was gone, leaving the others at peace in their catatonic states. On the screen, Spanky and Alfalfa were scheming, and as I stepped through the back door, Mike's voice followed me.

"Nice working with you, George," he said.

Up in the weather office, Zeebo was leaning back in his army surplus chair. The Old Crow flask was in his hand was down to its last few swallows. "You." He smiled. "I was hopin' it would be High-Pockets, himself."

"They want us in the boss's office," I said. "Haven't you had enough to drink already?"

He smiled, touched his fluffy collar on either side, removed his red ball nose and slammed it down onto the desk. "I don't swill all the time, no matter what you hear. Just when the rules of the game change – and by God, they've changed. In spades."

More cryptic hogwash. I wanted to scream at him, but it didn't matter. He had committed the worst sin that can be visited on a TV show. We would all be fired, and I would never get a chance to question Cuthbert. A stupid drunken clown had destroyed my career – both my careers.

"You were friends with Chris?" I said lamely.

"The only friend I have – damn it, *had* – in this space and time." His woozy gaze grew hard. "Hey – guess I need a new buddy. How about you, Sport? You game for plottin' a little revenge?"

"Revenge?" I finally lost it, and yelled. "How do we get revenge from the unemployment line?" I turned to storm out.

"Revenge for Chris." His voice was even, sinister. I stopped. "Who the hell do you think killed him, anyway?"

The clown rose, shoved past me, and went hopping down the stairs two-at-a-time, sure-footed in spite of his snoot-full. His announcement had me confused. "I thought it was a hunting accident," I called after him.

Maybe it wasn't. That thought sent ice down my back. If someone was after the marshal's plants in this place, then I was the only target left.

I weighed my options – of which I had none – as we stepped into the large front office, and I got my first good close-up look at one of the richest men in Central Texas. Emil Cadwallader was leaning back in his huge leather chair, a cigar in one hand and the wooden stock of a bullwhip in the other. He flicked his wrist back and forth, making that woven black snake writhe slowly. This would be our first and last meeting, I was sure.

On the far side, past the front windows, a door led to a small washroom in the corner. Behind the desk, built-in bookshelves housed stacks of papers and the twin of the large TV monitor in the lobby. On the wall opposite sat a massive leather couch. Andrea hated leather couches, but this looked like one of those expensive five hundred dollar jobs that she might tolerate.

"Sit down," Russell said from behind the door. Two cloth visitor's chairs sat out in front of the ornate desk. Off to the side, a taller, red-velvet seat had been placed in the corner near the washroom. Billy Dean seemed to read my mind, and nodded toward it.

"Russell's throne," he whispered. "That's why everybody calls him the Dauphin."

"Shut up, there," Russell bellowed. "Boss has the floor."

We took our seats. Cadwallader seemed to make a point of not making eye contact with me. "What do you mean coming down here in that get-up?" he asked Billy Dean.

The clown threw up his hands. "When Massa Russell calls, we drop what we's doing and come a' runnin'."

Russell growled. "You insolent--" he began.

"That's enough," Cadwallader cut him off. There was a moment of silence, then, to my horror, he looked straight at me. "Why the hell did you let him do that, Greenhorn?" he asked.

I sputtered, at a total loss for anything to say. "Sir, my name is George Blair--"

"Don't blame George," Billy Dean interrupted. "I'm sorry I did it. Say your piece and I'll go upstairs and pack my things."

"You ain't going nowhere, and you know it." The look in Cadwallader's eyes could have melted lead, and the white hair protruding from his ears might as well have been steam coming out. The bullwhip bucked. "We're going to see this thing through to the end." He pointed. "I just this minute got off the phone with my friends at the FCC. I called them before they could call me. This station will keep its license, but if you say that word on the air again, you will go to jail. You can't go gallivantin' around the Universe from a cell."

I took his measure, tried to memorize his looks, the way an alert undercover operative should. If this man's money was about to give birth to a whole new country, why the hell was he scared of the Federal Communications Commission?

The drunken, angry clown and the grizzled old man entered into a staring match.

"Chris was my friend," Billy Dean said.

"Yes, I know that. Those dummies should have waited 'til after the show to tell you."

"No they shouldn't. In fact, they should have told me right on the air who killed Chris."

Russell stopped sauntering and held out his arms. "Billy Dean, he fell on his deer rifle. The highway patrol said so."

"Is that so?" The clown turned in his chair. "The highway patrol? Or the Balcones Army?"

"That's enough." Cadwallader bit his lip.

One dumbfounding moment piled upon another. If everyone in this building knew I was a spy, why would they be so loose-lipped about their army?

Billy Dean leaned his elbows onto the desk edge, and his big red mouth twisted into an evil smile. "Stupid mistakes like that might cause your ball game to be rained out this evening."

Cadwallader looked away. "Beagle Benson's passing attack requires good weather. You want Sironia State to stay number one, don't you, Mr. Brown?"

No sooner did he pose the question than a clap of thunder shook the building. The hailstorm wasn't finished. Billy Dean looked upward, cocky. "Way I figure it, those State boys lost number one the minute Chris got killed."

"What?" The pressure was too much. The guy doing the yelling was me. "You all are talking football now? Football? What about the FCC? What's going to happen to us?"

"Very good, Mr. Blair." Cadwallader smiled and leaned back again. "I like a man who gets straight to the point, unlike some others." He leaned forward, clutching the whip in both hands. "State troopers say it was a hunting accident." The gaze was simply malevolent. "I want this storm system out of here by supper time."

I laughed out loud before I could catch myself. "Sorry, sir, but you talk like Billy Dean could tell a thunderstorm what to do."

Russell Crump collapsed into his throne, and glowered. The clouds rumbled again. Cadwallader twirled the whip, and pronounced sentence.

"The Zeebo Show is cancelled," he said. "Putting it back on the air would amount to declaring war on the Baptist Church. Michael can run cartoons for the kids every afternoon." He pointed the whip at Billy Dean. "The weather has to stay good, right on up to the Cotton Bowl."

"You're deaf, old man." Billy Dean stood, and snapped his fingers. "Good weather's over. I quit." He headed for the door.

I looked from one boss to the other. Cadwallader didn't blink an eye, but the Dauphin's face had beaded with sweat. So the idiot wants to resign? Let him, I wanted to say.

"Chris was my friend, too." Cadwallader's voice slowed the clown's exit. "It was a hunting accident, Mr. Brown."

"An accident on your deer lease."

The Dauphin pushed his glasses up on his nose. "No, he was out in the bushes near his house, Billy Dean. He fell on his gun, they think. One bullet, right in the chest. Hell, there's no reason the general staff--"

Cadwallader banged the whip's stock on the desk, and the weatherman grabbed the doorknob. "That's enough, Russell. Brown, if we can't work together, how do you expect me to stop the war games down between Sonora and San Saba next week?"

Billy Dean's hand lingered. "You're bluffing. The script don't have any war games planned down there. Not anywhere near Landview. I guaran-damn-tee it."

"Maybe the script's been re-wrote, Sergeant." Now Cadwallader's mouth twisted. Not a smile, a threat.

"No, *El Presidente*. It ain't."

They looked like two twelve-point bucks, puffed-up and facing off. I was shocked when Cadwallader was the first one to blink.

"You haven't given me a chance to explain the reason for this meeting," he said, his face blushing in some weird embarrassment. Billy Dean's TV utterance was fatal – why try so hard to keep him?

"You know that Frank Watkins, that ungrateful bastard, is going to Channel Twelve in Ft. Worth," the old boss continued. "I'm promoting Holiday to chief correspondent. He never was worth a shit on Zeebo, and he was a piss-poor weekend weatherman, but he can read a teleprompter." The cigar went to its rest in the ashtray. "Your equipment will be here soon, Billy Dean, but I need someone to train me a new weatherman before you leave, too."

The clown stared at him through bloodshot eyes. "You've finally gone crazy, Boss. You know nothin' happens that way." A nod in my direction. "You know that he--"

An explosion went off in front of the clown's face. I jumped back, and so did everyone else. Billy Dean was splayed back against the door, bloodshot eyes glaring out of that pale mask. Cadwallader reeled in the bullwhip, and I swear I saw a wisp of smoke drifting in the room. Chris hadn't been kidding about that weapon.

"Remember where you are and who you're talking to," the old man demanded. "If the whole place goes up in flames, so do you, with or without your lost property." He looked at me, and managed an awkward smile. "George, here, is going to learn the weather ropes, just like I say."

The clown took a step forward, fist clenched. "It don't matter what he does, as long as my equipment gets here. Pronto." He pointed at Russell. "This fool must have been talking to Victor again."

"Victor?" I asked. "That strange old Mexican man?" Cadwallader's jaw dropped, and all three of them seemed set back for a moment.

The boss came out of his stupor first, scratching his chin slowly with the rawhide. "How do you know about Victor, young man?"

I shrugged. "I just met him for about ten seconds, one night. If it's the same guy."

Cadwallader pursed his lips and nodded slowly. "Well, it's hard to explain, George, but Billy Dean here is wise in the ways things will happen in the – well, how they will happen in the future. But so is Victor. And sometimes they don't agree on what course things will take."

"Sometimes?" the Dauphin said. "This whole thing's a crock of shit."

"Shut up, Russell."

The staring match between the boss and the weatherman was back on, and I I still couldn't discern who held the power around here.

"Wouldn't you like that, George?" Cadwallader continued. "To learn how to forecast the weather? A whole new challenge."

I was dizzy. "A challenge?" I heard myself say. "You want me to be a weatherman on the air?" *But do you have any nukes?* – I wanted to add, but that question stuck on the roof of my mouth.

"Hear that, Zeebo?" Cadwallader taunted. "George is game. So you're going to teach him everything you know about the weather. You got two weeks or less--"

"Less," Billy Dean demanded. "You ain't slowin' me down."

"OK – days then, to pass on all that knowledge. All of it, Compadre. If I'm giving you the world, you're gonna at least give me a piece of it back." Now the whip pointed toward me. "George, you're gonna learn about the weather the way no one else on earth could learn about it."

Billy Dean's mouth twitched.

"What can you teach me that's so new about the weather?" I asked him.

"Nothin'," Billy Dean said softly. Then to Cadwallader. "You're a fool. You don't have me backed into no corner, and it sounds like you haven't heard a word I said for fifteen years."

"And you ain't the only one with all the secret knowledge," Russell said. He licked his lips, but pressed on, resembling a rodeo rider taunting an angry bull. "Victor talks to us, too, you know. Blood is thicker than—"

Billy Dean's flaring, red eyes stopped him mid-sentence, and I was getting tired of the secrets being passed on their little glances. I came in here to get fired, and to hell with it.

"Just keep that garbage maw closed, Russell," Billy Dean said. "This whole little weather-learning gambit's a waste of my time. And yours." It was as if I weren't even in the room. "I'll go ahead and teach the man-child a few tricks, but if this is some cute FBI plot to get a spy up my ass, just you remember: you'll never catch me. I've told you a thousand times how this plays out. You even try to come after me, you'll rue the day."

Cadwallader was on his feet. "Enough of our dirty laundry. Let's just follow the blueprint." Suddenly, he was all smiles. "George, here, had a rough start today, but he's a quick study, I can tell. We all gotta get back to work."

"Don't you worry about that." A nod toward me. "Be up in the office in ten minutes, Rookie. These boys want you to earn your keep, you're gonna earn it."

He swung the door open, and flapped down the hall on his long red shoes. The old man and his son-in-law stared past me. The tension in the air was thicker than custard, and somehow, I had missed something.

"Are you guys talking in code?" I said. "What's so special about the way he forecasts the weather? Doesn't he just get it off the teletype?"

A new clap of thunder answered me, rattling the windows behind Cadwallader's floor-length drapes.

"This storm," Russell Crump said. I looked at him. Pale and sweaty, his lips quivering. "You're listening to the only thunder in the whole state of Texas today." He advanced on me, and I couldn't tell whether he was on the verge of tears or a heart attack.

"You watch him," he demanded.

"Watch who, Mr. Crump?"

"That clown down there, for God's sake. Boss wants Sironia State to win the game today. They win, they'll stay Number One in the nation, on their way to a national championship for the first time. Keep that scrawny little bastard here up in his office, and if he starts into any hocus pocus, you come straight and tell me."

Cadwallader didn't protest.

"Yes, sir," I turned to go.

"George," Cadwallader said quietly. "I can imagine you've got your hands full right now. That's life, as they say. I just want you to remember one thing. You take this weather job, and you're working for us. Understand? Nobody else."

A pause, and I could feel him searching every thought that might be streaming from my own eyes. "A job like this will require all of your concentration. Follow my orders, sir. If you don't, the consequences are just too bad to imagine."

So what was so hard about learning weather forecasting? I wanted to ask. But I couldn't. I was numb, more certain than ever that they knew I was a spy, yet they were giving me a promotion, and they were letting the drunken clown keep his job. Something was indeed rotten in Denmark.

Zachary's words about "taking it in the shorts" came back. I got out of there as quickly as my legs could move. The hollow looks of those goons followed me – if Chris's death wasn't really an accident, they were just sizing up their next victim. I wondered if I were finally witnessing what Chief Lafferty said every cop would come up against sooner or later – the face of evil.

Chapter 10
A Sudden Storm

In the hall, I stared wistfully at the bathroom door. No
– my insides had nothing left. There was always the front door
– the marshal might criticize me for running, but surely he
would forgive me. Or maybe not. What would I be running
from? A promotion? On paper, an undercover man was
winning the game if he got a promotion. But signing up to be a
TV weatherman was just a diversion from my mission.

I gave up, and trudged down the long halls to the back
stairs. Hell, why was I thinking like a coward? I wasn't getting
my assignment done. Hadn't even started. So I decided to
change tactics. I opened the Weather Room door slowly. Billy
Dean seemed anything but angry, pitched back in his chair,
the broad clown smile still on his kisser, and he had found a
new flask of booze. My stomach sank – every moment I spent
with this bum was time wasted.

"So you want to be a weather monkey now?" he said.
"Career change like that's kind of sudden, ain't it?" He
laughed, too loudly for whatever joke he thought he had told.

"Been through a few of them lately," I said. My
patience was at an end, and I surprised myself when I spoke,
and laid all my cards on the table.

"Look, Mr. Brown, if I'm really going to be working under you, why don't we level with each other?"

I was out on the thin ice. I closed the door and leaned against the filing cabinet. I had him boxed in. Above him, and bigger. The physical advantage, Chief Lafferty would have described it in the Academy. Time was running out, I knew, so I made my play.

"You know I've never been on TV before," I said. "Who told you? Was it Chris, since you were best friends?"

The imp sneered, and took another swig.

I bulled ahead. "I'll do whatever weather chores you want me to do, Mr. Brown. But in exchange, I want information. Have you ever heard about the Balcones revolt? Are you mixed up in it? Because if you are, I'm sure I can work on some sort of immunity for you."

His chuckle turned to a gurgle when the next draw of whiskey hit it.

"Come on, Mr. Brown." I thought my front was pretty good, but I felt a line of sweat sneak down my temple. "You don't want to go to jail just because that old man down there couldn't find enough interesting things to do with all his money."

"I'll be damned. You got you a gold tongue in that mouth. I believe you could sell fleas to a tick hound." With another laugh, he slammed the flask down, got a rag out of the drawer and poured rubbing alcohol on it, and began to wipe off his clown grease. "You almost had me ready to turn myself in, by God."

"I'm not kidding, Mr. Brown." I made an attempt at looming over him. "We know Cadwallader's the money guy. But who's the kingpin? The brains? The commanding officer of this whole revolt? Tell me and I'll promise you to--"

The pungent alcohol vapors invaded my nose, but before I could press in any further, he flipped open the bottom drawer and pulled something out. A silver forty-five revolver.

He stuck it square in my belly. Every muscle in my body turned to mush. So much for the physical advantage.

"Word to the wise, Buckaroo," he said. "Don't try to corner a World War II vet. I been there before, and momma didn't raise no fool. If I thought you knew half of what you think you know, I might give you the time of day."

I stood there. For an eternity, composing my farewell to Andrea. But we never had intercourse. I had to die without ever becoming a real man?

I panted, and told myself, silently, that we lived in a civilized nation, and I had friends, and there were laws – but none of that carried any weight in those beady black eyes that stared up at me. He could pull the trigger, and likely Cadwallader would make sure my body was never found. I waited for the explosion that would bring down the night.

"OK. I take it back." I choked the words out.

He smiled – this time with his real mouth. Only a few white greasepaint streaks remained on his forehead. "Tell you what you're gonna do, Hotshot. Get your ass down to the parking lot and warm up your car. You're taking me to make sure that old man remembers who he's dealin' with. Same lesson you're learning right now. *Capiche*?"

"You – you're letting me go?"

"Of course not, Greenhorn. Cain't you listen to instructions?"

Shaking violently, I nodded.

"I'll swan. Thank God we didn't have boots like you in War Two. *Move--*"

I nodded, and backed up. No *boom*. Was he crazy? How did he know I wouldn't just head for the hills and call the cops? But confidence was oozing from his fresh-wiped pores as he un-cocked the pistol, and let me leave the room. I was halfway to the lobby before my heart started again. Outside, the raging hail from before had turned to a light rain, but I could only walk slowly. It felt good to get wet – I was still in one piece, and I wanted to run, get away from all of them, but --

I waited in the car, and the weatherman finally emerged, carrying a strange-looking leather purse that had been painted in splotches of bright blues, pinks, and greens. He opened the passenger-side door.

"That your booze bag?" I asked.

"You're pretty mouthy for a secret government agent," he said. I reached back and unlocked my own door. I couldn't trust what this guy's next move was. "To the lake," he said.

"Why the lake?"

The coyote smile. "They want you trained. Here's your first lesson. We'll also remind old High Pockets who's boss around here. Two birds with one stone, I call it."

I drove. Lake Centex abutted the rich part of town. Andrea's home sat not far away in the middle-class Mount Hope area. I took the road that followed the river, then the turn that went up the hill toward those neighborhoods. In a nodding moment, I realized my adrenalin had run out – the sound of the rain on the car roof was putting me to sleep. I had to talk to stay awake.

"You never answered my question," I said. "Which side are you on?"

He raised his cigarette hand to shush me. "Stop babbling, Boy." A gesture out the window. "The people who live in those clouds get irritated pretty easy. You don't want to make 'em mad right before you ask a favor from them."

"What people?"

His bloodshot eyes flared. "I gotta concentrate."

"What people are you talking about? Do the Russians have some secret reconnaissance plane?" No response. "OK, who lives in the clouds? Is it the Russians? The Chinese?" I asked.

He cracked the foggy window, to see better – drizzle soaked his forehead. "I'm kinda old fashioned, Boy. I call them the 'Thors.'"

"Thors? Oh, come on. What sort of joke--" He shushed me with a motion, then pointed down the long slope to the boat ramps, in the direction opposite the one I had traveled with Andrea the night before.

Billy Dean scowled. "Not here. Take me to the dam." That was another two miles, and more desolate. The hair went up on my neck. He probably brought his gun in that weird leather purse.

"Look, you got me," I said. "I already played my cards, and you seem to know what I'm doing anyway. They can find me dead at the dam, or right here on the street. Just tell me whose side you're on, for God's sake. And if it's theirs, then why in the hell--" The rain had stopped.

He stared at me with those piercing eyes. Didn't pull his gun, didn't open that multi-colored purse. He only lit a new cigarette. Not with the lighter in the dash, but with a metal-cased one like the one I remembered my father carrying. Except that on its side, this one had some sort of raised engraving – along with an unintelligible word written in Old English script.

"So how long were you friends with Chris?" I said, hoping to distract him from whatever scheme he had up his sleeve.

His eyes flared, and he sat up straight. "Just like I thought. This storm system is about give out. We'll give it a little re-charge." Then, thoughtful. "Everyone was friends with Chris. Went hunting and fishing with him. He knew everything about every animal alive."

"Did you two go hunting often?"

He ignored the question. "Knew how to talk to deer. And dogs. Could converse with them just as sure as we're talking here. Could hear the birds warn each other when a snake slithered into in the territory, but a college boy like you wouldn't believe stuff like that, huh?"

"Those sound like old wives tales. Not science."

He flicked his ash out the window, and sighed. "The old fart's bought his own army. But I expect Chris told you all that."

"Yes, sir. --" Now we were getting somewhere.

A sidelong glance. "Joe College, let's not start out behind the eight-ball, OK? So I screwed up and almost lost you your job. But if I'm going to teach you the weather, you'd better damn well pay attention. Now shut up and stay shut."

The sharp look again, and he passed his thumb over the odd purse. "Park by the roadblocks, on the top of the spillway," he said. "And keep the motor running. Watch every move I make, but stay close to the car in case the Corps of Engineers guy comes and tells you to leave."

He opened the door and climbed out, hugging the purse to his side. "If the gentle folk upstairs are in the mood." Before I could ask anything else, the weatherman shot out of the car like a rabbit, vaulted over the wide gate that closed off the spillway road, and clambered down the huge rocks that made up the water side of the dam.

I left my door open, but went as far as the hurricane fence, so I could keep him in view. Relief washed over me. If assassination were his intention, he would have invited me down to the water's edge before pulling the trigger. The sun was in and out of the remaining clouds, its rays throwing diamonds over the lake's green surface, some so bright they stung my eyes. If he planned to meet someone, had summoned any Balcones soldiers, they had not yet arrived.

Then I saw him down at the water line, crouching, digging inside that garish leather pouch until he pulled out something white. It must have been covered with glass flecks or glitter, because it sparkled in the sun like snake's scales. He started waving the thing – a stick or rod not a foot long – above his head, three, four times. The watchman could have come up behind me, but I didn't dare look away.

He moved lower, until his feet were covered with water, and swept the sparkling stick downward like a slow dagger. My vision blurred the instant he touched the white rod to the lazy water's surface, because the earth beneath us rumbled. Or was it just thunder?

A flicker pulled my gaze away from the scrawny weatherman – there, out over the lake, new clouds swirled into existence before my very eyes, twirling and puffing like new balloons, coming into being in a whirlpool motion and climbing into the sky until they were caught by the wind that had just kicked up.

Billy Dean still stirred the mud-green surface with his rod. For a moment, I thought I heard him moaning on the stiff breeze, but then the swelling gale wafted quiet – he was singing!

I leaned over the fence, but a bright flash blinded me and threw me back. A jagged bolt of lightning as wide as a fishing boat hit the lake's surface, way out in the middle. That was the negative-like picture imprinted in my eyeballs, anyway.

All hell was breaking loose, and I had to grab onto the wire fence to keep from slipping on the wet gravel. Still blinking, still blinded by that shaft of brilliant yellow-white electricity that was burned into my brain. I looked again at the middle of the lake – a sort of gaping maw seemed to open up in those milliseconds, carved out of raw air behind a new flurry of lightning. The vision was ultimate brightness, and darkness at the same instant – I had the impression of gazing into an endless cave behind a shaft of light, a cave that led into a new, impossible landscape.

With rapid blinking, my real vision returned. A cloud of green steam sizzled above the center of the expanse. Water conducts electricity, and when I looked back down the boulders, I fully expected to see Billy Dean's body stretched out down at the water's edge.

Instead, through the deafening, unceasing thunder that surrounded us, the weatherman, shirttails out, came clambering up those rocks just as the rain started anew. Fluffy clouds above us had gone gray and been unzipped all at once. Little bits of hail were mixed in with the heavy drops, and stung my face.

Billy Dean mounted the fence, and his leather pouch caught on the wire. I reached to help. "Don't touch, jackass," he cried and shoved me away. We scrambled to the car, landing in the front seat at the same time, both panting and reeking like wet mongrels.

"What happened?" I asked between gulps of air. "Jesus, that lightning might have killed you."

He glanced over. His coyote look, followed by a sinister laugh. "Baseball games are rained out all the time. Well, this will be one of the first gully washers to stop a football game."

"But why take it out on Sironia State?" I had to yell to get above the din of rain on the car's metal.

"'Cause that's his team." The weatherman tore open his cigarette pack, searching for one smoke that wasn't soaked. "They didn't have to kill Chris, so let's see how his precious ball team likes this."

The air hugged close, but the deluge was too strong for me to crack a window without getting wet. I guided the car out onto the road and drove slowly, like a blind man. "What the hell you did down there, Billy Dean? How did you know a storm would blow up just at that instant?"

He had discovered a single, somewhat-dry fag, and smoothed it and lit it before he answered. "That's your first lesson, *amigo*. The clouds are alive, and if you make friends with the beings who live in them, they'll do you an occasional favor."

I leaned my head against the cold window. A revolution was brewing, and I was stuck in a rainstorm with a drunken, chain-smoking nut.

"You're full of shit," I said, imagining that he might have killed men in the war for lesser insults, but not caring. He didn't respond, but whooped whenever we splashed into a big puddle.

"I'm glad you're having a good time," I said. "What's next on the schedule? You have a gun in that purse, too?"

He laughed harder. "Hells bells, College Man. You look sicker than a stack of black cats. You think I would threaten a bona fide government agent? Crap, I don't want the IRS down on me."

"Bullshit," I cried. Finally, it all came out, the fear of that huge black cloud, the thunder deafening my ears, the shuddering humiliation of being in front of the TV cameras. We were already on the Temple highway, and I swerved across the wet pavement, and skidded off into the muddy shoulder. I put my finger in his face. "Out with it," I demanded. "You already tell Cadwallader about me? Did Chris? Hell, somebody did."

His shocked look dissolved into a giggle. "Cool your jets, Punk. I never squealed on you." He tossed the forlorn butt out into the rain, got a handful of the cold falling water and washed his face with it.

"Yeah? How can I trust you not to tell?"

An angry look. "Because I ain't one of them." He looked for a new weed, but they were a lost cause, so out the window went the whole pack. "I got a shipment coming, see? Something that is rightfully mine is finally being returned to me. The only thing you need to remember – the only thing on this earth you have to worry about, *Mr. Apprentice Weatherman* – is making sure you don't get in the way of me getting my property back. *Capiche?*"

His eyes had turned into those of an eagle – or some evil bird of prey. My breath caught, and my head was spinning – I could no longer ignore the memory of that sight – clouds puffing up out of thin air.

Cadwallader and Crump were criminals – that I could believe. But who was this guy? He committed the cardinal sin on TV, yet they had spent twenty minutes in that office kissing his ass. And what was this about a shipment? Was he dealing in morphine? It was something the marshal should know – I was sure of it. Maybe there was no Balcones army after all. Maybe they were just smuggling something into the country. But what? He was a drunk, and carried a six-shooter around –

"Well? You got that clear, Punk?"

"Yes, sir," I heard myself say. A complete lie. Nothing – about anything – was clear.

"Now get out of this mud hole and take us back to the station. We gotta get ready for the six o'clock weather."

I drove, feeling as washed-out as the flowing streets. I still hadn't collected my first bit of usable intelligence, because I was sure his "shipment" was just penny ante. For some crazy reason, I believed him when he claimed he wouldn't rat on me. But then, they already knew, didn't they?

As for that other thing – the idea that this scrawny wreck of a human being had the power to invent storm clouds – even though I had witnessed it myself, or witnessed something – that wasn't really reportable, was it? I didn't want the marshal to decide I was a complete idiot.

So I told myself I had never seen what I saw, switched the windshield wipers to "high," and kept driving.

Chapter 11
Judgment Night

In the station parking lot, I turned off the ignition, but Billy Dean shook his head. For some reason, he'd had a change of heart.

"You look more washed out than a puppy crawlin' out of a storm drain," he said. "I'll do my usual. You get on home, and sleep it off. But be here on time, tomorrow. There's lots to learn, and I won't have you getting' up in front of those maps and actin' a fool."

The passenger door came open, letting in the deluge, but I grabbed his arm. Another wilting look.

"Mr. Brown, what was that you stuck in the lake water? Some sort of silver iodide, or – what? Did it really make those clouds?"

A disgusted smile. "Believe your eyes, or don't. Ain't no skin off my nose. Just be here in the mornin'."

I went and stretched out on the bed, commanding the crazy swirl of thoughts in my head to be still. Miraculously, they did, and I woke just in time to get ready to go to Andrea's for our usual Friday night date. I was driving down Sironia Parkway before I even remembered the events of the afternoon. Rain still fell steadily.

A few blocks from her house, I stopped at the Seven-Eleven pay phone.

"Marshal, I don't even know what I'm going to say. Either they're crazy or I am."

Silence on the other end, so I kept talking. "Marshal, did it ever occur to you that there may be no Balcones revolt at all?"

I heard him spit. "You hear the State score?"

"Did they lose?"

"They're losing." I heard him cuss under his breath. "Can't have a passing game when you're under water." Another cuss word, like he was talking to someone else in the room. Then, "Can't believe it's like they said—I just can't gol-darn believe it--"

"Like who said, Marshal?" I asked.

"Never mind." He was mad. In that moment, of course I thought I had done something wrong. Only later would I remember the tone in his voice – that sad, almost whimpering resignation. Something he had always been promised was coming true.

Another sigh. "OK, George. Tell me exactly what you saw."

"I saw a drunk bossing around the richest man in Texas. Then that same drunk went out to the lake and made clouds out of thin air. Or it seemed like he did. Marshal, what's really going on out at that TV station?"

His low chuckle gathered steam. "George, it's time we get things straight. This is Friday night and I'm on my second beer. There'll be no more second guessing the intelligence I've given you, y'hear? There is a revolt, and Cadwallader is one of the leaders. Bank on it. And yes, that Billy Dean is a crazy loudmouth—"

"Not just him, Marshal. All three of them are like a covey of bedbugs. And I haven't seen soldier one. This Balcones army is a figment of somebody's imagination."

"Aw, hell, get your head on straight, son." Another laugh. "I told you we already lost some boys who went scouting those tin soldiers out there. Those nukes Cadwallader's army possesses are the real McCoy. You ain't seen them yet, but you will. Now buck up and take it like a man. You signed on to do a job. I sent you in there to find out who their leader is. So get off your tokus and be more effective, startin' tomorrow. Clear?"

"Marshal, did you hear what I said? About him creating clouds out of lake water?"

"For God's sake, son, quit worrying about a pissing match between the old man and the clown. I promised to take the missus to the movies. Find Mr. Big. I don't trust my Washington boys any further than I could throw 'em. If we don't get results, like right now, they're gonna do everybody dirty. We're running out of time. You hear me?"

Andrea met me at the door.

"Did you forget how to dial a phone?" she said. "I've been a nervous wreck since Daddy's old army buddies started calling at six this morning. What's all this about Cuba, George? His friends say there might really be a war."

The hair on my neck bristled. Good. No mention of the Zeebo fiasco. Still, I was facing a whole night of more questions about the police station, and was losing the heart to keep this charade up. "Did something happen?" I asked. "I heard there were war games out west."

"You dummy. Cuba is east of us. I thought you were Mr. Smarty in Geography class. And this isn't a game, George. They might even bring up the reserves. If Daddy goes, are you going to be here for me and mom?"

"Of course I'll be here, Darling."

She kissed me, then reached inside the door, and brought out a large box, and shoved it into my hand.

"It's a dress. I wore it once, and I'm sick of it. Take me to Golden's. They're open another hour, so be quick, or I can't look at anything else." She settled in the passenger seat, tugged her dress properly over her knees, and looked straight ahead. I patted her leg, but she slapped my hand away.

"Drive, George Blair. I heard a nasty rumor about you today, and you just better hope it's not true."

Silence. She just sat there and sizzled. After a long, shuddering moment, I choked it out -- "What rumor?"

Still not looking at me. "First Janice said it, so I didn't give it a thought. You know what a dang pot-stirrer she is. Wants everybody to dance to her tune. But, guess what? I just got off the phone with Marie. Mom's pretty upset."

Oh, God. I took a deep breath, and remembered my story. "I was going to tell you tonight, Dear. Marie saw the show?" Of course she did – she was in love with Dobie Gillis, and that show came on right after Zeebo.

"What show?"

My breath caught. Slow down. Take this one easy. I tried a smile, stuffed my voice full of innocence. "What exactly is your mother upset about?"

A rifle stare. "Oh, no, Blair. You're not dodging me. First you're gonna explain what 'show' you're talking about, then you're gonna explain the rumors that are all over town that say you flunked out of the police academy. Start talkin'."

I took as much of a breath as my pounding heart would allow. "Well, I did flunk out. Sort of."

"Sort of? What kind of darn fool answer is that? Either you did or you didn't. I told her she was lying, 'cause I saw you graduate with my own eyes. So, dang it, Blair, tell me what's going on."

"Officially, they rescinded my appointment to the force."

Her jaw fell slack. She put both hands on the dash, and her belly heaved in and out. I thought she was going to hyperventilate.

Finally, a helpless whine. "I can't believe what I'm hearing. You said you were third in your class. Was that a lie? What in Lucifer's Hades is wrong with you?"

That was Andrea's version of blaspheme. The chips were down. It would be so much easier if I could tell her about my assignment. But I could only play the cards the marshal dealt me. I kept my eyes on the road, and braced myself. "I got a job on television."

I felt the ray gun beams of her gaze bore into the side of my head. She didn't speak. Neither of us breathed. I blinked, trying to shake the illusion that even the traffic was standing still.

"You what?" She collapsed against the passenger door, holding her head. "Don't go right. Go left. The long way."

"By the lake?"

"Yes, by the lake. You might as well drive into the lake, for all I care, because my life is over." Her eyes brimmed with tears.

"Andrea, I was going to surprise you. I've always wanted to be a reporter. I just never told you, I don't think. And it's the darnedest thing. They want me to do the weekend weather. Isn't that great?" Offense. Stay on offense.

"You're talking crazy, George. If there was insanity in your family, you should have told me before this." Her voice geared into a shrill scream, and she stomped her feet. "That's the second job you got on a silver platter and managed to foul up. You were going to get promoted. I can't stand this shiftlessness. Oh, the Savior, I can't take it--" She started weeping against the closed window.

We crested the hill overlooking the lake, the Costas' house to the right, Ludlum mansion on the left. Down below, near the boat ramps, she had let me take her parking a couple of times, until her father convinced her that parkers were regularly murdered there by hoodlums. I had seen more of the lake this day than I had in a year.

I let her cry, feeling for a gap in the tension, when she suddenly rolled down the window. My God, she was going to jump out –

"Don't, Andrea--"

"Look," she cried. "There he is. It's him. It's him."

Out on the dusky surface of the water, two small fishing boats rocked near the woods on far shore. I thought of Chris. The sportsman. What if he were not dead, but out there on one of those boats, lolling back, waiting to catch the big one? He just forgot to call home.

"Not there, idjit. *There*." She slapped my arm. Bright marking lights shone from either side of a large craft, a monster on a body of water this small. Its huge wake tossed every fishing boat it passed. Though the light was failing, I could make out the unmistakable form of an army troop carrier, like one in the movies, churning toward the ramps.

"What the hell is a troop carrier doing on Lake Centex?" I asked aloud.

"Oh, stop cussin'. That tall man is Mr. Cadwallader, the millionaire. That boat is called a *duck*, and he bought it from Army Surplus. It was on the front page." She bounced on the seat like a schoolgirl. The change of mood was amazing, but I had seen it before – whenever Andrea was confronted with Sironian royalty.

"Andrea, that's a troop carrier."

"Oh, you argue about anything. It's called a duck. Slow down -- see, that's him in the back." The road took a long slope downward, leading to the ramps. I pulled onto the shoulder, inches away from the cliff's edge.

"Nope. That's not Cadwallader," I said, playing it as cool as Kookie Byrnes. Suddenly, my poker hand was brimming with new aces. "I was in a meeting with him this afternoon, and his hair is all white. That guy's is brown."

She turned, mouth agape. "What? You were in a meeting with Emil Cadwallader? Oh, George now you've become a pathological liar."

"I told you, Dear. I got hired at his television station. They're gonna train me for the weather. They liked my audition."

"George Blair, you're full of shit." She had never used that word before. A flash of childish terror washed over her face, so ridiculous that I burst into laughter. Within seconds, she was cackling with me. "Oh, I'm sorry. That was so out of character for me." Serious again. Not serious, mad. "Now stop this fairy-tale-ing. What in Hades have you done?"

With a loud scraping, the duck banged against the boat ramp, and started climbing it onto solid ground. I gunned the car, heading up the opposite hill, and used her moment of consternation to recite my cover story about my unspoken dreams of being a newsman. I even improvised a postscript – it was my wise counsel that saved Billy Dean Brown's job after he cussed on the air.

When I finally checked to see how much of that portfolio of hogwash she was buying, Andrea the snake confronted me. Her eyes were slits. Not good.

"George Blair, you have never once told me you wanted to be a newsman. Something is wrong here. Bad wrong. And I can't believe you didn't know that stupid weatherman was a drunk. Everyone knows he used to be in and out of jail. When he ain't on TV, he's drinkin' and playin' pool down at the Brass Rail."

"Oh, there's always rumors about celebrities, Andrea." Why I was partially trying to cover for him, I'll never know.

"You're telling me you were in a meeting with Billy Dean Brown and Emil Cadwallader this afternoon?"

"I swear. It was touch and go for a while. I had to talk like a lawyer – it was all I could do to keep those two prima donnas from tearing each other apart." With Andrea, if you didn't embellish, you died.

"You're crazy, Blair. If he said the f-word on television, they'll wind up arresting him, anyway. You just watch." She jabbed home her point with two fingers into my side. "Wait a minute. If they send him off to prison, why couldn't *you* get the head weatherman job?"

The jabs hurt. She always picked the same place to dig in. But her ability to switch gears and aim right for the heart of any opportunity was simply Olympic-caliber. Good – she was blinded by Cadwallader's fortunes, but I wasn't out of the woods yet.

A hiss. "Old good-hearted George, full of Christian charity, as usual. For pity's sake, you're going in there tomorrow and telling them you're insulted they would take a cusser above you. You tell them you want a raise, and the top job. Heck, anybody can learn the weather, even you."

I maneuvered the car into the Sironia Center's parking lot. "I'm not so sure, hon. Everybody raves about what a good forecaster Billy Dean is. The farmers love him." I drew the line at that. She would never hear what happened out at the lake if I could help it.

"Don't 'hon' me. He's a drunk. An ugly, scrawny little dwarf. But you – you're handsome, George. I'm sure Mr. Cadwallader wants only good-lookers on his channel. Like Chuck Holiday."

"But I don't have any on-air experience, Dear. And Chris was sort of a friend of mine, and he lied about me working somewhere else. I'm going to take this one step at a time."

"He lied? And then he shot himself today? See what God does to liars? Who was he, anyway? You never mentioned any Chris." Her eyes narrowed again. She could sense a prevarication from a hundred yards.

"It's a long story," I said.

"I'll just bet." She cocked her head. "You know what your punishment will be if you're telling me a bunch of lies, George Blair."

Her look could have melted an iceberg. No, I never knew what punishments she ever planned, but when she made a threat like that, my mind flashed on movies about World War II.

Her lips pursed. Thinking. Conniving. "What's so hard about drawing squiggles on a map and reading cue cards, anyway? How long? How long 'til you learn that, George?"

An answer burst out of me with no antecedents. "Three weeks. Or four. And the weatherman doesn't read cue cards."

"My foot he don't. I've watched that Billy Dean Brown. He could talk the leg off a dog. He's gotta be reading cue cards."

"Maybe he's not as dumb as you give him credit for."

"Never mind that. Shut up and listen. So you're saying three or four weeks to get into that job? Let's make it two."

I pulled into the loading lane, and she opened the door. "You'll introduce me to Mr. Cadwallader, won't you?"

"Well, yeah. Andrea, I haven't even worked a full day yet."

"Next week, then." She hauled the dress box onto her lap, and suddenly kissed my cheek. Her glance was part flirtation, part mountain lion measuring its prey. "I don't know about you, Blair."

In her absence, I played the radio and shored up the details of my cover story. As I feared, when she plopped back into the seat, she opened fire at every weak point in my line.

"Are you going to the funeral?"

"What funeral?"

"Why, Chris's funeral, dummy. Was he your friend or not? And I still don't know from where."

"I'm sure I mentioned him before--"

"I don't want to hear it. Drive me by Dr. Kilgallen's. We might go past Rusty's again, too." The demure look. "I'm working on a plan."

I shook inside. That might be the worst thing she could say. "Andrea, I don't want to drive by their houses. We never see anything at your doctor's, and why you were ever fascinated with that plumber, I'll never know."

"You have no memory, Blair." Her jaw was set. "We've seen Missy's car at Dr. Kilgallen's house five times. And Rusty Carter is an air conditioning man, not a plumber. What are you so worried about? I'm not infatuated with him. We just clicked, somehow. He understands me." She clawed through her purse. "A girl can have guy friends, too, you know."

"He understands you after three hours at your house? Andrea, I'm tired of spying on people whenever we get in the car. I'd rather park somewhere and neck."

She huffed. "You've got a dirty mind, Mr. Lazy. We'll start by you driving me out to the Line."

"The Line? You mean the liquor stores outside town?"

"You heard me."

I steered in that direction, but her explanation didn't come. Finally, I couldn't stand the suspense. "Andrea, you don't drink. Are you getting something for your dad?"

"Don't spoil a surprise. Besides, you haven't asked me about my day." She spent the miles ranting about Janice's rare food shop, and the chocolate-covered grasshoppers they sold. I half-listened, seized with the wonderful notion that we were going to celebrate. Would she finally let go and come to my apartment without one of her friends? And why? How could she be warming up to my new career this quickly?

"I'll go in," I volunteered when we parked outside of Jezebel's liquor store. My favorite haunt back in college, though she would never know that. "What do you want?"

"No, let me do this."

I tried to squelch a smile while I waited. She returned, looking smug. "Burger time."

I wasn't having it. I moved across the seat, took her in my arms, and kissed her, long and hard. "Let's be friends. What's in the bag?"

"None of your business, George Blair."

"Andrea, this is the first time I've taken you to a package store. Are we going to celebrate my new job?"

She pushed me back. "I can't believe my ears. You know I don't drink. You just said so, yourself."

I drove, still considering fantasies that Andrea might at last be changing into the carefree, fun-loving, normal girl I knew she could be. A pumpkin transforming into a coach. I finally exploded. "Andrea, don't play coy."

"OK, numbskull. You don't have the patience of a rat." She jerked a flask from the sack. Jim Beam. "This is for you to sneak to that weather drunk. A little insurance. Let's be honest, George. That man sinned before God and every family in town. If they let him keep his job today, it was just for show. They have to fire him. If he's there tomorrow, you can get him soused before he goes on."

"Andrea, you're crazy. If Mr. Cadwallader found out I did something like that, he'd fire me, too."

"No, George. He'll thank you."

This was below the belt, even for her. I could sense her enjoying my froth, felt her loading more ammo. She wanted me to blow, so she could annihilate me. After five years, I knew her M-O well.

When the Burger Ranch came into view, she sighed. "We need to pick out our china in the next few weeks." A smile. The picture of innocence.

"Andrea." I spoke through gritted teeth. "How can I learn the job if I torpedo the guy right now? Sure he's a creep, but I won't offer booze to an alcoholic who can't help himself."

She smirked. "Don't be so self-righteous. A drunk is his own worst enemy. Momma's said that a thousand times. If he does himself in, that's not your fault."

In another swift movement, she took my right hand in hers, kissed my fingertips seductively, then opened my palm and shoved the flask of bourbon into it.

"You're the cross I have to bear," she said. "You promised your mother you would always take care of me, and look who's doing the protecting. Two weeks, Blair. You're on notice." Only the world ending would make Andrea forget the infernal vow I gave to my mother on her deathbed.

"So what do I do? Leave this bottle lying around the weather room? This sounds like a bad plot on Playhouse Ninety. I'm not doing it." I guided the car into the only open stall.

"Hold your horses, Mr. Television. You're the one who took a job without telling me. Our wedding's only eight months away, and if you don't want me to be one of those career girls, you have to get promoted, like it or not."

I flicked the carhop call switch. Andrea pouted while she played with my shirtsleeve. "You're destined to be a chief, George. Squaw want to marry big chief."

A deep breath. "I love you, Andrea." I laid the hooch on the seat. "I don't need to be promoted right now. We can get married just as well if I become head weatherman later. You know I'll make you a fortune, no matter what kind of job I wind up in."

She looked down her nose. "That might impress Mrs. Hobbs, but she's senile. You owe me, George." With a practiced motion, she grabbed my little finger and pulled it back until I wanted to scream.

"You order our burgers and promise me right now that you'll drive by the doctor's on the way home," she commanded.

His house was only a few blocks out of the way, so it was really no trouble.

Chapter 12
Speeding

Andrea spent the evening laying out her new plans – *our* new plans, which she concocted with a speed and agility that was amazing. The only trouble was that they all seemed to revolve around a very close relationship with Emil Cadwallader, his wife, and their whole social set.

"Wake the Hades up, George Blair," she yelled more than once. The most draining day of my life was weighing on me. At last she grimaced, and released me. I left her house just before midnight.

On East Austin Lane, red lights flashed, a police siren wailed, and I noticed I was three miles over the speed limit. I switched off my engine and waited for the officer to walk up. The night droning of locusts enveloped me, and the guy took his sweet time. I actually dozed off before he leaned in the window.

"What the hell are you doin', boy? Drivin' in your sleep?"

The flashlight beam stung my eyes. When he pulled it away, I recognized Homer Tudberry's barrel-chested shape. He began scribbling in a ticket book.

"Oh, come on. You're not really giving me a ticket, Marshal?" I yelled, suddenly awake. "I know I wasn't speeding."

"The night has a thousand eyes, George. If a spy sees me stop someone, he'll get suspicious if there's no citation to go along with it. I've been waiting all damned evening for you to leave your girlfriend's house. I've got an assignment. You're going to Chris Ellis' service tomorrow."

"But I didn't even know him, really. He just died yesterday. Isn't that pretty fast? Won't there be an autopsy?"

He squatted down, grunting. "Don't make me do all the thinking for you, George. Somebody paid off the coroner, likely. Cadwallader will be there, so maybe some of his army cronies will be, too. The closer we get to a missile launch, the more likely they are to post bodyguards."

"My God, did you hear something?"

"Shut up and listen. Chris had a military mind. They tried to recruit him, but he was too much of a patriot. My money says they tracked him on his way home from the deer lease to make one more try. They probably told him too much during their sales pitch, and when he said 'no' again, they shot him. Bastards. This wasn't supposed to happen."

I stared at him. "I don't guess any killing is ever supposed to happen. But, come to think of it, they might have already given me a sales pitch."

He tensed. "What? What sales pitch? Out with it, George."

"They want me to learn the weather from Billy Dean. Marshal, that was spooky, what he did out at the lake today – Wait. Aren't you supposed to be at the movies?"

"Mrs. Tudberry had one of her famous headaches. So they want you to learn the weather? When did this come up? "

"They want to put me on the air. Marshal, you're not listening. I think that weird guy actually made that thunderstorm happen this afternoon."

"Well, don't look at me. You're the scientist." He started pacing a short course, up and down, next to the car. "This damn train better not be running off the track," he said. A sort of mumble that, maybe, I wasn't supposed to hear.

"What does that mean?" I said.

"Nothin'. Get home and sleep. Dress up nice for the funeral. You never know who you might meet there."

He chuckled – strangely. Then pointed a fat finger. "You OK?" he asked. "Is your head still clear?"

"No, sir. I'm asleep on my feet."

Leaning down again. Peering into my eyes. "You'll make it, son. Just a few more days. But being undercover means following orders. Like I say, pay attention at that planting tomorrow. Get there bright and early. Don't miss a minute of it. Is that clear?"

"Yes, sir." My belly churned. He was warning me about something, without coming out and saying it. Why?

"Find Mr. Big. Clear?"

"Yes, sir."

He handed me the ticket and turned away. Any number of cars had passed us. He was right about the night having eyes. I called after him.

"Marshal, do I really have to pay this?"

"Look on the back, dummy."

Paper-clipped to the ticket was a twenty-dollar bill. I drove home.

Chapter 13
A Flash of Blue

I passed out immediately. A deep sleep. Until about
four a.m., when I woke and lay there, letting my apprehension
build to astronomical levels. Something was going to happen
at that funeral. Maybe the Feds were going to strike, arrest
Cadwallader, or his army officers, if they did show? But the
marshal should have told me to take a gun, in case things got
out of hand – the look on Tudberry's face started haunting me.
He knew something. Yes, and it would happen at the funeral –
but where in police tactics did it say you should keep your
only inside man in the dark?

That look – something was going wrong. But this was
Marshal Tudberry. He wouldn't let anything happen to me.

Would he?

Either Ft. Hood had sent a whole division to Chris's
funeral, or the rumors of the Balcones army were true. It was
quick to have a funeral this soon after a death, especially
considering that the autopsy report had yet to be issued. I
chalked that up as one more proof of Cadwallader's influence.
Maybe things were afoot, as promised. I watched the
uniforms, and wondered if Mr. Big might be among them.

"Hey, George. Sad day, huh?" Michael Lemmon, the director heir apparent shook my hand, and we ambled up the wide stone staircase together. Bodies choked the main entrance of First Presbyterian, the line moving slowly. "Did you know Chris very well?"

"Not really. Was he in the army?"

Michael shrugged. "Nah. Belonged to some hunting club. A lot of guys from Ft. Hood in it. He took me to one of their keggers last year. Man, those GIs can drink."

"Guess so."

Michael's somber countenance was offset by a mischievous twinkle in his eye. "Ready for this evening?"

"What's this evening?"

An evil smile. "Billy Dean says a novice has to sink or swim. You're doing the weather tonight, daddy-o."

The thought of stepping out in front of the camera's red light again made my belly convulse, but the sudden rumble of police motorcycles on the street distracted me. A hearse and two sleek limousines followed a squad of dashing young motorcycle cops. I could have been one of them, making ten bucks per funeral, off duty.

On the curb on the far side of the street, Billy Dean stood laconically, smoking a cigarette. He wore a seedy black suit, string tie, and his hair had enough grease in it to reflect the sunlight.

"You heard the coroner's report?" The question made me jump.

"What, they already had time to put one out?"

"Suspected homicide."

I caught my breath. Maybe the weatherman was right. But if Cadwallader was behind it, how would they let that out? "Not an accident? Who do they think did it?"

A shrug. "The shot came from at least ten feet away, so no way he fell on his gun. They're questioning every hunter in the club, but nobody's talking. Those army boys stick together. I bet they never find the jerk."

I remembered to be cool, not act like a cop. "No one had any grudge against Chris?" I asked. "He never got into trouble?"

Michael chewed his lower lip, and thought. "Once. They were out drinking last spring, and one of those soldiers looked cross-eyed at Chris's wife. Chris smashed the bum's motorcycle."

Before I could ask the obvious, Michael shook his head. "No. Not revenge. They sent that bastard to Germany. Boss saw to that." His eyes lit up. "Here she comes."

"Who?"

"Marilyn. Chris's wife."

A hush fell over the crowd while a woman with blonde hair was helped from the lead limo. The obvious family members around her wore muted colors, but she wore black. She climbed the steps in their midst, head high, face covered by a thin veil.

"Good grief, Charlie Brown," I heard myself whisper. Marilyn Ellis was a perfect black vector floating effortlessly up the stairs, surrounded by confused, teary-eyed chatterboxes.

"He kept her at home," Michael said, answering my unspoken question. "Nobody at the station really knows her, except maybe Billy Dean."

"I would keep her at home, too. " I couldn't see her face, but her shape, her bearing – there was something magical here.

Near the top step, her face was just discernible behind the veil. Striking eyes – were they blue? Not puffy, just sad.

"Move aside, there. Move, please." Russell Crump's wide frame wallowed out of the clogged doorway. Bodies fell back, and Cadwallader, himself, emerged from the church and extended a hand to receive the stricken widow. As she looked up into the old man's face, I could see from the corner of my eye that Billy Dean had crossed over to this side of the street. He threw his cigarette down and stood with his hands on his hips.

Marilyn Ellis recoiled, then seemed to steel herself, letting her demure white hand fall gracefully into the old man's weathered paw. At the same instant, she glanced in my direction and our gazes locked for the briefest instant.

Blue.

Those eyes, sterling blue. A flash passed between us – some feeling from her – I thought – I know energy was pouring out of me – so very strange and foreign, yet somehow comforting. Before I could even guess at the meaning of that gaze, she turned away, and let the rangy television tycoon haul her behind him. I exhaled.

Michael was staring at me, laughing. "She's a looker, all right."

"Any kids?"

"No. Poor Chris felt bad, always out hunting or fishing or playing poker. Never got rid of his bachelor habits, even though she deserved better. I never could tell they had a real love life at all."

I heard another sigh escape my mouth. "If they didn't, he was certifiably insane," I said.

We worked our way to the few remaining slots in the back pews. I sat on the end, purposely, so that I had a clear view of Marilyn Ellis when I leaned over. The veil complicated things. She might be twenty or twenty-five. Even thirty. I bit my lip, banishing my unholy thoughts. Not at her husband's funeral. Besides, I was engaged.

Cadwallader sat next to the grieving widow. Halfway through the eulogy, the gray head began nodding. The old codger was asleep.

"Sleazy disrespectful son-of-a-bitch." The voice turned me around. Billy Dean lounged, smoking, in the last pew, behind us.

"Shhh." Michael gestured.

I could smell the whiskey coming off him, yet I was the one who was drunk. Andrea and her mom would be at the mall cafeteria by now, and I didn't care. I could only gape, passing my gaze repeatedly over every curve, each movement of the woman wearing the veil.

"Where do they live?" I whispered.

Michael shrugged. "Somewhere out in China Bend."

I was mesmerized by the nape of her neck. Surely my gaze was heavy enough to make her look back. I wanted her to turn her head, stare at me, raise her veil with meticulous, purposeful fingers, make that eye contact again. Something told me that if I could look directly into those blue eyes –

While the others prayed and sang, I plotted a strategy. Where should I stand when she walked out? I needed just one more solid, quenching look. Mr. Big might well be sitting within yards of me, but my plan to memorize faces, the way the marshal would want me to, was out the window.

The preacher hushed, the organ swelled, and Michael wiped his eyes during the eulogy. I bided my time while the living strutted past the closed casket, but before the postlude was over, Marilyn escaped through the side entrance. I plotted a way to catch up to her, but when we crowded out, the lead limo was gone.

At the station that night, I didn't flub my on-air debut. Much. They patted me on the back and offered to take me out for beer, but my stomach was turning somersaults – only it didn't feel like the nerves I experienced yesterday. What, then? It reminded me of the way my head used to swirl at high school dances, when my body pushed up against a girl.

Either I was about to get sick yet again, or I was falling in love.

That thought burst upon me from nowhere. I shook. That can't happen when a guy is engaged. I know it sounds naïve, but that's the way I still thought. I chalk that up to life with Andrea, and her continuous offensive, her rough tirades that obliterated all daydreaming, all quiet contemplation. I'm certain the poor people of Europe didn't have any time to dream of Utopia while Genghis Khan was sacking their villages.

So what if it was love? The notion was impossible, because, besides the Andrea issue, Marilyn had been a widow for less than forty-eight hours. And there was no reason she should be attracted to a big goof like me, anyway. I wasn't Chris.

I locked those thoughts away in the back filing cabinets of my mind, resolved never to utter them, either for sympathy or threats. Because if a time ever came when I confessed to Andrea the wild imaginings about the Widow Ellis that – during that agonizing moment – bounced around in my soul, that hour would be my last.

Chapter 14
Frank Watkins

Another night of tossing and turning, and my one true assignment morphed in my pressure-packed dreams – from finding Mr. Big, to solving the puzzle of how to make time fly forward so a widow could come out of mourning early. I awoke to that new goal. As I snooped and asked around at the station, I would try to uncover information about both persons. That didn't mean I was second-guessing my engagement – I wasn't that kind of guy. Even so, a new sensation grew with every beat of my heart, uncontrollable: I had to meet Marilyn Ellis. Hear her voice out loud. Look into those eyes again. At least once.

The next day was my first in the newsroom – I would perform flunky duties when not working under Billy Dean. That was also the last day for Sironia's most legendary on-air personality, Frank Watkins. Chuck Holiday met me the door, friendlier, for some reason. "Here, George, I accidentally poured two cups of coffee. Have one."

Watkins, himself, was sitting at the largest desk in the room, engrossed on the phone.

"OK, Chuck? What's the deal?" Julie asked. "Has George gone to the head of the class?"

Cuthbert Thompson acknowledged me. His hair flew around like Medusa's and his tie might have been knotted years ago, and simply slipped over his head. "So you're finally in harness, eh, Spartacus?" he said. "Now I won't have to do any more of those blasted car wrecks. Who knows, I might stumble upon a real story, like nuclear war."

I searched his eyes. Was he trying to tell me something? None of the others had flinched, but the retiring legend suddenly straightened up in his chair, looked around in a stately cock-of-the-walk manner, and slammed the phone down with a loud *clack*.

"Shut up, Cuthbert." Watkins pointed his finger, the first time he had even looked at me. "Don't let them saddle you with traffic accidents and murders, son. Politics. That's the ladder you climb to the top."

"Politics? Yes, sir."

Chuck grabbed his sleeve. "Frank, your assignments are wrapped up. Get in there and get ready for your party."

The legend ignored him, and pushed right into my face until I could smell his age through the tobacco and stale mouthwash. "Don't be lazy like these guys, Blair. Sometimes, things are going on right under our noses, eh? Remember that."A meaningful stare at Cuthbert. He knew something. They both did. But when could I get him alone?

"Strawberry cake, Frank." Ryan came from the other side, slapped him on the back, and joined Chuck in hustling the legend out the door. Cheers erupted in the studio.

Julie sighed. "We won't see his like again."

"Oh, spare me." Cuthbert threaded paper into his typewriter, and kept talking. "Blair, I hope you are less loony than these buffoons. In other words--" a wink, "take the words of Herr Doctor Watkins to heart."

She erupted. "Well, well. We aren't jealous of Chucky-poo or anything, are we?"

"Bullshit, my dear." Cuthbert peered over his glasses at me. "Chucky-poo didn't deserve that promotion. He cut a deal with the old man. He's corrupt. Power corrupts, absolute power corrupts absolutely. Who said that, Cub Reporter?"

"Lord Acton," I said, remembering a question that had once flunked me on a test. "But some say Machiavelli, years before."

A sneer. "Thucydides of Greece." He made a checkmark in the air. "But good try. You came closer than anyone else in this intellectual vacuum."

Julie rolled her eyes. "Take it easy, Cuthbert. It's just a news anchor job, not the presidency."

Russell leaned through the doorway. "All right, people, we want the entire staff in for a shot at the end of the show."

Johnny's Farm Show was already in progress, with Watkins' farewell party in full blow behind the cameras. I followed Judy into the hall, but Cuthbert tarried.

"Aren't you coming?" I asked.

He shook his head and erased something. "Two-bit parties are how he keeps the peasants under his thumb. Parties, in lieu of salaries."

"Is that the way it is around here?"

"Go, Lord Acton. Some of us have work to do."

"Hail, Thucydides." I saluted, and turned down the hall, surprised to hear the snotty bastard actually chuckling.

The studio was so jammed – I never imagined Channel Three had this many employees. Then I saw a couple of faces I recognized from City Council meetings I had seen on TV, as well as a few lawyer types.

Everyone jockeyed for cake and punch. But no army guys. I looked for the people in power. Like Al Capone, maybe even an accountant would be the key. I introduced myself to strangers during the commercial break, then Paco gave the high sign and the crowd quieted when the red lights came back on.

Johnny introduced Cadwallader with fanfare. The old man sat next to the glum-faced Watkins while Johnny brought other Channel Three veterans on-camera one-at-a-time to tell anecdotes from the newsman's career.

Zachary motioned, and led me silently to the punchbowl with hooch in it.

"Wow, he's got quite a history," I whispered. "Do you know him very well, Zach? I'd like to ask him some questions later."

Raised eyebrows. "Ain't no later. The old fruit's hightailing it to Ft. Worth right after the party," Zach said.

Damn. I would have to act quickly. "What's the hurry?"

A shrug. "He and the man had a falling out about something. I ain't privy to the upper level politics of this dump."

"You called him a fruit – did they--"

"Naw, Cadwallader's an old lech, but not like that. Watkins had a big fight with that stupid general that's always hanging around. About a month ago."

"A general?"

Someone shushed us.

On stage, Cadwallader gripped Frank's shoulder in a brotherly gesture. "You've led us through a lot of history, Frank. But you never know when more history might be made. Are you sure we can't lure you into staying?"

Paco's hand came up. Commercial in thirty seconds.

Watkins met the boss's stare coolly. "For what's coming down the pike, Emil, wild horses couldn't keep me here."

For an agonizing moment, the crowd froze. I watched this face, that one. Embarrassment everywhere, but about what? Maybe they were all in on the joke, because the discomfort wafted through the crowd like a nauseous wave. But something didn't add up – if Watkins was leaving because of the revolt, Ft. Worth wasn't far enough away if nukes started exploding.

Johnny sputtered to life, flashing his pearly-whites into the camera. "When we come back, ladies and gentlemen, we'll see some taped highlights of Frank Watkins's career at Channel Three."

"Clear," Paco yelled. The commercial rolled, but the crowd remained suspended. The quiet was shattered by Cuthbert barging through the door, waving a dispatch.

"Johnny. A bulletin," he cried. "The sheriff issued a subpoena for three army guys wanted for questioning in Chris's death." He shoved the papers at Watkins. "Frank, want to take it? Your last extra?"

I watched Cadwallader make eye contact with Russell, who nodded, tossed his punch into the big trash can, then rushed out the door.

"I've had enough," Frank said, shoved Cuthbert's notes aside and stalked off the stage.

Johnny called after him, "Frank--"

Cuthbert stood, stunned, Paco chattered over his headset, but I moved. "Frank." I followed him into the newsroom. "What was the matter out there? What's going on?" He already had his hat on, and shoved an envelope into his coat.

"Mr. Watkins, stop, please. You showed up Cadwallader on the air, in front of everybody. When can I talk to you?" He brushed me aside like one would a panhandler. I gave chase. In the lobby, he tipped his hat to Sharon, and rushed through the door. I followed him out to the far edge of the parking lot before he turned around.

"Leave me alone, young man."

"The nuclear fallout can reach to Ft. Worth," I said. It was a gamble, but I hoped I had read him right.

His eyes narrowed. "True, my friend. But a hundred miles from here is a start."

"Let me buy you a drink. You know Cadwallader's plans, don't you?"

He opened his car door and threw the hat in ahead of him. "Get out while you can," he said. His coat came off, and he started rolling up his sleeves. "Even if he wins, what will be the spoils? That old man--" He pointed. "—is going to die soon, and that will leave that lump of a son-in-law. And they'll kill him."

"Who are they? Please tell me what you know, Mr. Watkins."

"You?" He sputtered, eyes wide, backing away from me as if I were suddenly a leper. He bent into the car, and when he straightened up, he pointed a nickel-plated thirty-eight at my chest. "I heard they were sending an equalizer. Well, the government could have sent you when I first reported this – but now I won't talk to anyone. You hear me?"

The gun flashed in the sunlight, and those grandfatherly eyes I had watched so many nights on the tube held me in check. He was capable of pulling the trigger, but he was also scared. I don't know where my confidence came from, but I looked over my shoulder, then stepped to cover the view of the pistol from anyone in the lobby.

"What are you doing?" His voice shook.

All my senses were open, and they told me this man wanted to do the right thing. "Who's in charge, Frank? We know it's not Cadwallader."

He flinched, lowering the gun to my belly. "Lamar Halliburton. Ever hear that name?"

"No. Is he Mr. Big?"

"Of course not." He wiped saliva from the edges of his mouth. "He was a reporter, and a damned good one. A Texan.

Helped break the Teapot Dome scandal back when there were still horses on the streets. He gave me a piece of advice: Follow the golden thread."

"OK. I've heard that before." I motioned for calm. "Golden means money. So Cadwallader is the kingpin?"

Frank squinted. "You misread 'golden.' It means power, as well as money. That's the real key, isn't it? Who has the power? Why do you think I carry this?" I didn't move.

"Please, Frank--"

"If you're a cop, then go to hell. Where were you a year ago? If you're a reporter, then report. Be a hero." He tossed the weapon onto the seat. "Come to Ft. Worth. I'll give you a job. If he brings down Armageddon, the stockyards are as good a place to die as any." His car roared to life, and I yelled after him.

"If it's not Cadwallader, then who's his boss?"

The vehicle paused, and he stuck his head out. "Who is the only person who ever has control over any man?"

I was stymied. "His wife?" I said.

A shake of the head. "Hell, no, young man. His mama."

The car threw gravel all the way to the highway. I sauntered back into the station, feeling elated, but for no reason. Watkins' clue made no sense. Even if Cadwallader's mother were still alive, she must be old and senile by now. My only hope was that somebody like the marshal would recognize what that sort of street-smart, old-fashioned code word might mean. On the lobby monitor, Frank Watkins' clips ran, as if he had never left the studio.

"Was he mad?" Sharon asked. I shrugged, and looked her in the eyes. What had she seen? I decide not to make a big deal about it, and headed for the studio.

But Cuthbert popped out of the newsroom door, still fingering his teletype sheet. "Lord Acton. Thought you might be interested in something."

"I heard about the subpoena."

Cuthbert gave a know-it-all sneer. "Not that. Someone else had to be holding Chris's deer rifle. But who? Just happens there was an entry about you in his little black book in his hip pocket."

"Me? What did it say?"

"A note to call you, right about the time they figure he was shot. But something else before that, too."

"What?"

"A note for nine-thirty that morning. Simply said, *Boss — deer lease.*"

"Jesus." I wandered to the nearest desk and sat down. "Cadwallader was out there? Is it possible?"

Cuthbert rocked back, obviously enjoying his private scoop. "Not at all, mi lud. The old man was here that morning. All morning. I saw him with my own eyes. I just thought a hired assassin like you might be interested in that information. Any comment on technique? Perhaps a colleague of yours?" His smile was insufferable. "Sending you a message, perhaps? A day's work done?"

I kicked the desk, unable to restrain myself. "Did Chris tell the whole staff I was a murderer-for-hire, or were some people off that day?"

My wisecrack didn't stop him for an instant. "What's the matter, your Royal Highness? Did you assassinate the wrong head of state?"

But he didn't slow me down, either. "Mr. Thompson, are you going to be a help to me or be a hindrance? Are reporters out for the national good, or just for themselves?"

Cuthbert clicked his tongue and addressed the typewriter again with those pudgy fingers. "You are green." The keys tapped only a moment. "But, being such a novice, how do you propose to stop a civil war, *mi lud*? If you came to shoot the King, go in there and shoot him. Should make great tape for the evening news. The only thing that could top the clown's faux pas of days gone by."

So I was naked, for all to see. Everyone knew I was a government agent. So why were Cadwallader and Russell even giving me the time of day?

"Are the boss and his henchman planning to turn me around to the Balcones side?" I asked, staring a hole through Cuthbert. "Did they already turn you?"

A crude laugh. "The day Cuthbert Thompson abandons his duty to the American people will surely be Armageddon," he said. "Maybe you're cute, standing there with all the secrets, deciding which of us lives, which not. But beware--" He shook his finger. "I, too, have friends in high places, and the Washington Press Corps might just run up your ass if you ever point a deer rifle at me."

The man seethed ego. Certainly a member of royalty in another lifetime. That was back when Americans didn't believe in other lifetimes, but I remembered watching his pudgy, stately stance, and thinking just that. So he had the wrong idea about me – I wasn't intimidated. I pressed him.

"If you don't want to find out what I can do to you, Mr. Thompson, I would advise you to cooperate." I spoke evenly, tightly. Quietly. "Tell me right now what you know about the military maneuvers in West Texas."

His smile evaporated. "You grow tiresome, Lord Acton. That was precisely what I wanted you to tell me."

Chapter 15
A Secret Summit

Johnny's Farm Show signed off, and the partygoers filled their plastic cups and drifted back to their offices. Chuck collared me in the newsroom with my first field assignment as assistant reporter. Julie accompanied me to the mayor's weekly press conference. Before we could leave, though, the phone at my makeshift desk in the corner of the newsroom rang for the first time.

"Are you coming to dinner tonight?" Andrea asked with no introduction. "Or do TV stars not mingle?"

"Sure. Nothing's changed, Darling." My biggest lie. I had never questioned my relationship with her before, but now talking to her made my skin crawl. When I closed my eyes to imagine the future, it was now Marilyn's veiled face – not Andrea's – that appeared on the inside of my eyelids.

"Get here at six. Mom wants to be in bed early. Or do we have to wait until after the news show?"

"I don't get off 'til six, but I'll rush. Hey, did you have fun with the girls last night? Weren't you going to watch my weather debut?"

"What do you care? You're not part of my weekends anymore."

"Don't talk like that. Did you see it?"

"George, I have never been so embarrassed in my life. That was the worst weather show I ever laid eyes on. Janice and Elaine could hardly keep from giggling. Did you give that freak the whiskey yet?"

I wasn't ready for such a damning blast, even from her. "No," I said. "You agreed to give me a little time."

"Well, I won't go into how humiliated I felt, George. I'll see you when you get here. Honey, try to do better on TV, if you care about my future at all."

Downtown, at the news conference, Andrea's words hung on me like leeches. I was a screw-up as a lawman, and even worse as a television star.

Then the thunderbolt. When Julie, Paco, and I pulled into the parking lot after our foray downtown, I hit the brakes until they squealed. Parked next to Cadwallader's Caddy, Andrea's mother's car shimmered in the afternoon sun.

"Either of you recognize that car?" I asked, hoping there were two of those old clunkers in the world. Shrugs.

Julie mentioned editing the footage we just shot, but I was steeling myself – surely Andrea would be sitting at my little desk, waiting. She wasn't.

Cuthbert attacked me as I passed him. "Lord Acton. Glad you're here. I've had a change of heart." He pulled close, lowering his voice. "We're both detectives, aren't we? Each in his own way? Let's sample the soup before it boils. You're coming with me to Ft. Hood."

His obvious excitement only made me more nervous. "Did you see a lady come in here?" I asked. Then it hit me. I leaned out, and stared at Cadwallader's closed office door. That meant nothing. It was always closed.

"Don't be rude, Acton, pay attention," Cuthbert said behind me. Then, he seemed to catch on. "Who are you looking for? That floozy who's closed up with our lord and master?"

I turned on him. "Floozy?"

He glanced toward Julie, then grew sly, and whispered. "Our fearless leader has an Achilles heel, mi lud. He – shall we say – samples the fruit without buying." A wink. "Especially Mexican fruit."

"The lady in there – is she Mexican?"

"Huh? No. White. Skin like a clam."

Had to be Andrea. I tasted bile.

"Well?" he demanded. "We've got the perfect angle. We'll quiz the base's commanding officer about those three GIs the sheriff's looking for. That's how we get on base – after that, we hunt down some real informants."

"What?"

"Pay attention, Cubby. Overflights today confirmed the Russians have missiles in Cuba, and my sources say the troops at Ft. Hood are moving. Get a notepad. Cuthbert J. Thompson will show you how to land a national scoop."

I reached for a pad, but at the same instant a loud *click* sent me back into the hall. Andrea was exiting the big office, walking arm-in-arm with the old man, himself. I don't know why I was surprised – I swear that woman could have snuck into Mr. Lincoln's box at the Ford Theater. I shoved past Cuthbert's mass, and caught them in the lobby. Andrea giggled like she'd been caught peeking into the boy's locker room.

"Hi, Dear. What are you doing here?" I asked through clenched teeth. Sharon sat quietly, painting her nails.

"Oh, George, are you still on duty?"

"I told you my hours."

The old man took her hand in both of his, and flashed me the biggest grin I had ever seen on his face. "Your little filly and I have been chatting. You have a real peach here, George."

"Yes, sir."

"I was just telling Emil how excited you are to be working here, George." She batted her eyes. "And how determined you are to polish your broadcasting skills."

Cadwallader lobstered her hand, just as he had Marilyn's at the funeral. "She's gonna spare you for a few days, George."

"Spare me?"

"You know," Andrea said, "for weather training." She pinched my cheek with her free hand. "I'll miss you, Dear."

They were a pair, somehow – her plump smile, and Cadwallader's gothic leer. If two more horsemen of the Apocalypse appeared now, the set would be complete.

"I'll miss you, too," I said, with no clue about what I was agreeing to.

Andrea reached up and hugged the old man like a grandfather. "In a couple of weeks, you'll have the best Nelson ratings in Texas."

"Nielsen," I corrected.

"Oh, pooh." She dismissed me, still flushed-up against her new friend. "I'm already used to his being gone weekends, though I have to admit – last night I was wishing for a little companionship." It was a confidence. A cry for help. The most syrupy, insincere little flirtation I ever witnessed, complete with eyelashes in fast motion.

"Andrea."

Cadwallader actually winked at her. "Don't you worry about you-know-who," he said. "When George gets back, we'll dispense with that problem."

"You're a bad man, Emil." Andrea laughed. He laughed. Secrets. First names. "Bye, darling," she told me. "Go back to work." She pinched my cheek again, and swept out the front door.

Cadwallader flexed his eyebrows at me. "Oh, to be young again."

"You got that right." Russell's voice made me jump. He had come up behind us, and he waved me toward the boss's office. "This way, George. It seems we've got a little change in your plans."

Inside the office, I apologized. "Andrea shouldn't have bothered you, Mr. Cadwallader."

He only chuckled. "A lady like her is no bother, son. Now listen to Russell. We've got a plan that has Miss Andrea's stamp of approval."

My stomach plunged to new depths. She had done it. The richest, maybe even the most experienced businessman in Texas, a man supposedly financing the first revolt against our country since the Civil War, was worried about Andrea's "stamp of approval."

I stood there between those two crazy men, cringing at the thought of whatever might be this infernal plan might be. It dawned on me in that moment, to my great embarrassment, that if Marshal Tudberry wanted secret information, he should have sent Andrea, not me. She would have done the job right, and in record time.

Chapter 16
Warnings

They pointed me to a chair, and Cadwallader's old-fool smile vanished. A reporter wearing a bow tie stared out from Cadwallader's office monitor, but the sound was off again, and I quit watching when his face was replaced by a map of Cuba. Rather than take his throne, the Dauphin half-stood, half-squatted in front of me, trying – and failing – to look shrewd.

"We should have whomped those goddam Horned Frogs by fifty points on Saturday," he said, arteries bulging on his neck. "Just how do you reckon it rained so hard that afternoon?"

I glanced at the old man. They knew damn well what caused the rain, though that was impossible, of course. "And that's my fault?" I asked.

Russell kicked the base of my chair. "I thought we told you to watch that sleazy little pool shark. I saw the both of you, thick as thieves, gallivantin' off in his car. Where'd you take him, son?"

My patience was at an end. Let them think they could toy with me like a rat between two cat's paws. Everyone else in the building – besides Billy Dean, of course – might grovel before them, but I spoke forcefully.

"He wanted me to drive him out to the lake. He has a gun, in case you didn't know. Keeps it up there in his desk with the booze. How was I supposed to stop him? Hell, he almost got himself electrocuted stirring the lake with white sticks when that storm blew up."

A visible wave coursed through both of their faces. They transformed from ominous sphinxes to deer in the headlights. Cadwallader groped quietly for his bullwhip, and Russell grabbed my arm. "Sticks? He put sticks in the water? Boy, tell us right now if he taught you how to do that?"

"Shut up, Russell." Cadwallader's voice was little more than a whisper.

"Boss, if that bastard tipped his hand, there may be a way out of this yet--"

"I said hold your tongue."

"Damn it to hell." Russell stomped around in a muddled circle. "Well, boy? You didn't answer me."

"Mr. Crump, I don't know what he did, or how, and I don't really believe I saw what I saw. Maybe he blew his stinking hooch breath up my nose and hypnotized me somehow--"

"Don't be an idiot. Go back – what did you say about him stirring the lake with those sticks?"

"One stick. A white one. Clouds formed. Like – poof – and the deluge started – and wind."

Russell threw up his hands. "God, Almighty. He's seen it." The fat man bent over the desk, begging with his hands. "Boss, you can't ignore this. He saw the little rat workin' his magic."

"It was magic--" Cadwallader's stare stopped me in mid-sentence. "At least it seemed like magic. Surely some scientific explanation--"

"Hell, yes there is." Russell seemed positively overjoyed. "There's got to be. Boss, this is our chance--"

"I said shut up. The both of you." He waved the whip. "And sit back in your chairs."

The Dauphin backed off, and took his throne. I watched the coiling cowhide, and waited. Cadwallader chewed his lip.

Finally, he spoke. "Listen, carefully. If he teaches young George, here, anything, then that's a feather in our cap. But he's not to be interfered with. Understand?"

"Goddam it, boss, if George can figure out what--"

"He can't." Veins bulged on the old man's scrawny neck. "Not in time, dunderhead. Or can't you grasp that?"

That was enough. I stood. "Look, Mr. Cadwallader, I don't care if you take me to the cleaners with that damned piece of hide. Billy Dean has something on you guys, obviously, and everybody around here spends half the day talking in riddles. Now I've already done a weather broadcast, and maybe Andrea's right. Maybe I can learn faster. If you don't like the guy, then fire him. Give me a raise, and have done with it. Either that, or tell me what the hell you two are talking about."

Eyes wide. I might as well have shot off a gun. A long, burning pause, and I was just about to turn on my heel and walk, when Cadwallader actually started chuckling. That turned into a laugh, though the Dauphin could only manage a twisted sneer.

"Gumption," the old man finally said. "I like that. Sit down, please, George, and I'll tell you what I know."

I shivered. Would he really?

He glanced at Russell. The fat man shook his head slowly. The whip settled on the desk, and the old man fixed me with a steely glare.

"Billy Dean Brown is employed at this station as a weather man for one reason," he said. "As you have no doubt gathered, it ain't his personality. But he's the best weather forecaster in Texas. You can check that out. There's stories in a paper or two, roundabouts. He's the best forecaster because, when he's wrong, he just goes out and changes the weather so that he winds up right."

He quit talking, and watched me. Then started nodding. "That's right, George. Billy Dean can control the weather. Up to a point, at least. And it is vital that you learn what you can from him. And fast, because he's going to be leaving us soon."

"So you are going to fire him?" I asked. This was indeed a madhouse – and somehow, I was certain the marshal knew that when he sent me here.

"Never mind why, or where he's going," the old man answered softly. "But after he goes, everything will be OK around here. If you pick up some of his tricks, I daresay things will be even better."

Russell collapsed back into his throne. "I never heard such a crock--"

Crack!

The air exploded over Russell's head, and I fell back. Cadwallader was hunched behind the desk, re-coiling his whip. "Fool, you don't know when to hold your mouth," he said. The son-in-law's lips were quivering. "Things are gonna be the way I say they are. Clear?"

"Yes, sir." The Dauphin's cheeks puffed.

Cadwallader pointed the whip handle at me. "George, be here at eight tomorrow morning. We'll put you on the clock. I told your little lady I was sending you out west to train."

"Out west? What town? What city?" I asked. "Ft. Hood?"

"Ain't much of a town," Cadwallader said. "Just a collection of buildings. It's called Landview. Don't look for it on a map. My mother's from that area."

A shiver rose from inside. What was that Frank Watkins said about Cadwallader's mama?

"How long is this assignment?" I asked. This old coot was truly crazy, but like a fox. Was he baiting the hook with promises of learning the weather, only to send me out there to get buried in the desert? Or were they just using Billy Dean to get me out of the way?

I got hold of myself – maybe this was my chance. The army was out west, somewhere, weren't they? If I took Cuthbert along, we might get enough interviews to uncover something.

"Just you and Billy Dean," he said, as if reading my mind. "Just for a day or two." He sat back, looking tired. "He'll give you some rigmarole about Indians and magic incantations, but you seem like the scientific type. Maybe you can figure it out what he's really doing. That's what your goal should be – learn exactly what he does." Bulging veins again. "This is important, George Blair. Do you understand?"

I didn't. "Yes, sir."

Russell had calmed down a bit. He wiped his mouth, elbows propped on his knees, like a weary ranch hand fresh from branding cattle all day, though it was doubtful he'd ever done an honest day's work in his life. "Study him, son. You don't learn what he does, we're all screwed. And that's all I have to say about that."

If that infernal whip had broken the tension, it was back now, both of those ghouls staring at me, as if their four collective eyes protruded off the same brain stem.

"That's quite a gal you have there." Cadwallader changed the subject. Or was it a threat of some sort? "You listen to me. Leave her be, tonight. Go to bed early. Tell her I said so. You're gonna need your strength." He waved me out. "Eight o'clock. Sharp."

I nodded, rose and walked out, even though I knew it was a mistake to agree to this infernal trip. Maybe the army was out there somewhere, but I had a nagging feeling they just wanted me out of the way. I had no experience whatsoever, but I could just feel that this damned Cuba/Balcones thing was coming to a head – if such a thing existed at all.

Halfway down the hall, a sound turned me around. The Dauphin waddled after me, fire in his eyes. Before I could take a stance, he grabbed my arm with force, hustled me around the corner and up against the soda machine. I looked down into the barrel of a gun.

"Know how to use one of these?" he asked.

I gasped for air, hoping a DJ would come out of the radio booths back there.

"Of course you do." He jabbed the hard tip into my belly, and smiled. "You take this just in case." His move was practiced, rapid. He lifted the flap on my jacket pocket and pushed the thirty-eight down inside.

"Talk to Billy Dean's Comanche woman," he was saying. "You hear me? Boss don't believe in all that mumbo-jumbo, but that squaw is the key."

"Squaw? Billy Dean's got a girlfriend?"

"Not exactly. More like some spooky gal who taught him his Injun weather tricks." He hit me on the shoulder, suddenly my best friend. "I hear she's a looker. You can get friendly with her. Know what I mean?"

I felt the heavy shape in my pocket. I wanted so badly to arrest him right then, for assaulting a federal officer. "Who am I supposed to shoot?" I asked.

"You figure it out when the time comes. Just don't come back without talking to that Indian. Tell her the big chief will pay if she teaches you how to bring rain. Even more for how to conjure a tornado."

"A tornado?" Our gazes met. He was serious. "OK, now you're changing your story, Mr. Crump. He learned weather control from an Indian?"

"I ain't changin' nothin'. We don't know where he learned it, but those crazy people down in Landview are neck deep in whatever scam he's runnin'."

No, I was looking at the crazy person. "I can't take this," I said, and dug the weapon out of my pocket.

He gripped my wrist, pushing the gun back against me. "Yes, you can."

"You want me to kill Billy Dean, don't you?" I said, keeping steady. "I'm won't shoot a man over rain at a football game. Even if you give me five thousand dollars."

Come on, you fat Dauphin, say it, I thought. *Offer to pay me, and slip the noose around your own neck.* Another charge, paying to have someone killed. Damn, I wanted to arrest the son of a bitch and be done with it.

"Drop in the bucket."

"What'd you say?"

"I said five grand is a drop in the bucket compared to what you might earn. Want to be Mayor of Sironia? How about Governor of New Mexico Territory? Of course," He chuckled, wiping sweat from his double chin. "That job's spoken for, but who knows? When the Balcones Republic is declared, we'll all end up with more than we bargained for."

With his fat hand, he overpowered mine and shoved the gun back into my jacket. "And don't play dumb," he said. "We know who sent you here, but you're working for Emil Cadwallader now. Tomorrow will be the most important trip of your life."

"So you're not offering me money, but a political office in a country that doesn't exist yet. Is that it?" No good. There was no law against bribing someone with bullshit.

A pat on the shoulder. "Be brave when you meet Rebecca Flock-of-Birds, boy. To her, a man's either strong, or he's breakfast." He guffawed, and waddled back down the hall.

Cuthbert looked up, and motioned me over when I entered the newsroom. "Never mind," he whispered. "You can't have both a woman and a career. It seems you've made your choice. I'm going by myself." He went back to his typing, and I hunkered at my desk in the corner and picked up the phone. Andrea was already home.

"Now don't say a word about me coming to the station," she said. "I know you're mad, but I did it for your own good. I was going to call you, anyway, to cancel dinner. Mother's not feeling well. Besides, you've got to get ready to go out of town."

I was feeling lost. "You want to get a coke, at least?" I asked.

A pause. "No, Sweetie. I'm adjusting to this new job that takes you away all the time. It's made me think. There might be some – changes in our lives, George."

"Well, that's a cryptic statement."

"Mr. Cadwallader said you would be back in a couple of days. When you return, don't just show up, call first."

"Don't worry. You taught me that a long time ago."

"Things are changing, George. Don't get mad at me about it, 'cause you started it yourself."

She hung up. After work, I went home, heated a TV dinner, and drank a beer. How would I explain to him that I had agreed to go out of town?

I packed, and never bothered to drive down to the Seven-Eleven to call. Three hours later, as I sat watching Ben Casey, I decided to do the only thing that made any sense right now. I hopped into the car and headed for China Bend, on the far side of the lake.

Off the exit, I plunged my jalopy onto narrow roads lined by grasses and canebrakes whose shadows towered above the car's roof on either side. In the evening breeze, the cane undulated like dark curtains. The only lights were my headlamps and the late summer swath of stars high above.

I kicked myself for not asking Sharon for Chris's address – but I banked on spotting his truck. Surely she hadn't gotten rid of it already. I twisted and turned through those treacherous, two-lane corridors walled in by cane, brush and forest for thirty minutes, maybe an hour. House after house lay dark, as if all the farmers, fishermen and retirees had turned in early. I cruised past a bait shop I had seen before. One weak bulb glowed above the padlocked minnow vat bubbling on the porch.

The scent of the river mixed with the odor of grasses, confounding my sense of direction. Going down another familiar path, I finally admitted I was going in circles, and stopped the car to plan my next move. The cane rustled in ominous waves, warning the sleeping residents of my trespass. The next thing I knew, I woke with a start, still sitting in the middle of the road, the car idling in park. The stars had moved.

The radium hands on my watch read two o'clock. I made a turn and miraculously found the highway, sleepy, maybe embarrassed. I would be worthless on the road tomorrow.

My heart throbbed in my ears, and the gun still hung heavy in my jacket. Did Russell really want me to shoot Billy Dean? Or was the weapon meant for someone I hadn't yet met? My undercover agent career was only days old, but any fool could tell this trip was a set-up. I looked for a consolation. Sucking it up and going seemed the path of least resistance. I might at least squeeze some useful information out of Billy Dean. Like where Marilyn Ellis lived.

Chapter 17
Flowers

I've often done my best thinking when I'm asleep. By the time my alarm rang, I had more perspective. I would phone in a report to the marshal on my way to the station, and quit feeling sorry for myself. I owned some old thirty-eight shells that used to belong to my grandfather. I found them in a box in the closet, and put them in my overnight bag. It might help to bring more ammo than they expected me to have. My marksman scores at the Academy were in the top quintile.

When I stepped down to the parking lot, a voice came from nowhere, almost sending me out of my skin.

"George. Thank goodness you haven't left."

I turned. "What are you doing here, Andrea?" She wore one of her sophisticated outfits, and held out a bunch of flowers wrapped in wax paper.

"Thank the Lord." She hugged me. "I was afraid you'd already gone." The smell of the roses was drowned in a cloud of Chanel.

"What's wrong? Did somebody die?"

"Of course not, silly. Can't a girl tell her man *bon voyage*? Here, I made you an egg sandwich." She pressed a paper bag into my hands. Still warm.

"Thanks. And the flowers?"

"They're for you," she said. Tears welled in her eyes, but rather than turn away, she wrapped around my neck again, crushing the blooms between us. "I'm sorry, George. You forgive me, don't you?"

"Andrea, you're scaring me. I'll just be gone a couple of days."

She pulled a kleenex from her sleeve and dabbed her teardrops. "I was too hard on you about this weather job, wasn't I? Do you forgive me for whatever I've done?"

This sort of meddling, dramatic performance happened a couple of times a year. Usually, they occurred when I was thrust into the center of attention, eclipsing her. Then she had some sort of epiphany, like a Catholic who had realized her sins, and I became the priest, until she figured a new way to defrock me, and grab the spotlight again. I wanted to tell her that going to Landview was no spotlight – it was a mistake that was taking me away from my real mission.

But as I stood in front of her, peering into her eyes, my paranoia returned. She was always afraid I would die on a trip. But this journey was different – what if Cadwallader told her something that would further that notion?

"Stop it," I said. "Don't tell me you've had another one of your premonitions. I'm not going to die in a car wreck."

She smiled, but kept wiping. "No premonitions. George, you know me so well. We're almost like brother and sister."

My skin crawled. "What's that I smell?"

"My perfume. Or the flowers." She shoved them in my face.

"Don't get upset, Andrea. I appreciate you seeing me off—"

"How could I be upset, you silly thing?" With her hands free now, she brushed her skirt down. "I just came to tell you that I love you." She hadn't said that in a year. "Well?"

Crows squawked in the trees, and she put her hands on her hips, waiting. "I love you, too," I said. "Thanks for breakfast."

"That's better, Blair." She kissed her finger and planted it against my lips. "Remember, call first when you get back." She made it out of the parking lot before I did.

I consumed the sandwich in ripping bites. Andrea had apologized before, but there was something very different this time. The hairs stood up on the back of my neck.

From the pay phone outside the Short-N-Snappy, I broke the news to Tudberry. "They know the government sent me, Marshal, but they're still keeping me on. You give me the least excuse, and I won't go on this trip."

"No clue as to how they found out?" he asked testily. I imagined him leaning back in his chair, anxious to get back to the sports page.

"What does that matter? This trip is a damned diversion. How can I collect intelligence out in the middle of nowhere?" I was yelling. "Say the word, bring me back in."

"Calm down, dammit." A pause. "Where are they taking you?"

"Out west. Landview, or some damn town nobody ever heard of," I said. The rest came out without warning: "I'm scared, Marshal."

Tudberry grunted. "George, this may be a chance we can't afford to miss. OK, they know. I know Emil Cadwallader, and he ain't crazy enough to shoot one of my employees--"

"Not shoot – what about Chris?" I screamed. "What about those other two?"

"Shut up and think logically, son. If you're skirting the Hill Country, I might have another job for you. The division with the experimental mobile launchers, for atom bomb missiles, was spotted out in that country. We could use a pair of eyes going through there. How long will you be gone?"

My heart sank. God help me, he *wanted* me to go.

I shuddered, peering through the convenience store window at the fresh-faced men and women, combing the racks, picking out a fast snack in the way to a busy day's work. Honest work. They were living normal lives. They couldn't see a whit of the yawning abyss I was about to fall into.

"Couple days." I groaned. "This doesn't feel so good, Marshal. The army doesn't like spies."

"Look at the big picture, George. The old man owns those guys, so they won't hurt anybody running with that goofy weatherman. Just keep a record mentally – don't write anything down. Count the tanks, and the missile launchers. You might even stumble upon Mr. Big. Keep your ears open."

I belched stale egg and started to protest. "I know your car. We have Billy Dean's plates on our books, too, so it don't matter which car you take. I'll have the highway patrol track you boys close. Call collect, if there's an emergency."

Call collect. Awful nice of him, I wanted to say. Instead, I just staggered inside the store, bought a Dr. Pepper, and even considered taking Andrea's flowers to Marilyn, if I could find her. I also thought about driving downtown and throwing them in the marshal's face. A goodbye bouquet.

To hell with all this – I finally came to my senses. That is, until I pulled into Channel Three's parking lot. Chris's old forty-nine Ford pickup was parked there, crooked, in a slot near the front door. Marilyn Ellis was here. And I was back on the job.

Chapter 18
A Flash of Yellow

I could barely take a full breath while I tucked my shirt in, and combed my hair in the rear-view mirror. How would I introduce myself? In the excitement, I almost started in without my overnight bag. When I opened the trunk, a glint of sun struck my eye. Andrea's infernal whiskey flask was lodged in its nook. I stuffed it into the bag, cushioning the glass bottle from the pistol with a pair of jeans. What was Marilyn doing here? Collecting Chris's last paycheck?

In the lobby, the first thing that struck my eye was the monitor – President Kennedy was holding some sort of news conference. The second thing I saw was Marilyn – walking briskly toward me.

"Bye, Sharon," she said, her cheekbones just as high as I thought they were. Skin perfect, freckles under each eye, blonde hair falling almost to her shoulders, and eyes so crystal blue. They wanted to laugh, those eyes, but she was still in mourning.

I held the door open and stood aside, and Providence intervened again – she stumbled on the entry mat.

"Oops." A sandal flew from one foot, and she grabbed my arm for support. My hands came up under her arms, and cradled her breasts. Our gazes met.

"Let me." I knelt to pick up the wayward shoe, after I set her upright. Boldly, I grabbed her foot. "Just like Cinderella," I said.

She let it happen, left her foot resting on my knee for a moment, a delicious eternity. I took my time bringing the sandal to it, like the Prince, trying to drink in every blemish on that leg, the color and depth of all that smooth, uncharted territory beneath the dress's fabric that it led toward. I looked up again, and what I saw in her eyes was anything but rejection or disgust. There was a new land lingering behind those eyes, a land, a realm I could only guess at.

But for that moment, I was on that map. She was studying me. She had noticed. Somehow, I had leapfrogged past the level of a kow-towing lackey doing a sudden favor. Maybe it was just puzzlement – she hadn't reached a verdict – maybe she was just being polite, or maybe she didn't yet know how a widow was supposed to behave. What did it matter? I had played my cards, and now I was a paralyzed imbecile, wavering on one knee, waiting for the volcano-blast of feeling that bubbled all around me to subside. She bit her lip, rendering herself even more desirable. I couldn't breathe.

I wouldn't have voluntarily taken my hand from her calf for a king's ransom. Bare skin. No nylons. Warm. I had never touched Andrea's leg like this. *My God, her husband just died*. She smiled.

"Then you must be Prince Charming," she said. "Thank you."

"I'm George."

"Nice to meet you, George." She pulled away and stood on the sandal. I pushed the glass door open again, letting in warm October wind, causing her bright yellow dress to ripple around those soft legs.

"I think I've seen you on television. The news?"

"No, Ma'am. Well, they've had me do a couple of reports, but I'm working on weekend weather--" I was botching this – "Uh, Chris helped me get this job. Maybe he mentioned me? George Blair?" Of course he hadn't. Why should he? I was stalling.

She leaned easily against the doorframe, like a schoolgirl waiting to be asked to her first sock hop. "Oh, you know Chris. He never talked too much about anything. Thanks for getting my shoe. Hey, maybe I'll run into you at the picnic."

"What picnic?"

"This Saturday at River Park. Emil is throwing a company picnic in memory of Chris."

"Great. I'll be there." She brushed past me before I could think of anything actually clever to say. A voice inside urged me to run after that yellow dress, jerk Andrea's flowers from my car, and make sure this woman would remember me, but someone cleared his throat loudly enough to make me turn. Russell Crump had his ass lodged against the corner next to Cadwallader's office. How long had he been watching? His glare said long enough.

I didn't care. I turned my back on the Dauphin, and watched the old truck churn out of the lot. I turned my back on everything – yes, I still had a mission here – but it had changed. If I lived through the trip, I would at least stay in this job until after the picnic this weekend. Someone would have to tell President Kennedy – if he wanted a war, he'd better put it off at least until Sunday.

Chapter 19
Parsifal

"You drive." Billy Dean threw me the keys, and spent the first half hour of the journey warning me about certain taverns as we passed them, which ones watered down the drinks, which ones the prostitutes frequented, and how almost every one of them had been founded by World War II vets.

I didn't listen, but thought about Frank Watkins' golden thread. Cadwallader was the money. There were only two things more powerful than that – military might, and love. Watkins' statement about his "mama" was dumb – if Cadwallader had a mother, she must be in her nineties, so how could she weigh in on a revolution?

"What are those words on the side of your lighter?" I asked. The man could not exist without a cigarette, it seemed.

He held it up in front of my face, but it wasn't an invitation to touch the thing. The metal figure tacked on its outside was some sort of castle. "That word is 'Aachen,'" he said. "Old German script. Old English looks the same." A puff. "Went through that town, once upon a time. Me and the Third Armored Division. Those Jerries slowed us down, and when I finally got in there, it weren't nothing but a pile of *rooble*." A long, dreamy look while he tucked the lighter back in his pocket. "Got this lighter off a German officer. He didn't particularly want to give it to me, but, well--" His smile made me shiver.

As if on cue, we crested a hill, and a long green line army trucks lumbered into view, traveling slowly toward us in the opposite highway lane. "Jeez," I said.

"Uh-huh." He scowled at me. "I figured you'd never spent a day in the service. Ain't too late, boy. Make a man out of you."

"So it's true." The sight took my breath away. A dozen tanks, each mounted on a large tractor trailer, rumbled past. "There really is an army out here. What are they doing? Tell me what you know, Billy Dean."

His spoke out of one side of his mouth. "Forget these tin soldiers. Those are all I need to know about." He pointed to rain clouds off to the west. Dark shafts extended down from them in haphazard angles, as if they were clumsy white-gray insects, moving on shadowy stilts.

"That's the way they walk across the prairie," he said, as if reading my mind. "On thin little spider legs. Legs of rain. A beautiful sight, ain't it?"

"Oh, yeah," I said. "I forgot. The clouds are alive."

"Don't patronize me, Punk." He flicked his ash and stretched over the seat to retrieve his weird bag. "You want to make rain, you're going to have to have these." He extracted a single stone rod, perhaps ten inches long, whitish and sparkling like rock candy. "Down to my last one," he said. "Need more if I want to keep raining on State's team every weekend." He winked, tickled at his own statement. "It takes this and a little communication." Gesturing toward the clouds again. "Gotta learn to talk to the people up there."

"Is that quartz?" I asked.

He bypassed the question, pointing. "See that cloud straight ahead, maybe twenty miles? The big one?"

"There's lots of them." The clouds ahead looked less dangerous than the group to the side. We were heading into brilliant, fluffy and white cumulus marshmallows floating lazily. It was a day to be lying in the grass, watching. "The one that looks like an alligator?"

He grimaced. "Are you here to learn, or not? I'm talking about the big, symmetrical one dead ahead."

"I see it, sir."

"You ever hear of the legend of Parsifal?"

"Do you mean Percival? It's an epic poem," I said. "One of those hero-goes-around-the-countryside-having-adventures poems."

His eyebrows went up, as if he were impressed. "Percival's name in German is *Parsifal*. It's also the name of the guy who pilots that cloud. Impressive *hombre*. Behave yourself in Landview, you might get a chance to meet him."

I searched his face for a bit of honesty. "You really mean a myth. Like Norwegian thundergods, right? OK, I'll bite. Just what does your *Parsifal* look like? Anything like Bucky Beaver?"

Another sneer. "Bucky Beaver sells toothpaste. Parsifal's an admiral of a race of giant beings who conduct campaigns in the sky. Watch out for these army jackasses up ahead."

I took my foot off the gas. We were bearing down on a wide army truck that dominated more than half of the two-lane road.

"Damn." I slowed, and had to drive off the shoulder to clear the thing. "Let's go back and take another road," I yelled.

"Too late for that," he said calmly. "Play it cool. This is our road, too."

Over the next rise, an even scarier panorama opened up. Armor stretched for miles, tanks and jeeps mounted with machine guns, some moving, some parked on the side of the highway. A roadblock lay ahead, and it was too late to turn and run. Billy Dean let out a low whistle. "Let me do the talking." He punched my arm. "Hear me?"

My pulse banged in my ears. I was sorry for ever doubting the marshal's word. The weatherman crushed his smoke. "Whatever happens, for God's sake don't admit to being a spy for Kennedy."

I eased Billy Dean's roomy Kaiser Frazier to a halt at the wooden spars that blocked the southbound lane. A large tent stood to one side, at the edge of the open prairie. Men with rifles stared down at us without humor.

Billy Dean put on his biggest smile and repeated, "Not a word."

"I'll keep quiet, but that doesn't mean our friend will." Next to the tent, a familiar red Ford sat in the dirt.

"Hell's bells, if it ain't Cuthbert."

The aging reporter looked disheveled, his hands were cuffed and he was being led into a tent by men wearing military police patches. He was hunched over, stumbling.

A sergeant tapped the hood with the butt of his rifle. "Get out of the car."

Billy Dean leaned to speak out of my window. "It's OK, gents. We're employees of Emil Cadwallader." More troops surrounded us, and I started to freeze up. The old man's name didn't seem to carry weight with any of them.

The sergeant opened my door. "The last guy who said that is a goddam spy for the Washington press. Get out."

My heart thumped. They would find the gun in my bag. I forgot my promise and started blabbering. "Didn't you hear the man? We're on assignment from Mr. Cadwallader. Your superiors know him. This is peacetime, so you can't stop us."

The sergeant's rifle bore a bayonet, and he twirled the gun like a baton and finished by digging its point into my hip.

"Peacetime, my ass. See that table over there? Go answer the man's questions."

The two-striper on Billy Dean's side raised his hand. "Hey, I recognize this one. He's that weather guy on TV."

The sergeant nodded. "Good, Corporal. Send him to that other table, and no funny stuff."

The corporal looked a little pale. "I don't think we're supposed to mess with him."

Billy Dean grinned like a smart-ass, and lit yet another cigarette. "He's right, Sarge. I'm like, hands-off."

A scowl. "I report to Lieutenant Geary, not any Cadwallader or even Rockefeller. Get over to that table."

Billy Dean side-stepped the bayonet, and moved right up into the man's face. "I don't know if you would have made it in World War II, non-com."

The sarge didn't flinch. "You won't get my sympathy just because you're a washed-up vet. Now *git*."

Their questions seemed harmless enough, but the men asking them were rattled. We had only been on the road a couple of hours. Did the war already start? A tarp-covered vehicle parked on the roadside – not twenty yards away – bore the alarming black and yellow nuclear material emblem on its side.

"I'm warning you gentlemen not to make us late in reporting to Mr. Cadwallader." I said it with no authority, and the sergeant came from behind, handcuffed me like a veteran cop, and shoved me toward the largest tent. "Son, you're going to be very late."

Perhaps I was a cop after all – playing World War II in the woods as a child came back automatically. I found myself studying the lay of the land for possible escape. This tent backed up on a dry creek bed. In darkness, a commando might slip out and be miles down that gorge before they were wise. Surely it wouldn't come to that.

But those thoughts coursed through my brain right beside a feeling of betrayal. Not from my country, but Andrea. She must have sensed something terrible would happen to me out here, otherwise why the flowers? She had never been stingy with her predictions of doom before.

At the tent entrance, I jerked out of the soldier's grip and pled with the MPs guarding it. "Please. Let us go home, and I'll put in a good word for you with the boss."

The college-aged one on my right, sandy crew-cut, seemed genuinely sorry for me. "Can't help you, sir. This is a top secret operation. Condition red. Every spy is to be shot. No prisoners."

I dug my feet in. "What the hell do you mean? That's crazy. We're not spies. Whose orders?"

A hesitation. "President Emil Cadwallader and the Balcones Council," he said.

"But we work for Cadwallader," I screamed, but the sergeant overpowered me, and pushed me through the flap and past a card table. The air reeked of canvas, but these weren't boy scouts. With one last shove, he sent me reeling into the corner next to a crumpled form. Cuthbert. He was lying on his side, his tears dripping through red gashes all over his face.

"Lord Acton." He seemed flabbergasted to see me. "They're going to kill us. You shouldn't have come looking for me. They found out I'm a spy. They had a file. Some fucker in Washington gave them my file. The traitor." He struggled closer, looking furtively toward the single GI who remained in there with us. He was paused at the tent flap, as if he could never be concerned with anything we said.

"They'll have a file on you, too," Cuthbert whispered. "Run for your life if you get a chance, because you know what they do to assassins."

I opened my mouth to console him, but my throat had dried up. Nothing came out.

He seemed to understand my difficulty, and more tears issued from those seasoned blue eyes. "I'm sorry you got sucked into this, *mi lud*. Fate is just too cruel. I honestly thought you had the potential for a respectable career in television news."

Chapter 20
Cuthbert Thompson

I tried to look away, but wound up staring at the dirt mixed in with the blood on the old newshound's face. A pudgy, middle-aged member of the fifth estate who probably couldn't fight his way out of a bar serving free drinks, yet these big, brave soldiers had pounded on him something fierce. When I first saw him, he had been handcuffed. Now his hands were free, and bruised. Guess they realized he probably couldn't even walk, much less run.

This was a dream, I told myself. Cadwallader and Crump were crazy enough – but they were more like little boys playing at being big shots. These army guys – a different caliber, altogether. Rabid. And the toys they wielded could ruin a civilization. I shook my head, praying that one of them would call Channel Three, and realize their mistake.

"What's going on here, Cuthbert?" I whispered. "We just need to get to a goddam phone and clear this up."

The soldier at the flap finished his confab and turned toward us. His main feature was a top fluff of black hair. "Sorry, boys." A sickening, cocksure smile. "Looks like you hired on with the wrong team." With frightening swiftness, he crossed the ground and put his boot into Cuthbert's stomach. The seasoned reporter yelped like a baby.

"Goddam you." I tried to rise to my feet. "Quit picking on a helpless old man, you jackass. When I tell Emil Cadwallader about you, you'll be peeling spuds for a hundred years."

He pushed me back into the dust with one powerful hand. "Don't worry about me, sumbitch. Executing a spy for the U.S.S.R. won't get me court-martialed in any man's army."

"You're crazy," I yelled. "He's not a spy for Russia."

"Sorry, son. Your buddy confessed." Black Hair strolled away, grabbing a newspaper off the card table as he did, and settled on the tent's single folding chair.

Cuthbert lay on his side now, gasping for air like a fish. "You confessed to working for the Russians? Are you crazy?" I said.

When he grimaced, his grimy gray eyebrows came together. "I am a spy. Not normally, of course, but when the old king started playing army, the Soviets offered me a stipend to give them occasional reports."

"The Soviets? Goddam you, Cuthbert. The communists?"

"And the Italians. They just wanted my scoops before I put them on the air."

"But America doesn't have a beef with the Italians. Shit, tell these maniacs I don't have anything to do with that."

The veins on his forehead bulged with his speaking effort. "These are diplomatic friends I met, OK? I'm a patriot. Now, *mi lud*, if you could get medical help, I would be most grateful. I don't wish to die while bleeding." A smile, a cough, and then a trickle of blood eased out of his lips. Internal injuries.

"Hey," I yelled at Black Hair. "We need a medic over here, pronto." The thug glanced up from his newspaper, as if to say *what's the point?*, and resumed reading.

The old newshound's eyes closed and he started repeating, "We're going to die."

"You're not going to die, goddam it." But he was. The trickle of blood wasn't getting any thinner.

At the academy, they taught us to stick your cheaters wherever you could; your boot, your cuff, down your drawers. A cheater could be a blackjack, a derringer, a shiv. Mine was in my back pocket – a bobby pin.

"Just keep quiet until Billy Dean straightens them out," I said. It was unthinkable that they wouldn't come to their senses, but the looks in the eyes of everyone in uniform out here was strange, panicked. "Think you can get up and run?" After dark, we might indeed sneak down that ravine, where cooler heads might prevail.

"Like the wind, *mi lud*," he said. His eyes were shut, breathing labored. He didn't have until dark.

I twisted the bobby pin, and scraped it into one of the keyholes. They taught us that all cuffs were the same. It would be too cumbersome to make sure everyone had keys for different locks, so a handcuff key was basically a straight piece of metal. Keep paperclips clipped to the edge of your pockets, they told us, in case a bad guy ever turned the tables on you. A bobby pin was even better, and Andrea was my supplier, though I doubted she ever knew.

"Take a letter, Julie," Cuthbert mumbled, like someone having a dream. "Robert Jensen. Washington Post. Remember that name. Tell Robert Jensen what happened. They're going to kill the communists."

"What?"

"The communists in the government. Moscow's in on it. Some Russian general – brave new world. Free money. Balcones Council over here, Ukranian... " Droplets of blood sprayed out with the words.

"What about Cuba? What's going on there?"

Eyes fluttering. "Missiles to launch against Texas. Fat little Nikita doesn't believe Kennedy can handle these boys."

"Here." A loud voice made me jerk upright at the same instant one of my cuff locks clicked open. I kept them behind me. A handful of soldiers barged through the tent flap. The lead one – wearing lieutenant's bars – carried my overnight bag, plus Billy Dean's quartz pouch.

He dumped his booty on the card table. A rapid *zip* and he jerked Russell's pistol from my clean clothes. "Who were you going to plug with this, buckaroo?" A sneer. "Or should I say, Mister Cosa Nostra?"

My insides froze. "The gun's for protection, Lieutenant. I wasn't planning to kill anyone."

Cuthbert grunted.

"No?" The officer opened Billy Dean's crazy purse, and pulled out the quartz rod. "What's this shit? Uncut diamonds? You guys smuggling diamonds? Or could it be uranium?" It seemed somehow unnatural, that snide soldier handling one of Billy Dean's little treasures.

"I don't think you're supposed to touch that," I said.

He stared warily at the rock, then shoved it back in, but he left my bag open, with the gun butt sticking up in the air. A glance at Black Hair, who still stood at attention. "Private, be ready to bring them out. The firing squad will assemble shortly."

"Yes, sir."

"Wait." I scrambled to my knees, careful to keep both hands behind me. "Are you crazy? You can't just shoot us." But the flap closed behind them. "Lieutenant," I screamed. Even Black Hair watched the opening for a moment, then retreated to his seat.

"Sit down," he commanded.

Cuthbert's voice was a soft moan. "Did he say firing squad, *mi lud*? Perhaps we shall go the way of Eddie Slovik?"

"For chrissakes, Cuthbert." My stomach convulsed violently. This was for real. I settled to my knees, trying not to stare at the pistol butt, trying not to telegraph my move. All the bad-cop stories from the academy came back, tales of how they trapped criminals into going for guns in this same manner. First they unloaded the weapon. When the criminal made his move, *bang.* But the lieutenant's voice boomed outside, so I didn't have the luxury of figuring out another course of action.

"Billy Dean," Cuthbert muttered, then sank back into his funk.

"Where is the bastard?" I said, scraping the pin into the other lock. I was wasting time. One wrist still wore the shackle, but my hands were separated, free. Outside, things were on the move, roaring engines drowning out the lieutenant's squawking. Then, his voice again: "Line up over there."

They were going to do it.

I nudged the newshound. A whisper, "Wake up, Cuthbert." Black Hair stirred. The ground shook. Engines revved, the only confusion we could hope for, and I heard the marshal's voice echoing from so many years ago, chatting loudly with my grandpa: "I tell my men, if you're going to do, do. Don't think about it."

I did.

I reached the card table in one jump.

"Hey." Black Hair stumbled to his feet, but the gun was in my hand. Another leap, and I brought the barrel across his forehead.

He gurgled something, so I hit him again. And again.

The army man crumpled. I needed him to be quiet, so I knelt and hit him once more. He went to the ground, tongue hanging out.

"Come on, Cuthbert." I had his collar. He wouldn't budge, so I slapped his swollen cheek. "Go."

"Shit." He leered upwards, eyes blinking. "OK, *mi lud*." He lunged on all fours, me pushing his rear. We crawled, squeezed under the tent's back border, and emerged into a world of dust kicked up by the roaring troop carriers and missile launchers. Unseen, so far. I pushed toward the ravine. Cuthbert coughed, and I clasped my hand over his mouth, then we were over the lip, sliding into the dry creek bed, me supporting the newshound's ass, using all the strength I had to lower him to a soft landing.

"Free, *mi lud*," he said between retches.

"This way. Keep down, and run." I pointed toward the southwest, where the bed wound like a snake into an oblivion of dust. He wobbled, but actually made it over the scattered rocks for a moment. Then, the unmistakable sound of running above us.

"They're here," someone cried.

I raised my hands, still gripping the pistol – bad mistake. Thunder broke the air, and Cuthbert's shoulder jerked, blushed crimson. I wheeled. A figure knelt above us, rifle scanning. Without thinking, I aimed and pulled the trigger. The form went down, in fast motion. Yells.

"Help," Cuthbert cried, scrambling against the wall of the river bed, pawing dirt, and I hated him for not knowing where he was going, hated his helpless stare as I ran past him. Another explosion, and he fell. I could still make it down the ravine, but I spun around first and fired toward the noise. A shadow crashed out of the dust onto the limestone at my feet.

This is it. The thought echoed in my head. Yes, I was a child again, playing war, flying on adrenalin, knowing the jig was up, but never quite believing it. Shadows shivered in the dust clouds above , but no clear targets, and then fists, legs – two, five, a hundred of them digging my face into the chalky dry streambed. I knew I should feel pain, but the air crashed out of my lungs and a knife appeared at my throat.

"Stop. I give." The blade dug deeper.

"Halt."

They dragged me to the center of the ravine, and I looked up to see that same lieutenant above me, and a score of rifles trained my way.

"Churchill's dead." A man stood over the second guy I had shot.

"That tears it," the lieutenant said.

They pulled me up the incline. One GI groped at the set of handcuffs that still hung from my left wrist, but let them go. The officer waved until they formed a line several yards away, then my handlers backed off.

"Lieutenant Geary," a new voice called out.

Geary twisted away and snapped to attention while a crowd of olive uniforms invaded the mass of khaki. "Captain, this man is to be shot as an enemy spy and murderer," Geary said.

From behind the captain, someone pushed Billy Dean forward. He also wore cuffs, but they had been courteous enough to lock his hands in front. The weatherman regarded me with a wary look, and sauntered toward me, digging for a smoke with his wrists locked together. "Looks like you accounted for yourself pretty good, Hot Shot." He managed a cigarette and, amazingly, a GI leaned forward with a light.

A thin line of blood came away when I touched my neck. "Cuthbert," I said, but couldn't continue.

"Let these men go," the newly arrived captain said, and stared at me. "On condition of their absolute silence about this incident. Gentlemen, you will sign a pledge."

I started to speak, but Billy Dean elbowed my ribs.

Geary was crimson, pointing. "Captain, this man is a hired hit man. The one in the ditch was a confessed spy."

"Lieutenant, follow protocol."

Geary stretched up onto his toes, and yelled in a phony cadence. "Sir, I protest and officially advise *you* to follow

General Raven's orders. Nuclear units operate under rules of no tolerance of spies during wartime." Pointing at me. "That traitor spy shot my men."

"Lieutenant, these are employees of the Balcones president, himself."

The junior officer boldly unsnapped his holster and extracted his pistol. "Sir, we cannot risk a breach of security. Not at this late stage."

"Hey, kid, why don't you listen to your superior?" Billy Dean snorted smoke. "We got friends in high places. Like him." He jutted his chin toward the wide, oblong cloud that had settled above us, blocking the sun.

The rabid lieutenant brought the gun up and aimed.

Billy Dean didn't frown, didn't flinch. Didn't seem worried about anything. Instead, he just smiled his insipid smile, raised his hands in the air, spat his cigarette into the dust, and called out in a shattering yell,

"Parsifal!"

In the next moment – I don't think I even blinked – the world froze like a photographic negative – in that first millisecond, my mind told me I was dead – no, everyone was dead – the firing squad line, the snotty lieutenant, the chugging tanks. Then the world tumbled, the air became a wave I couldn't stand against, I turned a somersault, and came crashing into a mob of falling GIs. We thudded to a halt like tangled tree limbs. I thought I saw Geary crawling like a baby through the morass. Only the weatherman remained standing, a smart-assed tower in the middle of writhing casualties.

Through the wall of sound in my ears, and the image burned on my retina, it was a guessing game to determine what was real. Did a lighting bolt from that cloud really cut the chain of Billy Dean's handcuffs?

The captain was one of the first up, coughing dust. "Release them. Put them in their car and get them the shit out of here. Hurry."

Troops fumbled like bewildered munchkins after the wicked witch disappears. The corporal I had seen in front of the tent propped on one elbow and spoke. "I told you SOBs we shouldn't mess with that guy."

A bulky man removed my handcuffs, but refused to touch Billy Dean's. I took the key and did the honors. The cuff on each wrist was still hot, the severed chain between them scorched.

"Well, you're pretty sharp, after all, Joe College," Billy Dean said. "Thanks for taking care of my kit."

To my amazement, his multi-colored leather pouch hung under my left arm. I had been holding it through the whole shootout and didn't ever remember bringing it out of the tent. A recruit stuck my own overnight bag into my hands, while another shoved Russell Crump's pistol into my face. I zipped it up safely in the bag.

"What about Cuthbert?"

The weatherman poked me in the ribs again. "We gotta pick which war we want to fight, son."

Wide-eyed soldiers opened a path for us. Billy Dean had the car keys. We drove for three miles before the green-vehicled convoy fell behind us. I didn't count the tanks. There were too many.

Chapter 21
The Road to Landview

"Take us home," I said. "For god's sake, we've got to get to the authorities. The marshal will know what to do..." I was rambling, and didn't care anymore who knew what – just this side of passing out, crumpled against the passenger side door.

"And miss a date with the enchanting Rebecca Flock of Birds?" Billy Dean chuckled, and turned the car south.

It occurred to me that a truly smart soldier would just put some bullets through our doors. No one would ever be the wiser, but I felt groggy. In shock, perhaps. I watched the last pieces of convoy dwindle behind us on the roadsides, and knew I would never convince this greasy little bastard. He was taking us to Landview, come hell or high water.

He smoked. Still shivering from an unearthly fear, I panted, using my fingers to wipe away the caked filth and dust from my head and neck. The deep breaths, and the sound of my pulse slamming in my ears had me in some sort of spell. Somewhere in the dizziness, I dozed, fitfully.

"No, Billy Dean," I screamed once when I woke. "Cuthbert. He's back there. Who are we gonna tell he's dead? For God's sake, his family – find a pay phone--"

My demands fell on deaf ears. He kept driving.

But I wasn't being honest. There was something hanging over me. Hovering, about as heavy as an airborne hippopotamus – until it finally crashed down, and the world warped even further:

"For God's sake, I killed a man. I heard them say – oh, Christ, maybe two--" Tears came, so fast that I started bawling before I had any chance to think. I blubbered like I hadn't since that time three days after my dad died in that wreck. Billy Dean only peered over, with new contempt, if that were possible. I didn't care. I wailed.

"I'm a murderer. Who am I kidding?" I screamed. "Take me in. Put me in jail. Tell them what I did--"

"For Cripe's sake, stop your sniveling," he bellowed, and let a fully lit butt sail out on the wind. "That was self defense. My God, I'm glad you weren't in my outfit in the war. The Nazis could hear your baby screams from ten miles away."

I wept some more, but his words slowly hammered home. He had been in a war. A bad one. Now I had joined his ranks, like it or not. Besides, even that wasn't the real issue, was it?

"What the hell is going on?" I yelled, once I had composed myself. "I swear to God I saw you make a cloud come out of that lake. Then today—the lightning bolt – what in Hades are you, anyway?"

The lighter flicked fire. He took a puff, and pushed harder on the gas pedal,. "I'm the monster that's about to throw you out of this car at a hunnert miles an hour if you don't stop your caterwauling. Now shut up and go back to sleep."

I did.

When I woke, Billy Dean seemed to think it was funny. He reached into the back seat and produced a canteen. I was sure it was filled with hooch, but my thirst got the better of me. Water, thank God.

"Why are we going down to this little one horse town, anyway?" I managed to ask.

"I told you, Rookie. We've got to replenish my supply of quartz rods."

I digested that for a moment. "And Cadwallader's giving you time off for that?"

Another chortle. "Not just that," he said. "We're also running an errand for him. Making sure things are set. An errand for his mother, in fact."

Again, his mother. Maybe Watkins was onto something. "His mom lives down here?" I asked.

"Naw. She's up in Sironia. But she was here a number of years." He fixed me with a weird look I could not read. "These are her people. The Landview folks."

His strange behavior at Lake Centex wouldn't shake from my mind. "I've read about interesting experiments they're doing, seeding clouds with silver iodide," I said. "Does the quartz work like that?"

He studied me, then grew thoughtful. "You ever see a tornado in person?"

"Just the ones you pointed out to me on radar. I thought I heard one once, though. Sounded like a freight train up in the clouds."

A nod. "Probably a big one." He smiled, cig in lips, pushing back against the seat. Our conversation took place at high volume, to beat the wind coming in his window. "You ain't lived until you've stood out in a field with one, close enough to smell it, feel that pressure playin' your ol' eardrums like a bellows. A lucky few even catch a glimpse of its heart."

"OK, I'll bite. The clouds are alive, and tornados have hearts. Is that it?"

The coyote sneer. "If a cloud's alive, a tornado's even more so." He pulled both hands off the steering wheel, and formed an oval shape with his fingers. "If you get near the tip of the vortex without getting blown to kingdom come, look up. There it'll be, like this, up in the storm's middle. Like a little sun, almost, but made out of lightning. Sometimes, when yokels report golden flying saucers, I wonder if that's what they were looking at."

I laughed. "Now why does it not surprise me that you're mentioning UFOs?"

But he was earnest. "Inside a tornado's heart – that's where you can do some real travelin'."

He crushed the butt in the ashtray, which was so full, he wound up digging the whole mess out and tossing it out the window. Out came a fresh smoke, chased by the Aachen lighter.

I tried a different tack. "You learn to predict the weather in the war?"

He nodded. "Weather Corps. Learned a little bit more from an old German colonel. Weird old duck. Big scientist for them, it turns out. But everybody's weather methods take a back seat to my lady's."

"You mean the Comanche woman?"

"Her name's Rebecca," he said, peeved. Then suddenly, "You believe a guy could go backward and forward in time?"

"No. It would violate the laws of relativity," I said.

A shrug. "We held that colonel in a basement all day before we shot him. Well, not we, actually. Just me."

"Why did you shoot him?"

Again the coyote. "Because if we hadn't, somebody in the German Reich would have found out what he gave me. And what he gave me is why you and I are here today. Got it?" This time, his laugh was way too loud.

"No, I don't *got* it." I smelled a clue. "What did he give you?"

"Shut up." A scowl. "Just don't forget what I just told you. Now, I'm pulling over. I want you to do the honors of driving our procession into Landview, the capital of the Cosmos. Take the wheel, and turn right at that sign up there."

I got the car going, and gazed at the sun in the west. We were driving through a dream. A nightmare that promised a stunning horizon, rolling hills, grazing cattle, but behind every bush my crime squatted. I was a murderer now, and going to Hell. I thought of Andrea with her flowers – the dream turned sour. Then the vision of Marilyn Ellis – a flash of hope – too late. I was condemned.

We entered Landview from the east, and might have missed it if the gravel road had allowed any speed. The trio of three-story buildings caught my eye first. Spread in a semi-circle to the right of the main road, none of them bore signs of any kind, but the entry awning in front of each made me think automatically of hotels. Porches and the lawns in front of them were well kept, but deserted.

"Like the tree house?" He waved for me to slow, and lit yet another smoke. The road split around a narrow structure. Billy Dean pointed, indicating the right fork.

"Screwiest house I ever saw," I said. It was as tall as the hotels, but no wider or deeper than a single room.

"Keep yer eyes open. You might see her."

I almost asked, but it could be no other – the treehouse was where this Rebecca lived. Through the large window on the ground floor I glimpsed a steaming coffee pot inside. A frying pan, spurs and sombrero hung on the wall.

"Hells bells, where is that woman?" Billy Dean motioned for me to park on the lawn in front of the first hotel. When we climbed out, I could more clearly see the two structures on the south side of the road. One, a long open-air pavilion, had a crazy roof that swooped upward in dozens of points, a bit like uneven Chinese pagodas. They were all asymmetrical, as if the architect had been drunk when he drew them, the carpenter drunk when he built them. Under that bizarre roof, clusters of worn wooden tables stood on a dirt floor. "Farmer's market," he said. "If we stay until Friday, you'll get to see it."

"No." I almost shouted it. "I mean, it won't take that long, will it? The company picnic is on Saturday."

A sly look, as if he fully understood the reason I wanted to be back for that. "Whatsa matter? Your girlfriend bake you cakes on Friday nights?"

I wanted to tell him that it was he who was dense, and that if we stayed out here in the boondocks too long, we might return only to remnants of a civilization. Instead, I pointed to the lone structure, farthest away from the hotels.

"What's that? A depot with no train track?" The squat building sat just beyond the market pavilion.

"Whaddya know? You musta been outta town before, after all, Hot Shot."

Farther out, beyond the depot, lay a forest of scrub, stubby live oaks and mesquite that sloped down a long hill. To the west, the lonely road we had traveled continued on. Beautiful scenery, but it didn't lift my spirits, because my curiosity about this Comanche woman had disappeared, replaced by ferocious longing to see Marilyn Ellis again.

Beaten-up suitcase in hand, Billy Dean was already walking toward the entrance to the first hotel. "We'll stay in this one tonight," he said over his shoulder. "Hey." A stern look. "Here's your marching orders, Pancho. Get your room at the front desk. Then eat something, then go get cleaned up, and rest a while. Hear me? Take a nap, and decide to be a man again. You'll need all your strength to meet Rebecca. She might just take a shine to you."

Chapter 22
Guillermo

The high-ceilinged lobby reminded me of the old western-style hotels that my grandparents had dragged me through on our trips to New Mexico. Wood-paneled walls, and the requisite wagon wheels and mounted longhorn racks. Leather chairs and couches filled the lobby, large fans rotated overhead, and a smaller one droned on the registration desk, where a husky Mexican man sat, scribbling.

"Mr. Brown, you never bring guests with you." The desk clerk looked up and smiled with big crooked teeth.

"Well, I did this time. Guillermo, say hello to George Blair."

The gun and the whiskey clanked together in my bag when I shook hands. Both men looked down.

"What is in the bag?" Guillermo asked. "A cuckoo clock?"

"Nah," Billy Dean answered for me. "He probably was afraid to leave Sironia without his girlfriend's picture." He peered down his nose. "Or did you bring your own bottle of beer?"

"No, sir." Sweat trickled down my neck.

"Well, there's no need," Billy Dean continued. "Guillermo, here has the best food and liquor in West Texas, and it's all on the house. Right, my friend?"

The man behind the desk grinned. "As always, *mi amigo*. Can I show you to your rooms?"

"Give us the ground floor," Billy Dean said. "We'll let my partner here make the climb when he's a little more rested." A look passed between them.

I protested. "What climb? We're already on top of the tallest hill in this whole area."

"Just hold onto your jockeys." Billy Dean waved me away, and threw a thumb over his shoulder. "How is she?"

Guillermo slapped the keys on the counter. "Nervous," he said. "She is always afraid you don't come back, my friend."

The weatherman grimaced. "She worries too much. I've been keepin' my promises for fifteen years."

"We are men, aren't we? Don't men break promises?" Guillermo laughed at his own remark. Billy Dean only shook his head.

"Speak for yourself, Amigo."

Guillermo led us down a hall and invited us to lunch. My room was one-zero-six, directly across from a substantial wooden staircase that led up into shadows. Billy Dean kept walking.

"Can't eat with you. Gotta hot date, you know?" An insipid wink. "See you later, alligator."

I found the room decent, though the bathroom was at the end of the hall, and the trickle of water from the faucet barely big enough to fill my hands after a full minute. Hell – was there enough water pressure for a shower tomorrow morning?

I reported to the kitchen, where the pungent smell of cilantro filled the air. A large woman pulled tamales from the oven, and shucked them on a plate with artful fingers impervious to heat. Guillermo waited at the stove, then ladled chili from a steaming iron pot onto the plates next to the tamales.

"He said you liked beer, Mr. George. You wanna beer?"

"Sure, why not?"

He pulled two Falstaffs from a cooler, and settled across the table from me. The lady served the plates, and I dug in, famished. Only a few hours ago, I had imagined I would never eat again.

As far as that went – what gave me the right to eat now? Killers should simply starve themselves to death, for the good of the race. What would the marshal do? Arrest me? He sent me down here for information, not blood. But those worries backed away when I tasted the spicy food.

"So, how long have you known Billy Dean?" I asked.

"Since the storm."

"Which storm?"

He studied me with placid eyes as he chewed. "We met in the tornado. If you are traveling with him, surely he told you about the tornado?"

"Billy Dean was talking about tornados just today. Are you talking about one in particular? Did it make the news? I might remember it--"

Guillermo extracted a church key from his pocket and punched holes in the beer cans. "Are you a student of physics?"

"I took a few science classes." The hardest thing about interrogating someone, they taught us in the Academy, was keeping him on the subject.

"Did Mr. Brown change your view of commonly accepted natural laws?" He wiped his mouth, eyes shining with what might be mischief.

"Change my view? Physics is physics, right?"

A shake of the head. "Not with tornados. What about that one in Wichita Falls a few years ago? The splinters. How can physics explain those splinters?" He put down his beer can and belched. The old woman finished wiping the stove, and stepped out a back screen door without a word.

"You lost me," I said. "My God, if you're talking about controlling the weather, just say so." That made Guillermo flinch, so I pressed. "I don't know crap about tornados. What I really want to know is how many people live in these buildings? Has the army been here? Do you know anything about the Balcones revolution? Is Billy Dean just a messenger – like, is he bringing information to some officer down here?"

Guillermo chewed. And scowled.

I thought out loud. "Just as I said, you're on a hill here. Seems like a good place for a command post."

"That's why we picked this place. But, my friend — " Another belch, followed by a bite of tamale. "My job is not to talk about armies, but give you a lesson of physics, especially pertaining to tornados." He raised a hand, squelching my next protest.

"In Wichita Falls, a family canned some peaches in mason jars, and put the jars in the storm cellar. A tornado tore the house down. Even tore the door off the cellar. They were lucky the monster didn't suck everything out of the cellar. That has happened before, you know."

"OK," I said. "Sounds like a bad storm. But Guillermo, there are some serious things going on just up the road--"

"When they opened the jars," he continued, waving a piece of tamale on the end of his fork for emphasis. " — they found wood splinters mixed in with the fruit. Splinters, painted the same color the cellar door had been painted. How would a physicist explain that?"

I watched him rise, amble to the stove and scrape another helping onto his plate. I didn't answer for a moment, content to let the exquisite beer salve my over-spiced tongue. "Were the jars broken?"

"No."

"Well, the seal had to get corrupted, somehow. Maybe from the shock of the storm."

Another shake of the head. "No. The lids were vacuum sealed." He pantomimed with his fingers. "You know, *pop*. None of them had been popped open at all."

"Then someone's telling lies. It's a hoax," I said. "We'll never find out. Now, I played your game, so what about answering my questions?"

He devoured the new tamale, studying me all the while. "You don't listen so good, my friend. Have you seen a picture of a hay straw driven into a pole or a steel spar, after a tornado has passed?"

"I might have seen something like that in the newspaper--"

"Yes? Is that also a hoax?"

I slapped the table, as much to keep myself awake as anything else. The food rumbled in my stomach, the beer had me woozy, and behind everything that fought for focus in my mind, the realization – I had killed a human being. My God, would that thought hang behind everything from now on?

"What is your fascination with tornados, Guillermo?" My patience was at an end. "I'm not trying to be rude, but do you have a TV? The president might declare war tonight, and I'm looking for--" I stopped. Why should he betray his old friend to a complete stranger? Surely the army had been here. Probably still was, hiding out in the mesquite. Billy Dean said he was running an errand for the boss, so he had to be making contact with someone – my gut said it was Mr. Big, himself. "Have any soldiers checked in here lately?" I asked.

He shook his head slowly. "No soldiers. No TV or telephones. We want to experience the world as we were meant to experience it."

"Who's 'we?'"

Both hands spread out. "The people in this town. Me. I only mention tornados because they can twist the air in ways the physicists can't explain." His eyes were suddenly earnest, innocent. Sad, almost. "I am thirty now, but when Mr. Brown brought me here, in nineteen forty-seven, I was fifteen years old. Do you know when I was born?"

I did the math. "Nineteen thirty-two?"

A sip of beer. "I was born in Hermosillo, in the year of our Lord, eighteen eighty."

I felt the wind leave my lungs, and started laughing automatically. "Eighteen eighty? Very funny, Guillermo. Either you Mexicans have a different calendar, or he gave you orders just to give me the runaround. I need answers. We – all of us – don't have much time."

A sheepish smile. "And how do you know I'm not answering your questions, George Blair? The unspoken ones, the ones you need to know?" He settled back, and dug out his own cigarette, and lit it with a match from one of those little books. His look was deadly serious.

"Mr. Brown instructed me to tell you all about Landview, so I thought my studies of tornados would summarize it for you. We came here from my father's farm, in eighteen ninety-five, in a tornado. It was after the fiesta." After only two puffs, he crushed the smoke out, rose and began clearing the table. "That is, we left the farm in eighteen ninety-five. A few moments later, we arrived here, in the modern era, in nineteen forty-seven. We rode a tornado. Mr. Brown was doing the driving--"

He stopped himself, then looked upward and crossed himself, like a devout Catholic. "I mean, *they* were doing the driving, but driving wherever Mr. Brown wanted to go. He is a singular man, George Blair. He has that kind of power."

"Oh, shit." I buried my head in my hands, searching for a retort. But what could I say? Maybe this wasn't a war, but a monstrous practical joke – a joke in which I had become a murderer? Before I could cuss the big man, he plopped a new beer down in front of me. In the next instant, Billy Dean crashed in through the lobby door.

"Hells bells. You guys done eatin'?" He took the Falstaff Guillermo offered, sucked in a huge swig, slammed the can on the table and looked at me. "Change of plans, Hot Shot. You nap later. First, we're gonna go find us some quartz."

Chapter 23
A Singing in the Air

The late afternoon sun came in the front lobby windows, and that didn't help any. I was dead on my feet, and didn't think I had the strength to make it to the front door. Before I knew it, I found myself following that little rat on the green, well-kept rolling lawn that lay in front of the three buildings. Then we crossed the gravel road. I had neither seen nor heard a single car drive by since we arrived. The interior of Rebecca's tree house was blotted out by the glare from the low sun.

I wanted to tell him that Guillermo's smoke screen had fallen on deaf ears, but I wasn't in the mood to give him any satisfaction. Let him think the big man never said anything.

"This way." Billy Dean carried that colorful pouch hanging from his shoulder, and he led the way through the airy pavilion with the crazy roof. We walked between rows of wooden picnic-style benches on either side. Their cleanliness and the smooth dirt surface beneath them indicated that someone tended the place regularly. We took a narrow path worn through the chaparral, and as the mesquite grew thick, my adrenalin kicked in again. Was he taking me to see Mr. Big? Or worse?

"Where's Rebecca?" I asked, trying to keep up with the short man's pace.

"I tried to get her to come with us. She's shy."

I stopped in my tracks. "Look, Billy Dean, I'll play this little game only if you promise we can be back by Friday. If the planet doesn't blow up by then – or maybe you know there's no real danger of that?"

He waved me on. "Why you so desperate to get back to that girl of yours, Hot Shot? You need poontang that regular?" He laughed crudely. "Law, she must be something. I heard tell the old man was pretty taken with her. Better watch out. Money has a way of turning a girl's head."

I stood my ground. "Why don't you go on? I think I forgot something." I had. My gun was sitting in my bag, back in my room. A fatal mistake. I was no undercover man.

He drew closer. "I don't have any time for your sniveling nonsense, Mr. Pseudo-Government Agent. Boss says he wants you trained in the weather, you do what I say. Quartz is a big part of that training. You gotta know where to find it."

"Come on, Billy Dean. You're not taking me to find any quartz. Where's the general's headquarters? Who's running this horror show?" I shoved my fist right up to his nose. I had already been in a fight today, and I wasn't scared of him anymore. "Either you introduce me to him, or shoot me. And keep that jackass with the funny tornado stories away from me."

Something flashed, and for the second time that day, I found myself lying in the dirt, looking up at the world through Johnson grass. Billy Dean was unclenching his fist, and my jaw was throbbing.

"Sorry about that, Sport. Reflexes, I guess. Can't let anybody get too close. Gotta complete my mission, you know." He resumed his walk. "Come or don't come. But if you don't learn about the weather, Boss'll fire you, sure."

I got up, and followed him.

Every few yards, our footsteps flushed quail, sending them skittering away, peeping loudly. Billy Dean led down into a dry creek bed, and we were forced to trudge along limestone slabs that sometimes cracked underfoot. I decided to call a truce and get him talking again. "What was that crap Guillermo was spouting back there?"

He put his fingers to his lips. "If we're gonna find quartz, we both gotta shut up. Ever hear a tuning fork?"

"Yeah. So?"

"Well, it sings if you hit it. Quartz is kind of like that, only it sings when the air moves over it. And air can even be under the ground, so when you're looking, you gotta listen." He kept going, more than a mile, it seemed, down the creek bed. Finally, the angle of descent increased, and the creek bed walls grew higher around us. What a perfect place to shoot someone. I gazed at the top. If the army were up there—

"Over here," he said, and pointed.

A small cliff stretched up nine or ten feet. I squinted against the sun, noting reflections flashing near the top. "I don't hear anything, but this wall sparkles."

"Bingo," he said. "See what happens when you settle down and quit yammering for a few minutes?"

He produced a small hammer with a claw on it and began digging at eye-level. "Popcorn quartz is fine, but we gotta find a vein. Quartz is a crystal. That makes it real easy for it to break off in little chunks and balls. The Indians used those chunks, too, but I don't really know how. Big pieces are what I'm after. Long, sturdy ones."

"So you just get those and dip them in a lake, and that makes rain?"

His fingers worked, brushing dirt away before each strike of the claw. "Not that easy. You have to concentrate.

Pipsqueaks like us don't make rain. The quartz does. Rather, we make the quartz sing, and the Thors come to hear it." That coyote smile. "Manipulating the weather is like getting your job at the station. It's not what you know, it's who you know."

"And the Thors are--"

"The people who live in the clouds. I told you that. And don't act like I'm crazy. Folks mention the cloud people all the time. Everyday Joe Schmo knows they're up there, even if the scientists, governors, and priests won't admit it."

I leaned against the rocky wall and wiped my forehead. What a mistake – drinking two beers before hiking. "Sure, I've seen those old cartoons on TV that show gods up in the clouds, fighting, or throwing lightning bolts, even bowling. Those are old wives tales made up to lie to kids, so they won't go bonkers about thunder. Tell me something real, Billy Dean. What's the scientific basis of these native practices? Did this Rebecca dame teach them to you?"

He grinned broadly, and answered only what he wanted to. "Bowling. Ninepins, to be specific. That's their favorite game, by God. Now, be quiet. I got one here."

He worked, and I rejoiced with each plop of a craggy, awkward-looking piece into his bag, hoping it would be the last. But he paused at one point, looking disgusted. "Dang if we don't need a few more." He gazed up and down the creek, and I saw this whole nightmare stretching into eternity.

"I'm about to die, Billy Dean." I backed up and pointed to the high patch of sparkles above us. "What about up near the top?"

He patted me on the back. "Too high up. Are you gonna give me a boost, or make me hang off the top?"

Reluctantly, I braced myself against the wall, and let him stand on one of my outstretched knees, like a stool.

"Whoo-eee," he cried, after a moment. "I think the quartz likes you better'n me." He worked until his weight started pains shooting along my thigh. Sweat poured down my face, and rocks where I held on to the cliff face cut my fingers.

"Why the hell didn't we bring a canteen?" I yelled, trying to ignore the pain.

"Just a few more," he said after an eternity. "And you can have another one of Guillermo's beers."

"It better be quick. I'm falling asleep on my feet."

"He brags about their beer back in the old days. I never heard of a Mexican beer that was worth a damn."

"Oh, yeah. The old days. When was Guillermo born, really?"

"Same year as Rebecca. They're cousins. Late eighteen hundreds. Don't worry. She's about your age, even if she's eighty-something." He swung the pick and laughed as a new hail of dirt rained down on my head. I had reached my limit.

"I guess you can convince country hicks of anything."

"Hells bells, boy. Ain't you got any judgment of people?" He hopped down, and I collapsed against the cliff wall, rubbing feeling back into my leg. "The people of Landview are the decent-est folk you'll ever meet. I'll bet Guillermo's read more books than you. Here's a good one." He held a sparkling chunk up to the sun, then packed it away.

Icicles of pain radiated from my knee, and I fell back on my butt. "Fine. So we dug some quartz. Is that all it takes to manage the weather, Billy Dean? Polished quartz and a lake? Can we go home now?"

"Cool your jets, Hot Shot. Now we go back and get you cleaned up. You got a hot date with the prettiest Indian lass to ever grace the plains of Texas."

I'm sure my jaw dropped in horror. "A date with Rebecca? You pervert. A war might start tonight, and we're out here wasting time."

He glanced over, wearing that twisted coyote smile. "Only way a war's gonna start is if you make Rebecca mad."

Chapter 24
A Stormy Sea

After a half hour of rock-solid sleep, I followed Billy Dean's edict and made my way to the bathroom to clean up. Thankfully, the tub's water flow was greater than the sink's, and I lay in the suds, dreading meeting this Rebecca person. I wasn't thinking about Andrea, either. But the warm water helped arouse me with fantasies of Marilyn.

The sun sank behind advancing clouds, and Guillermo's mother served tongue-stinging enchiladas, as promised, and I made the mistake of getting ahead of Billy Dean in the number of beers.

"So, explain to me about when you were born," I asked Guillermo, when I could get a word in edgewise between them. The big Mexican was also deep in his cups, and his only answer was a hiss through his teeth.

"What does that have to do with the subject?" Billy Dean downed the last Falstaff and started on the six-packs of Lone Star. He pointed at his old friend. "Now tell this son of a bitch that aged, heavy beef is better than veal."

Their culinary argument grew heated, punctuated by thunderclaps of a storm approaching from West Texas. I got drunker, convincing myself that beer would replenish the salt

I had lost that afternoon. Then, from somewhere in the fog, I heard Guillermo ask a question, his gruff voice on the verge of weeping.

"When do you think we can go home, *Patron?*"

My eyes flew open. Billy Dean was shaking his head. "Soon. They're bringing it. Flores ready? What about Alfalfa?"

"Are you talking about the kid on the Our Gang films?" I blurted.

Billy Dean winced. "Shut up, College Boy. Hell, my friend here's showing you hospitality, and you fallin' asleep. Come on, let's go to our rooms so we can get an early start tomorrow, polishing those stones into sky daggers."

There had been no more mention of my "hot" date with Rebecca, but the beer had made me curious. "Look at this," I cried, "--you've gone and gotten me too drunk to meet that Rebecca broad."

"Watch your mouth when it comes to the Princess of the Prairie," he said, and shoved me against the wall. He grabbed my chin, and directed my view toward the staircase just across the hall from my room.

"See those stairs?" was all he said, then staggered off to his own room.

Lightning outside threw shadows around the walls. Rolls of thunder followed, and I lay counting, dividing the number of seconds by five, the way Billy Dean had suggested, realizing the thunderheads were coming closer. The window panes rattled in the wind, until a shuddering boom made it sound like the old bricks were coming right out of the walls. I sat up, gripped by an uneasy feeling: What if this wasn't just a storm on the horizon, but nuclear war?

I pulled on my jeans and t-shirt, and found a light switch. It didn't work. Neither did the one near the stairs. I must have been asleep before, because I wasn't sleepy anymore, and decided to venture up the steps, holding onto the rail and navigating by lightning flashes.

The second floor hall's layout seemed identical to the one downstairs, and the door to the room directly above mine lay open. A couplet of bright strikes showed the bed was still made, and empty. I groped my way in, and crept over to close the window someone had carelessly left open, letting in wind and rain. I looked out.

Across the road, a light burned in the tree house's window. Visible through a universe of falling raindrops, in the middle of the strange structure's living room, a woman stood. She had long black hair and was clad in a floor-length, old-fashioned dress, and her dark eyes were looking directly at me, as if she could see me here in the shadows. A jolt went through my body. Her face was thin, angular, lovely, but almost menacing. I couldn't shake the ridiculous feeling that she had been standing there for some time, waiting for me.

I stumbled back, hitting the heavy bed, then knocking over a lamp table in the process. If that was Rebecca, she was beautiful – if a bit scary. I retreated to the hall, but instead of fleeing logically to my room downstairs, I went upwards, climbing to the top floor by feel. Same layout. As below, the door directly across was wide open, and the window in the room, as if it were the housekeeper's job to make sure rain would come pouring in. I stepped carefully across the wet floor. This floor was more exposed, of course – that had to be why the wind felt like a full gale up here.

I braced against the window -- the view showed the tree house at a steeper angle – but the dark-haired woman inside was now nowhere to be seen. Still I stood, letting a spray of chilly rain blow all over me, until a marvelous sight stole my attention: Each time lightning illuminated the sky, the crazy roof atop the market pavilion across the road appeared to go into motion.

I focused my gaze on those uneven pinnacles, pagoda-like peaks that swooped with each lightning strobe, transforming the caddy-whompus roof into an illusion of a heavy, roiling sea, as surely as if they were rolling waves instead of stationary spires. I gripped the slippery windowsill, spellbound.

"You're doin' fine."

The voice made me jump a mile. Billy Dean's silhouette flared in the doorway behind me. He cupped his hands, to be heard over the wind. "She's pitchin' and tossin' tonight. Come on up to the roof and let me introduce you to the captain."

"No," I bellowed. He blocked my retreat.

"We're on a cloud ship, and I want you to meet a Thor captain." He motioned. "Make it snappy, boss."

I yelled through clenched teeth. "Get the hell out of my way." I clawed across the mattress of the room's wide bed, and barged past him, but he grabbed my arm on the stairs, and pulled me upward with a warning. "You came down here to learn. If you don't follow Cadwallader's orders, you'll wind up like Cuthbert."

I was too dazed or drunk to resist. The steps ended flat against the ceiling, but I heard him fiddling with a metal latch in the darkness, and a trap door flew open above us, letting in a stiff breeze and all the brilliant stars of a hill country sky.

"Where's the rain?" I asked, even as he pulled me to stand upright on the softly swaying roof. A cabin lay close by, some sort of rooftop utility shed, and I experienced a weird sort of vertigo – the loud storm hadn't stopped at all, but was mostly audible from downstairs, through the trap door. I looked down into that darkness at the very moment the staircase lit up, bathed in a lightning flash. I tried to stand straight. Over the roof's side lay a carpet of dark gray clouds so thick, it seemed you could vault over and walk on them.

Billy Dean gripped my arm like a vice. "Shut up and listen. You're about to meet an admiral. He's really just a young buck, but he's the pride of the whole country. Cloud people live life at a much faster pace. They live their lives in segments, and one segment might last only a few hours."

The roof swayed more, enough so that I wondered if the whole building were coming down, but I braced beside the runt and looked all around us: We were high in the air, the earth a dark mass that came intermittently visible in the gaps in that gray carpet that stretched out beside the structure. Above the fluffy landscape, huge thunderheads towered, moving. But these were not clouds, but great ships, with wispy riggings of clouds that towered over decks and cabins. I looked directly upwards – my God, this building had sails, too.

My breath caught. "This is a dream, you bastard," I yelled, and slapped Billy Dean on the arm.

He returned the favor, only his hand stung the side of my face. "No, it's not, Numbnuts. Pay attention, or you'll get us both killed. For the last time, this ain't a hotel. You're on a cloud ship."

He waved his arm, beckoning me to look around us again. There were dozens, hundreds of these great cloud crafts spread out in every direction. Gray/black bottoms with fluffy white sails above them – and then I saw the "admiral." A giant, human-looking beast draped in a short robe that seemed like an animal skin, yet with the consistency of clouds. The image it evoked was of some ancient Neanderthal, or a primitive Greek god. He towered over the cabin nearby, manning a sort of helm made of roiling cloud-spokes. The sight stopped my heart. His face was bony, misshapen – not human at all. In fact, my senses immediately concluded this was some sort of primeval animal who could never be controlled by humans, nor even befriended. Even so, Billy Dean didn't seem scared, but smiled like a fool.

"George Blair, meet Admiral Parsifal," he yelled above the whistling wind.

My teeth chattered, and I reached for the cloud-covered railing of the ship automatically, for support. It felt solid enough. And I looked out over the other ships, the nearest ones only fifty or so yards distant. Each one was peopled by its own giant, clad in those same cloud robes. The male captains wore full beards, like Parsifal. The garments on the females seemed more gossamer, less like animal hide, and more like a nightgown. Each one fell down to expose one breast, but their countenances, like the males, were fierce and foreboding.

Billy Dean was dragging me. I grabbed for the railing, but it came apart as wet cloud, then air, like trying to grasp cotton candy. "Stop it," I cried. "This is a nightmare."

I gasped for air, giddy with the conviction that this was just a dream, and that I could command my arms and legs, even if I couldn't control this snide runt who had the power to do or say whatever he wanted, waking or sleeping. The wind blew, and the deck beneath us pitched with each roll of thunder, and I could have easily tumbled over the side into oblivion, but didn't care. Nothing could hurt me – except for the weatherman's iron grip on my biceps.

He pulled up, right in my face. "Don't hee-haw like a danged donkey," he said. "You've got to meet this guy and if he don't like you, the jig is up. Now shut up and be polite."

Chapter 25
Ninepins

It had to be a dream – but the spray of rain on my face was real, the aching of my muscles, and the pedal-to-the-metal smashing of my heart against the walls in my chest while Billy Dean held me against the side of the shed that lay just behind the middle of the cloud ship's deck – real enough. The hard wall felt like wood, yet not wood, and when I squinted my eyes to examine it, little puffs of cloud seemed to peel off of it.

Billy Dean stood on tiptoes, peering above the cabin's roof in the direction of the giant. I willed myself to wake up, told myself I was still in bed – somewhere – but nothing happened except his infernal grip on my arm. Who was in control of this dream, anyway?

"What the crap are you doing to me?" I screamed, but the wind filled my lungs, smothering the words. "I want to wake up."

He pulled me around the corner of the cabin. Its walls, too, were firm, yet at the same time cloudy and spongy. The he was in my face, eyes mean and cold. "Listen up, Hot Shot," he said. "This is a test. What do you do when you see an ant?"

My teeth chattered too much to answer.

"Well?"

"We used to burn ant beds with gasoline."

"No good. For pity's sake, get that out of your mind. What about spiders? It's bad luck to kill a spider."

My grandmother had taught me the same thing, but I was too mesmerized with the way the wind toyed violently with his greasy hair to answer. Still chattering, it finally came out. "Don't kill 'em. Get a jar and take 'em outside."

"That's better. Hold that thought in your mind, 'cause our kind is no better'n pesky spiders to these guys."

He grabbed my sleeve just as a large flash overhead lit up the sails of our ship. Those cloud masts were the very picture of grace – stretching upwards, reaching almost to the stars. My prayer came from deep in my throat. "Please, Billy Dean. Let me wake up. I'll quit. I'll never tell a soul about the army--"

"You think that's a nightmare--" He pointed. On the wide deck, the giant humanoid deserted his ship wheel, and stepped out on the wide expanse of the front deck. His wide-set eyes darted back and forth, seeming to check the craft's progress through the wind. Not Greek, maybe, but maybe like a crude Norseman, or someone from biblical times – the historical images swirled in my mind. Only this sailor was fifteen or twenty feet tall.

My lungs felt close to bursting, and so were my bowels. I broke the weatherman's hold and crept backwards on my hands and knees, my fingers digging into the cloudy-firm deck, until I lodged against the puffy ship's railing again. "Christ Jesus," I said, though I couldn't assemble a prayer to save my life.

Billy Dean spoke close to my ear. "I told you not to cuss. Get your sea legs and get back out there."

As we watched, the great beast-captain leaned over and opened a large locker that lay on the deck. From it, he pulled a huge, bright pitchfork made of pure, vibrating lightning. I shielded my eyes.

"Pay attention, if you want to survive." Billy Dean turned my head until I could see, far down the long deck, right in the nook of the ship's prow, a host of bowling pins, each as tall as me. The giant poised the pitchfork over his shoulder, then heaved it like a javelin just as the ship hit a cloudbank, sending drops of rain over us like ocean spray. The pitchfork sizzled and crackled through the mist and plowed straight into the standing pins, sending them flying every direction.

The sky disappeared in a white, blinding blaze.

"Hells bells, look out," Billy Dean yelled – in the next instant, he clambered on top of me, and the air filled with sizzling fire. We crumpled down just in time to be slammed against the rail by an explosion. The air fixed, and an all-encompassing roar stuffed my ears, taking away all my senses.

I may have passed out. It seemed I was in that bright-loud for an eternity. Then the world grew dark again, and through the railing, I could hear the progress of the thunder as it galloped away into the clouds below us.

I blinked until I could see again, but it took longer seconds for the ringing in my ears to abate. The weatherman lay back on the deck, on his elbows, like a man reclining at a picnic.

"Damnation, I wasn't paying attention, trying to nursemaid you, you little bastard." He rose to a squatting position, and pulled me up. He shoved, guiding me closer to the monster, who was busy extracting another lightning pitchfork from his locker. From the corner of my eye, I saw it – the fallen ninepins had disappeared in the blast, but now a new set was growing slowly, magically, up out of the deck.

"Wake me up," I whined.

He slapped my face. "Quit sniveling. You gotta meet force with force," he said.

More shoving. When we reached the middle of the deck, that giant turned toward us, the blazing pitchfork poised over his shoulder. His massive head bowed, and he looked at us. The pronounced brow over his deep-set eyes made him clearly look Neanderthal, yet his pupils glowed with fire. From the corners of my eyes, the other ship captains were throwing at their own ninepins, blasting out their own thunder strikes. The storm was cranking up.

"Concentrate." Billy Dean's voice came out of the fine mist that poured over us with each thump of the great craft. "Smile, but look him square in the eye. Think spiders. You don't want him to squash you."

As if he were listening, the giant took a step toward us. Another. He covered ten feet in each stride, and I retreated until my hands were one with the railing. I couldn't even scream. The weatherman scuttered toward my feet, but the giant bent over, and swung a great backhand that struck the entire side of my body.

"No." I felt the jolt. Then I was airborne, racing the lightning bolts all around me. *This is it*, I thought. Yes, I'm dreaming, but tomorrow, they will find I died in my sleep – I thrust my hands through the air, scrambling for the ship's rail before it flew away from me – I caught a piece of the fluffy substance – it didn't give way! – and I hung there, legs flailing over a deep, pitching abyss, with pain pulsing up my side.

But the firmness of the wet rail didn't stay – as if some force suddenly remembered I was supposed to fall to my death. Edges of it began peeling away in cotton candy clumps, and I had to grab, and re-grab, and the angry clouds pitched below me like sharks waiting for their dinner, flashing on and off, like monstrous Japanese lanterns. Between the mounds of fluff, through patches of dark – farm houses were dotted by yellow-lit windows, and lonely car headlights streaked through the rain-heavy roads.

I cursed myself, for I should have recognized the signs of approaching death, though I had never died before – the way the world sped up, and went cockeyed after that old

Mexican man appeared at my door in his sombrero, after I graduated only to have the marshal scuttle my job – I was beyond screaming, and could only think about how I would never get to really meet Marilyn, and Andrea would have to find herself another breadwinner. Dream or no, this was how it all ended – how unfair life was.

My fingers finally gave way, just as I felt a tug. Billy Dean's face was in mine, and he hooked his arm under mine, and hauled me up onto the deck. He crushed his hand over my mouth, smothering my scream. Behind him, the giant was back on the deck, holding his new pitchfork, ready to throw another frame.

The weatherman bellowed into my ear. "You did good, son. I think he likes you."

"You're crazy, you son of a bitch," I yelled. "He tried to kill me. Let me out of this dream – am I dead already?"

"Hush. Here he comes again."

My heart froze. The big man scored another deafening strike, and we cowered while he turned toward us again.

I whimpered. "We are dead."

Billy Dean nodded. "Not yet. Look."

A shadow emerged from behind the cabin – the woman from the tree house. She walked gracefully onto the rolling deck, keeping perfect balance. For a moment, she stared at me, smiling, her long dress flying out behind her like a flag in the breeze. I had never seen anyone so poised. So utterly unafraid.

"That's Rebecca?" I whispered. Billy Dean slapped me.

"Watch her."

I could watch nothing else. She kept moving, and yanked at some cord at her neck. The action loosed her dress, and it flapped in the wind and fell to the deck like a crippled albatross, leaving her naked. The monster turned around.

Billy Dean tensed, and I thought he might actually spring to her aid, but it wasn't necessary. The beast moved closer, then crouched down in front of her. Rather than smash her aside, the giant extended a hand, like King Kong's invitation to Fay Ray.

"He's going to grab her," I warned.

The frightening scowl on the giant's face melted into a pained expression. His open palm neared Rebecca's face, and I could see a bright red, pulsating streak that coursed along it, perhaps where the lifeline on his hand should be.

"Watch how she does it," Billy Dean ordered.

Rebecca nodded, and her appendages looked tiny as they sank into that great palm. With a sure motion, her fingers traveled directly to the giant's red streak, which he offered gingerly, like a wound. Her fingers worked quickly, picking little lumps of red matter out of the oozing injury, and then, to my horror, she glanced over her shoulder and motioned for me to come to her side.

"What does she want with me?" I cried, gripping Billy Dean's arm for dear life.

"Get over there, Hot Shot. Make it snappy."

A muted roar filled my ears, and the ship's crashing on waves of air made it impossible to walk upright. Riding a kite must feel like this, and I had to remember it was a dream – or I prayed it was – but some inner drive told me I was going to approach that monster no matter what, and Rebecca's hand beckoned again, and my legs moved. I took drunken steps, tasted cold water droplets in the air and marveled at the fleet of cloud ships all around us, each one flashing yellow-white explosions as their respective captains knocked down pins. I detected the scent of flowers as I approached the long-haired woman's side.

Her body glistened with rain, but the giant quickly stole my attention from her enchanting vision. His arm, his whole body pulsed with a biting magnetism, and as I drew close enough to touch the wide hand, I realized he could crush us with one tiny move. She held the thick red stuff in her hands, and nodded for me to feel it with my fingers. Its consistency resembled that of clay, or Play Doh. With another motion, she directed me to collect some, myself.

"It's a gift," she whispered. "You must take it."

I avoided looking at those great fire-eyes under the heavy brow, and focused on the hand of this now docile creature. I scraped at the red clay with my fingers – once, twice, three times. When I had all of the stuff that could fit in my hands, Rebecca pressed against my side, nudging me back with her body, and thankfully the creature stood and crossed the deck in the blink of an eye, and climbed back to his locker, seeking another lightning fork to throw.

Rebecca's eyes glowed with delight. "Watch him," she said, and nodded.

I turned to see Billy Dean down among the ninepins, wearing an impish grin. With ceremony, he bowed and pushed one of the heavy pins until it fell, creating a minor clap of thunder that shook the entire craft. Rather than explode in fury, however, the giant gripped his great belly with one hand and let go with a laugh, which itself resembled thunder – a loud version of the warped sound like that you got when you run an audio tape in slow motion. Rebecca's hand closed around my wrist, for my own were too full of clay to grip anything. She pushed me toward the trap door.

"You need to sleep," she said.

A gentleman would have helped retrieve her dress, but I remember only stretching my foot into the dark square opening, touching the top step awkwardly, and being consumed by darkness.

I awoke in full sunlight, my head throbbing, the sheets soaked wet with sweat. Thoughts swarmed through my brain in no order. I was uncontrollably horny, and lay for a moment before I rose and stumbled down the hall, to the bathroom to wash my face under that pitiful trickle of water. Only then did I notice my fingernails were caked with red clay that even the hotel's Lava soap couldn't dig out.

Chapter 26
Rebecca Flock-of-Birds

As I half-walked, half-staggered to the kitchen, it became clear what must have happened. First, they drugged me somehow – then Billy Dean must have slipped into my room during the darkness to stick my hands in clay. Obviously, hypnotism, or some sort of suggestion was involved. That thought relieved me – he must have performed the same feat when we were out by the lake.

But yesterday was no magic spell. That was real blood I saw gushing out of Cuthbert. What in Hades was going on?

The image of the Comanche woman popped into my mind, naked and lithe – I couldn't ever remember seeing a grown woman naked, totally. "You're gonna like it more, if you wait for it," Andrea always said. But who could look? I was about to die when it happened, and my sore jaw, the aches all up and down my side, were testimony that it really happened. But what happened? That pitching, crazy pavilion roof – I was always handy at putting facts together in logical order, but all that was gone.

This must be the way insanity takes hold. That thought echoed in my brain. I wanted to slow down everything that had happened since that morning I walked into the marshal's office.

I shook my head – to hell with the self-pity. If they wanted to make me crazy, I wasn't going down without dragging the little bastard with me. I was bigger than Billy Dean, and this time, he wouldn't get the drop on me – but when I entered, the kitchen, Guillermo's mother was the only one around. She set a plate down on the table, as if she knew the moment I would appear.

"Huevos Rancheros," she said, with a thick roll of the 'r.'

"Muchas gracias," I thanked her, and sat down to the pungent breakfast. No need to take it out on her.

As before, the old lady escaped out the back screen door before I could ask a single question. I turned my head, and saw Billy Dean blocking the doorway, his suitcase in one hand and the multi-colored purse in the other.

"Where are you going?" I asked.

He beckoned. "Pick up that plate and come with me," he said. "First, breakfast with Rebecca. Then I decided to go easy on you, get you home in plenty of time for that hot date."

The little bastard was committing the only possible act that could keep me from cold-cocking him on the spot. I followed him.

Rebecca Flock-of-Birds sat alone at the nearest table under the pavilion, and I fairly ran across the lawn, balancing a dish of butter atop the tortillas, trying not to slip on the rain-slick grass. She looked identical to the woman in my nightmare – young, noble face and long black hair. Ravishing. Again, the vision of her lightning-lit naked body returned from the dream, and a shiver crawled up my spine.

She smiled as I approached, and stood to brush off the bench opposite her. "You did well last night, George Blair," she said, in the same melodious voice she possessed in my sleep. "You will be a great weatherman."

I smiled and offered her the plate of tortillas that accompanied my breakfast. She picked up a knife on the table, spread butter, rolled it inside of one, and passed the plate back. "It's nice to finally meet you." I extended a hand, but she only laughed.

"Must we be so formal?" she asked as she prepared one for herself. "I thought we were already friends."

I took a deep breath. My anger had vanished in the glow of her beauty. Even if she were Billy Dean's accomplice, there was no way she was responsible for his jokes. I took a large forkful of egg.

"Why don't you both--" I said between chews, "--explain to me what the hell sort of trick you're trying to pull, here?"

Billy Dean stood apart, smoking a cigarette and looking at the horizon, but she giggled, tearing at her tortilla. She smelled of lavender, and once she took a bite, she lowered one hand to cover mine. Another shudder coursed through me.

"It's not a trick, but a surprise, George Blair," she said, and produced a leather pouch from down by her own feet, this one made of softer leather, without the garish paint of Billy Dean's. "This is yours, to commemorate your first voyage." She handed it over with ceremony.

"It looks brand new," I said. The lacquered leather smell stung my nose. Its edges were tightly sewn, its sides imprinted with odd symbols, snakes and eagles, reminiscent of the Mexican flag.

"I just finished it yesterday. Open it," she said.

I pulled the flap over, and looked in. In the bottom sat a wad of newspaper which I unwrapped to reveal a large ball of red clay. I touched it, then looked again at my fingernails. "I can dig clay in Sironia," I said.

"Yeah, but from now on, when you dig clay you better be careful you don't blow your head off." Billy Dean put his foot up on the bench next to her. "Thank the lady."

I felt my face flush. "I was just going to. Thank you, Rebecca. I didn't mean to be rude."

"You gathered it last night." Her voice was full of softness. "It was a grand first voyage, a good omen. The grandfathers will accept you."

"Grandfathers? Are those what Billy Dean calls Thors?"

The weatherman sat down on the end of the table, flicking his lighter. "Don't play dumb, College Boy."

Rebecca clicked her tongue at him, and he shut up. A smile. "He's right, you know. You know how to use the Thor-blood. The captain told you last night when we collected it."

"He told me nothing--" I caught myself, and they both cackled as if I had told the funniest joke of their lives. "I don't even want to hear how you know about my dream. When did you give me the post-hypnotic suggestion?"

"Spare us, for Pete's sake." Billy Dean tugged on my shirt. "Let's get going. You two lovebirds can chat more next time."

"Why do we have to leave right now?" I didn't want to trade sitting here, across from one of the most beautiful women, for a long car ride with that asshole.

"Because you aren't quite ready." Rebecca's hand came across again, entwining her fingers with mine. "You were so tired after your meeting. It's not our time, yet, anyway. We follow the timeline of the Grandfathers." My motor was running, to say the least, but I was out of ad libs. She watched me in obvious amusement, and shook her head slightly. "Soon," she said, and softly ran her fingers through my hair.

It's not that I had forgotten that I was engaged – or forgotten Marilyn, either – no, all that was a shambles now. Marilyn had dislodged my feelings from Andrea. Now was I doomed to be a horn-dog? Start lusting after every female I met?

No, I told myself. This woman – so different than anything I had imagined, though I wasn't sure I ever imagined her at all – was perfect, other-worldly. I wanted to kiss her lips. I settled for kissing her hand, then stood, and walked back to the hotel to get my bag.

We didn't see army vehicles until we were almost to Highway 81. He drove most of the way, and my body cried out for sleep, but the cry of my curiosity was louder.

"What is this all about, Billy Dean?" I finally asked. "These weird visions in my sleep, everyone acting like they know what's going on, the army gone crazy--"

He chuckled, enjoying my frustration, it seemed.

"Dammit," I said. "What's going to happen when I tell the cops what happened? Am I going to jail?"

A flare went through his eyes. "You ain't tellin' nobody nothin', Numbnuts. You're the cop. Don't you know self-defense when you see it? Those guys are a treasonous, foreign force, technically, so anybody you done shot was just a favor to your home country."

"Oh, yeah?" I yelled. "If you're so blinkin' concerned about my home country, then tell me who's behind this goddam revolt. Why can't you point me in the right direction?"

A look. A laugh. A puff on his weed. "All right, Hot Shot," he finally said. "You ready for it?"

My whole body tensed – was he actually going to be straight with me?

He gestured with his cigarette, while it flared hotter and hotter in the wind from the windows, and he had to yell to be heard.

"In the war, the American and Russian governments took something from me. They stole it. And I've worked all these years to get the leverage to make them give it back."

I felt my jaw go slack. "So what? What does that have to do with Cadwallader starting a whole new nation?"

"Creatin' Balcones was the only way he could figure to force both countries to give my property back."

I studied his eyes. "You're lying. Cadwallader hates your guts. Why would he want you to have your sacred property? What is it, a goddam sword with a swastika on it?"

He laughed, took another puff of the rapidly disappearing cigarette, then threw it out the window. That was the way prairie fires got started.

"I never said he wanted me to have it back," he yelled over the wind. "He ain't got no choice in the matter."

"Please stop being a smartass," I said. "How can you make that old bastard do anything? Why in the hell would the whole army revolt?"

"You're a cop, ain't you? That's for me to know and you to find out."

He grabbed another smoke, and dug out his Aachen lighter, and waved it at me.

"Archimedes said give me a lever and a place to stand—"

"I know, I know, and he'll move the planet," I said. "So what's your lever? What's so all-fired important that you have to get it back?"

A knowing look, and he flicked the lighter. "I could say the key to all the past, and all the future, but you'd just say I was a drunk," he said. "Now shut up and take a nap. When we get to Temple, you're driving."

I lay back against the door, trying to formulate my next question. But I fell asleep before it came to me.

Chapter 27
True Confessions

In the Channel Three lot, I hustled my gear from his car to the trunk of my own. Billy Dean started for the front door and called over his shoulder. "Ain't you comin' in, College Boy?"

"Tomorrow," I said. "You tell them about Cuthbert. I won't."

He drilled me with his gaze. "I told you – ain't neither of us sayin' a damned thing, Punk. Not to nobody."

I drove home and went to bed without even taking off my dust-caked jeans. My nap was fitful, perforated with visions of running through dream ravines, dodging the *zip* gunshots. And lightning bolts. And each time I woke, I fought to erase that last look at bloody Cuthbert from my mind, only to have the vision replaced by supreme embarrassment – how could I let Billy Dean convince me that he was the cause of all this? No way could he be Mr. Big.

In late afternoon, with my head throbbing like a jackhammer, I picked up the phone. Andrea's mom invited me to dinner. It was that time of the week, but why did *she* call, and not Andrea?

While the receiver was still in my hand, I almost dialed the marshal – but to say what? To turn myself in? He would say I had killed in the line of duty, wouldn't he? Self defense? But what if he wasn't in control of that – what if the Washington types running his end of things decided it didn't look good to dust off a couple of army guys?

Driving the car, my stomach doubled up in the sharpest pangs of guilt I had ever experienced. Bad timing, because Andrea always got mad if I didn't eat what her mother dished out.

"Well, that was a short trip." Andrea pecked my cheek when I stepped through the door. "I figured that idiot would at least keep you a couple of nights. Did you learn about the weather?"

"Some," I said.

"Oh, George." She was on me suddenly, hugging me tighter than she ever had. "Daddy talks about Cuba on the phone every hour or so. Will there really be a war? What do they say at the station?"

"They don't know any more than the rest of us."

She seemed to come to her senses and pulled away. "Doesn't matter, Blair. I've been busy. I told you your new job was going to cause a few changes around here. You never did intend to give Billy Dean that whiskey, did you?"

"No. You said I could wait."

"Well, we gotta talk, but first, you're going to see my father. And don't you even dream of yelling at me for introducing myself to your boss the other day. And don't tell Daddy about it, neither. Tuck your shirt in."

In the den her father stood, highball in hand, gazing out the back window. The yard was ablaze with lights.

"Oh, Georgy, we're so proud." Mrs. Wiggins put her arms around me and kissed me full on the mouth. "You're doing such a good job on TV. And you're handsomer than Ed Murrow."

"Oh, Mother, George ain't a *news* man," Andrea said.

Mr. Wiggins offered his hand. "Son, take a gander out back. I'm digging a bomb shelter."

"No kidding?"

"Get him a Dr. Pepper." He motioned, and Mrs. Wiggins scrambled into the kitchen. "Yep, I thought this Cuba thing would blow over, but now my connections have me convinced. We're gonna be living like cavemen for a while, George --" He glanced around, and continued, even though both women were still in earshot. "Hell, we got five more orders just today. I've had the boys out here at night, working overtime. If you were still with the company, you'd make a bundle – but, I guess pretty soon there'll be no place left to spend it."

He stepped closer, whispering. "Hell, we all knew nuclear war had to happen sooner or later. If that asshole Kennedy could only stall this thing until most of the populace has time to protect themselves. Tread water six more months, then let 'er rip."

"Daddy," Andrea scolded, and took her normal seat at the table.

"Which brings me to the favor I need to ask."

"Sir?"

"If you're not busy in the evenings, do you think you could help me with the troweling down here? Aces is here most nights. And Jack. They'll be happy to see you. It'll just take a few days."

I swallowed.

"Say no, George." Mrs. Wiggins swished in with the serving platter. "You're a busy man, now. Albert, he's on TV. Leave him alone."

Albert Wiggins' stare did not waver. I had always hated working for him. But now, sitting in that tattered secretary's chair in his contracting trailer, listening to the carpenters talk about their beer busts, beckoned to me like a cabin near the lake. At least that job made sense.

"Sure," I said. "I guess I could use the exercise." I patted my stomach.

Andrea grunted. "I'll say."

I stuck my tongue out at her. She replied in kind. I didn't mind. It felt good to be home.

Yet that feeling didn't stay long. A hollowness was growing in my belly. Andrea was talking too fast for me to identify the change. But afterwards, she lay on the couch with her head on my lap, thoughtful, the coffee table full of bride mags, forgotten.

"You are good at reporting the weekend weather, George," she said, almost wistfully. "Wouldn't it be crazy if you've found your calling?"

"Thank you."

"That first night, you could hardly get the words out."

"Thanks for reminding me. It's in the past."

She reached up and patted my cheek. "You're so right. The past is the past, Dear. Right?"

"You keep saying things like that. I'm sorry I've screwed up our weekends. Maybe we should go back to the past. Think your father would hire me again?"

"Lucifer's Hades, you're going to be helping Daddy every night, but I won't be here most of the time. I keep telling you."

"I mean work for him full-time – wait, why won't you be here?"

She slapped a pillow on the floor. "Don't ride me like that overbearing Tommy Benson does Laura. I'm just going to be busy. You started this change of life, Mister. Come on, drive me past the doctor's. I'm not a girl to waste away. I've got some – some new ideas. But none I want to share with a Nosy Nelly. We'll take Mom's car."

She started for the door, but I stayed put, watching her dress flow around her legs, and thought of Marilyn. "How would you find an address?" I asked.

"Whose address?"

"Chris's house. I never knew where she – uh, *he* lived. Just thought I should take some flowers by or something."

"Look in the phone book, idjit."

"I did."

"Well, he just died last week. Check the obits."

"Never mind." I feigned disinterest. "Hey, would you have a copy in your papers?" Andrea kept the social pages and obituaries for weeks at a time.

"Lazy." She started for her room. "Man in the hall," she cried. She claimed that was their code to warn her mom not to wander around naked, but I long ago figured out it was a signal to her parents that we were going to the bedroom, and to check up on her in a few minutes. "What day did he die?"

She dug and found it. The address had five numbers, just off China Bend Road. "I know where this is. Wait." Her first suspicious glance. "It's too late to take flowers to decent folk. Call Baxter's tomorrow."

I shrugged. "I just wondered where he lived."

She handed me the keys. "I swear I don't remember you talking about any Chris. Let's see if Missy's car is outside Dr. Kilgallen's."

"God, I love the feel of that air conditioner," I said, once we were on the road. These little things – tiny luxuries – those were what I should focus on, I told myself. Not the vision of Cuthbert in the bottom of that draw. Not the soldier that I hit – I was a marksman at the Academy, but hitting those bull's eyes never happened under fire. I just held the damn gun, pointed it – the bullets went where I wanted them to. The soldiers were gone now, and Billy Dean was right, to a point. Maybe over time, if I buried myself in the little things of life, the air conditioners, and lawns and bomb shelters and going out to the drive-in with my girl – maybe the sin of killing those living, breathing creatures would fade. Over time.

"After you get promoted, we'll buy you a real car." She giggled. "Might be sooner than you think, big boy. Your boss and I have an understanding."

"You haven't been listening, Andrea."

"Shows what you know. You're better off working for him. Treats a girl like a lady. And that big Roman tub in his bathroom --" She stopped, mid-sentence.

"When did you ever see his house? Some deb party?"

Her eyes shot sparks. "Blair, my daddy's a builder."

"Your dad didn't build the Cadwallader mansion, Andrea, so don't be so puffed up."

"Never mind, you impossible snoop. Turn." I let her direct me, though I could have driven to Kilgallen's in my sleep. She smelled good. Tonight was good. Let time work on me.

The doctor's house loomed ahead. "Look. No car. She's not there, George." Andrea fairly bounced on the seat, then looked at me with all seriousness. "I have a yearly check-up Friday, so I might be too tired to see you Friday night."

"Andrea, Friday nights will be the only nights we can see a movie or go to dinner. At least for a while. Can't you change the appointment?"

She laughed – a carefree, full-throated laugh that was rare. "Don't you know that every woman is in love with her gynecologist? Poor, naïve, George." She chucked me under the chin with her hand.

"Let's go out to China Bend," I said.

"Only if we check up on the big man, first." Hand up. "Mr. Cadwallader's, Jeeves."

The Cadwallader mansion was the showplace of the elite Garden Vista Estates. When we rounded the corner, I saw Andrea's jaw go slack before I saw the reason. The huge manse glowed with a hundred lights, as if the biggest society do imaginable were in full swing. The only vehicles in front, though, were moving vans.

"Oh, my God. Go slow." She practically crawled out the passenger window. "Do you see that?"

The front yard was filled with moving men lugging chairs, desks, couches in the stark light. "It's furniture." Andrea gasped.

"So what? Maybe the Cadwalladers are getting a new living room suite. They can afford it."

"At this time of night? No, you idjit. *Look.* That furniture's going out, not in."

"So?"

"So, it's all masculine. Did you spot a single vanity? That big leather couch over there belongs in a hunting lodge." She bounced, even higher this time.

"Andrea, I'm happy for you. After years of driving around, we hit the jackpot. What do we win?"

"Those pieces are *his* furniture, Dummy. Your boss is leaving his wife." It was just the sort of soap opera intrigue she would invent for any activity.

By the time I turned around in the cul-de-sac, her demeanor had transformed. Feet on the seat, her eyes glazed, and she muttered, "The Lord is answering my prayers. Right before my eyes."

"What are you talking about?"

"You wouldn't understand. Go to his ranch, Blair."

"No deal. We're heading for China Bend."

"Oh, poof to China Bend. If you don't drive the car where I tell you, I will."

The moving vans in town had a sister, and it was parked next to Cadwallader's sumptuous ranch house, which lay about seventy yards back from his split-rail fences. Not barbed wire. A true sign of wealth.

"My Savior," she whispered.

It galled me to admit, but her theory was gaining plausibility. Then the headlights hit something new, and I stomped on the brakes.

"Are you crazy?" She cranked her window closed. "Keep moving, or they'll see us."

I turned to shine the lights through the white fence beams and into the huge, immaculate barn. Inside, Cadwallader's fabled troop carrier, plus a huge army tank sat side-by-side.

"My God," I said. The shadows of the two soldiers came rushing back into my mind.

"Stop cussing, George Blair. Haven't you ever seen a couple split the sheets before?"

This was definitely something to report to Tudberry. "If they really are divorcing, I wonder who gets to keep the heavy artillery?"

She bubbled like hot champagne, too excited over our discovery to protest me finishing our search mission. Sironia's society crowd would be polarized by this, she said. Who would side with the old lady, who with my boss?

"Nobody," she said. "Nobody likes Emil. But that's because they don't know him. It doesn't matter. He's a real man. He can take the consequences."

"Andrea, you're getting way ahead of yourself. Why do you think you know so much about a man you talked to for thirty minutes?"

"Oh, pooh," she said, and I could hear the wheels turning in her head. Obsessing. I didn't grill her any more, because the soldiers I shot kept appearing out ahead, just beyond the shine of the headlights, along with those sinister vehicles with the black and yellow radiation signs.

As I turned into the wooded shadows of China Bend, she was counting on her fingers the number of society matriarchs who would likely join a boycott of Channel Three after this news came out. I pretended to listen, and this time immediately found the mailbox with the right numbers on it.

So what? The desolation of my situation only sank in deeper. Chris's truck sat, lonely, in front of a small frame house. A shed-like structure and an old tractor stood to one side. A single light burned on the front porch, and another in one of the back rooms, and I thanked God that Andrea was with me. Otherwise, I might have sneaked through the unkempt grasses to look in one of the windows. It was at least a quarter-mile to the nearest dwelling, someone's trailer home.

So this was Chris's empire, the one he had worked more than a decade to build. Working for a miser in life, he left a beautiful woman behind in death. And it was my fate to meet her for a few precious moments, back when I was still pure. I might have deserved her then, before Cadwallader's dirty little game sucked its pound of flesh out of my soul. Before I became a killer.

I turned the car around for the main road again, and Andrea stopped her counting, and suddenly started to weep. For a sick instant, I imagined that she had just read my mind, and could see the bodies of those soldiers lying in the dust.

"Oh, George. You know, don't you? I'm so transparent, and you're always so wise. You'll forgive anything, won't you? Just driving me around wherever I want to go--"

"Andrea, I killed a man."

She raised a hanky and blew her nose. "I'm doing it for our future, and it's just for a while. Please trust me." She caressed my arm.

"Andrea, did you hear me?"

"Don't talk about killing, George. You're not a hothead, no matter what you'd like to think. You could never really have been a policeman." She wiped her eyes and looked away. "And don't humiliate me. Either you trust my judgment, or it won't work between us, anyway. We both need time to think."

She gripped my arm, her look heavy, strange. "I've grown up, George. It's been my destiny to step into society, like the women I just mentioned. A house doesn't stand without its pillars, and I can't help it. I can't help that it would happen this way, and not with you. Take me home. We've both gotta think about our new relationship."

"What are you talking about? I didn't say I was *going* to kill anybody. I said something terrible happened to me and Billy Dean on our trip." I stopped the car. Up ahead lay the road to Crawford and Abilene. Behind us, Marilyn's house was a small, dark shadow in the rearview mirror. Andrea only wept and shook her head.

"Damn it, Andrea, every time I try to pour my heart out, you force me to play twenty questions. You have to tell me you understand that I couldn't help it, or we're going to sit right here all night."

"Oh, stop playing games, George. You know what I did. Don't make me say it."

"I know what?"

She stomped her foot.

"You know I'm not a virgin anymore. You know I slept with Mr. Cadwallader last night. OK, I confessed. I'm being totally honest, though the Lord knows what kinds of secret things you were planning to do if that weather drunk had taken you out on the town during your trip."

Some organ clenched deep inside my stomach – hard – but when I stuck my head out the window, the sky and its stars were closing in on us. I couldn't breathe, so I drove.

We were both silent. What could be said? She had finally flipped, moved into her fantasy world where she could be rich, since I wasn't cutting the mustard. But why would she pick such an old cuss? And why would he sleep with her? Hell, maybe I was the daft one, dreaming about giants on ships – We turned onto her street, and she finally exploded.

"Don't you dare say I've betrayed you. I haven't betrayed anybody. That old man is over sixty, and I'm just looking out for the future, like I said. Our future. I was meant to be wealthy, George, and when you just went ahead and chose the wrong profession, well, I guess, God must have seen fit to intervene. This doesn't stop us – I mean, you and me – by a long shot.

"We were meant to be together, George. And we will be. Eventually. We just gotta change our plans. A little."

I didn't reply, but got out and trotted to my own car. This was not the Andrea I knew. And yet it was. What irony that on this night when I had finally reconciled myself to a happy, sedate life with her. Right when I was about to sell my soul all over again to her father, she had committed the single act that would make that foreordained life impossible.

I drove away, and watched her in the rear-view mirror, straddling the driveway like a scorned colossus, waving her fist and babbling threats I couldn't hear. I headed for my apartment, head throbbing, heart skipping beats, my brain bouncing between an aching desire for sleep and the notion that I ought to go back there and slap the crap out of Andrea. I imagined Mr. Wiggins storming into the living room, carrying his shotgun – but then I would tell him what Andrea had done, and hell, he would jump right in and help me thrash her.

Hells bells, as Billy Dean would say.

I was hyperventilating. I stopped, turned the car around, and headed for China Bend.

Chapter 28
Moonlight

On the way, I stopped at R.J.'s Drugs, the only store open 'til midnight, and bought a bouquet of fake tulips. In China Bend, I cruised past Marilyn's house repeatedly. Down to the river, past the bait shop, then back again.

Then, at ten-fifty, the porch light switched off. I panicked. The only light still burning was in the back room. Her room.

In a fog of slavering heat, I parked out by her mailbox, crossed the scruffy lawn and gravel drive, and walked quietly up the steps, sweat pouring down my temples. I rang the bell. Not a bell, a buzzer. I heard shuffling. Lights flared on.

Finally, the door opened, and Marilyn Ellis stood before me, clad in a nightgown that cast a blue shadow, holding a twelve-gauge shotgun across her left forearm.

"Yes?"

I presented the flowers. "I'm George. From the station. Remember? We met the other morning. I came to pay my respects – uh, condolences."

Her silence grew and stretched, and I couldn't think of anything pithy to say, like Clark Gable or Dobie Gillis or James Bond might have. I could not read her gaze, and finally just wished she would shoot me and close the worst chapter on the life of an idiot.

Then she smiled.

"Yeah. Prince Charming. You were at the funeral, too. Come in, George."

I opened the screen door and stepped across the threshold, my pulse echoing up and down my body.

"Nice house."

A normal country house, well-kept, but no piece of furniture matched another. Andrea would never stop criticizing if she saw this place. My God, Marilyn was wearing her nightgown. Not even a robe over it. "You saw me at the funeral?" I asked.

"I saw a lot of people." She let the shotgun point straight down, and reached for the flowers with her free hand. "What are these?"

"They're fake. Sorry."

She leaned over and set them on an end table. "Then I won't have to water them."

I tried to be discrete, but my eyes sought pay dirt automatically. The nightgown wasn't sheer enough to reveal anything but curves. Lord, what was I doing here?

"I'm looking at pictures," she said. "Want to see some of them?" Simple. As easy as if I were an old pal.

"Pictures?"

"Chris's pictures. You know, hunting trips." She laid the gun on the couch. "If you're one of his buddies, maybe you're in some of them."

A light gesture, and she started toward the kitchen, her bare feet extending below the nightie's hem. I followed, watching those naked appendages cross the worn carpet of the living room, onto the faded linoleum of the kitchen. Her blonde hair brushed her shoulders. She switched off the living room light behind us, then swept through the kitchen and into the bedroom.

"In here," she said. The kitchen light went off, too.

Photos spilled out of a shoebox on the neatly made bed. The closet door was open, and a rocking chair with threadbare upholstery stood next to another doorway that led into a short hall. Andrea would call this house a cracker box.

"Come on," she said. "You must know some of the guys in these."

With an ease that was maddening, she threw herself down on the bedspread, propped on her elbows and grabbed a small stack of the glossy prints. I stutter-stepped around, like a moth sensing that wherever he lights the surface will be too hot. She smiled and patted the mattress.

"Here."

I eased my rear down, then leaned. One-by-one, she held up pictures, or shoved them at me, and I was thrown back to childhood. We were like two seven-year-olds, I thought. Innocent, as if I had just moved into the neighborhood, and our parents were making us socialize.

"He liked the coast." The one she thrust into my hand showed a grinning Chris standing knee-deep in surf, with a stout-looking fishing rod in his hand. "I feel bad, because I usually wouldn't travel with him to Galveston, so he didn't go very often."

"Don't you like the ocean?" I asked.

"It's not that. Whenever we went somewhere, he always had to bring his buddies along. These guys."

She tossed down a print of six smiling men. Overgrown teenagers really, displaying different-sized fish, Chris in the middle of all of it.

"You're amazing," I said, and let myself settle deeper into my side of the soft mattress.

"Why amazing?"

"You're so – friendly. You don't know me from Adam, but you're being nice to me."

A tiny shrug. "I can tell about people. Sometimes." Her gaze stayed glued on the photos, and I was thankful for that, because my eyes were at it again, flitting from the pictures to her cleavage, deliciously ample, now that her breasts were hanging down.

"Are you sad all the time?" I asked. "I mean, since his death?"

A glance, then back to the pics. "Not sad," she said quietly. "But my figuring is all slanted. You know, as if the way things happen has been changed. Not like before, when Chris was here."

"What do you mean, figuring?"

Her smile turned into a giggle, and she even blushed. That made her face so grindingly beautiful, and it was so impossible that I was really here, not dreaming.

"I'm always doing figures in my head. Adding things up, you know? Adding up the probabilities." She reddened so much, I had to laugh, too.

"That sounds pretty weird. Are you some kinda math whiz or something?"

"That's what Chris used to call me – the whiz. Not really. I made a B in school. But they made me stop at the third grade." A sigh. "That's all we had back then. Besides, it's not really math, just figuring."

"I still don't get it."

Pensive, now. "Like--" She looked away. "I figured you would come."

I almost fell off the bed. "Me? How? I didn't even know I was coming until a little while ago."

"You weren't here with all the others last week, you know, at the visitation, so I just predicted you would come by yourself. Chris never wanted to hear my predictions."

I was getting confused. Now she was talking like the people at Channel Three. Maybe it was the blood raging up and down, inside. Her nightgown lay, silky smooth, over the round of her butt. What do you say to a widow in this circumstance?

"How long were you in love with Chris?" I blurted.

A smirk. Finally, a suspicious look. Then a sigh. "I wasn't. But then you're new to all this. I keep forgetting." She dropped the photos remaining in her hand, then pushed the whole mess toward me. "You'll probably never believe it, but we weren't married. We just lived in the same house."

My head spun. What did she just say? I couldn't listen, because two of the top pictures contained familiar faces – Cadwallader and Russell in hunting gear. "What?" I sputtered. "You lived together? As man and wife, but not really--"

Now I was way out of line, but she only laughed, and sank down on one arm, the look in her eye full of meaning. Though I couldn't guess what that meaning was.

"We never knew each other as man and wife, George Blair. That was the rule when I moved up here."

"You moved here from where?" I asked.

"Landview."

I shuddered. "You're joking. I was just there."

Her eyes widened. "Oh, then you met Rebecca?"

"I – yes."

"Did anything happen between you – and her?"

I couldn't breathe. "What do you mean--"

She shook her head. "It doesn't matter. Rebecca is my best friend. Like a sister. A friend for life."

"Nothing happened. Why would you--"

A slight smile crossed her face. Then a new sparkle in her eye. "I moved from Landview, and I'm supposed to live here, until—"

I looked away. The whole world had become hieroglyphics. Used to be, I seemed to catch on fast – to anything. Not now.

Questions raged inside me. Was her Landview connection another clue? Her eyes stayed on me. Deep. Full of something unbearable. Irresistible. The questions would have to wait.

"Guess I'd better go," I said. "You're going to the picnic, aren't you?"

"It's OK. I'm almost always up this late."

I told my body to move, but it didn't.

"Look how many fish they caught." She giggled again, recovering a new photo.

"I killed a man." It came out easily. Even if it ended everything, I was glad it came out.

Silence. Then, "How did that happen?" If my confession worried her, she poured all of it into that picture, her voice, so soft.

"It's all this army stuff. I was with some friends. We were going to be executed. There's a war brewing, Marilyn, and everything's gone crazy. Did Chris ever say anything about that?"

No answer.

"But of course, you must know all about it--"

"Chris killed someone, too." She was forming the photos into little stacks, like playing cards. "Fight in a bar on our first date."

"Wow. What a way to start a love affair."

Her grimace was more sultry than the night air. "I told you, it wasn't like that. But we had to keep up appearances."

She looked into my eyes, and kept staring, and not until that moment did I realize how heavy my eyelids were. The bed felt so good. I felt her look away from me, heard the photos *plop* back into the box, heard the top of the box fit into place. My eyes jarred open when she moved off the bed.

"It's too late. Time for me to go." I tried to say those words, but instead of exiting my mouth, they rattled around in my head while I stared at the floor fan. It hummed so nicely, turning its lazy face back and forth, sucking in fresh night cool from the open window.

Then the lights went out.

I blinked.

She came back and stood between the window and the bed. A silky monolith, glimmering white in the moonlight that poured through the window's upper reaches. Her hands dropped below her waist, gripped her gown, and pulled it off over her head, in one exquisite movement. I stopped breathing.

She poised in the moonlight for a long moment. I don't know if she was watching me, or drinking in the night, or doing the impossible: inviting me to look. My gaze roamed from her perfect breasts, down her slim belly, to the thick patch of hair. After a whole lifetime without seeing anything, now I was given the gift of a naked woman for the second night in a row. Only this time, there were no storms, no monsters to suck desire out of the air.

Except that I was the monster. The man who had killed, and if I never had, maybe I never would have known how to do what I did next: I moved slowly off the bed, undressed, and climbed in next to her.

"You and Chris –" I began. She put her fingers to my lips.

"Never him. It's only us," she said in a whisper. "Finally--"

Sheets so cool. Marilyn's body, so hot to the touch. She beckoned, and I lay on top of her.

"Am I too heavy for you?"

"No." A whisper. "Girls are made to support the weight."

She led me, and I followed with no reservations. Somewhere, out beyond the cane breaks that surrounded this house, somewhere in the night was the girl I had loved for years. But her infidelity made guilt impossible. Marilyn's kisses made guilt impossible.

The music of crickets lilted through the window, grace notes to Marilyn's grip, her urging breaths, and groans. In a world gone mad, the gods had taken away my innocence when I pulled the trigger yesterday. Tonight, they were giving it back.

She was already in the shower when I woke. Dawn. I sat up in bed. The deed was done. So Andrea had lost her virginity? Well, I –

To my delight, she emerged naked from the bathroom. Completely unashamed, as impossibly free as she was last night. The world had changed – it was finally as it should be. I watched deliriously as she went about selecting underwear and socks from a drawer, and began to dress.

I crawled out, pulled my jeans on, grabbed her arm, and hugged her. She looked up, into my eyes, and permitted one strong, sealing kiss. "When can I see you again?" I said.

"Don't know."

"At the picnic, do you want to take a walk?"

"Don't know if I should. I'm supposed to be in mourning." She grimaced. "If the neighbors see you leave--"

"Shh. They won't."

I started to break away, but she held on, laughing an embarrassed little laugh. "Seems my whole life is live with things I'm *supposed* to do."

I laughed, too. "Maybe you're supposed to be with me."

Her eyes grew dark, and she let go, and walked toward the kitchen. "That's what they told me."

"Marilyn what does that--"

"It's OK, George. It was good, not bad. Hurry. You need to get your car out of here."

She was right. We might be hidden by the scrub and the river, but this was still Texas. We kissed one more time, and I walked out, and drove for my apartment.

I hadn't called the marshal, and I didn't even know if she would ever see me again. Or if this had been a mistake. Because it wasn't – it felt right in every way. A chilly October wind whistled through the window, the Thors' big ships were floating peacefully above me, and all the hubbub about nuclear missiles seemed a childish fantasy – they could never fly in this sky.

My heart soared as my mind replayed every move from last night. Every perfect touch. Every helping squeeze. Like last night, my soul was an eagle, soaring through the heights of the absolute cream of what we poor earthlings can experience –

My joy should have been complete, but the eagle remembered something, and it brought him back down to the cane breaks.

Yes, it was real, what I saw last night – something besides the perfect moon-bathed alabaster of Marilyn's body. A small, tawdry vision that I had shoved away, into the back reaches of my mind while my body bloomed into the very cosmos, riding each touch of her fingers, her lips.

But now that I was heading back to my frustrating reality, that little vision came knocking at my memory, and would not be dismissed. It – they – were in her photos last night. A half-dozen candid shots of happy outdoorsmen lounging on boats, around back yard barbecues, standing beside trees in forests, dressing out deer carcasses. Little glossy chapters of Chris in his happier times – Cadwallader and Russell Crump, too, with shotguns and fishing poles, along for the perennial Texas sporting experience.

Running around with his boss and the Dauphin – all that was predictable, understandable. But there was another face – a companion, an obvious "buddy" whose girth and smiling face stuck out like a sore thumb.

That other hunter, the other fisherman was Homer Tudberry.

And if that weren't enough, the eeriest snapshot of them all – I only glimpsed it for a moment, but there was no mistaking those aging images – was a wide-view nighttime snapshot of the old tycoon, the son-in-law, and the lawman seated around a campfire, beer bottles raised to the night. Behind them, the haunting face of Billy Dean peered out from behind the flaps of a tent in the background.

The weatherman's face – drawn and snide and ruthless, and looking just a bit younger than he did now – wore the same impish leer he had when he was hiding behind that giant's bowling pins.

I was ranked highly at the Academy, at least grade-wise. Everyone, from my grandfather to the mailman, always said I was smart. So how had I missed the clues? Acting mysterious, never really explaining anything – adults behaving like petulant children. Like crazy men.

Why didn't I put the puzzle pieces together before?

They were all in this together.

The marshal was in cahoots with the whole bunch, and Billy Dean was Mr. Big.

Chapter 29
The Replacement

I showered, though when I climbed out, the heavy humidity instantly replaced the sweat I had just washed off. By the time I drove to work, I was a useless wet rag, barely able to keep the car on the road for all the shivering, consuming visions of Marilyn exploding in my head.

I sat down at my cramped desk, allowing only short glances at the neatly placed pencils and notepad on Cuthbert's desk. Julie, Chuck Holiday and Ryan, the sports guy, were arguing.

"It *is* better now, Chuck," she said. "Heck, the president's on a campaign trip to Connecticut. That's routine. He wouldn't be doing normal stuff if we were going to war."

"Read the UPI reports, Doll," Chuck answered quietly. "They were burning the White House lights all night. Limousines coming and going. The crap is in the fan."

"Don't say that. The army trucks left Brownwood. My aunt told me on the phone last night. It's all winding down."

"Julie, a woman can't analyze these things the way a man can. I don't like it that they moved out. I would rather know where they are. Out in the woods, they might be doing anything. I'm telling you, this is coming to a head—"

"Where is he?" Julie pointed to Cuthbert's desk, and looked at me, as if I should know.

"Probably fell off the wagon," Ryan said. "He wasn't in yesterday, either." To me: "Weren't you guys back by then?"

"The poor bum." Julie sighed. "He always builds up his interviews, and they turn to crap, and he can't admit it. That probably happened out at Ft. Hood."

Chuck nodded. "This is all the excuse Russell needs. This is no time to fire Cuthbert. Here we are, needing his Washington connections like we never did before."

So Billy Dean hadn't told them. I felt tears welling in my eyes. For him, yes, but more for the shambles my life had become. Andrea betrayed me. Then I betrayed her. But that didn't matter anymore, did it? Marilyn wasn't a betrayal – she was the first step into the promised land. Last night really meant something, didn't it? Sure, she was in mourning – but if she never lived with Chris as a wife –

Doubts returned. They were married. Somebody was lying about something.

A wide body appeared at the newsroom door. For an instant, I imagined it was Cuthbert, and that the whole trip with Billy Dean had been a dream. Only Russell, hauling a fresh-faced young man by the arm.

"Ladies and gents, meet Lionel," he said loudly. "Just graduated from TCU last spring. He's going to take Mr. Thompson's place on the city desk."

Julie gasped. "Cuthbert's not coming back?"

Russell ignored the question, the new guy gave a sheepish smile and a little wave, then began shaking hands, starting with me. But my gaze could not leave Russell's. He knew – but then, the army would have reported the whole thing to Boss.

But it wasn't that evil secret that made me stare. His pudgy face brought back visions of the photos last night. They were four, including Billy Dean and the marshal, and they had an army. What the hell were they cooking up? And why on God's green earth did the marshal agree to act as their shill, and drag me into this under false pretenses?

Russell seemed to be reading my mind, because he stopped lecturing Lionel, and brought up the company picnic tomorrow.

"Dang, I guess we'll have to have someone stay here and mind the store. You wouldn't mind missing the picnic, would you, George?"

My body tensed. Marilyn would be there. "Billy Dean sort of expects me to go," I lied.

His eyes flashed. "Izzatso? Billy Dean don't usually make any of our celebrations." He patted Lionel on the back, guiding him out the door. "But hell, we'll decide that later."

A cheap, veiled threat. He knew it, and I knew it, and I told myself never to forget that they – the four of them – had put this whole thing together, so they knew their plans for me, and I didn't. I needed help, but my only backup was part of the screw job.

It didn't matter. I took a deep breath. All his little threat did was help me make up my mind. After work, tonight, I would go back out to China Bend. Let them start their world war, they weren't going to keep me away from the woman who was my destiny.

Chapter 30
Dead Men's Friends

That afternoon, I showered and shaved in fast motion. Yes, her neighbors would be aghast if they saw me coming over for the second time, but I thought about the photos – she had some more answers for me, whether she knew it or not. Who was I kidding? She had – everything.

Ryan's face gazed from the TV screen, touting a special wrap-up show after the big game, Sironia State versus its eternal rival Texas. Add that to the picnic, and Cadwallader had his hands full tomorrow. Maybe we were safe from nuclear war for another day.

I buttoned my shirt and reached for the doorknob, ready to walk out, silently rehearsing what I would say when Marilyn answered her door, but fell back when a knock shattered the air at that same instant.

I made sure the chain was in place and opened it a crack. "Who is it?"

A pistol barrel dug into my forehead. "Open the door, assassin."

"The – the chain."

"That's OK." With a loud *crack*, the entire side of the sill came crashing in. I saw uniforms, but they had me bent over the couch before I could react, hands pulled behind me, pain shooting up and down my back. Three army guys, including the crazy lieutenant from the prairie.

"What the hell are you doing? I thought you guys learned your lesson."

When they had me handcuffed, one shoved me down onto a kitchen chair. No name tags – a bad sign – but I remembered the officer's name: Geary. The guy who tried to have us shot out on the prairie. His neck was covered with scrapes and scabs from the incident. He perused my apartment with a smirk.

"So, the big Mafioso lives like a normal human being, eh?" he said.

"Why do you keep calling me that? I'm not some goddam hit man. What happened out there in that riverbed was self-defense."

"Nice try. But those men were under my command." His smile hardened, and he drew the pistol from his belt holster with ceremony. "Killing in the service of our country is fully legal, especially if we're getting rid of a hired assassin."

"If you shoot me now, it's simple murder, Lieutenant."

"We're on duty. U.S. Army Intelligence, and I—"

"Balcones, sir!" The door-breaker shouted it in a drill instructor's voice. For a moment, Geary seethed.

He cleared his throat. "Correct, Corporal. We are Balcones Army Intelligence, and the traitor Christopher Ellis told us who you were before his – accident."

The subordinates chuckled.

"He was wrong," I said, wondering if I could make it out of the window in one jump – but even if they failed to hit me when they fired after me, how far could I get on the outside with my hands cuffed? "Are you the ones that killed Chris?" I asked. "Did Cadwallader order you to kill him?"

A sneer. "I was going to ask you the same thing, Mr. Apprentice Weatherman."

"Why?" I demanded. "Why kill Chris? He was in on everything with Cadwallader." In the academy, they told us to try and buy time if we ever got in a fix like this, but my chances were slipping away fast. "I've got new information on the conspiracy, Lieutenant. I know who the ringleader is, and it's not Cadwallader."

"Sit down," Geary told Doorbreaker, never taking his eyes off me.

"Sir, I found it." Guy Number Three re-entered, carrying Russell's revolver. Pretty thorough. I had stashed it in a new hiding place – in the attic within arm's reach from the little trap door in the ceiling in my closet. He laid it on the end table, almost within reach. I felt my back pockets – like a damned fool, I had neglected to snag more bobby pins from Andrea before her confession. Once again, the unloaded gun trick. Surely it really was unloaded this time.

I talked. "There were four of them. Thick as thieves. Cadwallader is using his money to hijack the army. They're using you, and risking the whole world in the process--" My voice was loud by then. It had his attention.

He leveled the gun at me. "Four? Which four?"

"I mean five, including Chris--"

The gun barrel touched my forehead.

"That thing Billy Dean had in the war," I screamed. "It's all about something they took from him – he's a goddam devil--"

"Shut up," Geary cried, and swung the pistol. I heard the *thud* before I felt the pain. Stars flew through the air, and Doorbreaker leaped up and grabbed my shoulders to keep me on the chair.

"None of your dodges," Geary was saying. "We know he's got something. And he's waiting for some other piece to make it complete. So what is this device that Brown covets so much?" Geary gritted his teeth. "And where is it? Does he carry it with him? Does he hide it in his office?"

Now the three monsters smelled blood. My tactics were losing me ground, not gaining it.

"I don't know--"

"Bullshit. You're his confederate. He's adopted you, because he's about to throw the President over, anyway." Geary shoved the gun back into its place, and slapped me. "That's why we pretended we were going to shoot you out at the staging area, asshole. That bastard won't talk, so we were going at him through you--"

He hit me again, this time with his fist. Pain piled on top of the ache already throbbing in my head. Woozy now, I couldn't think of any more lies. "Don't know, don't know," was all I could say. "He never told me – just that they took it from him, and that I'd better not get in the way of his getting it back."

His face was in mine. "I'm going to ask you just one more time. This is your last chance, understand? Where is the piece that came from Washington, and what is the piece the Russians are going to deliver?"

I was doomed. I had always imagined that the worst death of all is to be murdered because someone thinks you know something when you don't. I didn't have to play dumb, I was dumb – but my swirling mind warned me that if I came out with any more dumb questions, I would hear a loud bang, and nothing after.

I took a breath, and the only answer came in my memory of the marshal. That kind old bastard who got me into this, and who had been lying all the time – the vision of his jowl-y face smiled inside my brain. "You're an actor," his look said. "So act."

"Nuclear--" The word came from nowhere.

Geary shook me. "Yeah? Nuclear what? Goddam it, spill--"

"It's a small nuclear device. Like a bomb. It's a bomb, I think--"I reigned myself in. They had showed me films of interrogations where liars' fabricated stories got wilder and wilder. I had to avoid that. They still hadn't pulled the trigger.

"What kind of bomb, you bastard? A suitcase bomb?"

"I've heard of those," Doorbreaker chimed in.

I never had, but the very concept sent a shiver up my spine. Of course, a tiny A-bomb that you could cart around might be much more dangerous than a big one.

"But it's bullshit," Geary continued. "Our government may have already built one of those. Why would they give one to Billy Dean? And why the hell would the Russians be involved?"

"They have something they took from him," I said drunkenly.

Geary whipped out the pistol again. "Listen, you sack of shit. We know that. We have intelligence saying the Russians are delivering an integral part of Mr. Brown's bomb – or whatever it is. But that doesn't make sense. They don't have any better technology than we do – you're hiding something."

I shook my head.

"What is it?" he demanded. Gun barrel up to my temple, bearing down. "Last answer, jackass--"

"He can control the weather," I blurted. The stupidest idea in the world. Instead of fighting, as I always imagined I would, always knew I would, I closed my eyes and waited for the bullet--

Nothing.

A deep breath, and I opened my eyelids a crack.

Geary looked dumbstruck, his minions pale and blinking.

"You're lying," Geary finally screamed, his face flushing red-purple.

But the third guy touched the lieutenant's arm. "Sir, remember that lightning strike," he said. "The handcuffs?"

"Shut up. Stop saying that was lightning--" But all three of them fidgeted in slow motion, their gazes meeting painfully.

I struck, trying to nail my ruse in place. "That's what it is, you imbeciles. The piece that Washington gave him allows him to control lightning. When he gets the Russian piece, he might be able to make whole thunderstorms. Those stupid Russians didn't invent it, the goddam Nazis did. That's what all this is about, and I'm an official agent of the U.S. government assigned to make sure he doesn't get it."

Geary blinked. The weapon, still pointed.

"I'm not kidding," trying my best, sourest Hamlet face. "The CIA guys figured that when the little rat puts the two pieces together, he'll have some nuclear device that makes clouds and rain. Tornados, even." OK. Stop. I was laying it on too thick. "Ask your superiors, for God's sake." I gauged the distance to the window again. A poor Plan B.

Silence.

Doorbreaker broke the stalemate. "Fuck, Lieutenant. That's the only thing that makes sense. You told us, yourself, that the big cheeses were hot and bothered beyond reason."

"So?"

"Well, what else could be bigger than a damned portable nuke? Weather control."

"Shit," Geary finally muttered. Slowly, he holstered his weapon. He paced, all the way to the kitchen, then back. His eye lit on the phone. Then he was back in my face, shaking his fist. "I'll check it out, and if you're lying--"

"Lieutenant, maybe he's on our side," the third guy said.

"No, he ain't." Suddenly, the officer was inspired. "This is the way you're gonna play it, Mr. Apprentice." He pulled the chair close, sat, and looked into my eyes.

"Think logically," he said quietly. "No nation can last forever. If a new one wants to rise up out of the prairie, it has that right. That's what Texas did once already. This time around, it's called Balcones." His gaze, unyielding. "I'll give you one chance to survive."

"Sir?" I said.

"You gotta stay with that criminal Billy Dean a little longer. If you can work for Kennedy, you can damn well work for Cadwallader."

"I already do--"

"Shut up. Your loyalty is in the wrong slot. Your job is to find out how he manipulates the weather – if he does get this Russian piece, how will he work it? That's your only ticket out of this. Understand? You have until the Russians show up. The hour he puts that device together is his last. By then, if you can't give us the working formulas, we'll just shoot you in the head, and let our scientists figure it out the rest."

"But surely--" I looked around, from one stone face to the next. "Stopping the nuclear war comes first, right? Then we can worry about his weather toy?"

Geary leered. In the same moment, my telephone rang, sending a shock wave through the room. Except the lieutenant, who didn't bat an eyelash, but stepped over and yanked the phone cord until it whipped out of the wall.

Then, even more surprisingly, he lifted Russell's pistol, leaned over, and shoved it into my belt.

"You do what I say, when I say," he said. "You go to that picnic. Bring that piece with you. You're working for the old man, is that clear? But as of this moment, I'm your immediate superior. And your nation is Balcones, not the USA. Got that straight?"

"Yes, sir."

"Don't worry, Mr. TV Star." A pat on the arm. "You think you can bullshit me. But the time has come – for you to take a blood oath. You know, kill someone to show good faith to those who are your new comrades in arms." Close to my face again – "To show all of us you're ready to play in the Big Leagues, Mister U.S. Government Spy."

The other two drifted toward the door. I could have pulled the pistol, but still believed they had removed the bullets. I was that close to them leaving – that close to surviving, but my long lost sense of truth came back, out of nowhere.

"I already killed someone, Lieutenant. I won't do it again. Not for you," I said.

He shrugged, and smiled. "That's up to you, Big Boy. Somebody's going to be carried out of that picnic today on a platter. It could be you, instead of your target. Your choice." He patted his own holster, as if daring me to draw. Doorbreaker and the third guy were tense again.

"OK, I'll bite," I said, clenching my teeth. "Who am I supposed to shoot now?"

"Russell Crump. The noose has got to be pulled tight. Cadwallader himself may come after that, if he picks the wrong cabinet, but first things first."

"You're an idiot." I seethed. "What good will killing that blowhard accomplish? We've got to stop this Cuba thing, stop this revolution, too."

Geary tapped his chest. "You're not paying attention. I am the revolution."

I shut my mouth. The lines had been drawn. Cadwallader invents a fake revolution to get the Russians to deliver something top secret. I started to believe my own lie – maybe this whole mess did have something to do with weather control. And maybe the old man was just part of a ruse – get the commies to deliver, keep the thing, and the U.S. would have another leg up in the cold war – the whole damned thing was too convoluted to figure out.

But when you dance with the devil, you have to pay the piper, my grandfather always said. Maybe there was no real Balcones Republic, in Cadwallader's mind. Didn't matter. The new nation had become a reason for living for this young renegade officer, and he was bound and determined to hijack the whole thing, if necessary. And if he had control of the weather, who could stop him?

"Now, you'd better get that door fixed." Geary smirked. "Wouldn't want any more break-ins. Come to think of it, I figure you're probably planning another rendezvous with that little honey of yours. Am I right?

"Well, cancel your plans. We're watching her place, too. Pretty interesting stuff you can see through that back window of hers." His two minions wore sick smiles.

"Get some supper, Mr. Assassin, and go to bed. We'll shoot both of you if you get anywhere near her. We need you fresh for tomorrow. Can't be bleary-eyed when you pull the trigger." He pointed a finger. "Crump, understand?"

One-by-one, they stepped through the splinters of the broken door, and disappeared.

Chapter 31
The Picnic

I was a man, I told myself, and not the kind who would bow to threats. But this had never happened before, and they weren't just threatening me, but *her*. I didn't even know whether she had a phone – there was no listing for Chris Ellis in the book.

I sat there, like a coward, until well after dark, weighing my options. I had none.

The next morning, I drove through streets I had known all my life. Yes, I had been to Galveston, and the Alamo in San Antonio, and out the Big Bend territory. I even took a summer trip in college – to New York City. But it was the streets of Sironia that pumped through my veins, along with my blood. The houses, old and new. The bars, the ice houses, the run-down grocery stores.

Today, those structures all shared a new glow. The world was new. This was the morning I would kill a man on purpose. But no it wasn't – I had thought all night, until the plan finally descended on me: how I would take Marilyn to Mexico, how we might live, how the old life, Andrea, her father, that lying Tudberry, Zeebo – all of that was gone forever.

But what if that new glow that vibrated behind everything was just what happened on the morning that you die?

I caressed the pistol on the seat next to me. Fully loaded. Extra shells in my pocket. I wasn't really working for the U.S. government, was I? No way the Feds could save me from Lieutenant Geary, or Cadwallader, or the marshal, or anyone else. But most of those jerks would be at the picnic, and if they didn't let Marilyn leave with me, then I would do my damnedest to settle as many accounts as possible. I didn't want to live in fear in Mexico.

I belched up bile. It was a plan, but would it work? No way out. The evil lieutenant would keep his promise. He expected something. This was no police trap, I was sure. He didn't want me to shoot Russell and get arrested for it. He wanted me free, might even help me stay free, so he could use me to milk Billy Dean for information. He was a madman after the Lost Dutchman's mine – the weather control machine I had created in a moment of panic. Even if I did kill Russell Crump, Geary would eventually find out my lie, and I would wind up just as dead.

An idea exploded in my brain. At Nineteenth Street, I turned the car around, swerved through the Piggly Wiggly parking lot, cut across to New Road, and headed for the highway, and Channel Three. The air was electric, the sky spotted with cumulo-nimbus clouds that hung waiting. If the Thors were real, did they know about my assignment? Would there be a way to ask them to help?

I passed a phone booth – empty – I was two or three calls behind to Tudberry, but my twinge of guilt was easy to dimiss – surely, by now, he knew that I knew he was part of this.

He – and Andrea, and anything I had ever cared about – had all been replaced by Marilyn. Her body. Her face. Her silken hair. Her body. Her body. I wondered again if I should feel guilty for betraying Andrea – no, the betrayal wasn't mine. Though what that old man could see in her, I could not imagine. Hell, with his riches, he could surely have Marilyn if he wanted.

Only a couple of cars remained in the station's parking lot. Poor chumps who had to mind the store. They were probably bunched in the control room, drinking beer and watching the golf tournament. I didn't want to run into anybody.

The lobby lay empty, except for the huge monitor. Sure enough, this afternoon's game of irons and woods had pre-empted the preparations for nuclear war. It was nice to know the networks had their priorities. I hustled down the deserted hallway, climbed the stairs and entered the weather room – Billy Dean had left it unusually tidy. In a few hours, I would be here, putting the evening broadcast together, assuming I wasn't under arrest for murder. Or dead.

I opened the filing cabinet drawers, one at a time. Nothing. Then the big desk drawer. The overhead light hit the most garish colors: green, blue, that awful pink. I almost had to force my hand to touch it, but I finally poked at the painted leather of Billy Dean's strange purse. The zipper moved with effort, and I could only imagine what punishment the little scrapper had reserved for anyone who meddled with his treasure. At the moment I pulled it free from the drawer, a creaking noise made me freeze. I listened. Just the cheap building settling.

The purse was crammed full -- rods of quartz, bunched together, were crowded to one side by the rounded clumps of red clay. I had no idea what to do with the latter, and had no wish to get it under my nails again.

I pulled one of the rods – gingerly, certain it would break. It came loose -- a single shaft of sparkling quartz, just longer than the span of my hand, carved and polished so smoothly, it looked like a cylinder of diamonds. If I couldn't figure out how to use the thing, I would bring it back here before he missed it. Assuming I was still alive.

With care, I slipped the rod into a deep inner pocket in my jacket. In the other pocket, the gun Geary and his buds had foolishly left me. I had been wrong. It was loaded all the time.

I exited, and drove. The rod and gun were hard lumps pressing against either side as I passed under the old stone lions gazing down at me from the park entrance. A happy place where my grandfather used to bring me, but today the guns I would be playing with weren't toys.

The River Park playgrounds and ball fields were packed with kids and families, Saturday in a world under nuclear threat. Before turning up the steep slope to the clubhouse, I passed Jacob's Ladder, the winding, switchback stairway that led straight up the cliff face, interrupted by numerous landings that provided great views, and places to rest. On its stone benches, couples grubbed regularly, out of reach of parents and friends. My dream – until now – had been to catch Marilyn on one of them.

I turned uphill, until I came to the gravel parking lot that lay across from the large white-boarded clubhouse. My heart leaped. Chris's old pickup was lodged against the curb. I took the gun out of my jacket, and stuffed it in my belt, covering the bulge with both shirttail and jacket. On the wide lawns, a sea of now familiar faces. My new colleagues, along with their families, were smiling, drinking beer, playing badminton, horseshoes. Kids swarmed the food tables, or dared the paths into the woods where I had played as a kid.

Only the presence of a score of uniformed troops on the porch of the clubhouse seemed out of place. But though these guards appeared watchful, none of them ventured out to search me, or anybody else. Some of them were even drinking beer, and laughing. Balcones needed a lesson in executive security.

Through the grillsmoke, I scanned the tables, looking for Marilyn and trying to familiarize myself with the potential battlefield. Geary and his henchmen were nowhere to be seen. No Russell, either.

I felt for the quartz rod. Still in one piece. Why did I bring it? The only answer was some fuzzy thought about giving it to Billy Dean – maybe he could confuse the army with it somehow. My plan needed work.

"Hey, George." Michael strode straight for me, holding out a beer can that dripped ice. "You're late – Zachary's already getting soused."

"Thanks." I took a swig, and the cold liquid made pathways into every part of my body before I remembered that alcohol would only sully any chance I had of getting the drop on Geary. "Is Russell here?" I asked, my voice shaking.

"Inside. With the boss and some army brass."

I got in his face. "Michael, this is a company picnic. What are soldiers doing here?"

He patted my arm. "You're an apprentice weather man. They don't pay you to ask questions. Me, either." He sighed, and looked around. "Chris always loved the picnics." Michael shook his head. "Too bad he ain't here to enjoy the one in his honor."

The big double doors of the clubhouse swung open, revealing even more soldiers – the entire ballroom inside was packed with them. My stomach clenched. This would be harder than I thought.

I stared him straight in the eye. "Don't look away," I said. "Those army guys in the house – do they have any guns?"

He shrugged. "I don't know. Maybe some of them have side holsters."

"You see any rifles?"

"Jeez, who put you in a grumpy mood?"

"Is Billy Dean here?"

"George." Gail waved and headed our way.

"I don't think he's coming," Michael answered.

But Marilyn was here – and I had to find her.

Chuck Holiday sat at one of the stone tables, waving a piece of teletype paper over his plate of food, preaching to any who would listen. "Look at this, ladies and gentlemen. The Chicago Sun thinks Kennedy's flu is a sham. The army is moving troops. We're going to have war with Cuba, just like Cuthbert predicted."

Zachary slammed his beer can on the table. "They have every right to do whatever they want for their own self-defense."

Chuck ignored him. "Where is that bum, anyway? Did he go to Dallas or Washington?" Different employees offered different opinions, and I stared at the few troops left on the porch, wondering why these same folk were accepting the army's presence.

Did I dare plunge into the clubhouse? Russell was in there, but Marilyn might be, too. If a fight broke out, how would I get her out of the way? Hell, I still had no idea which path I would choose – the disastrous road to murder, or a worse one to death.

One of the big doors stayed open, and I didn't have to decide. Mr. Cadwallader filled the doorway now, and waved at me.

"Hey, George, get your butt in here, boy."

Chapter 32
Mr. Big

The old man preceded me through the crowded ballroom, and respectful troops stood aside, raising their cans of beer as he passed. I wondered if any of these guys had been in the shootout in the ravine near San Saba. We passed into a smaller, den-like room in the back, and my gut turned over. Geary's henchman, Doorbreaker, was leaning against the wall. A smug smile. "You know what to do," he whispered when I strode by.

"This way, George." Cadwallader waved me along, and Russell Crump waddled directly toward me from the other corner of the room. My heart leaped to my throat.

"Folks," the old boss said, raising his drink in toast to the bevy of soldiers and a couple of gaunt-looking men in expensive suits who held their own drinks and sat in two of the large armchairs in the middle of the room. "Russell has been called away on an emergency."

My God—My God—My God, my brain buzzed. The boss was in on this, and the next thing he would do would be to ask me to give Russell a ride. I would have no out. They had played this brilliantly.

"Say goodbye, Russell." Cadwallader gestured.

The Dauphin tipped his Stetson, as if confident he would be missed. "Leave me some beer, just in case I make it back."

"George?"

I was a statue in a trance. "Sir?"

"I need you to meet some people. Come back to the smokehouse room." The Dauphin rumbled past me, an odd smile on his face.

Everything happened too quickly. I didn't have to shoot him, did I? I had an excuse. Even that slavering asshole Geary had to allow an excuse – I had Doorbreaker as a witness.

"Yes, sir, Mr. Cadwallader," I said, too loudly. A glance at Doorbreaker – he seemed devastated, as if he would receive the same punishment I did. I shrugged my shoulders at him, and followed the boss.

Cadwallader led through the dance hall and into a back room furnished with cushy leather chairs and sofas. A man with two general's stars sat at a table near the center of the room, drinking a highball. Still no sign of Marilyn, and that worried me.

"General Raven," Cadwallader said, "this is George Blair, the weather prodigy I've been telling you about."

It was the second time I had heard the name – the first, on the prairie. Hair pasted down with Brillcream, beady black eyes reminiscent of Hitler. He did not extend a hand but remained seated. Only a couple more officers were in this room, anchoring either side of a sofa, drinks in hand. Three younger soldiers sat strategically by the windows. Watchdogs, armed only with beer.

"This the same guy who killed two of my volunteers?" Raven asked quietly. I took a breath. So the second guy was dead, for sure. Geary wasn't lying.

I put my hands on my hips, gun in reach. The idiots hadn't searched me. "Self-defense, sir. Your boys went crazy. Want me to spell it out for you?"

Cadwallader shook his head, ever so slightly.

"Sit, Mr. Blair," Raven said. "I accept your plea, because I need your services. The next time you are detained, you stay put, is that clear?"

"They were going to execute us, General. That bastard of a lieutenant—"

The general's eyes flashed, shutting me up, and he put his hands together under his chin. I sat, leaving space for free access to the gun. "Mr. Blair, the president," a nod toward Cadwallader, "tells me you're quite the scientist, though you've never really had any experience with nuclear fuels. Is that correct?"

Cadwallader jutted his chin, urging me on.

"I saw the missiles out on the prairie. That's the only time I've been near anything radioactive," I said, not caring if I made a liar out of the old man. When faced with a powerful crime boss, they taught us in the academy, show strength.

A worried look. Loud voices outside, and someone had turned up the music. A soldier at the window signaled 'OK.' Where was Marilyn?

"I don't like you, Blair." Raven's eyes narrowed. "But if you're the only one Mr. Brown will in instruct in the operation of his weather devices, then you may deserve a place in this government. As long as you can take orders." My God – was my fable about the weather device really true?

"Answer me this, and be careful you start out telling me the truth. The absolute truth, understand?"

All eyes were on me. I nodded.

"You admitted to Lieutenant Geary that Mr. Brown can indeed control the weather." Raven's gaze drilled into me, though Cadwallader just seemed bored. My God – yet another flip-flop. Geary had already reported to this S.O.B. Who was working for whom around here?

"That's not news, General," I said, and pointed at the boss. "Mr. Cadwallader – uh, the president, and I believe, Mr. Crump, all know he can manage some control already. They know he ruined the Sironia State game, anyway."

Cadwallader's eyes had a wild look I could not decipher. I almost felt sympathetic, as if he were a lesser evil than this pompous commander. But they were birds of a feather, and maybe I was feeling too big for my britches, because I had a gun, and I didn't see anyone else with one. Maybe I could stop this revolution right here.

I played my card.

"Before I answer anything else, I have a question." I looked directly into those black eyes, my hand on my side, ready to go for the pistol. It was a fair bet I could plug the bastard, and the old man, and make it out that back door before anyone moved. Of course they would chase me, but I knew these woods, and the cliff below Lover's Leap.

"Am I to take it," I continued, "that you are the brains behind this revolution? I know Mr. Cadwallader will be the president of Balcones, but are you the guy really in charge?"

First a blank look. Then that hardened, pointy face actually blushed, his expression almost humble. "Me? No, sir." He rose suddenly, scraping the chair back. My hand fell to the lump under my jacket, but he motioned for me to turn around. "Not I, Mr. Blair. But I'll be happy to introduce you to the person who is. The planning genius behind the greatest revolution in the history of North America--"

Against my better judgment, I let go the gun grip, stood and turned. A door in the wall had opened – I had assumed it led to the kitchen – but it was a hall of sorts, and Marilyn stood in the doorway, wearing a frilly white blouse, looking more like a goddess than a widow.

"Mr. Blair, I want you to meet Mrs. Ellis, the lady who planned both our revolutionary strategy, and the founding of a new nation. Mrs. Ellis, this is George Blair, the man we are interviewing for the post of Science Minister of the Balcones Republic." He was waving his arms around, all proper and formal, but I sank into a morass, part disbelief, part desire.

Marilyn stood blinking in the doorway and didn't speak. Raven moved to my side, jabbering into my ear about her credentials, but I was searching her eyes for denial – or confirmation. Raven turned jolly, addressing Cadwallader. "Tell him how much Washington wants our hides, Emil. By God, if the feds stop this revolution, they'll put us both in the hoosegow for life. But this little lady?" He stepped forward, raised Marilyn's hand, kissed it, then looked directly at me. "They'll hang her."

His words hit like a body blow at the same instant the door to the ballroom banged open. I grabbed the gun by reflex, almost pulling it out, but the frantic colonel who rushed in accosted Raven instead of me. "General. The news is out that the Russians finally challenged the blockade of Cuba with one of their ships. Kennedy has informed the press that they turned the ship back--"

Raven and Cadwallader exchanged a meaningful glance, then the colonel caught his breath, and finished.

"Was that the one, General? Did they make a mistake?"

The superior officer seemed almost as perplexed as this new guy, though he kept his cool. Again, staring at Cadwallader, as if asking for advice. Marilyn only looked at me – almost floating above the floor, above this uniformed riff-raff.

"I can't be sure," the old tycoon finally said. "But I think it's OK. This would be too early, wouldn't it? It's only a couple day's sailing from there to Corpus." Scattered debates broke out in the room, as if every one of these army yayhoos pictured themselves experts on a foreign navy's movements fifteen hundred miles away. My attention stayed on Marilyn, whose gaze sank to the floor. Someone clapped his hands. Raven brought them back to order by raising his voice.

"Make sure the honor guard is ready," the general ordered. "Move them out of San Antonio early, if you have to. We' can't leave the Russian couriers exposed so some hot CIA punk gets any ideas about interfering," Raven twirled his hand, some of the other officers drew into a small circle, and the frantic colonel spun on his heels, saluted first me, then Cadwallader, then exited through the back door. I reached out my hand, and took Marilyn's.

"You guys don't need us," I said. "I'll take Mrs. Ellis out for some air."

There was no protest. Marilyn looked up at me – the most incredible look I ever saw on a girl, before or since. It combined guilt and hope, deception and nakedness, fear and trust, and impossible *allure*.

A ridiculous notion – that she had planned this tempest in a teapot revolution. Yet, somehow, it made perfect sense.

"Let's go," I said, and led her outside, and towards Jacob's Ladder.

Chapter 33
Jacob's Ladder

I had only a moment – the time it took to lead her through the clubhouse's bustling kitchen – to try to digest what I had just heard. Sharon, the receptionist, looked up from her work on a huge bowl of potato salad, gave us both the once-over.

"Made in heaven," she said, and smiled.

A casual remark, maybe. But everyone working at that damned radio station was getting creepier by the day. Marilyn hadn't denied the details of General Raven's flowery introduction, but quizzing her about that wasn't what I wanted her on the ladder for.

Looking back, maybe I might have helped myself if I had stopped and asked the right questions. But no, I was in the stupor of love. Only twelve hours before, this vision of pure femininity had ushered me into adulthood. The idea of her touch, and repeating our deed over and over were all that mattered. Even Geary's threat had lost its sting, though I expected him to pop out from behind ever tree.

An escape plan was forming in my brain. First, I had to kiss her. Cement the foundation we started to lay two nights ago. Mentally, I counted my money in the bank. But that was unreachable on a Saturday, so our I had to figure out the best way to keep us both alive until it reopened Monday. Then – Mexico. It was the only place that might be safe from these Texas idiots.

We stepped off the clubhouse's back porch, and I put my arm around her.

"Careful," she said. "I'm still a widow in everyone's eyes."

"I don't care," I said.

She stopped. "Well, I do. Where I come from, the way a girl is regarded is everything. Please understand that, because it's not something I can afford to forget, no matter how your world does things."

"Where you come from? Is that Landview?"

"Just accept the fact that I'm going back there. OK?"

She squeezed my hand, and the euphoric jolt from that shut me up. The cliffs were just a few yards ahead, and we followed the well-worn path that wound through dogwood and cedar trees, toward the top steps of Jacob's Ladder. The winding staircase fell with the cliff below us, all the way to the bottom, where a stretch of blacktop cut a path through the thick underbrush that covered the riverbank. Below that, the wide Brazos eased along, as if it didn't care that Geary might be following me, that I was in love with Marilyn, that nuclear war was imminent. It flowed on, as if it had seen all this before.

Even though we were high up, trees covered most of the view of the ladder below. In the few patches I could see, other couples were scattered. Some were people I recognized from the station, others just teenagers, out for a secret weekend rendezvous. Marilyn again squeezed my hand for support as we took the steps down, and I looked over my shoulder.

We went down two flights, to the first landing. I nudged her to sit down on a stone bench, and had her cradled in my arms before she even flinched.

"Darling," I said. "No one's going to hang you. I promise. Let's go to your house and pack some things. We're going to have to get out of here, you know. Until this stupid revolution is over."

She tensed, staring at me through tears. "I don't care what Raven said." She sighed and closed her eyes.

"Bingo," I yelled. "He's full of shit and so is Cadwallader." I kissed her, long and hard, not caring that other picnickers might pass by. When I pulled away, her fingers still gripped my biceps.

She looked up, blushing, then closed her eyes. "Go home, George. All this is too confusing. I have a feeling you never asked to be drawn into this--"

"Drawn into what?" I looked for the truth in her eyes. "Was the general serious? Are you part of their planning?"

She shrugged, looked thoughtful. "That's hard to say. I know it sounds crazy, but all of this was predicted, so my job is to keep them all on course. God knows the general can't do it. As for Emil--"

"You? Keep a whole army on course?" I laughed, but her admission had opened a hole in my stomach.

"Marilyn, this is crazy. Why didn't Chris tell me?" I didn't know where to begin. "How can you be a factor – what is this revolution all about, anyway?"

She looked at me steadily. "I thought they told you. Don't they have you studying the weather, so that after —" Her voice trailed off.

I took her by the shoulders and shook her. "Damn it, what is going on here? This can't be all about Billy Dean. I don't care if he gets his precious cargo. Run away with me, Marilyn. Maybe you trust the soldiers, even Cadwallader. But

I promise you that's a mistake. Even if there's a nuclear war, we'll live longer down in Mexico. Monday. We gotta go."

Her steady gaze searched my brain, sent the hairs up on the back of my neck. Automatically, I turned. Geary and Number Three were standing at the top of the steps.

"Come on," I whispered, and jerked Marilyn to her feet. We started down, dodging two couples coming up. Yes, Geary was giving chase.

"My God, what is it?" Marilyn said.

"Those guys want to kill me."

"Soldiers? Emil will stop them."

"He's not here, is he? I told you they couldn't be trusted, and Cadwallader may want to act like your best buddy, but it's just guilt about Chris."

I stopped talking, winded now. She was dragging. "Darling, they'll shoot us. We gotta pray we can hitch a ride down there."

"George, Emil Cadwallader's--"

"Hurry," I said, and pulled her around another landing, then down again. She seemed in better shape than I, But I didn't hear any cars – what was I going to do at the bottom?

"George, why are they after us?"

"Army intelligence, as far as I can tell." We spoke between gasps for air.

"Then you're going the wrong way," she cried. "The general will tell them to stop."

"Damn it, we're in a trap," I yelled. Tree limbs hit my face, and we raced past Michael and Gail, hand-in-hand, on their way up.

"George – what the hell--"

"Those army guys behind us," I yelled. "Stall them if you can."

We hit the asphalt at the bottom, and the answer came – there was the river, and I had a quartz rod.

"To the water."

I pulled her across the empty road, between two majestic cottonwoods, down the riverbank.

"George, I'm not a good swimmer." She pulled back.

"You won't have to swim, Lady," a voice answered. Geary, to my right. He nodded, until I looked around and saw that Number Three had flanked us from the other side.

Geary continued, "And the only swimming your boyfriend's gonna be doing is the dead man's float."

"George--" Her whisper, breathless. Her body, tense, as if she froze from the ground up. "It can't happen like this. Everything will stop--"

"Let's have your gun," Geary said, bringing out his own, and kicking through the high grass on the bank. I saw no need to warn him the grass was laced with poison ivy. "Since you decided not to follow orders, you won't need it anymore."

"This is a set-up," I answered. "Crump left as soon as I arrived, and I think you and your buddies made it happen that way. You never wanted him dead, did you?"

"Dream on," he said. "Too bad, little lady. For a minute, I thought we could spare you, but you see how it is, if you watch us shoot this traitor—"

She shook her head. "Go ahead and kill me. I've only wished it for fifteen years. Just one thing--" She straightened up, her voluptuous breasts, those enchanting hips re-defining the cosmos – and I realized I had finally reached madness. Here I was, facing this guy's gun for the second time in as many days, fully aware that I had no chance to escape this time. Her body was the last vision I wanted to see.

She leveled her gaze at him, a look as seductive as Eve must have projected to Adam. "That thing is this," she continued in a sultry voice. "The Universe is like a rubber band, and I'm about to snap back. You couldn't kill me with all the nukes in China, Tin Soldier."

His eyebrow rose, and somehow my body knew this was my only chance. I already had my hand around the quartz. I gripped it – not too tightly –

"Down, Marilyn," I yelled, and dove into the Johnson grass, stretching my arm for the flowing water. I hit hard, and the rod went flying out of my fingers. It sank into the green, slimy water with barely a burp. In the next instant, a fish leaped up – in the exact place the rod had vanished. Its splash went all over my face.

"You're a dead man--" Geary yelled.

I hunkered down. A *blast* filled the air – *the end*, I thought – but instead, the water came alive, spurting and smoking. I turned. Billy Dean stood above me, biting off chunks from a round handful of the red clay we had collected, and spitting them into the Brazos. Each *plop* of the substance went off like a firecracker when it hit the water, and sent up little spews of it, like miniature fountains. Geary hadn't reacted yet, and the weatherman kept biting, spitting, and the fountains hissed bigger, and smoke rose from each spray, until it mingled above the water, forming a cloud.

I leaped to my feet at the same moment the cloud tripled in size. Geary was still paralyzed, but I knew we were out of time. Number Three cowered against a tree, his eyes wide.

"Parsifal," Billy Dean cried to the heavens, "they need another lesson. A little one."

Heavy clouds farther up, above everything, rumbled, and the world turned yellow.

"Christ," Geary cried. Light and heat – I went down again, my upper back slammed into the solid, wet ground. My skin crawled with fiery ants that passed over, singed the grass, then came back on me again. I scrambled for Marilyn, but she was hunkered down. Geary was screaming, scrubbing his arms and legs, trying to put out the sizzling electricity, then he went down, his hand hitting the water with an audible *hiss*.

On our other side, Number Three had quit the tree, and was in the river up to his ass.

"You boys are gonna miss dessert," Billy Dean yelled to them above the fading rumbles. "Now, git!"

They did not stay to retrieve their weapons, but moved out of the water, Number Three wincing and limping, Geary nursing one hand.

Billy Dean watched them retreat, then shook his head. "You did good, College Boy. You just gotta learn to hold on to the damn thing when you touch the water. The quartz is alive, you know. Like a fish. Now why don't you two lovebirds pull yourself together, and come back up the hill? This picnic's for Chris, after all. Tch-tch." He made a shaming sign at Marilyn. She only smiled.

With great effort, I sat up straight, and with each deep breath I took, the river's nauseating flow calmed down, and the tunnel that surrounded me began to widen out to both horizons. I heard Billy Dean chuckling as he climbed off through the underbrush.

After a long while, Marilyn looked at me. All of those strange, desperate walls she kept inside were gone again, for only the second time.

"We almost died," I said. "Is that what you meant by snapping back in the Universe?"

Her arm came up under mine. "No, that was your plan, not mine. The quartz confused them." She wrapped around, and kissed me, long and firm. Before I could reply, her lips were against my ear.

"We have to be a team, if we are to save the world," she said.

I took her in the grass by the water. That fishy green water slopped up, soaked my jeans all the way through to my knees. Cold breeze, her lips hot – we both burned with a freedom, a wild thrusting I had never even dreamed about. Maybe someone up on Jacob's Ladder could see us, but I didn't care.

So that was the second time we made love. Which was the one that counted, you ask? The one in her soft sheets, or this one, down in the green Brazos? I think I know, but it doesn't really matter, does it? In that moment, I could only hope, only believe that I'd found my destiny at last – the real one – and that she and I would repeat the act a thousand million times.

Chapter 34
Traffic Stop

The clouds rumbled their congratulations as we made the long climb up the concrete steps. I couldn't hear that sound now, without thinking of ninepins falling. No rain yet, but my whole left side – shirt and pants – was wet with river water, and we shivered, and clung together a couple of times, stopping on landings.

She smiled, and searched me with her eyes, and came out with a whisper that chilled me ever further to the bone.

"I think you've done it," she said. "But is it enough?"

"Done what?"

She only giggled, and pulled hard at my arm, leading me up the stairs. "We're from different times and places, George Blair. Assigned to do God's will..." She stopped. Kissed my lips, soft, spinning my head. Another whisper. "You see how you can't get around Him. He works in mysterious ways."

The hairs on the back of my neck were only getting stiffer. "Stop this, Marilyn. Stop talking like--"

But she let go my hand, and raced up the steps. Over her shoulder, she caught my eye. "I will never forget this afternoon, George."

She outraced me. By the time I reached the top, she had disappeared. But Chris's truck was still parked over on the road.

Halfway across the huge lawn, I realized what a fat target I was, if Geary and the others hadn't learned their lesson – and then the big doors opened, soldiers crowded out into the first of a light rain, followed by Cadwallader, General Raven – and Marilyn.

"Hey." I started trotting, but the old man put his arm around her back. They hustled over, en masse. She turned, gave me a short wave, then climbed into Cadwallader's huge car, with him, Raven and a couple of the GIs.

"Wait," I cried. But Doorbreaker appeared, stepped into my path, got in my way. He was flanked by two soldiers on either side.

"Not for you, smart boy," he said. "Top secret." He bore no scars, for he hadn't been down at the River, but when he pushed me back, I clocked him. In a flurry of arms and legs, they punched me in the stomach, and then I was eating grass, gasping for air.

A sharp voice yelled from somewhere, "Leave him alone."

So they just held me there, smothering, while I watched the car speed out of sight.

They let me up. The limo was headed toward the main street, but I knew the roads in River Park like the back of my hand. Including roads that were now covered with ivy. I might cut them off – I ran for my car.

It was not to be. Around the second turn, a siren began blasting behind me. The marshal's car filled my rear view mirror. It was against my better judgment, because forest covered any view of us from anywhere. I knew not to trust this man any longer, but it's as if my body, and two decades of friendship overruled me.

He waddled up to the side of my car, spitting tobacco into the brush, just as slow as if he'd finished off a plate of my grandma's chicken fried steak. Any hope I had that there'd been a mistake, that he might be on my side, evaporated.

"Well, well, the wayward spy," he said. "You ain't been answerin' your phone, George."

"Marshal, I'm in a hurry."

"And you ain't been calling in your reports--"

I stared straight ahead, refusing eye contact. For some reason, I didn't want him to lie to my face.

"I know you're with them, Marshal. And you're trying to stall me. Just let me get Marilyn and get out of here."

His lips made a line, and he squatted down by the car.

"Why were you afraid to tell me, Marshal? We've got history, I thought. Am I still a ten-year-old to you? Somebody you can just tell to dance to any tune you whistle?"

He spit again.

"Damn it, Marshal--"

He sighed. "What were you going to do if Russell hadn't left the picnic? Would you have shot him?"

"Don't know. How did you know about that? Plant one of those listening devices in my apartment?" My stomach fell. "My God, you're not in with that insane Geary are you?"

He laughed. "I ain't completely dumb, George. Give me a little credit." Out came his tin of tobacco. He dug a thick finger into my elbow. "But you ain't dumb, either, and everything's been secret up 'til now. I want you to go down to the Austin Building with me. You know, across from the Federal Building? Got a prisoner who might clear some of this up for you."

"What prisoner?"

"Russell Crump. Got him for speeding when he drove out of the park. Don't scowl, George. If I didn't nab him, he would have been gunned down before he could ever get near the station. There's always a loose cannon in every operation, and that crazy Lieutenant fits the bill in ours."

Finally, I met his eyes. "So you admit that you're part of Cadwallader's operation? What's he gonna make you, head of the Balcones FBI?"

"Come downtown like I say, George. You're still under orders."

"Whose orders? Washington or Balcones?"

"My orders. Plus, Geary's still on the loose, and the rest of us can't shield you forever."

"Shield me? I was almost killed twice today."

"Listen to me, George. You can't know everything yet, but I've talked them into giving you a glimpse of the problem we're trying to solve."

Now I met his gaze. "That's a damned lawyer's building, and I don't need a lawyer. I just want Marilyn, and I'll be a monkey's uncle if I set foot anywhere near downtown unless you tell me exactly how deep you are into this mess."

"No lawyers, son. He's in one of our secret holding cells, and he's got something to tell you."

Those kind, understanding eyes. I guess that was my first moment to understand evil – to witness a man who was working against everything he claimed to love, and yet could lie about it in cold blood. I reached for the pistol I had tossed onto the front seat, and pointed it at him.

"Get away from me, Marshal. You got no secrets I want to know, and neither does Russell Crump. If you want to run, I'll give you a head start. When I get out of here, I'm driving straight to the FBI office, and turning you in. You're not trying to stop the revolution at all."

He sighed, took a step away from the car, and folded his arms, as if to reassure me he would not draw his own gun.

"Son, I thought you might have trusted me by now."

"I did. That's gone."

Silence. Not the shifty silence of a lying jerk, but the heavy quiet of a boulder. "George, this revolution is made up of regular folks like you and me – trying to deal with something much bigger than all of us put together."

"Bigger? Bigger, you say?" I waved the gun, and tried to feel the same way I did out in that ravine. I could pull the trigger, couldn't I? Even shoot the man who had been around for as long as I could remember? "If a world war is bigger, it's their fault. They started it. Don't you dare follow me, Marshal. I'm going to the real authorities."

"You'll never see her if you don't go downtown."

I gunned the engine, peeled out, gravel and leaves flying, and made it all the way to the hidden curve, before I screeched on the brakes.

Of course, he was right. Somehow, they fooled Marilyn into going with them. If they wanted to, that old bugger could hide her anywhere. Or worse.

I turned it around, and rolled toward him until my fender could almost touch his massive legs. I shifted the gear into neutral, and jammed the gas a couple of times.

"Stop playing, George. Time's a wastin'."

I revved it. "You can't predict what I'm going to do."

He blew out, puffing his cheeks as he did, "I do know what you're going to do right now, George," he continued. "You're going to go down there with me. Then, tonight, you'll drive out to Marilyn's house. But if you don't go listen to Crump right now, she won't be home. They ain't taking her home, until they hear from me."

I revved again, the pistol still in one hand. "You may be a traitor," I said, "but you won't let them hurt her."

He waddled. Got into his car. Pulled out in front of me. I followed him downtown.

Chapter 35
The Hunting Party

In movies and TV, even in the academy, criminal suspects were questioned under harsh lamps. The interrogation office in the Austin Building was nothing like that, packed only with filing cabinets and old, stained desks. The Dauphin sat at one in the middle of the room, his wrists free of cuffs and chains, drinking coffee.

"Hello, Russell," I said.

A fat finger jabbed at Tudberry. "Marshal, I told you to bring in a radio."

The marshal stormed out, and Russell's look permitted no questions, so I didn't ask. He stared at the door until, finally, Tudberry returned with a nifty new transistor job no bigger than a sandwich. I remember marveling that they could stuff a radio into a box that small.

"You're daft," Tudberry told the fatter man. "I told you we didn't have any microphones on you. Turn this on, and you'll have to yell, and everybody out there will hear, anyway." He left, slamming the door.

"OK, Russell." I settled down in the chair, determined to get through this. Then, if Tudberry went back on his word, I would shoot him. This bastard, too. Some operation – they hadn't even taken the gun out of my belt.

"Are you gonna tell me about this Balcones revolution? But first, what excuse did they use to arrest you? Can't we get this all settled?"

Russell ignored me, fidgeting with the radio dial until he tuned in Glen Miller or Lawrence Welk -- some damnable station of lounge music.

"In case they have those recording devices," he explained. "Homer's too stupid to use them, but I don't trust those goddam G-men."

I chafed on the hard chair. "Russell, why do those soldiers want you dead?"

He smirked. "They don't give a damn about me. They want to get to Boss through me. If a team of nuns worked for him, they would chop through them one-by-one. Likely, that's the only way they can get to Billy Dean – through Mr. Cadwallader."

"Oh, come on," I said. "If they wanted Billy Dean dead, that damned lieutenant could have shot him this afternoon."

He sipped coffee underneath the most condescending look I had ever seen. "Billy Dean makes them shit their pants. You know that. Got any more stupid questions?"

I started to ask something else, but a wave of his fat hand shut me up. He reached for the pot that sat atop a hot plate at the end of the table, poured another cup, then lit a cigarette.

"You're a snot-nosed punk, as far as I'm concerned," he began, and followed up by mumbling something that the swelling band music drowned out. Then, "I don't think you're George Blair at all. You're some government plant. Or else this whole thing is a lot of hooey."

"I don't have all day, Russell."

A frown. "They want me to tell you what started all of this. I was there, so I'm qualified. But if I say more than I'm supposed to, old Tud-banger will shoot me between the eyes." He leaned forward, oozing a vicious look. "And if I do tell you too much, he'll have to shoot you, too."

I scooted my hard chair back, and patted the protruding butt of my own pistol. "They want to shoot me, they'll have to be quick," I boasted. "Get get on with it, for God's sake."

He blew smoke, and started whispering: I had to lean in close, my hand wrapped around the pistol grip, straining to make out the words between choruses of *Volare*.

"A long time ago, after the war, Boss bought a radio station. I married his daughter, and I had finished two years of college, so he promoted me to program manager. He took me out hunting to celebrate. Me and Chris, and one other guy."

"Chris worked for you then?"

"He was eighteen. I just turned twenty-one, and 'Lizbeth was pregnant. She lost the baby, probably because she was so upset, because I was upset. That was later. Upset about what happened that day. We were out on one of Boss's ranches down near San Saba."

"Was the other hunter Billy Dean?" I said it loudly, and he slapped the table.

"Stay close to the music." He motioned with his cigarette. "It was that tub of lard out in the hall. Shut up and listen. We hadn't found deer one for about three hours, and then it started raining. Hell, we were laughing and talking, and we'd had a few beers. And we didn't care, but it started hailing, too. Chris told us to unload our guns, and high-tail it. He was the only real hunter in the bunch.

"Then a funnel cloud dropped out of the overcast, all black and green and spinning. I had always heard about those, but never seen one. It was incredible. As if God had decided to step down onto the Earth. I stood there in the deluge, watching while it pointed at one of those windmills that pump water out on the prairie. That damned contraption set to dancin', bent right and left, popping bolts 'til its metal squealed like a trapped pig. Then the whole derrick jumped right up into the sky, like some Olympic pole vaulter. Right into the nozzle of that black funnel. It was like watchin' an anteater turned into a vacuum cleaner."

"So you saw a cyclone," I said. "My grandfather worked a farm in Arkansas. He had better storm stories than that."

"Yeah? Well I bet he wet his britches, too, if he ever got as close to a tornado as we were." Russell leaned in more, close enough for me to smell the onions on his breath. He glanced right, glanced left, cocked an eyebrow as if he were divulging the biggest secret in the world.

"We jumped down into a long dry creek bed. Chris yelled at us as soon as we did it. He said that was stupid, because flash floods are common in that country. So we climbed out again, up the wet grass banks, hailstones flying like a rock fight, and then we seen it."

The fat man's hand rose and he stared up into the dirty, faded-paint corner of the room, as if he were witnessing the event all again. His whiny voice rose loudly, above the din of his screen of radio music. "High above us, floating on the air, coming right out of that tornado was a man and two women, holding hands and standing straight up together. They looked like square dancers, cool as cucumbers, peering around for more dance partners in the sky." He licked his lips like a preacher sitting down to supper.

"Russell--" I started to laugh. He was parroting the same idiocy Guillermo tried to sell me in that Landview hotel.

He raised his cigarette hand. "Swear to God, George. Read the books. It's happened before."

He took a breath and settled back in his chair. "I'll never forget that sight. The wind put those three folks down on a grassy rise, gentle as you please, but the grass was white with hailstones, and when that twister shrunk back into the clouds like a bull's dick after the fifth cow, Mexicans started coming out of the woodwork."

"Mexicans?"

"People from Mexico who couldn't speak English. Boss is pretty good at Spanish, and so was Tud. But they could hardly savvy these yahoos, 'cause they was all wailing and crying for help. All dressed up they were, like they just came out of some fiesta with piñatas and cake, and their clothes soaked through with icy rain."

He wiped his own brow, breathing heavily. I didn't prod. His description of those people gave me the willies, perhaps because I couldn't understand why anyone would make up something like that.

He shook his head, falling further into the memory. "Then Boss was crying – I actually saw him weep. One of those three people – the first ones, the ones holding hands – one of those two ladies was his mother."

"His mother came out of that cloud?"

"Sure as hell—"

"Oh, come one, Russell. That tears it. You're saying that Emil Cadwallader's mom was flying out of a tornado? What – did you guys smoke a bunch of reefer?"

Another disgusted look.

"Was this near Landview?" My voice was rising. What bill of goods were they trying to sell me? By then, *I* was pounding the table. "I thought she just lived there. You're a lying son-of-a-"

"Shut up," he yelled, drowning out everything. "I don't like this any more than you. But if I don't tell the exact part I'm supposed to tell, they'll stick a hot poker up my ass. So shut up. I hope I never see you again, anyway."

The room fell silent. Even the radio. Until early strains of *Begin the Beguine…*

"As I was sayin'," he started up again. "We stood there in Noah's own deluge, watching those people floating on the air, like something out of the *Wizard of Oz*, but when ol' Boss ran up to his mom, you could'a knocked him over with a feather. His jaw dropped a foot. We were yellin' at him, tellin' him he was crazy, begging him to come the hell back to the house, so we could get outta there. And him just on his knees, snivelin'."

"Who was the other woman? And the man with them?" My teeth chattered when I asked it. I wasn't sure I wanted to know. "The first ones you saw?"

"That Comanche gal and Billy Dean, of course."

My body felt heavy in the chair, as if I already knew the answer. His idiot story made some twisted sense, though I couldn't decipher exactly what part. Not yet.

Russell, on the other hand, seemed suddenly proud. He sat back, sucking his weed like a used car dealer who just won a dickering match.

"I don't understand." I choked when I said it – the air was hot, stuffy. They were all together in this, intent on making me crazy. I slapped the desk again. "Why are you telling me this, Russell? What is all this bullshit? Even if a bunch of people got pulled up into a tornado, what cause is that to start a nuclear revolution?"

He looked at me, picking at a shred of tobacco in his teeth, until he got it. "You're not tracking me, College Boy. Mr. C's mother was already dead by nineteen forty-seven. Yet, there she was, dropping out of that cloud. How do you figure that?"

I didn't try to answer. He didn't wait for an answer.

"Billy Dean rode a tornado back in time to bring Cadwallader's mother to the present." The fat man's face bulged red now. "So, I just give you the answer. You don't have to tax that swelled college boy head of yours any further."

He stared, jowls shaking, teeth stained tobacco yellow, a satisfied, gloating look in his eyes. But he was scared, too. They made him read a script. Maybe he screwed it up.

He leaned across the table, staring through the smoke, his hands open in a pleading way. "Don't you get it, you stupid fuck? Billy Dean is holding Boss's mother hostage until they give back his property," he said. "She's alive here, right now, in nineteen sixty-two. And Billy Dean's the only human being alive who knows how to get her back to the eighteen nineties, where she belongs. She don't get back there – well, you should hear what those Princeton scientists say will cut loose. All-out nuke-leer war ain't nothin' compared to it."

I muttered, without meaning to. My pulverized brain was trying to fit the puzzle together – "Guillermo – eighteen eighty-five – or something…"

He stared at me. My tongue was thick. I felt like I was going to sleep. I remember wanting to gag, peering into those wild, sick eyes of his, smelling his fat stench – the pattern of this joke was all too apparent. First, they got me believing all their lies, then they hit me with nonsense, like this. Of course they had listening devices, and the guys in the next room must be rolling in the aisles by now.

"Don't you get it, Mr. Lake Charles? Cadwallader's mother will never give birth to him unless Billy Dean takes her back. Then ain't we in a pretty mess?"

The desk was one of those ancient, heavy oak jobs, and I realized my fingernails were digging into it. "You're full of shit, Russell"

Slowly, he stood up, and pointed his blimpy index finger, jabbing each word for punctuation. "The goddam world will end. That's what we did all this for. For fifteen damned years we have danced to Billy Dean's tune. Half my life. My wife's a drunk because of it. Hell, I'm a drunk because of it, and now the army wants you to shoot me to earn your first merit badge. And all I goddam did was put up with that snotty little greaseball, to try to save Emil Cadwallader's mother. And him. And my wife. To try to save the world--"

Behind me, the doorknob clicked, and I almost jumped a mile. The marshal leaned in, with a doleful face.

"Very funny, Marshal," I cried at the lawman. "He's wasting my time." I grabbed Tudberry's arm, and leveled my gaze. "So are you. Marilyn better be there when I go home."

He didn't respond.

"You forget, Marshal. Ol' Russell here said you were there. You gonna tell me the same story? Or are all your deputies having a laugh about this down the hall?"

Russell switched off the radio, pulled a pack of cigarettes out of his pocket and waved me away. "Take me back to my cell. I done my part."

I let go of Tudberry, but he grabbed my arm in return, and successfully pulled me out, through the door.

"Stop it," I yelled."Have you gone totally crazy? Why make up this stupid tale? Are you trying to outflank the Russians or something?"

"George--"

"What? Billy Dean knows how to time-travel? Controlling the weather wasn't enough?"

He only stared.

I pointed at the defeated blob in the room. "One thing I do believe is that the army wants this bum dead. Serves you all right." I headed for the outer door, keeping the heel of my hand atop my gun the whole while. "I don't care about the army. Call them, and tell them to drop Marilyn at her house."

"You're a damn site smarter than me, George." His voice, soft, followed me down the hall. "I'll bet my last twelve paychecks you've got everything figured out by now."

"Bullshit. A smart man can't figure out crazy people."

A deputy opened the lobby door. The sky was overcast, clouds promising a rumble, but not delivering.

Tudberry was behind me. He stopped on the stairs, his look – sad. "Just add it up, son. Add it up."

This wasn't the Homer Tudberry I grew up with. This was some shell of a creature who never cared about me at all, had nothing for me, and I knew his next lie would be about helping Kennedy defeat the Russians, or some such crap. I didn't care anymore.

"We ain't playin' around, George. This is the real thing. God works in mysterious ways."

My head was spinning, and I kept asking myself why they had let me go. What could it possibly profit them to let me remain at large, just waiting for the government to stop this little gambit they were all staging. All they had to do was pick me up, and stick me in front of a grand jury.

I climbed in behind the steering wheel, and turned the car toward China Bend, all the while praying she would be there. I didn't want to have to come back here and blow that old lawman's brains out.

Chapter 36
The Visitor

I drove like a man possessed – not under the illusion that I could save anyone, but determined to stop being part of this sick little game. People disappeared sometimes. They told us that at the Academy. Re-located, went straight and started new lives. That's what Marilyn and I would do.

In China Bend, I parked carefully on the lawn, but Chris's truck was still absent. Never mind, some soldier would probably deliver it from the park later on.

But her back window was dark. I peered in at the rumpled bed where I had lost my virginity. Did the marshal lie to me? They must still have her. But why? The army had geniuses to make their plans. No way Marilyn was really calling the shots. And if Tudberry was part of this ridiculous conspiracy, why did they put Russell up to that little story-telling session? Even if any of it were true, what part did Marilyn and I play in this?

If it were true – time travel – the very concept made me shudder. There was no way in hell. It was yet another ruse – to hide something diabolical. But what? A nuclear first strike?

Frantic, I drove. All the way back into town, to Cadwallader's mansion. The large ironwork gate on the driveway was locked tight. I pounded my head against the top of the car – of course, I was an idiot. If they wanted to hold her hostage in some way, it would be out at his ranch, not here. I drove the fifteen minutes out there – the ranch house appeared dark as a tomb, with no sign of the limousine they had taken her in. Even horses in the corral refused to take notice of me.

I gave up, and headed back toward town. Finding her would take some detective work, but I couldn't ask the marshal for help. My worries blew up into full panic when I reached to unlock my broken door. It stood ajar, and I remembered pushing it closed as best I could. Was Geary back? My mouth went dry – what if it were Marilyn? I didn't remember giving her my address.

I backtracked as quietly as I could, crouched down by the laundromat, and pulled the pistol from my belt. It was my nervous habit to open the cylinder and make sure all six chambers had bullets in them, but my hands shook so violently, I spilled the shells all over the parking lot concrete, and bent down to recover them, certain that someone would see me and call the cops.

I crept along the apartment wall, praying with each step that it was Marilyn waiting inside. A deep breath – I pushed the door, raised the gun and flicked on the light.

"George. What are you doing?"

I gaped. "Andrea?"

She rose from the couch, rubbing her eyes, wearing the matching black pedal pushers and sweater I bought her last Christmas. She flinched. "George, were you going to shoot me?"

"Of course not. How did you get in?"

"You gave me a key. Two years ago, remember?"

I closed the door, and stuck the weapon in my belt. "But you never used it. I'm not taking you back, Andrea. I'm sorry, but there it is."

Her mouth screwed into its little twist, and her hands went to her hips. "As if I would have you, George Blair. After all I've done for you, and here you are brandishing a pistol at me. I've half a mind to call the police."

I sank into my favorite chair. "I am the police."

She grimaced, but instead of sitting back on the couch, she slinked toward me.

"What are you doing?"

"I'm thanking you, George." She pushed my hand away, and sat in my lap. I started to protest, but Andrea in her pants outfit moved more quickly than I thought possible. She kissed me. Hard.

I let it happen, feeling no guilt. Marilyn's kisses were Everest. This was the mound of garbage in the alley behind my parent's old house down on Broadway. Finally, she pulled away.

"Andrea, please. I've had a long day."

Her eyes flared, and she stood up. "I can't believe you would humiliate me like that, George. Ooh." She stomped her foot. "You did me a favor. Now I'm sorry I returned it, you ingrate." She stormed to the door, then remembered her purse.

"Calm down, Andrea. I'll bite. What favor did I do?"

She blushed, looking proud. "I don't know what you said to him, but he's not going to see any of his little girlfriends anymore. He's taking me to the next game."

"Who? Cadwallader?" I'm sure my jaw dropped. There was no end to the insanity.

"Yes, dummy. Why do you think I came all the way here?" She bit her lip. "See how well we work together?"

Before I could flinch, she was back in my lap, pinching my mouth, jabbering in baby talk. "Don't you see that it will all fall into place eventually, George? Emil told me you got promoted in his new government. I'm so proud. That old man will do right by me, and then he'll die. So what if I have to be his – his girl for a year or two?" She turned beet red as she giggled. "It will be sort of like an undercover police assignment. George, any mature man knows that there's a little – *prostitute* –" More giggles. " – in every girl."

I looked away, but she used the opportunity to whisper directly into my ear. "George, after he's gone, we'll be rich. He's the president now, but he said – and don't you dare breathe a word of this – that they're thinking about making the whole thing a monarchy. You know what that means?"

I stared. "Andrea, you're always so practical –"

"It means I will be queen, Dummy." Loud again. "And when the old King dies, I will be in charge. Like Elizabeth of Britain." She laid a hand on my shoulder, with ceremony, as if it were a knighting sword. "And that will make you Prince George. Or King George. However they do it. And our children--"

"Damn it, Andrea. I never thought you would go as nutty as they are. You go ahead. Have the life you've always wanted. I'm taking a different fork in the road."

"Now you stop that ungrateful talk--"

I pushed her away, sending her plunging to her butt on the carpet. "I found another lover, Andrea. Face it. You made your bed, and it's got a cadaver lying in it, so the joke's on you."

"Oh." She rose, nostrils flaring. This time she didn't forget her purse, but I knew she would twirl around in the doorway. Last words were her forte. "You are the worst human being I ever met, Blair. He said both sides would be after your hide in a couple of weeks, but I begged him to save you. He listens to his woman, George, unlike certain skunks I know."

"Wait." I caught her on the walk outside. "Who'll be after me? What did you tell him to do? How is he supposed to save me?"

She spoke through clenched teeth. "He's going to fire you, George. You can go back to work for my father and earn an honest living. They'll be building shelters from now on, so there, I've made your fortune, too. Now let me go. My future is waiting for me, and when you see another prince on my arm, well tuffy wuffy."

She stormed down the walk, and I yelled after her. "Shut up, Andrea. I want you to give this new lover of yours a message. Tell him to let her go, or I'll go to the Feds."

"I'll do no such thing."

"Oh, yeah? You'll do as I say. You're not going to have much of a life if your sugar daddy is sitting behind bars."

She jerked her car door open and stuffed herself in. When she peeled out of the driveway, she burned rubber all the way down the street. Of course, my threat didn't pack much punch. But if Andrea got worried enough that his fortune might slip through her fingers, I was confident that she could nag him into doing anything.

Chapter 37
The Note

Andrea was a fool, on a fool's errand, I was thinking.
But why would Cadwallader say those things to her? Was he
truly smitten? No – he was crazy. But I couldn't waste another
moment on either one of them – Marilyn had to be
somewhere.

I tried to guess what road that big black limo might
have taken out of the park. No, that trail was colder than ice.
By the time I got back behind the wheel of my own car, I was
frantic. I would start in China Bend – again – and work
outward.

I drove right up into her front yard, no longer caring
what the neighbors thought. Another walk around the house. I
banged on the front door. Then the back. Only then did I see
the piece of notebook paper tacked up at eye level:

*George, gone to my sister's. Be back home Wednesday or
Thursday,* it said.

How in the hell had I missed that before?

Dusk was quickly approaching. From Saturday to
Wednesday was a long time. And where the hell did her sister
live? I sat on the back steps, not believing a single word of it.
Yes, it was a female's handwriting, but hers? They had her.

I sat on that broken little porch, figuring my next move
– if I had one. The birds out in the cane breaks sang their
China Bend songs, and the smell of the river pierced the pre-
dusk air. Her message was addressed to me – as if she didn't
care who saw that. Surely there was no sister. This was a weak
diversion, but I was already a good three hours late to work
and this was a dead end – for now. Perhaps someone at
Channel Three would let something slip. It was futile to go
back there – but I had no other cards to play. Time to pass, and
wait for their next bid--

When I walked into the lobby, Sharon sat staring at the
big monitor, tears streaming down her face.

"What's the matter, doll?" I asked, alarmed. Maybe
that was the first moment that I realized that Sharon was a
tower of strength around that place. An unflappable witness
to everything that happened. To see her upset like that sort of
shook the whole building.

She turned slowly, eyes as glassy as one of those
automatons in a flying saucer movie. "Douglas Edwards just
said the president is going to make a speech tonight. They're
predicting he'll declare war. George, it's getting worse."

"It can't be that bad," I said, too flippantly. Didn't she
know the crisis wasn't real?

"If they would just let the congress spend more on
defense." A nod toward the big man's office. "After all he's
worked for--"

"Yeah." I stopped in the hall, and turned around.
"What did you say? He's here?"

Cadwallader's door swung open, and the old man,
himself, stood there, twisting his bullwhip. A nod. "Let's talk,
George."

I followed him in. Other than him, the office was
empty.

"Where's Marilyn?" I demanded. "Give her to me, and
I'll be out of your hair."

He tapped the whip handle on his palm while I found my place. "I never would have met Andrea without you, but you know what happened today. Guess I thought you would hold up your end of the bargain, keep your mouth shut and take all the things we were offering you. I'll include an honorarium in your severance check." His gaze met mine. "That's right. I'm firing you."

"I had nothing to do with Russell's arrest," I said automatically. "You're going to fire me because Andrea told you to? Well, her little plan is moot – I'm not going back to work for her father."

His arm flexed, and the whip cracked, exploding above my head. I tumbled to the floor – automatically. A quick feel of my head told me I wasn't cut – but I was through being intimidated. If he fired me, I might never get back in, and there would go my chances of finding Marilyn. But I thought of one more tack to take.

"You can't fire me." I stood up. "I threw away a career to come over to your side, Mr. Cadwallader. I do want to learn the weather, though God knows why you picked me. I'll do your dirty job, even if it means working for a new government. But you're going to have to pay me."

A sudden, puzzled look. "Is that so?" he said. "How much do you think you're worth?"

"Listen, old man. My life's not worth a plugged nickel. You know that, but maybe you don't realize that yours isn't worth much more. Not with traitors like Geary running around."

"You still haven't named your price."

"Give me Marilyn, and we're square. I don't care what shit is going on around here. Why would Russell make up fairy stories about people flying through the air? Once upon a time, I believed fantasies like that. Not anymore."

He nodded slowly, coiling the whip for another strike. I folded my arms, bluffing.

"Not convincing, George," he finally said. "Your ex told me how you fib when you're caught with your drawers down."

I raised my hand. "Swear on the Bible. You need people you can trust around you, sir. Your cash-on-delivery army's planning to betray you. But somehow, I think you know all that. Can't you hear, old man? I'm saying launch your first strike. Rebel. Commit murder and mayhem. I'll just stand by – won't call anybody, won't testify anything. Just give me Marilyn."

He wiped his lips with a single finger. By God, he was considering it. "What I'm wondering is if you would have done it," he said.

"Done what?"

He studied me. "Shot Russell, if we hadn't shipped him off to jail?"

"Of course not." That, I think, was the truth.

"No." He stood and paced, brushing my shoe with the whip's tassle. "I'm starting to think no one can learn the weather like that little skunk, anyway."

"Mr. Cadwallader, I know how Billy Dean makes it rain. I know where he gets his quartz, and I've seen some other things that you might just not believe--"

He stopped, and looked at me. A look full of history. There was a heaviness in that look that sort of summed up everything, if I had just been able to decipher it. But an insane mind can't be read for very long, I reminded myself.

"Why don't you just tell me?" I said. "Are we all going to be blown up, after all? Wouldn't you like to see Marilyn be free of that, after losing her husband, and everything?" A weak ploy.

"You know Chris wasn't her husband," he said. After another searing moment, it was his turn to speak in little more than a whisper. "Her husband's not dead yet."

In three quick sweeps of his hand, he coiled the rawhide tightly. "OK. You got your second chance," he said. "Go upstairs and fetch that little punk. No use waiting. Vamoose to Landview today, if you're serious."

"I don't want to go to Landview. I want to save Marilyn."

A heavy nod. "She's down there, visiting her best friend. I think you've met her already." Of course I should have doubted him, but those gray eyes projected a quiet desperation. It did make sense, after all. Landview seemed to be the place he stashed all of his secrets. Standing there, sensing those unreachable feelings shift inside him, I actually pitied the man, almost as much as I hated him.

"You'd better hurry. The army's not gonna wait forever, and neither is Kennedy," he said.

"What's this bull about her best friend? Do you mean Rebecca? And why do I need Billy Dean?"

"You wanna face that rogue lieutenant by yourself, if he shows up?"

"No, sir," I said, and rushed out the door without waiting for any more answers.

In the lobby, a rerun of *The Real McCoys* flickered on the monitor. Sharon seemed more composed. I pointed. "Darlin', tell the newsroom they'll have to read the weather tonight. Billy Dean and I have another field trip." I trotted up the stairs, a rabbit fully aware that I was being bounced between two snakes, but devoutly believing that my pure heart would help me outsmart them. I only had to keep them believing that I was on board for a while longer. Once I found Marilyn, no army and no cloud ships could move fast enough to catch us. I would jump out of their trap.

Chapter 38
The Treehouse

When I reached the weather room, I thought I had it all worked out. "Hey," I yelled, pushing the door open.

"Well, look what the cat dragged in."

Billy Dean was on his feet, shirt tucked in, taking a swig from his eternal flask. But his demeanor seemed sharp – he had just started, perhaps.

"You ain't gonna make any kind of weatherman, 'less you show up for work on time," he said, sneering. "Just for that, I'm doing the show tonight."

"No, sir. You gotta go with me. Cadwallader told me that Marilyn is down in Landview," I said. "He wants me to go get her, and said you would give me another weather lesson."

A long stare – he could tell I was embellishing. "Oh, he did, did he? Well, he would know where Marilyn is, if anyone does." Then a smile. "That picnic today sort of turned into a cluster-fuck, didn't it?" Before I could answer, he motioned to a transistor radio on the desk – a serious-sounding voice was coming from it.

"Hear that?" he asked. "Ol' Kennedy announced he's going to quarantine Cuba, not let any Russian ships pass a certain line. Can you believe that?"

I shrugged. "No war declaration?"

"Sounds like the sort of pussy thing he would pull." An insipid wink. "Only one boat I want to get through, anyway."

The jitters were overtaking me. It was time to get going, and he could tell me more of his lies in the car -- "For God's sake, Billy Dean, are you serious? The Russians are sending a boat just to deliver something to you?"

A Cheshire-cat smile. Rather than packing up to go, he sat down in his chair. Cripes, I didn't want to go down there by myself. Not in the dark.

"Listen, Billy Dean. We gotta get going. Please. Russell told me a story. The marshal's been playing both sides, and I'll bet that lieutenant will shoot me first next time, and ask questions later. Now you got me into this, and I know you care about Chris's widow, so help me go pull her out of this bullshit." His look only hardened.

"You're a neophyte, College Boy. None of your education has brought you within a mile of the Truth, 'cause that's the way they want it. A college boy learns too much, he might be a threat to their world order." He was lighting a cigarette while he made his little speech, and he stood up, waving the smoking weed in my face.

"I'm a rebel. They have all the power. The big governments run everything. And they're run by big money. Never does a little guy really get to hold the baton. Well, that fat-cat German officer slipped up. Nobody gave him a program, I guess--"

By now, the cigarette was sticking out of his lips, and he pulled close, talking up to me through the spiral of smoke. "I'm the rare bird – a little guy with a baton." A finger raised. "One chance. And most dumb bunnies woulda just bent over and took whatever medicine those scumbuckets dished out.

Not me." His fist flew sideways, in a fast arc, slamming my arm, knocking me into the pole that divided the room.

"I'm Prometheus, Mr. George Blair," he yelled. A mad smile spread across his kisser. "I grabbed the fire, and the gods took it out of my hands. But I figured a way to get it back. You're an actor, Ol' Tud-boy said. Huh? Well, by God, let's get down to Landview, and play out the next scene."

He pocketed his flask, pulled the leather purse out of his bottom drawer, jerked on his coat, and waved the smoking butt in a circle above his head. "Come on, Cary Grant. Your leading lady is waiting for you."

He led the way down the steps, down the hall, kissed Sharon's hand ceremoniously, and held the front door open. But he stopped me when I tried to pass through. "Hey, Mr. Grant – just don't forget one thing."

"What?"

He whispered. "Actors, the really great ones, all have more than one leading lady."

"What's that supposed to mean?"

He slapped my back. "It don't mean shit." His roaring laugh followed me down the walk and to my car, where I fetched my overnight bag and the pistol. At that moment, I was still under Cadwallader's spell – I truly thought that Marilyn had gone to Landview, that he had no good reason to lie to me. Looking back, I wonder why I believed almost everything that each of them told me. Perhaps I was just horny, and ready to go to the ends of the Earth to find Marilyn, and carry out my escape plan.

"Makes sense she would go to Landview, even at a time like this." Billy Dean had his head halfway out the window, gazing at the clouds in the sky, the way he always did. "She and Rebecca, they're like sisters."

"The note said she was visiting her sister," I said.

So I got into his car willingly. By that point, I flattered myself that I could pry the real truth of the Dauphin's story out of Billy Dean, that I could get the drop on this little weasel, and take this very car away from him in Landview, and whisk Marilyn away to Mexico in it. I could wire the bank to send me my money. I had no intention of coming back to Sironia. True love creates fantasies of survival.

He made me drive, promptly went to sleep at the outskirts of town, and stayed that way. I didn't have the guts to wake him, to start my interrogation. It wasn't a lack of guts, really – in the silence of his quiet snores, I was consumed by my imagination of the future life Marilyn and I would create – where we might go in Mexico, where we might live, what I might do for a job, how fast I could learn Spanish.

Over every hill, my stomach tightened, expecting an army roadblock, but we traveled without incident – until hours later, when we reached great open fields that had been singed by fire. Tire tracks and debris, and clumps of smoking embers ran all through those fields. Ranch houses here and there had been torched. The devastation got worse, looming out of the darkness on either side of the road, until every dwelling we passed had been burned to the ground. It was an eerie feeling, and when I stopped the car on the shoulder, Billy Dean woke up.

A look around.

"They all like this?"he asked.

"More, the last while --"

"Go on." He motioned, face grim. I drove.

When we crested the rise that I barely remembered, the lost majesty of the hotels of Landview came into view. The far one – on the west end of town – looked normal enough. But the other two, including the one we had slept in, the one where I climbed the stairs into a dream of a cloud ship, had been chopped into jagged, leaning towers, still smoldering from an obvious artillery barrage.

"Cadwallader," I cried. "Why would he let them do this?"

The scrawny rodent-man only sat, smoking, lips tight together. "Wrong, College Boy. He's the one person on this Earth that wouldn't have done this. I think I smell that ambitious bastard of a lieutenant."

"Jesus." I flung the door open. "Marilyn. Where the hell is Marilyn? Would he have stuck her in one of those hotels? Where are the houses in this infernal town?"

"Shut up." He pointed. "It's even worse."

Rebecca's treehouse had been hit, too, its bottom floor demolished in a pile of timber. The tree still stood, the top two floors of the odd structure hanging onto it for dear life. I turned toward the ruins of the first hotel, but he held me by the elbow.

"Gimme the keys," he demanded. He opened the trunk. Automatically, I reached into my bag for the pistol, and shoved that into my belt. He pulled out his gaudy leather bag, and draped it over his shoulder. But the bag Rebecca had given me lay there, too. He zipped it open, and showed me the red-clay balls were still in it, wrapped in wax paper. In a swift motion, he closed it, and strung a rope through the metal rings on either side, jerked me closer, and hung the bag over my neck.

"Don't you abandon this bag again, or I'll shoot you with your own *pistola.* This stuff is magic, or did you forget?" He took me by the shoulders and aimed me toward the treehouse.

"I know the hotels," he said. "So I can search them without falling into an elevator shaft and breaking my neck. If the Mexicans are holed up somewhere, I can find them without getting shot. You – shimmy up that ladder and make sure no one's hiding there, then find me. I'll start lookin' in the only hotel that ain't blown to pieces."

"Billy Dean, I'm sure no one's left in the treehouse. Look at it."

"Follow orders and move your butt," he cried, and started off across the wide lawn – in the dimness, I couldn't make out much of the debris on the grass, save for the flagpole, which now lay on its side, the yellow and red flag of Balcones crumpled in the mud. "Whoever did this might come back at any time."

This was a fool's errand. Marilyn had to be in those hotels, if she was anywhere. Whoever did this wasn't playing by any combat rules I ever heard of. This little collection of buildings was no military target.

Piles of wood still smoldered, glowing nests and little campfires scattered from here to the horizon. One still burned under the treehouse, too, and I kicked wood off to the side, so that the fire wouldn't find its way to the tree and finish the destruction. Short, fresh planks had been nailed into the tree, the sort of makeshift ladder we used to craft as kids. I tested the bottom rungs – they seemed to hold, so I started up, into the wide dark opening of what used to be the second floor.

The entry space was too wide – I almost couldn't step to the remaining floor of that level. The room wasn't that big, of course, and the light from the fire below was worthless – I had to feel around – a mattress lay in the corner, soaking wet. A bucket clattered to the floor. So someone had hauled water up here to quench the fire. I felt along a desk – the wood was splintered, with pockmarks – I shuddered. They must be bullet holes.

"Who is it?"

The whisper almost sent me tumbling out of the jagged hole. The sound came from above.

"It's me," I yelled. "Marilyn?"

I raced up the rungs. This highest level was strangely untouched, though the floor was piled with cushions and a chair and quilts and kitchen utensils, likely from below. The blind on the single window was shut, leaving the light that seeped in totally inadequate for me to make anything out – except for the dark form standing in the middle of the room.

"George Blair," she said, her voice quivering. "Is that really you?" Not Marilyn, but Rebecca. Something in her hand – she tossed it down with a *thud*, and laughed. "I don't want to shoot my rescuer."

Before I could move, she did, and melted into my arms. Automatically, my hands were searching. She was wearing only what felt to be a thick quilt.

"Rebecca, are you all right? Are you hurt? What about Marilyn? Is she with the others?"

My hands wandered with a mind of their own, until they cradled her back. Hers worked higher, caressing my face softly, and the quilt fell away. Maybe she could be a tower of strength when facing cloud giants, but now she was shivering, obviously shell-shocked.

"It's OK, now," I said. "I'm here. Billy Dean's here. We'll get you out of this place. Where's Marilyn?"

Her arms closed around my neck, and she rose on her tiptoes and whispered into my ear, "It's all coming true." She disengaged. "You're really here, and it's all coming true." With one hand, she squeezed my own. With the other, I could hear her open a cabinet – not a cabinet, but a stove full of burning embers.

"George Blair, you are here, and I will do exactly what you told me to do, a long time ago--" Her hand reached gingerly into the little stove, and pulled out a clump of some grasses or plants that were smoldering.

"What?" I said. The smoke smelled like sage or rosemary. She waved the burning bouquet under my nose. I coughed.

"Breathe it in," she commanded, squeezing my hand tighter.

"Rebecca, the soldiers may be --"

The flavorful smoke choked me. With unexpected strength, she held me in place while she waved the smoke under my nose twice, three times. She threw the clump back into the stove, and by now the whole room was smoke, filling my eyes so that I could barely maintain my balance.

"Hey – hey--"

She was adept. She knew what she was doing – I remember that distinct certainty in my mind as she wrapped one leg around mine and we tumbled down onto yet another mattress – only this one was dry. Expertly, she maneuvered me out my pants, and in another second, we were making love, with her on top, leaning over, kissing me, kissing me.

"No, Rebecca –" Half complaint, half a whimper, half ecstasy. I closed my eyes, falling down a well, and her tongue played in my ears between her whispers.

"Be still, George Blair. It's just as you told me – we were written in the stars long ago--"

"Hmmm?" I could no longer speak. She pulled and moved expertly. I wanted to scream Marilyn's name, wanted to know when I had told Rebecca these things–? Wanted to know when the world stopped being real.

Everything melted, refusing analysis, for even gravity had ceased to exist on the slanty, cockeyed floor, and with my hacking coughs of the smoky air, even my guilt about Marilyn fell away – perhaps I could have resisted, but I was defeated, my will extinguished, and the musky smell of Rebecca's neck – for an instant, it seemed the two of us were on a cloud ship again –

Then utter darkness returned, and she lay draped over me, heaving, her cheek against mine.

A smile. "It was every bit as magical as you said it would be."

Coughing, gasping. "When did I say such a thing?" I scrambled to my knees, yelling. "What are you talking about? What is anyone talking about? The world is coming down around us, and I'm the only one who can't figure why --"

I pawed at the shutters, jerked one side open, then the window, anything to get a clean breath of air into this den. She had seduced me artfully, gracefully, and I never really fought it. Now the dam of guilt broke. Rebecca was perhaps the most voluptuous creature on Earth, but I had Marilyn – now *this*, just at the moment I might have convinced her to escape with me. Maybe I had always been a fool. God to damn me to hell, I wanted to yell to the firmament. But he didn't have to. I had dug my own grave.

"When, Rebecca?" I managed to ask. "When did I say something like that to you?"

"You didn't, directly. But you sent the message – your intermediary has told me this time and again."

"And just who is my intermediary – that bastard Billy Dean? He's always wanted to push me on you --"

"Where the hell are you, Hot Shot?" The voice of the bastard, himself.

We scrambled. I crawled to the opening in the floor, and could just make out that despicable smile in the smoldering light below.

"Got your business done?"

"Shut up," I cried. "Maybe you can create thunderstorms, but when you mess with people's emotions, you're looking to get busted."

"Yeah? Well, we'll both get busted if we don't get back. Mission accomplished."

Rebecca was pulling on her jeans. I grabbed her hand, squeezed it. That was all I could do. Clumsily, I put my feet on the wooden rungs – but she crouched next to me, holding on.

"I'm sorry Rebecca. Sorry that some frustrated people can't let the rest of us just live our lives. If it were any other time, or place--"

"Stop for a moment," she draped her arms around my neck, and whispered. "I'm in love with you, George Blair. I have listened to that little black eagle down there --" she motioned, "—for too long, but his commands could never make me love someone. You – I love you freely, with my own heart, and I am glad that it happened this way. At least it happened."

It was just another strange, unconnected thing to say. I kissed her one more time, and clambered down to the ground. She didn't follow. By then, Billy Dean was halfway to the car.

"Stop right there, Mister. Where's Marilyn? I'm not leaving without seeing her."

He flicked the butt into a scorched patch of grass, and called over his shoulder. "Not here."

"What the hell do you mean? You're lying. As usual. Where's Guillermo? I'll ask him." I turned back toward the intact hotel.

"Such a dumb ass," Billy Dean cried. "Ain't nobody in them buildings. The townsfolk are hiding out in the mesquite. A punk like you will never find them."

I wheeled on him, fist raised. "Marilyn. You tell me where she is right now, or I'm gonna ignore your buddy Parsifal and take my chances."

He leaned against the car, casual as you please. "She's probably back in China Bend, sippin' an iced tea, College Boy."

"Shut up," I said. "Her note said she was seeing her sister. Doesn't that mean Rebecca?"

A sneer. "And if it do, what does that make you, Casanova?"

The fist was still clenched, and I stuck it right in his face. "Don't you dare start with the riddles again. I know why you brought me down here. And so what if you finally got your sick little way. Marilyn is still the one I love." I raised that fist up to the sky. "Hear me, Parsifal? Your ol' friend is about to get a whuppin'." Now we were nose-to-nose.

"OK, you son of a bitch," I said. "If Cadwallader knew she wasn't down here, and you knew it, why pull this shenanigan when the world is about to end?"

He didn't move. Didn't twitch a muscle. The scrawny little bastard – with one kick, I could have sent him flying over the car, but those black eyes of his – the sheer animal sheen of them – kept me at bay.

Finally, a little chuckle. "The world's not going to end, Boy. I brought you down here to make sure it doesn't."

Before I could swing, he whipped out the pack of weeds, lit a new one, then jerked a thumb to one side. I followed the motion, and saw Rebecca, leaning back easily, ravishingly against the base of the tree. She giggled, then waved goodbye.

I wanted so much to walk over there, take her in my arms again, but the sheer math of everything made me catch my breath. "I'm not completely dumb," I told him. "You're trying to make me believe you knew she was going to seduce me. Fine. But that can be planned without time travel."

I started pacing. "And speaking of that, I'll swear to one thing: when we pulled up here, you were surprised to see the damage to the buildings."

"Yes. I was surprised," he said, measuring me.

"So if you know what's gonna happen ahead of time, how do you explain that?"

Cool. Intense. Blinking in the grotesque shadows from the car's cabin light. "There are always mavericks." He propped a foot up on the fender. "The more I mess with it, seems like fate has some tattered edges. Time ain't set in stone, just aspic, sort of."

He picked at a shred of tobacco stuck to his lip. "Maybe that lieutenant did this. Maybe somebody else. All I care about is them returning to me what is rightfully mine. They can throw all the curve balls they want. I'll just hit 'em out of the park."

I stepped, threw a punch, but he was ready, and moved, becoming a shadow behind the car. Too quick. I braced for his counterattack. It didn't come, but Rebecca giggled.

"You know," Billy Dean said, "for a smart guy, you sure learn slow. Turn around and wave goodbye to the little lady."

I waved, climbed into driver's seat, and gunned the engine. He slipped in the other side. We both knew the fight was over. "Be honest," I dared him. "You can't really travel in time at all, can you? You didn't know they would bomb the hotels. How can you be sure we're not leaving Rebecca to a fate of getting raped and murdered?"

That insipid chuckle. "You've seen how she handles herself with the king of the sky. How the hell you think a measly army's gonna scare her?"

In the rearview mirror, the second woman I had ever made love to disappeared in a swirl of night dust.

Chapter 39
Reunion

It was my duty to do some more probing – but hell, that would just be for myself, for I had no more duty. Duty to whom? A duty to Marilyn to confess the truth about what had just happened – that I was determined to carry out. But the heaviness of the night, the sight of the ruined hotels, the dying cricket songs, the sweetness of Rebecca's lips – all of those things conspired to put me on the run, as if I were determined to keep it all from Marilyn. God, Cadwallader probably still had her –

"What the hell if she is in China Bend," I said loudly, over the highway wind. "How do you know she is? Is she still working with you four idiots somehow?"

No answer. Billy Dean was curled up on his side of the car, sleeping the sleep of the dead.

Back at the station, rather than put up with the weatherman's groggy jeering, I fetched my bag, and peeled out for China Bend. My resolve to grab Marilyn and head for Mexico was shaken, however. First, I needed some sleep. And it still amazes me how I automatically believed Billy Dean's claim that Marilyn would be waiting at her house.

The smell of the river survived the frigid air – a cold front had passed through – and dark splotches of moss still hung in the trees. In the dark, the clumps of cane on either side looked like a million staffs planted by medieval knights, forbidding passage to the river beyond. The truck was sitting in front of the house, the light was on. My heart was in my throat.

"Oh, hi," Marilyn said, as if I lived here, and was just coming home from work. I yanked the screen door open, and grabbed her. Her freshly folded clothes tumbled to the floor. When she finally pulled away, her face was crimson. A little smile. "I didn't think you'd be back until tomorrow."

"How did you know I was gone?" I asked.

"Emil told me." She picked up her laundry, blushing.

"Come here." I locked my lips on hers, until her words sank in. "But where were you? Did you go to Landview? To see Rebecca? Were you there at the same time we were? Or do you really have a sister?"

A smile. So innocent. "Rebecca is the closest thing to a sibling I've ever had. Did you see her?" She seemed excited by the very thought.

I froze.

"Tell me about it," she said. Not so innocent.

My God. "Marilyn, if you already know, you'd better tell me. You're the one I love. No matter what happens, or who you might think I care about."

Brightness in her eyes. The blush on her cheeks deepened, then she walked over, and grasped my forearms, and collapsed against me in one of the sweetest hugs I ever experienced. "Then it is done," she whispered.

I think that's what she said. She might as well have hit me in the belly with a baseball bat. My thoughts swirled – all the guilt of a priest who's broken his vows, all the disgust of a rat who's on display in a breeding experiment. I grabbed her.

"Go to bed with me. Right now," I demanded.

She looked down at the floor.

"But George, I don't know you."

"Marilyn, how can you say that? After what we've had? Am I going crazy?"

She looked up, the gaze in her eyes neither condemning, nor approving. "Two things," she said, holding up a pair of fingers. "There's a flashlight in the kitchen drawer, next to the sink. Get it. I've got to get my boots on."

Fool that I was, I fetched the light. She met me at the front door, and led me out, under sparkling stars.

I caught up to her in the back yard, and recovered my bearings, for just a moment. "Do you know what time travel is?" I asked.

In the glare of her back porch light, she licked her lips. "How much did they tell you?"

My God. She was with them.

"Goddam it, Marilyn, there's no such thing. I don't know where all this shit started, but it's not scientifically possible. You just helped them because they fed you a bunch of fairy tales. What else did they promise you?"

She recoiled. In the darkness, I couldn't tell if she was mad, or hurt – but I'd had a long day, and it boiled over.

"Tell me, Darling. What have they made you do? What did they fool you into doing? Have they ever forced you to have sex?"

"What?"

Now the darkness didn't matter – Considering what I had just done, I was a total ass. She backed up, a motion that possibly saved me from being clobbered with the flashlight.

"Marilyn, I'm sorry--"

"You listen to me, George Blair. I don't care how time has changed, or what your people in this God-forsaken place do for recreation. Take your birth control and your car dates – yes, I know you've been on them. And I can only imagine the things you've done, regardless of what you say. Or what Victor says."

"Marilyn, please, I--"

"You shut your mouth before you crack the Universe apart single-handedly. I'm just trying to help you understand—because you've been good to me. Without flaw."

I fell to my knees. Wrapped my arms around her legs. Tears were starting. "I'm sorry for saying that. I'm under pressure, and you're the dearest thing – for God's sake, forgive me. I won't say anything like that again--"

She squeezed my arm, bent down, and enveloped me with her arms, her mouth. Without warning, she slapped my roving hands. The flashlight clicked on, inventing a cloud of gnats and flying bugs, and I shivered in the night chill, because I had learned that October was late for these critters to be alive, that the door of winter would soon slam shut on us, and it had become a daily ritual to wonder if the same thing was about to happen to the human race. She plunged toward the dark cane stands, but stopped at their edge, and turned around, and now the bright light boring into the thick grass created an obstacle I dared not step over.

"We were children a few days ago, George. No longer. And your suspicion of my virtue is like a weather forecast. I will go back where I came from, but I fear the disease of this time is sleeping inside me. I'll go back, but I won't be the woman I was supposed to be."

"You're not supposed to 'be' anything, Marilyn. You are a beautiful woman whom I love, and I will be there for you, and protect you always, even from these diseases you fear, if I can."

"Please listen." Tears in her eyes reflected the light, tiny against the dark foliage, the twinkling stars, the buzzing of insects in my ears, distant frog songs. I wanted to take her now, but she held the flashlight like a sword.

"I'm explaining my fate, George. You betrayed me, and it's not important how I know. But you did it because you were forced to. You're too sweet to catch the sickness of now. You're actually more old-fashioned, maybe, than I ever was. I know how devoted you were to that Andrea woman. Emil told me.

"But what you said a moment ago – you knew, somehow, and I was afraid you told them. We are close, you and I, in spite of the little time. You can read me. You know your world has the power to make me consider becoming a loose woman --"

"For God's sake, Marilyn--"

She stopped me with a wave.

"What you just said about me – was it a prediction?" She took a deep breath, covered her eyes. "While you were gone to Landview this time, I almost betrayed you, too. I went over to Josie's, down at the Bend. A man tried to pick me up--"

In the darkness, I reached for the flashlight, wrapped around it, and her fingers.

"Don't," she whimpered. "It's all right. Emil showed up, and stopped me. He knocked the boy out."

"Seriously? I didn't know the old fool had it in him."

"He doesn't. He could manage it only because his discipline is paramount, George. To you, he's just a gruff old man. But he's the only steady force in this whole tragedy. It's his strength, the purity of his heart – like your purity. Don't think badly of him--"

"So nothing happened?"

"That's not the point, George. I *wanted* something to happen. Don't you see? I risked it all – you, me, but so much more. Because of the disease. It's in my head. And even when I go back to my real home, I fear I will want other men."

I hugged her, squeezing hard. "Shut up. I know that feeling, too, but when you settle down with the right man – I should have resisted Rebecca--"

"Oh, George." She screamed the words, and pulled away. "Don't you see? I have the disease of *now*." She sobbed quietly, then shook her head. "Don't tell me I'm good. Don't say anything. You must see this--"

She pushed a few stalks of cane aside, and shone the light in, moving quickly, along a barely discernible path. I tried to keep up, afraid that some rattlesnakes and water moccasins might still be moving above ground.

"We going to the river? What's there?"

We passed through the tight passage, cane leaves slicing at my arms. The river smell increased, as thick as a cloud of tear gas, until we emerged in a flat place filled with high grass and dark scrub cedars that hung their branches around us ominously. The buzz of the bugs subsided a little, giving way to the sad, hollow song of a night whippoorwill.

I caught up with her, took her by the shoulders and kissed the back of her head. "I don't want you to worry. Why did you bring me out here?"

She shrugged my hands off and shone the light on another wall of cane. "There it is. My castle keep."

Odd colors streaked the night from the flashlight's glare, and I worked my way into a hollowed-out space in the cane that contained a tiny wooden table no bigger than a footstool. I scanned the light around. A damp, dirty quilt lay spread on the ground beside the table.

She was at my side. "I've never shown this to anyone. Not even Chris."

I took a step into the cramped, stalky cavern, and plopped down. The moist fabric beneath me reeked of river and rodents, mixed in with the sweet odors of grass and Marilyn's perfume. "Why not Chris?"

She sat down, legs folded, across from me. "He made me come here, sometimes. You haven't done that yet."

"You're talking Greek, Darlin'. If he never knew about this place, how did he make you come here?"

She let me take her hands. "I followed Billy Dean's rules. Emil's rules. So, you see? I was forbidden to let Chris touch me. But there were those nights that he tried, especially when he got drunk. This was the place I could hide, where he couldn't find me."

I pulled her closer. "Forget Billy Dean. See? You are virtuous."

"I couldn't help it." She broke into tears, and buried her face in my chest. "I shot him, and I couldn't help it, because Billy Dean – they all said I had to wait for you."

She was a warm mass against the night chill, and my body pressed into her, feeding off of that warmth, and everything she was, but my ears rang with her words.

"That morning, he wouldn't take *no* for an answer." She spoke between gasps. "He said this was all a lie. We had been hypnotized, said he really loved me, always had, and he was going to break the spell--"

"Marilyn, you didn't shoot him--"

"I did," she cried, sobbing heavily now. "What else could I do? It was the very wrong day, because you had come. It's like God wanted to test me one more time. You appeared right when Billy Dean said you would. When Victor said. That--"

She gripped me hard, choking out her words. "When you came, it was like Chris couldn't hold it anymore. He reached his limit. He even talked about you that night after you showed up, saying the very words – saying--"

"It's not true. The army shot him." I draped my arms around her shoulders.

"I came here. I was running. What else could I do? He got drunk before, and got all touchy, but that morning it was too early for him to drink, and that look in his eye was different -- I shot him with his own rifle. Oh, George, what if he *was* telling the truth? What if this is all some horrible dream?"

Shaking, sobbing, she clung to me. I wrapped her in my arms, then my legs went around her – but we both needed protecting. "My God," I whispered. "Are we all just trying to cover up some sort of murder?"

"Don't say that," she cried.

"I didn't mean you. I meant Billy Dean – Hell, I don't know what I mean."

I pulled her away, to face me, but all I could see were the little reflecting stars of tears on her cheeks. "If he was trying to rape you – I mean, you were married, but – oh, hell."

I shut up then, because a wife couldn't prove self defense in court if all her husband wanted was a piece of ass. Could she? But my mind was working for a change, my logic kicking in and overpowering her perfume, if only for a moment. What the hell had the marshal delivered me into? This was like one of those weird nudist cults. These people were all living some sort of passion play that made no sense, but had rules that they all obeyed.

I put my fingers over her lips, stopping her from breaking my train of thought.

"OK," I finally said. "Let's calm down. This is easy – what happened before? We just take it one step at a time. All you have to do is think back, to what happened before you met Billy Dean. Or however this all started. Did you live in Landview? Were you born there? Did anyone ever hypnotize you? Think, Marilyn, think."

She wiped her eyes, breathing hard. "I was a girl. I was just a girl." Again the tears started, but she fought. "My father bought cattle. El Paso. We lived in El Paso."

"On the border?"

A nod. "We went down to – to Juarez. That's where her father --"

"Whose father?"

A soulful look. "Rebecca's."

A charge of electricity went through me. "Rebecca was what? Like an aunt to you?"

"No. We met that night. It was her coming of age party. My dad had never taken me on one of his cattle trips before, but it was this huge event, and he had promised Rebecca's dad. Punch, cake, I wore a new dress Daddy bought me – it was wonderful."

"OK. So when did your dad move you to Landview?"

Quiet. Her hands dropped from their death-grip on my arms. The whippoorwill mourned.

"He didn't. Billy Dean--"

"What about him? Focus on your childhood, first, please."

"No. He ruined it."

"Your childhood?"

"The party." Her eyes sparkled in the darkness. "And I guess that means he ruined my childhood, too."

"But Rebecca's name – Flock of Birds?"

Marilyn sighed. "The Mexicans – so many of them had Indian names, too, and she chose to go by hers when we got to Landview, because she claimed the great Grandfathers had borrowed her life for a while, so – anyway, her father was also called Sanchez, and Senor Sanchez was just proposing a toast, and it was my first toast, and I had champagne in my glass, and couldn't wait to taste it, when that bastard walked in, carrying his big rifle, and kidnapped us."

"What bastard?"

"Billy Dean, of course. He promised to shoot Senor Sanchez if Rebecca and I didn't come with him."

"Didn't anybody fight him? Mr. Sanchez should have done something."

"No – he told everyone to be calm, that he would deal with this monster later. His eyes got so dark, I believed him. At first, I wasn't even afraid. Can you imagine that? The look on Mr. Sanchez's face was so strong and cold. I knew he wanted to avoid bloodshed, so he would let this wild gunman who wore a strange uniform leave the house – but he would follow us, and save us--"

A deep, shuddering breath.

"That's when Guillermo lost his temper."

"My God. I met him."

"He's Rebecca's cousin. He started running after us, and so everyone ran with him. But I only learned that later – I was so terrified when Billy Dean took us out into the fields. The sky was black, like the devil's own eye. The stars had been sucked out of it." Her fingers gripped my arms tighter as she remembered.

"When we made the fence line, something even blacker came – a tornado. A wind reaching out of the clouds, and I thought I would go deaf, 'cause 'Becca and I were screaming, and that horrible little mad monster jerked us up to our feet, and the storm sucked us into the sky, right before Guillermo jumped over the fence. But it got him. And everyone else, too. But I didn't know that until we landed. And suddenly, it was daylight. We must have spent the whole night in that horrible wind."

Another shudder, and the night sounds returned to my ears, slowly replacing the squishes of my beating heart. I felt lost. Never closer to this goddess, but she had parroted the same story that Russell had told me, only from another angle. She was still with them. She would always be part of this conspiracy. Who was this woman with whom I had fallen in love?

She relaxed now. The tension – it filled the whole world just a moment before – slowly seeped out of her body. I felt it in my arms, my legs, my insides. It was as if she were saying goodbye.

"This is the year Nineteen, Sixty-Two," she whispered.

"Yes."

"The party was in the year eighteen ninety-five. I was fifteen."

"Marilyn, please. You've been hypnotized, or whatever they've done to all of you—You have to let that nonsense go. Stop being part of *them*. Try to be part of me."

Her hands rose until they caressed my face. Then she was patting my arm, as if I were the one who needed consoling.

"It's OK. It will be OK..."

"What will?" I asked.

"This isn't a dream. I wanted it to be, but it's not, and if it's not, I know what I have to do."

She rose, and led me back to the house. We made love for the third time. Somewhere in the kisses, my guilt about being with the beautiful Indian woman evaporated, because my love was really here – with this lady. I collapsed beside her.

"Let' sleep," I said. "If they don't come out of the night and get us, let's sleep 'til morning, then run away once and for all. We can even go back Juarez, if you want to."

After a long moment of thoughts that I could not detect, she rose on one arm, and kissed my lips. "That was the third time."

"For us? Yes, I was counting, too."

"Victor said there would be three."

My drowsiness, the ultimate bliss of satisfaction, crumbled into a tight ball of fear – by now, I was used to it – it inhabited my gut the way a piece of sand lives in an oyster. "What the hell part does Victor play in any of this? What is he to you?"

She tried to fall back on her pillow, but I grabbed her shoulders, and shook her.

"Answer me, Marilyn."

She chuckled, and ran her fingers through my hair. "Silly. We can't leave yet. There's going to be a peace conference, and Boss said to make sure you and I both come."

"Peace conference? Between whom?"

"Washington and Balcones, of course."

"Marilyn, how do you know this? Who told you?"

For a moment, she blinked. As if I were a stranger, not her lover. As if she had never seen me before.

"We'll get an invitation tomorrow. Victor told me that, too."

She turned on me, taking all the power once again. Using that smile, those eyes, her hair that fell all over me, to suck all the oxygen out of my protests.

My sudden wakefulness evaporated, and I was sinking deeply into the pillow. "When did that stupid old Mexican tell you these things?" I heard myself mumble.

Hovering above me, she looked dreamy. Then thoughtful. Then sad. She whispered, "A long time ago, George. Before you were born."

I tried to hang on, ask what crazy language they were all speaking, a language that made it seem that everything was already said and done, as if we were finished with Time, and looking backward. But I lost my grip, plunged into darkness, riding the sound of distant thunder – yet another October storm approaching – and I knew I would dream about the huge monsters on their sailing ships ---

But no – it was Marilyn, lying on top of me, smothering me with kisses anew. My body tingled, surged back to life.

"But that was the fourth time," I managed to say when it was over. My eyes could barely open. "I thought Victor told you three."

She smiled, and buried her head in my chest. "He did. I think you're teaching me to tempt fate, George."

Chapter 40
An Invitation

I woke before she did, made a pot of coffee as quietly as I could, and wound up pacing the worn carpet in her living room, the chipped linoleum in the kitchen. A dozen times, I started to go out the door, clean out my car's trunk, prepared to give her the bum's rush – make her pack up, and come with me to Mexico.

Only her weird announcement about a potential "peace treaty" stopped me. Was if all this was over? I could call the marshal. Maybe Billy Dean would stop his charade, maybe they'd already given him his little prize, and let him go with it, waiting for the day some government operative would sneak up behind him and blow his brains out. No one ever told me the government worked that way – I read it in a secret agent novel.

Gulping coffee, I completed another circuit of the living room – she appeared, blinking against the light, in the kitchen doorway. Draped in her nightgown. Perfect and sleepy. I didn't want to go to Mexico. Here was home.

"You have to go to work," she said.

"Who says?"

A look of consternation.

"Don't tell me. You got a secret message from your sacred Victor." I plopped down on the couch. "I'll go to work when I want to."

A knock on the door sent me back to my feet. I rushed to the closet on the other side of the living room, where she kept her shotgun and a baseball bat. For some reason, I chose the bat, and made it to the front door before she could.

"Who is it?"

"Reed's Flowers, sir."

I opened the door. The bouquet was large, and the teenager set it on the porch, smiling uncertainly. "Here's the note," he said, handing it over.

Marilyn, it said on the outside. I tipped the guy, and ripped open the envelope.

The scrawl on the little card made me shudder:

I am always thinking about you...

The signature belonged to Russell Crump. I tossed the card at her.

"What the hell—How could he sign this? He's in jail."

A grimace. "He's always doing that. It means nothing. They never told me about this. I should have shot him, instead of poor Chris."

Such an instant, frustrated, fluid excuse had me believing her. But another envelope was nestled between the roses. This one I let her open.

"*Signing of a peace treaty between the United States of America and the Nation of Balcones*," she read aloud. "They're doing it at Emil's house. The ranch house. Tonight."

She took a deep breath, then sighed. "At last." No tinge of gloating in her voice. "Now. Time for you to go to work."

When I walked through those glass front doors of the station, Sharon gave me the sweetest smile I had ever seen on her face. Somehow, she had the same gravity, same detachment that Rebecca did. She was a survivor.

I almost stepped into the newsroom. But Cuthbert wasn't there anymore. And I feared that if I went up to the weather room, Billy Dean would only succeed in roping me into something worse than the way I was feeling now. I had thought a lot during the night. Thought all the way out here. I asked to be admitted to see Cadwallader.

"Not here," she said. "I'm not supposed to say, but I'll tell you. He's out at the ranch."

I pondered. Crump must be out of jail now. "Is his son-in-law with him?" I asked.

"I don't know." Was she blushing? "I have something to ask you, George." She rested her elbows on the desk, taking care to brush her perfect brown hair back out of her face, and put her hands primly together, like someone conducting an interview. "I want to know why you brought your girlfriend here."

"Who? Andrea was here again?"

"I mean why you brought her in the first place." The stoic, soft, impervious indestructible poise I was just admiring flew out the window, and her hands were pounding on the table, her green eyes flashing. "She's been here for the last two days, re-decorating his office. And some of the other offices. Sure, the girls in advertising love having a carpet, finally, but the color that hussy picked – sorry, George – makes everybody want to puke. *I* always took care of his office, before this."

I shrugged. "She's not my girlfriend anymore."

"It's not just the decorating. I don't think you know what's been going on behind your back."

"You mean between Andrea and the boss?"

Perfect skin, soft eye shadow, the correct amount of mascara, her cheeks growing more crimson by the second. "They've *done it*, George." She gulped back a tear. "I shouldn't have said that. But I really think you're a nice guy. I wanted to make sure you knew."

"Sharon, why do you care who he sees?"

Her tears came in earnest now, smudging that mascara. "She ruined everything. You don't really know him. He's a little schoolboy who tries hard to be good, and she's like a vulture preying on him. Now he won't even buy me that car I picked out."

"But you're just a receptionist here--" A thoughtless remark, since I had seen how many things she held together – I did the math. The floor could have fallen out from under me. "You? And Emil Cadwallader?" The profligate old lech. She was sobbing.

"It's not like that, George," she said. "But he was mine, nonetheless. Not now. Not with her in the picture."

"Don't worry, Sharon. I'm going to put a stop to all this nonsense. Including Andrea." I turned. Someone called my name, but I didn't look back. I had an appointment I was determined to keep.

I did a drive-by first. The gun was cozy in my belt, and Cadwallader's car sat in the circular drive. I knew full well I was about to ruin Andrea's dreams once and for all, and I was almost sorry, but I climbed out, opened the gate, and drove in as if I'd been invited.

A single GI guarded the huge front doors. My first obstacle, and I didn't have the guts to go for my gun. He saluted smartly, and I knew that in the next instant, he would frisk me. Instead, amazingly, he simply opened one of the doors for me.

"Go on in, Mr. Blair," he said.

I stepped into a large entry hall, and the door conveniently closed behind me. Voices droned somewhere in the distance, and I pulled the pistol and stealthily followed the sound. The living room was bigger than my entire apartment. I found them in a den in back, Cadwallader propped behind an antique bar, a man in uniform sprawled in one of the plush leather chairs that Andrea and I had seen them moving in that night. Raven.

"Hello, General." Out the windows lay a large swimming pool and the expanse of his ranchland.

"George Blair. What's the matter?" The sight of the gun sent his arms up automatically, as if this were a bank instead of a vipers' nest. Cadwallader surely had a weapon behind that bar, but somehow he wasn't as scary without his bullwhip. I stood where I had a clear shot at both of them.

"Gentlemen, you will both accompany me downtown, where I will personally lock you in a cell. That is, unless somebody starts telling me the truth."

"George--" Raven sputtered, but the old man gestured, and the impotent soldier clammed up.

"That's right," I said. "Don't start with any of your bullshit stories. It's jail, or a bullet, or both. Take your pick. Last chance to spill your guts to a human being. J. Edgar Hoover's boys won't stop to listen." I turned the weapon on Cadwallader.

"What do you want to know, George?" He spoke calmly.

"Everything."

Raven fidgeted, still reaching for the sky, but Cadwallader shook off little Hitler's pleading stare, and gazed into the drink he held in one hand. "In World War II, Billy Dean Brown was in a company of soldiers that liberated the Nazi's only functional heavy water plant. Our government didn't know it at the time, but their scientists had succeeded in creating the world's first fusion battery."

"Fusion?" I almost yelled it. "Boy, you guys like to pile bullshit on top of buffalo patties. How high do you think you it'll stack? Nice try, Mr. Cadwallader, but fusion is impossible. At least with today's technology."

Raven raised one hand higher, like a kid in school. "He's telling the truth, George. I was there. I mean, after they killed the scientists."

"Billy Dean killed scientists?"

"No," Raven said. "His job was to save them, and he was a good soldier, up until that one afternoon. The Nazis were the ones shooting scientists – orders from Hitler himself. One of their colonels escaped with the only functioning battery. Thought he would trade it for his life, and maybe a lot of money. Just his bad luck – and ours—that he ran into Billy Dean the one time that scoundrel had a lapse."

"That's what all this is about? A fusion battery?" They were leading my mind a merry chase – fantasy had become a way of life with them. I waved the pistol, slowly this time. "I told you bastards I wanted the truth."

Cadwallader set his cocktail down. I tensed. "That really happened, George. Billy Dean's unit went after the colonel. Trapped him in a cellar. None of our officers were present, but Billy Dean was a non-com, and the fool colonel surrendered it to him. Well, you know Billy Dean by now – he thought the battery was his private booty. The Army saw it differently, and relieved him of it, after a fight. This was in the Russian zone, and the commies heard about the whole drama, of course, and demanded half of the battery. They wanted a crack at figuring it out, too. But that was bad for both sides, because the damn thing doesn't really work without both parts."

"I'm going to shoot you," I said, breathing deeply, trying to keep control of my trigger finger. "If this nonsense were true, Kennedy would just order someone to kill the little jackass, and everything would go back to normal."

Raven licked his lips like a drunk in a brewery. Cadwallader was still cool – he wasn't making his move – yet. "Like I've been telling you George, that scrawny little bastard learned to control the weather just so he could get an angle on us. We can't shoot him, because he'll destroy the world if we do."

"Learned to control the weather. Just like that, huh? What – did he send off for a correspondence course?"

Raven's face was so red, I thought he might have a coronary then and there. "That's another thing the Nazi's were working on. Sergeant Brown had that colonel alone to himself about three hours before he shot him. We don't know for sure, but we're pretty certain that colonel gave him a few pointers, and he mixed that with whatever he might have culled from Rebecca Flock-of-Birds' people."

"The Indians had some pretty smart witch doctors," Cadwallader chimed in, then bit his lip, measuring his words. "I don't think the knowledge came from Rebecca, but someone close to her."

"Oh, please." I kicked an end table, sending a stack of china coasters crashing to the brick floor. They looked familiar, from one of the shops in town. Andrea was no doubt having a field day buying trinkets for the old geezer. "You're both too pitiful to kill. Nobody can destroy the world with a thunderstorm. What's he gonna do, conjure up a couple of hurricanes from beyond the grave?"

The old man swallowed hard. "You met the Indian girl, George? Did Billy Dean tell you what year she was born in?"

"He told her to lie," I yelled.

"He brought her from the past, George. He discovered something out about storms that science hasn't figured out yet."

"Hell, it wasn't the Indians or the Mexicans," Raven blurted. "Those Krauts taught him something."

"Shut up." I kept the gun trained on Cadwallader. "So you're claiming that Rebecca is what – eighty years old?"

"No, sir." Teeth yellow, some gold, certainly most of them false. Andrea was kissing that mouth. "I told you he brought her from the last century. She's still young, and if he doesn't take her back to her own life, then Time, itself, will be messed up. Messed up bad – by what the Washington boys call a time loop"

"A time loop? Did you actually say that?"

"Exactly. Don't ask me how it works. I just listen to what the physicists tell the government—That's why I assigned you the weather job, wondering if a smart boy like you could figure it out." A large drop of sweat worked down his forehead. "They also call it a *temporal rip*. Everything goes. Everything changes. We all die, 'cause everything that happened to our ancestors would be changed, y'see?"

Raven lowered one hand to point. "That's if he doesn't take those people back, George. You, me – we might not be here anymore. The Russians claim to be bringing their half of the battery right now, but if they don't, we hit 'em with everything we got. Ka-boom. They're double-crossing commies. We're holding Cuba hostage, so they know we mean business."

I would have bet Fort Knox that I had read ten times the science fiction books any of those asses had – except you can't read ten times more than zero. Now I was really seething. "You dumb asses. If you actually knew what a time loop was, you would realize it's not scientifically possible."

They stared, like diabolical sphinxes who'd been caught out in their little trick. The sweat crawling down the old, rich geezer's face confirmed it. They were all part of a hoax, an elaborate play-acting – of course there was an agenda, but it wasn't tornadoes and time travel. Didn't

Lafferty himself explain how hardened criminals used straw dogs?

It didn't matter that the marshal was one of them. They likely fooled him. Marilyn, too. Or made big promises. My resolve was in stone now – time to ante up, be a man. The marshal would be proud of me for taking action, even if he was one of the scoundrels who would go to jail for this.

"Gentlemen," I began, keeping the gun steady. "Billy Dean's not waiting for any package. Unless it's a payoff that all of you yokels will split up. I gave you a chance to let me go. I just wanted Marilyn. Ever hear me say that?"

This was my moment. I had to make a speech every bit as good as those victorious cops in the movies.

"But no, you jerks never listen to anything but your own nonsense. Mexicans falling from the sky, quartz rods and magical Indian weather spells. We'll let the FBI sort you bums out. They might not know it yet, but I'm about to save them a lot of money. Maybe even stop a nuclear exchange. Come out from behind that bar, Mr. Cadwallader. And no funny business."

A loaded gun trumps even the president of a new country, it seemed. The old man did as directed.

"Now. Single-file. We're going downtown, to where the real Feds work. And then I'll drive out and fetch Billy Dean, and Russell, too, if I can find the fat fuck. Tell that soldier out there to vamoose, if he doesn't want to get shot."

"George Blair, don't do this."

Cadwallader's hands were raised, his eyes teary. "We ain't been lying to you, sir. You gotta stay with us, for just a little while longer."

"Bullshit. Start walking. You're taking a ride, sitting up or lying down."

Raven actually started marching. At least I think so. The only thing that I'm sure happened next was Cadwallader dropped his hands, and stared at me with a sort of disgusted frown.

"You've forgotten one thing, George--" He said those words.

Then a rumble of thunder shook the house. I shivered, and the world lit up in a flash.

After that, all I knew was that my head hurt like fire, even though my arms and legs were sunk into something soft. Somewhere in that darkness, I smelled Marilyn's perfume. When I finally managed to open my eyes. She was there, rocking in her chair, dusk seeping through the blinds behind her.

"You OK, Sweetheart?" she asked me in that soft voice. "You've been out for hours."

Mouth dry, but I managed to speak. "Did I arrest them?"

A little chuckle. "No, my foolish warrior. You can't do that yet. You know that. Get up and take it slow. You have to have your strength for the Peace Summit."

"OK." My body had no strength left, only a feeling of being drugged, and falling. Into something soft.

"Tell me one thing."

"Of course, George."

"Did Billy Dean sneak up on me?"

"Yes, my love. But he'll leave you alone soon. Just get dressed. Drink some water. You'll feel better in a few minutes." She kissed my cheek. "Do it for me, George."

She said it so sweetly. I couldn't refuse.

Chapter 41
The Treaty of Balcones

I got up and moved around, drank a gallon of water, it seemed – wanted a drink in the worst way, because I had the worst hangover of my life – without a drop of alcohol to earn it. Marilyn watched me, laughing while I dressed, and when she finally went to the kitchen and mixed an alka seltzer, I started to feel almost human.

"Don't worry. You'll perform famously, tonight, George," she said.

I wanted to ask how much she knew – was there anything in her crystal ball about the two of us escaping this madhouse?

I liked it when she tended to me like that. Whoever invented the legends of vampires must have known a woman like Marilyn. All fire, and alluring glances on the nights we slept together – but when morning came, and sunshine, she turned into a driven, focused creature. Housework, or revolutions – her eyes seemed like steel to me. If I could live with her the rest of my life, what would we talk about?

When I had my shirt and shorts on, she started pulling Chris's suits from the closet and holding them up to me. Finally, she kissed my cheek and grimaced. "You need a

tuxedo, George. Don't worry. I ordered one down at The
Evening Place. We'll get it on the way."

She proceeded to the closet, and got dressed in a
stunning gown. I paced between watching her dress in the
bedroom, and going into the living room to glance at the TV.
Commentators argued heatedly about the latest development
in Cuba. A Soviet ship had been let through the American
gauntlet.

Marilyn gasped when she came in, and squeezed my
shoulder. "Isn't that great?" she said.

"Why great? Does that mean we lost the standoff?" No
mention by the press about the supposed state dinner tonight.
Of course not. This rebellion was off the map.

After the tuxedo shop, I suggested we go for ice cream.
In the car, my hands started roaming.

"No, George. We have to be on time, and you need to
keep your wits about you."

I was still on cloud nine, for the first time actually
enjoying the motions of a couple in love. We were practically
playing house. Not until we pulled onto Cadwallader's road
did I come down from that cloud. Both sides of the road were
lined with cars that issued Sironia's elite, dressed to kill. A trio
of GIs signaled me to halt.

"Do you have any firearms in the car?" A curt private
unsnapped his holster.

My own pistol rested in my belt from habit. I decided
to come clean. "Yes, sir." Marilyn turned pale.

They pulled us both out and searched the car without
asking. He put the gun in a duffel bag and wrote a receipt.
"You can pick it up after dinner, sir."

Marilyn took my arm at the bottom of the front porch
stairs. "You might be worse than Chris," she said.

A line of guests snaked out the front door. I studied their faces. City councilmen and their wives. The owner of Brazos Trucking, and other pillars of Sironian society whom I had either seen on TV, or to whom Andrea had introduced me over the years. The music and laughter lilting through the front doors sounded more like a cotillion than world-shaking peace talks. When I spotted Andrea at the head of the receiving line, that image was complete. I nudged Marilyn. "That's her."

Andrea had draped herself in a peach-colored monstrosity, and commanded the line, patting Cadwallader, rubbing his shoulder, or giggling at him between introductions to the passing snobs who would not have given her the time of day a few weeks ago. We almost made it to the front of the line when Marilyn pulled back. "Wait. I'm going to the ladies room."

This was my second time here today, and I felt my jaw, the back of my head, wondering which one I had hit when I went down. I had noted a restroom just inside the door on my first visit here, so I motioned her toward it, and stepped out of line to wait. A tap on the shoulder shook me. Russell Crump stood there, grinning sheepishly.

"Russell, what are you doing here?"

"Hi, George. They let me out right after you left."

"Congratulations."

Sweat dappled his chin. "Damn if I didn't lose fifteen pounds in that rathole. So, how does it feel to be heir to the throne?" He studied my face and chuckled. "Don't worry about me. I had time to think, sittin' in that jail cell. My days as Mr. C's lackey are over."

I shrugged. "How can I be the heir without a country? I thought this was a peace treaty signing."

"Yeah? You see any McNamara?" I looked around. America's famed secretary of defense was not in attendance. The Dauphin shook his head. "That's right, I smell a double-cross. They promise a big gun, he don't come. That's why we got so many troops on the ground, just in case the feds launch an assault."

The hair stood up on my neck, partly because I had to admit the fat man was talking sense. The band played, and the crowd in the big room was growing boisterous. This was how the feds would probably set things up before they lowered the boom. Another trick from the spy novels. Marilyn emerged from the bathroom, and Russell actually staggered backwards. "You're here with – her?"

"Why not? She's been mourning long enough."

He grimaced, and a heavy hand pounded down on my shoulder. I twirled. Cadwallader's face was in mine. "You brought her here? Are you crazy?"

Marilyn took a step, but green uniforms crowded between us, holding their coats open to block her from view of the ballroom.

Cadwallader had me by the collar, his whisper taut as a bowstring. "Get her home, now."

"She's my guest, Mr. Cadwallader."

"Damn it, George, you don't know what you're doing. Russell." He whipped out a ring of keys. "Take her."

"George?" Marilyn was clawing her way through the clogging GIs.

The Dauphin's fat fingers grappled, then dropped the keys. I pushed bodies away. "Leave her alone."

"Hurry."

More troops filled the space between us, and an officer gripped my arm, speaking coolly. "Mr. Blair, I'm Colonel Falk. We are both due in a meeting. Right now, sir. She'll be safe."

Cadwallader was in my ear. "Go with this man or Marilyn could be killed. They're looking for her."

"Why? There's no war anymore, goddam it."

He seethed. "Fool. The general already told you how important she is. If they get her, they win everything." The klatch of soldiers pressed me back, and my gaze met hers for an instant. The Dauphin was already tugging her away, and Boss jerked his chin at the colonel. "Send a squad with them. Give them plenty of ammo and a radio."

"Yes, Mr. President."

How did it happen? How on God's green earth did I let that moment slip through my fingers? I still ask myself that. I let her disappear behind a phalanx of GIs, mesmerized by the importance of the moment, fantasizing that I could protect her more by staying, believing Cadwallader's rigmarole in spite of the fact I knew all this was some sort of play-acting.

In the receiving line, Andrea squealed with delight and gave me a big wet kiss, flavored with tears and champagne. "Darling George, it's so good to see you. Save me a dance, dear one."

"You look lovely." I smiled, while Cadwallader's face started to regain its color. "Peace talks with a dance. Sort of novel, isn't it?"

"Stop being silly. This is General Grofsky," she said, introducing the first man to her right.

The man smiled. "She pronounces like a Russian," he said. "You are the man learning the weather processes, yes? Tomorrow, His Highness," he nodded toward Cadwallader, "is taking us to see football. It won't rain, will it?" Andrea found the remark uproariously funny.

"Arthur Bain, Lemco Tools." The chubby man next to Grofsky shoved a hand forward. Executives from Tiger Industrial, Avia Aeronautics, Combine Steel, every giant company in the country followed him in quick succession, all eager to shake my hand. Finally Andrea delivered the man I wanted to talk to.

"George, this is the Under-secretary of Defense of the United States, Rufus Hendershot."

I extended my hand.

"Oh-ho." Hendershot looked me up and down. "So you're the genius apprentice, eh?"

I pasted on a smile. "I need to talk to you, Mr. Hendershot. About amnesty."

Andrea elbowed between us. "The secretary will be glad to listen to your little secrets after the signing."

Hendershot shouted over his shoulder as she dragged him into the ballroom. "Congratulations, Blair. If that old faker got what he wanted, it's because of you. I'm honored to meet the guy who started all of this."

Andrea nudged him ahead. "Oh, Georgy didn't start anything, Mr. Secretary."

Colonel Falk took me the other way, to the far side of the big room. I had missed this room when I was here earlier, but the whole house had made quite a transformation during the afternoon. The walls were crowded with Cadwallader's heavy furniture, and the middle of the room had been filled with folding chairs, set around tables with white cloths, wine glasses and vases of flowers, all ringing a small dance floor.

The chairs were filling up, mostly with men in uniform. Around the room, though, the cotillion theme echoed. Crepe and garlands hung on drapes and walls and the refreshment table. A large sign sagged over the dance floor: "Welcome Robert McNamara," it said. The cheap decorations were Andrea's hand – if I squinted my eyes, I might have thought I was back in high school.

"I have to talk to Hendershot," I said, flushed with the sudden certainty that if I could get one sober ear from Washington that I might save Marilyn yet, but Falk shushed me with a move of his head and then motioned me to one of the front tables. The Under Secretary and Andrea stepped onto the makeshift platform in front of the band.

"Gentlemen." Hendershot raised a glass, as if he were on stage, and not about to dance with the most ambitious woman in Texas. "This is October, an important month to our friends from the U.S.S.R." A handful of drunks in the back cheered.

"October is a month for signing treaties." He produced a small notepad – my God, he was making a speech, and Andrea just hugged up against him, pinching his elbow, leering at the mustering audience. Hendershot read from the pad.

"It is my privilege to announce to all here top secret executive order number nineteen sixty-two slash one-one-niner-five, which decrees as follows: The proposed disarmament treaty between the United States and the Soviet Union, a treaty that would have reduced military forces on both sides by ninety percent, is hereby vacated.

"In its place, Rufus Hendershot – that's me – lieutenant to Secretary of Defense Robert McNamara, is hereby authorized to sign the Treaty of Balcones, which orders the forces calling themselves the Army of Balcones stand down and be re-assimilated into the United States Armed Forces, and which further requests the U.S.S.R. to remove their offensive weapons and reserves from the Peoples Republic of Cuba, and which further authorizes an increase in forces of the armies of the United States and the Soviet Union, by a measure of two divisions each. Signed, John F. Kennedy, President of the United States."

A whoop went up, and Andrea threw her arms around the Under-Secretary's neck. "Oh, Rufus." The uniforms rose to their feet, champagne glasses raised and quaffed.

I turned to Falk. "What just happened here?"

A grimace. "Boost in military spending. The Soviets and our government were going to make peace break out by gutting both militaries. But it would have left us both defenseless."

"So this rebellion was a ploy to protect the military?"

Now, a sheepish smile. "Well, the crisis presented an opportunity, so, uh, we sort of took it."

"OK." I kept my temper in check. "So what was this *crisis* that started it? Billy Dean's precious treasure?"

"Sorry, above my pay grade." The colonel smiled and headed for the bar. I remained, panting, wanting to scream. What was this infernal secret that everyone was protecting? I rose, and sidled toward Hendershot, hoping to get him out of Andrea's clutches.

I caught him at a table in the corner. "I need someone protected, Mr. Secretary." The band had cranked up loudly and he was already further under the weather than I had estimated. He slapped my shoulder and laughed out loud, bathing me in a cloud of gin vapor.

"Son, things are more complicated than that. We leave that sort of thing to the U.S. Marshal's office."

"But the local marshal's insane. The person I want to protect doesn't deserve to go to prison." I said it loudly. Heads turned, but Hendershot was unruffled.

"I know who you're talking about, son." He glanced at his watch. "Just relax. This will all be over soon." A grotesque smile. "They tell me you already did your duty, Mr. Weatherman." He laughed. Officers at the table laughed. Something was real funny, but I was already moving.

After one drink, I could still maneuver, but I knocked a waiter down on my way out. Guards swarmed the floor, and General Raven waved for me to halt. I socked him in the eye for good measure. Miraculously, that act caused the MPs to holster their pistols and back away from me in unison. Rather than wait for them to change their minds, I bolted through the wide front doors. If they hadn't already kidnapped Marilyn, Chris had left enough guns and ammo in the house to hold off a small army. That's just what I intended to do.

Chapter 42
The Death of Royalty

She was standing in the door, stone-faced, like she had been waiting for me all night. I felt a wave of relief. They didn't take her – but neither had any of Cadwallader's troops stuck around to protect her. Unless they were hiding in the cane. Something felt odd.

"I'm sorry--"

"Don't touch me." She couldn't have recoiled faster if I were a snake.

"Marilyn. I said I was sorry. I shouldn't have let that happen. They're coming. If Raven isn't chasing me, then Geary's probably out there in the weeds, watching us. We have to get the hell out. I don't know where, but the way that Defense guy acted, they'll be here tonight."

I heard her lock the door behind me, and by the time she made it to the back room, I had two suitcases out of the hall closet.

"Put those down and come to bed." Her movements slow, deliberate. She looked as tired as I felt.

"Darling, I'm not kidding. We have to go now."

"They're not coming. Get in bed."

"But you just said not to touch you."

"Get in bed and sleep. Just sleep, George. It'll be all right."

I did as she asked, but only long enough to plan where we might go, how I could write a letter to the bank, asking them to send a check – but where? I could slip it under the bank's front door on our way out of town. But did I have enough for a hotel? The next thing I knew, she was jarring me in the ribs.

"They're here. Hurry and get dressed," she said. Daylight crashed in, and the air filled with full-throated police sirens, a noise alien to these quiet river bottoms. I barely had my trousers on when banging on the door started.

"George, goddam it." Tudberry stormed into the living room, followed by deputies and blue-suited patrolmen.

"What are you doing here, Marshal?" He turned upon me with a look that would blacken melons on the vine. A deputy pushed Marilyn into a corner.

"Mrs. Ellis, we'd like to look at your husband's guns, if you don't mind." Her hands fell to her sides.

"I know where they are," Tudberry said, and led the parade of lawmen into the bedroom. Others combed the rest of the house, throwing stuff around. I pulled her out of the cop's grasp and hugged her. Then I stalked back to protest. Shotguns and rifles were spread out on the disheveled bed.

"What the hell's the matter, Marshal?" I asked.

He motioned me onto the back porch and fixed me with a grim gaze. "A farmer found Russell Crump's body out there in the Johnson grass an hour ago."

"Shit."My stomach tightened.

"Supposedly, he left the party with Marilyn. True?"

"Yes, sir. But she wouldn't--"

"Why didn't you take her?" The gray eyes bore into me.

"Cadwallader told Russell to. The army did it." I stormed out into the yard, trying to think. "That Geary jerk said they had her place staked out."

Tudberry followed, and punched a finger into my shoulder. "So you came home later? Did she say anything?"

"No, sir. She didn't kill him, and neither did I."

A sigh. "I know you didn't, George, but damn you, if you're gonna philander--" He shut up, then dug into his shirt pocket with a pencil. It came out, avoiding stray fingerprints: a bright yellow casing for a spent rifle shell.

"Thirty-ought-six?" I asked.

"Gotta test it, but I know damn well it's the same kind of bullet they killed Chris with. Same gun, too, I'll wager." He let me stare another moment. "We checked her shells – they're all that dull, copper color. Not bright like this one."

"Marshal, it's those goddam army guys. You know they were gunning for him."

A harsh look. "George, you swear she was in this house when you got home? And she didn't say anything?"

"That's exactly correct." My heart was sinking. He obviously didn't suspect her in Chris's murder, and of course the Dauphin tried to force himself on her when he brought her to the house. Probably convinced their army guard to am-scray, then made his move, and she simply dealt with it the same way she stopped her fake husband.

The other deputies filed out, combing every foot of yard space, but I doubted they would find anything. Marilyn was too smart. Before long, they were loading back into their cars. I touched the marshal's sleeve.

"Can't this all be over now?"

He shook his head, a helpless tone in his voice. "Russians ain't brought the booty yet." His car was the last to leave the driveway.

Marilyn emerged onto the back porch, and I walked her back to the bedroom. Without a word, she started leaning the rifles back into the closet corner, one-by-one. Then she turned on the shower. "I'm going to be busy tonight."

"Busy?"

"Yeah. Go home to your apartment, and call before you come back tonight. If I don't answer, I'm not here." The bathroom door was wide open, and she began to disrobe. I watched, holding onto the doorsill in the hall, because the floor was turning to quicksand.

"Busy with what, Marilyn?"

"I've changed my mind. I'm through with all this, George, and I don't have to tell you anything else."

Her underwear dropped, and she climbed in, leaving me alone. I paced the hall, but for only a few moments. I had had enough. I pulled the shower curtain open. "Damn it, who are you going out with? Oh, shit--"

She looked up from the wounds she was tending – bruises and cuts up and down her left side. "What in God's name?"

She jerked the curtain back in place, blocking me out. "I fell off the porch before you came home. Got a date tonight. Danny Stehl. He called last night."

"Danny Stehl? The lumberyard Danny Stehl?" Danny was two years ahead of me in school. A tough, known for getting in fistfights whenever he drank.

"His dad sold the lumberyard. They've got an appliance store now. I told you that you woke up the demon in me. I give up on ever going back."

My vision blurred. Just when part of me was starting to give credence to the whole bullshit scenario all of them had concocted, now the love of my life was declaring it over. I saw red. I had become Chris. "What brought this on?" I yelled, then got hold of myself. I opened the curtain, leaned over, my head full into the stream of water, and kissed one of the largest bruises on her hip. "Russell did this to you?"

"George, I'm going out tonight. You and I are not married."

"Then let's get married." My head pounded and my mouth tasted like stale champagne. She ignored me. I walked to the living room and flicked the television on, but couldn't stay in my seat. The expression look on Richard C. Hottolet's face prompted me to turn the sound up.

We have confirmation that Cuba has shot down a U-2 spy plane, he was saying. *Word on the fate of the pilot is still forthcoming, but this raises the level of tension between the United States and the Soviet Union, a tension that one State Department official described as "white-hot."*

I bellowed at the screen. "Haven't you heard they signed a treaty last night?" Hottolet smirked, as if he had heard me. I couldn't take any more, and I rushed the set and put my boot through the picture tube. Sparks and glass flew, starting a small fire on the carpet. I stomped it out, and pulled the plug.

"What was that, George?" she called out.

Then I saw it – right where the faded kitchen linoleum met the beige carpet of the living room – a stain, five or more inches at its greatest width. Brown, irregular, with a fringe of green Ajax cleaning powder. How could the cops have missed that? I knelt to touch it. Wet.

The shower was still full-blast. I moved through the kitchen, back to her closet. Her shirts, but mostly Chris's clothes and boots. Then the arsenal. I started with the shell boxes. But they had just looked through those. I stuck my fingers into a pair of boots. Then I looked up – a trap door, identical to the one in my apartment closet.

I hustled to the kitchen and grabbed a chair. Atop it, I could just peer into the attic. My hand hit something. Cold metal. A rifle, with grabs of insulation all around it. Then pay dirt. A box of shells. I heard the water turn off with a squeak, but I had to get the top off.

I struck gold – bright, yellow shells, brothers and sisters of the one from Tudberry's pocket. There went any hope of denying it. But how did Tudberry keep those trained officers from looking in such an obvious place? Did he know this in advance? Did these suckers know the future and the past? I took one of the bullets, retraced my steps, and was drinking orange juice in the kitchen when she came in, wrapped in a towel.

"What did you and Russell talk about last night?"

She must have started coffee when the police were here. A grimace as she poured a cup. "Chris bought me that TV." She sat, and pulled her hair back. "You don't have to play dumb anymore. I've killed two human beings now, just saving myself for you. No more. If I start sleeping around, as you moderns call it, then maybe this whole nightmare will unravel."

"And what about the time loop?"

"I don't care anymore. Russell I didn't mind so much. He was scum, and he cheated on Elizabeth before. I just know it. But Chris – he was a real person. He didn't deserve to die."

"How did you drag that fat body out of the house?"

She bit her lip. "I shot him in the leg, to get him away from me. Then I ran out to my castle keep. He followed. I feel sick." She clutched her stomach and ran to the bathroom.

The sound of her retching filled the house. I took a deep breath and sat down. A real cop would figure the best way for her to turn herself in, but I was thinking how we could cover it up. My corruption was complete, but the phone rang before I could fully grasp that thought.

The telephone crackled, and a voice spoke from far away. "George. Tudberry. I had 'em patch the radio through. There's trouble. Part of the rebel army won't surrender. General Collins has taken over the ninth and eighty-third divisions. They're marching on the holdouts in the woods near Landview. There's gonna be a fight."

"Landview? Jesus. Is Cadwallader's mother still down there? What about Rebecca?"

He didn't answer – only crackling.

"What about the Russians?"

He yelled, barely audible over the straining of his old car's engine. "They're on high alert. George. I'll need you to meet me out there."

"Hell, no," I said. "Let the army get them. I'm finished with this shit, and so is Marilyn."

"No, you're not finished. Because the rebels' commander is that goddam Lieutenant Geary. If we can get you in his face, make it personal, we might have a better chance." The phone froze in my hand.

"George, they have nuclear weapons that are primed and ready to go, remember? Bring whatever weather equipment Billy Dean gave you. Meet me in Brownwood. That's the staging area. Leave now, dammit. We gotta pull out all the stops to recover this fumble."

I realized I wasn't past caring for that man, but for once, I thought about me first. "No, Marshal. I'm not coming."

Silence. Then, like the perfect strategist he was, he turned the tables. "George, a new federal warrant for Marilyn was issued as of this morning. You said you wanted to take her somewhere safe. Well, now she's killed Russell. You and I both know it, and pretty soon, the DA will, too. If you want to save her, this will be your only chance. Savvy? Bring her with you. That's an order."

He had me. I laid the phone down, and went into the bathroom. She wasn't there, but I found her in the bedroom doing a turn in front of the mirror, wearing a freshly pressed calico dress.

"Get some blue jeans on," I said. "Call Danny Stehl and tell him you can't make it tonight. I love you, and I'm going to prove it by marrying you. If you want sex so much now, I'll give you all you can handle."

She looked up, maybe considering, maybe giving up on everything. Then she blushed, and covered her eyes. "See what a fool I am? It's started, and here I am thinking I could just escape."

"Marilyn, change your clothes, and get ready. The marshal needs us. I have a feeling this is coming to a head – but you already know that, don't you?"

Another look in the mirror, then she reached into the closet and extracted a smaller suitcase I had never seen before. She gripped it in one hand, turned and faced me primly, as if posing for a picture.

"I'm sorry for what I said, George. It's OK. I think Danny expects I won't show up, anyway." She picked up her purse, thrust the suitcase toward me. "I packed it last night."

She held my hand all the way to the car.

Chapter 43
Santa Ana

"My God." Marilyn pointed when we crested a rise in Brownwood. In the opposite lane, army vehicles were strung down the highway for as far as the eye could see, engines quiet, standing still. I pulled her close to me when we rolled up to the first roadblock, but the reception was friendly. The GI even refused to study my license. "You can go on through, Mr. Blair. It's a schoolyard. A mile into town this way."

"Thanks. Why aren't you guys moving?" I asked.

"They said stand in place when that company broke away. Might be some shootin'."

Tanks surrounded a school playground, and a jeep pulled out in front of us, and led to where a large tent was surrounded by cafeteria tables stacked with papers and automatic weapons. Billy Dean sat between two soldiers on a truck gate, smoking a cigarette.

"Hey, Hot Shot. I'll bet you didn't bring your bag, did you?" His own colored purse hung under his arm.

I gave him a thumbs-up, and opened the trunk. Next to Rebecca's leather pouch lay the gun. My breath caught – I had been sober when I left the party last night, and never went back to the soldiers to claim the pistol.

When I rose, I noted the strangest look on Marilyn's face. Of course, she was the only female within a mile, and the eye of every GI who wasn't occupied by equipment was focused right on her calico dress.

Billy Dean noticed it, too, and let out with a crude laugh. "Marilyn, doll, you look like either a scared rabbit or a little girl in a candy store. Which is it?" She said nothing, but tightened her grip on my arm.

The top brass were huddled over a card table behind the pitcher's mound of the school baseball diamond. General Raven gave me a curt nod in spite of his swollen eye, and Marshal Tudberry emerged from their midst and shook my hand. "I knew we could count on you, George."

Out near second base, Emil Cadwallader stood alone, gazing toward the southern horizon. An officer was rattling information to Raven. "Just got word of more defections. They're losing troops."

Billy Dean craned his neck to look at my car. "Think your jalopy can make it to Landview, Hot Shot?"

A commotion out on the perimeter prevented my reply. "White flag," voices said.

Two jeeps rolled in under white banners, both packed with armed men. The second had a trooper mounted behind a fifty caliber machine gun. "Let 'em come," Raven said.

They came to a stop in left field and, like Santa Ana's minion giving the Alamo defenders their last chance, Lt. Geary himself stood up in the jeep, and unfurled a scroll. He began to read in a loud voice. Marilyn pulled close to my ear. "George, I'm afraid this is a trap. I don't want it to happen."

I whispered. "What? Nuclear war?"

"They're going to separate us. I'm not sure what happens to you. They never really explained what will happen to you. You can still run." She panted, the blue of her eyes seeming to shrink.

I wrapped my arm around her. "Stop talking about me in the past tense. I'm here, this is now, and they're not taking you away."

The idiot lieutenant was preaching about the potentials the nation of Balcones might have if it were not betrayed. He pledged amnesty for all troops present. The revolution must proceed. Raven interrupted.

"Lieutenant, surrender your nukes and we can talk."

"No, sir, General. I demand that you admit to your troops that Kennedy's precious blockade screwed up and let a ship through, and that ship landed at Aransas Pass just a few hours ago. Russians are on Texas soil this very instant."

"What you say is true." Raven half-goose-stepped into the outfield, looked around at the troops, maybe sizing them up, then spoke loudly over their murmuring. "But the Russians are just coming here to watch your surrender."

Geary threw down his scroll and pointed. "You're a goddam traitorous dog, Raven. That commie is on his way to give you your marching orders. The nation of Balcones will never surrender." The jeep revved, throwing him down into his seat, and they sped off. A wave from the general let them escape the playground.

To my astonishment, he turned to the weatherman, rather than to his senior officers. "That bastard's down to less than a hundred men, Billy Dean. He won't withstand another night of artillery."

The weatherman clicked his tongue. "Maybe so. But if they're still shooting up Landview, what's the point? I go back with the same ones I came with." He threw his smoke down and stepped on it. "You ready, Hot Shot? We've got some citizens of dear old Mexico to rescue."

"Mexico?" I blurted. Marilyn dug her nails into my arm, and I looked at her, but she seemed beyond speaking. "Why do we have to go, Billy Dean? That's the army's job."

"They see more army, they're gonna fire the rockets, George," Tudberry said.

I felt a pressure in my head, and just the sight of the lawman made me see red. "So what, Marshal? You said you would help me get her out of here."

Raven was muttering instructions to a couple of officers, while Cadwallader turned on second base, and walked straight toward me. He seemed suddenly older, sweat on his forehead, one hand shaking.

"This is it, George Blair," he said. "Federal troops have reached Abilene on their way to arrest us. Down south, they're getting ready to launch missiles on Washington. This is your moment. You gotta go. Lots of people counting on you."

The glum faces punctuated his words, and the bodies around us began to move, like a crowd of hopeful fans, shuffling us toward the cars. Marilyn took my hand, and Billy Dean tugged playfully at the strap of my leather bag. "Got your red stuff? By God, we'll see if their ICBMs can float." He waved me toward my own vehicle. "Two cars. One of us has to get through."

He gunned his engine and pulled away first. I followed, with Marilyn hugging tight to my side. As we passed, General Raven came to attention and saluted.

Chapter 44
Rooble

Billy Dean drove hell-bent-for-leather, and I did my best to follow him, scrambling along roads old and new toward Landview, swerving sometimes down shortcuts huge military treads had cut into the prairie. How Billy Dean knew which ones to take, I had no idea. Always in the back of my mind: I would hit the highway, bypass Landview entirely, and take her to Mexico.

"Thank you for not making me stay there," she said, lying across the bench seat, pressing against my shoulder. "I'm supposed to be in Landview with you."

Chilly yellowed ranchland extended in all directions, and the effect of her words was even colder. "Quit talking like them, Marilyn. There is no pre-destination. There's only the love between us."

She gripped my leg, a jittery bundle of fear, yet her excitement was unmistakable, too. "But it's like he said, George. Everything has happened, just like he said – one-two-three. Maybe it's not a dream, after all."

"Marilyn, calm down. Quit worshiping at the altar of Billy Dean. We have our life to live. You and me. Right after this stupid revolt is over."

I took a hard turn, trying to keep the weatherman's sedan in sight, and she stretched up, and buried her face in my neck. "George, I know I've been having unholy thoughts. But I don't want to lose you. I promise."

A wave of warmth surged up inside me. But she retreated, just as quickly, and settled for holding my hand.

"Just remember I said those words."

We hit scattered groupings of jeeps and tanks, but no one impeded us. I expected roadblocks, anyway, and I knew that at any second, Kennedy's troops could rush around the bend and take us both to prison. She watched the road ahead like an excited little girl.

"There's no real reason for me to trust Tudberry anymore." A notion took root – her goal was finally the same as mine. "But maybe he'll come through. I know I can get a job in Mexico, and work my way up. I won't let them take you from me."

She blinked, as if I were speaking a foreign language. "But if they do, just don't forget to come get me."

"Prince Charming won't forget."

With the sun dodging clouds on the western horizon, we crested a hill and I thought we had indeed traveled back in Time – to World War II. The valley beneath us lay dotted with scorched tanks and trucks, too numerous to count. Smoke still rose from those metal corpses. This battle had to be recent, and it was obvious that the Army of Balcones had finally met a foe on the field – Americans fighting Americans. The sight of GIs and bodies being carried on stretchers, and the oily, burning smoke invaded the windows and made me want to puke. Marilyn dozed against my arm.

On top of the next hill, Billy Dean flashed his lights. I pulled over, disoriented, but only for a second. This was Landview. The roof of waves lay crashed-down into the market tables beneath it. A shambles. The depot stood in one piece, pocked by bullet holes and scorch marks, as did hotel number three. The first and second hotels, though, had been reduced even more than before – into huge piles of what Billy Dean would call *rooble.*

"Christ, Billy Dean, why did they pick here to fight?" I asked him when our vehicles stood side by side. The orange ball was disappearing on the horizon, and clouds had begun to growl above us, dropping sprinkles. The weatherman didn't answer, only smoked. He seemed stunned, but in a quiet, coyote way that made my skin crawl. A handful of men came out of the remaining hotel.

"Hells bells. They got bodies." Billy Dean ran his hands through greasy hair, and I saw what he meant. The well-dressed men were lifting three obviously human bodies, wrapped in sheets.

"Oh, no." Marilyn's hand tightened around mine.

"Shit," I said. "What if one of those is Cadwallader's mom?"

"Don't look at them, Hot Shot. Look at that." The southern slope of Landview's promontory fell away in a forest of mesquite. Perhaps a mile or two distant, the ominous nose of a missile stuck up above the scrub trees, gleaming orange in the dying sun.

"My God."

Billy Dean pulled Marilyn from my grip before I could react. "We're in a hurry, College Boy. They've let us come this far, but I'll bet a case of hooch they've got a few boys aiming at us from that tree line. Go get your gear and make sure Rebecca's not in her tree house. Search the whole thing."

He kissed Marilyn's hand as they hustled away. "You think you can come help me look after the wounded, Darlin'?" She let him drag her, glancing back helplessly.

"I'll be right there," I yelled.

I retrieved the gun and leather bag, and waded into the sharp splinters and glass of the tree house wreckage. The two higher floors had been blackened by fire, but remained intact.

A rumble froze me in my tracks – not artillery, but the clouds that towered above the scene like fantastical mountains.

I picked my way through pots, pans, books and sticks, finally winding up at the ladder – also more scorched than before. I called out. "Rebecca?" The sharp smell of burnt wood made me cough until I spat. I climbed.

"Rebecca?" The second floor surrounded me like a cave – empty, its few chairs and small tables had been upended. A loud *creak* from the floor above startled me, and I almost lost my grip. Then silence – only the sound of growing rain. Again I climbed. "Rebecca Flock-of-Birds?"

"Freeze, Mr. Minister of Science."

In the dim light, Lt. Geary was poised, one arm around Rebecca's waist. Her eyes were wide. A gesture, and I quit the ladder for the slanting floor of the third level. "I know you're carrying that pea shooter," he said. "Take it out and toss it down that hole."

I met Rebecca's gaze, wondering if she were capable of struggling if I gave the signal. But she was too scared, and Geary knew what he was doing. With minute movements, I dropped the pistol through the ladder hatch. It *clacked* into the rubble on the ground just as a rush of rain started on the roof in earnest.

Geary grimaced, and made the walkie-talkie on his belt screech to life. "Hey, Dexter, do you read me?" He left the radio on his belt, pressing the button with his gun hand and yelling to be heard. I didn't get the feeling he was here for hostages.

"Yes, sir," Dexter answered.

"We are go and go for launch," Geary said.

"Go and go." Electric chatter, but Geary wasn't interested. "Got one more assignment for you, Mr. Minister. But you won't get out of this one. Go down there and tell Brown I have her. Tell him to stay away from this tree, and that she's dead if he doesn't send you back with the treasure. Both parts. Tell him that, exactly."

"Treasure?"

"Don't play stupid. Both parts. Either I get his whole weather machine, or she dies."

A flash outside lit the scene from below. Then a crash of thunder – rain started pelting the outer walls. I looked at Rebecca, but she shook her head, almost imperceptibly. As I put one foot on the ladder, I noticed it led all the way up to the ceiling, and there, though I never saw it before, was a trapdoor almost identical to the one Billy Dean had taken me through last time, in the first hotel's roof. The Russians weren't here yet, so the weatherman didn't have both halves of the battery, but there was no convincing Geary of that. A diversion was necessary, but would likely earn me a bullet in the back.

One more look into Rebecca's eyes. I thought I saw her permission, and took a deep breath. I patted the bag under my arm. "Here. You want this stuff, instead?"

"Shut up and do what I say, Blair."

Another blast in the sky, and Dexter's panicky voice raked the radio. "Enemy patrol spotted at zero-nine-zero. How long do you want the countdown?"

Hand on the button. "Idiot. Ten minutes. Follow procedure. Haven't you started it yet? Report distance of that patrol. Deal with the situation, for God's sake." Geary sneered at me. "That's all the time you have, Mr. Minister. Run."

Rebecca's eyes widened, and she gestured upwards with her eyebrows. She had read my mind. A new flash flared through the ladder-hole below my feet, half-blinding me. Geary, too. I made my moved to match the thunder. "Yes, sir." I gripped the steps and climbed.

"Goddam it," Geary screamed. "What are you doing?"

The surprise was enough. I was up, and through the trapdoor in two great vaults. I don't know what I expected to do, once I was on the roof – and, looking back, I don't know why I wasn't more surprised: maybe I somehow expected to be standing on the deck of one of the great cloud ships, for that's where I found myself. A wet spray came over the side, and I grabbed the railing, and yelled downward through the hole. "Come up and get me, Lieutenant."

"Hey, fucker. Don't you understand they're going to launch?" It didn't matter. Up here was my only chance. Lightning crackled through the sky, and the great cloud sails billowed above me. This ship's monster pilot was invisible – behind the cabin, perhaps, or wherever they go. But what would I do if Geary didn't take the bait? I heard Rebecca's voice, but couldn't decipher it.

"We're coming up," the soldier said.

I crouched, knowing he would expect an attack. But I was ready. A boot to the face might end this whole thing. Focused on the hatch, I went through the catalogue of moves they taught me at the academy, even tricks we made up fighting imaginary Germans in childhood. The key was to empty the mind, and act like it was your last moment on Earth. Hell, it probably was.

A motion caught my eye, and the misshapen giant at the ship's helm moved into view. I had no idea how I had suddenly started this dream, but the sight of that great, ugly face erased all that – this was another world, and the dull, sharp gleam in the monster's eye gave me a strange hope – let me die, it didn't matter – this guy was in charge up here, and he would take care of Geary. The words my grandfather had whispered on his deathbed came back to me: There were worse places to die than this.

Chapter 45
The Battle of Landview

"Goddam you, Blair."

Taking short, silent breaths, I crouched low, putting all my chips on one kick. I expected a rush, gun-first – but Rebecca came through the opening. I signaled to her, and she wisely didn't flinch. Then Geary's hand, gripping her ankle. He took two rungs quickly, and had the gun pointed at me before I could move. I retreated automatically, acting contrite, and nodded my head, hoping he would look at the monster.

Bolts of electricity crossed the sky, flaring the boards of the broad deck, making them look like hard wood, and illuminating every blemish on his angry face. His mouth fell open, eyes wide, obviously dazed by the surroundings. I kicked him solidly in the head. He disappeared down through the trap door instantly, and the crash of his weight shuddered the structure – or maybe the ship had hit a wave. I grabbed Rebecca's arm. "Hurry." I dragged her forward through the spray, straight for the stand of ninepins.

"You're crazy." She wrenched out of my grasp, then took my face in her two hands. "We're not safe here. Clear your mind and come with me. The captain will take care of us."

A screeching noise shut her up – Geary's walkie-talkie. We looked back in unison. He already stood on the deck, pointing the gun. "You bastard. You're wasting fucking time. There's no way down from here. What kind of roof is this?"

I shoved Rebecca behind the ninepins at the same instant he pulled the trigger. The bullet whizzed over my head.

"No." Rebecca cried out, too late. She stumbled into a pin, and couldn't stop its fall. A blast of thunder knocked us all off our feet, and when I regained my footing, I saw the Thor captain moving down the bridge steps, his fiery gaze fixed on me. Geary was down, too, scrambling for his pistol.

"He's coming," Rebecca said.

"Distract him. I'll lure the soldier over here."

She gave me a horrific look. "To be near the pins is death, George Blair."

Geary stalked toward us, ignoring the screeching calls on his radio, but he faltered when he glanced over the rail. Below us, clouds, and dusk failing over the vast Texas ranchlands. His face registered bafflement, and he straightened up, finally taking stock of the legions of ships that spread out in all directions around us, each one spitting lightning and rumbling as if powered by colossal motors. He glanced at me from the corner of his eye, gun limp in his hand. "Where the fuck are we?"

Billy Dean's voice bellowed out of the ether. "Use your Thor's Blood, George. They're about to launch."

I ducked behind the end-pin. Rebecca had disappeared, but across the deep chasm below, Billy Dean perched precariously on the railing of another ship – perhaps fifty yards off our port side. His arm was looped around a gossamer streamer of rigging, and in one hand he gripped a quartz rod. In the other fist, a lump of the red clay. "Throw your Thor's blood into the rain," he yelled.

"Fuck you, weatherman." Geary grappled across the rolling deck to the railing, and fired the gun repeatedly across the abyss. *Click. Click.* He was out of bullets, but the damage was done. I saw Billy Dean fall backwards, and only then did Marilyn appear, rushing out from behind the cabin of their ship. She caught him in her arms, and dragged him back, away from the rail.

Geary wheeled to face me, shoving new cartridges into the revolver.

"He's going to throw, George." Rebecca's voice came out of the air, and I could see the Thor raise his sizzling pitchfork at the same instant Geary rushed me. I dodged through the ninepins.

"Come get me, Lieutenant."

Geary followed, yelling above the radio noise. "You're too late, Hit-man. Because of you, Washington is going to be a cinder."

"Run, George," Rebecca screamed.

I grabbed one of the huge pins with both hands, and slid it sideways, right into his path. He raised the gun. I turned and ran, and prayed.

We hit a wave. The pistol discharged. I heard the bullet whine, and went stumbling toward Rebecca. She caught me at the starboard rail, just as the lightning pitchfork struck the pins. The sky whited-out, and we rolled, grabbing for anything solid. I threw myself over Rebecca's legs, trying to keep us both from flying over the rail. When we stopped, I looked back – pins lay scattered over the deck. No Geary.

Rebecca was gasping. "He's over the side." I backed up to the rail, and watched the great, fallen pins dissolve, just before a new set of nine began to grow up from the deck.

"Hurry, George." This time, Marilyn's voice. I rose, staggered across the deck. The giant was picking a new pitchfork, so we had to hurry. Marilyn waved from the other cloud ship, yelling through cupped hands. "He said to use the blood now."

"I can't see," I answered, blinking my eyes to dispel the white and yellow circles that filled my vision. I pulled clumps of newspaper out of the bag, while a light rain fell, making it even harder to separate paper and clay.

"Over there." Rebecca leaned over the rail, gesturing. I squinted. Dark shadows had taken over the landscape below, pierced only by bright military lights in a single location, framing ominous pointed shapes. Two missiles. I tasted bile.

I waved at Marilyn. "What do I do?"

She bent down, disappearing. Obviously, Billy Dean was down on the deck, still able to give her instructions. She reappeared and called out. "Pull off little bits of the blood and throw them into the rain."

Rebecca looked past me. "Do what she says. I'll stop *him*."

The giant was advancing behind us, perhaps finally pissed at our invasion. I hunkered against the side while she curtsied in front of the growling monster and whipped her dress off in one motion.

"Look. Fire, George." Marilyn yelled.

On the distant ground, a small flame had sprouted. "Launch," I cried. "Damn it."

Rain came down in sheets now, swirling down from the turbulent air above our ship. I pinched off thumb-sized clumps of the clay and threw them furiously overboard. I kept throwing, but they were worthless pieces of dirt, and the missile was no longer a harmless pencil in the gloom, but a dagger, growing as it approached us. "The clay's not working. What's supposed to happen?" I yelled.

Marilyn didn't have to answer. As the pencil of fire climbed, the falling pieces of Thor blood started to sizzle as they mixed with raindrops. Now they were hot coals, spewing sparks. I kept pinching, throwing. Below, the ground lit up with tracer bullets, and I knew the American troops were making an assault, but too late to stop the terrifying ICBM, and whatever city it was pointed at would be a killing field in a matter of minutes. But the sparks from the clay kept spitting, swelling, growing into tiny campfires. "My God, they're joining together," I yelled.

"Don't stop, Hot Shot," Billy Dean's voice came through the air.

"Work, goddam it," I screamed, not really sure what I expected the sparks to do now.

Yes, they were joining, swirling, until they resembled a cloud of lightning bugs, growing exponentially, swelling like a balloon. Their hissing paled against the rocket's roar – now the weapon was pulling as high as our ship, and tipping over, turning, I was sure, for its trip to Washington – or Havana.

My chunk of clay was small now, and in my panic, I flung the whole thing into the deluge – the ball exploded like a bomb, merged with the other cloud of light, and I instinctively knew what it became, though it was the stuff of legends only: ball lightning. The rocket arced ahead of it, but the lightning ball rolled, and rose on the wind.

It cleared the tall ship's masts at the same time the nuke did. The lightning ball spread out like a blanket now, tracking the missile as surely as a hound runs after a quail. The blanket of fire-lightning struck, drawing a curtain around the streaking missile, blinding everything, shielding the weapon from view. Not a curtain, but the swirling walls of a tornado took shape as I tried to watch through shielded eyes. The twister's cone drew tighter, and the plume from the missile's tail disappeared into it.

Automatically, I braced for the nuclear blast, locking my arms over the rail for dear life. The storm could not have been a mile away, but it only swirled, lilted, and bounced in the wind like a rubber ball. The cyclone raised its tip, but still the blast didn't come.

Then, slowly, a glow lit up the inside – not an explosion, but a warm, yellow-white flare. If that was the nuke, it had been tamed. I thought back to Billy Dean's description of a tornado's heart, bracing again for the inevitable blast. But the sky filled only with a steady roar – like that of a locomotive rushing headlong down a track. When I looked again, the tornadic coils spun out like a top, lost cohesion, and flew apart into strips of white-gray that threatened no one.

I turned toward Rebecca, afraid of what I might see, but the giant was kneeling, only a foot or two away from her. Before I could figure out how to pull her away from there, Marilyn's voice called out again. "The other one, George."

Back to the rail – yes, the second pencil below was lit, and rutting into the air. I threw up my hands. "Tell him I'm out of clay," I screamed. Then I realized – Rebecca –

I turned to see her standing there, a vision of radiant nakedness in the lightning flashes. The creature still knelt behind her, and when she extended her hands, I saw she had collected a whole new ball of the stuff, still warm to the touch. I snatched the mass, and started throwing.

Like a valiant roman candle, this missile reached for a lone patch of stars in a break in the clouds above us. I peeled bigger chunks off, hurling them ahead of it. Sparks caught on the wind, showered back on us, and down the side of the boat.

This time, they gathered more quickly, like a swarm of furious bees looking for somewhere to go. "Make a tornado, damn it," I cried to the firmament, and tossed out the last of the blood. The wind whistled shrilly, and the clouds sucked together into a swirl.

"You're doing it, George." Even from this distance, I could see that Marilyn was smiling.

It was true – the twirling clouds had already formed a black vortex – with a roar that once again blotted out the noise of the wind and the rocket, the cyclone rose rapidly above the ship until I could look directly up through the point of its cone. This time, I saw the demon cloud's heart clearly, smaller than the lighting ball the sparks had created, but brighter. This twister seemed even more energetic than its predecessor, and poised above the soaring missile like an eagle flapping over a pool of fish, picking its target carefully.

Rebecca nudged against me, and my arm went around her waist. We watched together as the angry funnel struck at the roman candle. A flash. A *boom*. We rocked, and I tried to keep my footing, but wound up tangled with Rebecca on the cold deck, half blinded.

"Did the nuke explode?" I asked her.

She pointed forward. Pins were falling every which way. The Thor captain reached for another fork. The blast was only the monster at his game.

Chapter 46
The Dream of Children

When the Thor captain turned away, I staggered to the opposite cloud railing. Tracer bullets still marked one area of the ground, but racing clouds prevented me from seeing whether any more nukes were ready to launch. I prayed there were not. Marilyn's ship had moved well away, and neither she nor the weatherman was visible. Perhaps she was tending to his wound, or maybe they had descended back through the trapdoor leading into the top of hotel three. I tried to think of a physics that would allow these moving clouds to stay connected to stationary landmarks on the ground – I would have to figure that out another time. Back over the rail, the rolling hills of Texas had come alive with floodlights that illuminated soldiers scrambling into the trees.

Rebecca stifled an embarrassed laugh, and tried to cover herself with her hands when I looked down at her. "One must bare herself only when one volunteers to lighten the Thor's sorrow," she said. "The clay is their sorrow, the rain their tears. When the two touch, it turns to anger. That is the stuff of storms. Well, that and the bowling games." The captain bowled another frame, but this blast only ruffled her hair. "You must learn to bare yourself to them, too," she said. "Their sorrow is not so different from ours."

She fetched her dress, and put it on.

"I hope Billy Dean's all right," I said.

She peered over at their cloud schooner, then stepped down onto the ladder. "They will meet us on the ground." She squeezed my hand. "Praise to the Grandfathers, our time of waiting is almost over. Because of you, George Blair."

Compared to the cloud ship, the third floor of her treehouse now felt solid as a rock. Time must have passed, because fingers of daylight poked through the cracks in the walls. How long did that battle take?

Before she could step back onto the ladder, I took her in my arms. "Rebecca, I could love you, do love you, but Marilyn – she'll be back, won't she?"

She giggled, then stretched up to whisper in my ear. Her hair smelled of lavender. "You have two lovers, my sweet, ignorant man of the future. Yes, my sister is your destiny, but you will always have my love, too, even though I must go back home. The other night, I had the dream. We have done what we were ordained to do. The one thing greater than love is obedience to the grandfathers."

"Some on, Rebecca, all this being mesmerized by Billy Dean's little quest has got to stop. He might be dead now, for all we know, so maybe you aren't going anywhere. What dream did you have?"

"The dream of children. It comes to any woman in my tribe when they are with child. I had it the night we made love. I am carrying your baby, George Blair."

"That's scientifically impossible. It can't happen that fast."

"I'm sorry to jeopardize your world view, my love, but the dream of children is never wrong." She smiled, kissed each of my eyelids, then climbed down the ladder. On her way, she glanced back up. "Victor will thank you for this," she said.

"Who the hell is Victor, anyway?" I called after her. Then, I panicked, not knowing what our next move was, if Billy Dean were actually dead. "You don't have to go with him," I cried out. "Stay here. I want you both."

She stopped, a few rungs above the ground, and laughed. "No, my love. A strange man came for me when I was only a girl. My family came here with me. I would have run home, but my home was long gone. Then the old Boss paid us money, assured us we still had a chance to return, and we were told the stories, the prophecies that have now come to pass.

"You have come to pass, George Blair. For once in your life, recognize your own strength. You are a man who can call the tornados."

Chapter 47
Laws of Physics

We climbed down the ladder into the ruins of her house in harsh morning light. "Ahoy." Billy Dean sat on a hillock of grass across the road. His bandaged arm was in a sling, but he rose, and advanced to the edge of the debris to help us out. On the hotel lawn, a cheer went up. I gazed at the heretofore-invisible citizens of Landview – they were clad in formal Mexican attire, like a rich family going to a fiesta.

Gray and heavy clouds were now scattered in a blue sky. I bent over and pulled Russell Crump's pistol from its resting place on the muddy ground, next to a broken porcelain doll.

"Good job, Hot Shot," Billy Dean said. "You really accounted for yourself this time. Old Cadwallader will hire you for a hundred years. *Have weather, will change it,* that's your motto. Paladin of the goddam skies. You'll have better ratings than that Jethro on Channel Nine, for sure."

"They just winged you?"

"Yeah. Marilyn patched me up as good as any sawbones. Bullet's still in there, but I'm too busy to get it fixed now."

Marilyn came striding across the wide lawn, and I met her halfway. A deep hug, but no kiss, as if she had heard

Rebecca's claims of maternity. Billy Dean and Rebecca exchanged silent messages with their eyes. Hell, the whole town knew.

"You OK?" Marilyn asked.

"I guess." She let me take her hand.

"You still want to come get me?"

I shook my head. "I won't have to, Marilyn, because I'll never leave your side, no matter what happens."

She smiled, and we walked. "I know a guy named George," she said, "who has learned much, but still needs to learn the thing that is lacking most in his scary new world."

Her tone frightened me somehow. "What do I need to learn?"

"Patience."

When the four of us neared the hotel, various townspeople took turns slapping my back and shaking hands. "Congratulations," one little old lady said.

"So what now?" I asked the weatherman. "Is all this shit finally over?"

Billy Dean regarded me with one eye. "Hells bells, College Boy, I forget we sometimes have to drop a house on you. I'm going back to Mexico to take these good people home. You did your part, so now I'm a free agent. We're just waiting on those Russkies to remember not to double cross me."

"Senor Brown, a car." More cheers rose spontaneously.

"That'll be the general now." I had never seen Billy Dean's grin so wide. He snapped his fingers with his good hand. "And hot damn, he's got a special guest."

As we watched the vehicle approach, a line formed – the clean, eager citizens lugging baggage down toward the old depot. Guillermo broke out of the parade and grabbed my hand. "Senor George, it was a pleasure to know you. We will enjoy telling our friends about the crazy Gringo college scientist who disproved the laws of physics, and won a glorious battle." His big mitt almost crushed my fingers.

Several others joined in his laughter, until four men came, hoisting a moldy, scarred casket – it had obviously been taken out of the ground. I shivered, but Billy Dean was waiting for my glance. "We only lost one in all these years. Three more in the shelling the other day. Gotta take 'em all back, one way or t'other."

Rebecca was on the hotel steps, pulling clothes out of a steamer trunk, stuffing the ones she chose into a suitcase. I wanted her again, badly. Yet, she seemed already to have separated from me, smiling and embracing the townspeople, talking in excited Spanish. One of her kinsmen carried the case for her, and she came down the hill and threw her arms around me.

"I will never forget you, George Blair of the future. I will make sure your son is prosperous, and a leader of men." She gently kissed the palm of my left hand, my lips, then she took my right hand and boldly pressed it to her breast. I could feel her heart beating rapidly. She looked away, and fell into line. The citizens were almost uncontrollably festive.

"Rebecca." I called after her, but Marilyn's hand was hot in mine, and just as I squeezed it harder, she pulled away, and started to pace a short circle on the grass. Her face was wan, and when I caught her, and tried to put my arm around her, she only gripped my bicep. "It's happening, George. We're really going."

There were of course no train tracks, no matter what these well-meaning yokels had planned. I imagined some army transports were on the way to pick them up. The whole atmosphere was confusing, like a cult of worshipers getting ready for the Second Coming. But I had made up my mind. I took her hand, and approached Billy Dean.

"I'm not letting her go," I said. "I'll come back to my senses and shake off this stupid hypnotism, or whatever you've done to me. Go wherever you want with these poor people, but Marilyn stays with me."

The weatherman winked. "It don't work like that, Hot Shot. I only told you a hunnert times. She came with us. She goes back. I didn't make the rules. Besides," he gestured, "let's see what the general says about your notion."

The roaring car stopped just short of the baggage line, and familiar forms piled out. "Well, I'll be damned." Marshal Tudberry crowed, and slapped his hat on the front fender. "You boys sure got their number last night."

The young GI in the driver's seat stayed put, but Cadwallader and Raven ambled forward. They were followed by two more figures – both wearing similar odd uniforms, their breasts covered with medals. The stouter man was all smiles. At my side, I could feel Billy Dean tense up.

"This is General Barsukov, of the Soviet Army," Raven said. The depot line wavered, broke, and the citizens formed a large circle around us. "He has something to give you, Billy Dean."

With actions more in keeping with a harried suit salesman at Golden's than an ominous Soviet officer, the Russian general stepped up, and his companion hustled after him, and held up a briefcase and opened it like a servant, even though his own shoulder epaulets were appointed in brass.

The higher ranking officer seemed nervous, gave a little smile, and his hands shook through his fanfare. He extracted a wooden box from the briefcase. With shaking fingers, he opened that small box, and pulled out a smaller glass case.

"With the compliments," Barsukov bowed once more, "of the people of the Soviet Union." He beamed while he raised the glass box, displaying it for everyone present, like some Soviet athlete might show off an Olympic medal.

Billy Dean stood stone-faced while *oohs* and *aahs* escaped the crowd. Visible through the glass, a small greenish moon, a thick disc about the diameter of a dime, glowed like dials of a radium watch. An unearthly light in full sunlight, it took on an eerie glow when a cloud bathed us in shadow. Barsukov placed the glass case into the weatherman's outstretched palm.

The Russian licked his lips as he watched Billy Dean study it, then suddenly snapped to attention, clicked his heels, and saluted. "Sergeant Brown, as requested, we have restored your property to you. The Supreme Soviet, the Soviet Academy of Sciences, and the Soviet Army hereby relinquish all title to the battery, and extend our offer to help you research its construction at any time in which you might need our services."

"That's a battery?" I asked. Cadwallader stood behind the Russian, watching me instead of the tiny moon.

"A fusion battery, College Boy. One half of a pair. Help me, here." Billy Dean pulled his cigarette lighter out and handed it to me. Along with the motion, he leaned forward and whispered. "If any hero jumps out and tries to grab this, you'd better hold on." With his good hand, he gestured for me to pull the roller and wick out, as if he wanted to refuel it.

I took a step back. "Billy Dean, that's just glass. If that's really a fusion reaction going on in there, we'll all die of radiation." The nearby travelers flinched.

"Stay where you are, folks," Billy Dean commanded. "Never you fear, my educated friend. Ain't no radiation coming out of this thing."

Barsukov agreed, and lectured to the crowd. "Ladies and gentlemen, the energy bud is almost entirely inert, until a magnetized wire is wrapped around it. Were it otherwise, I would be dead after carrying it so far."

The lighter finally popped open, and I held its inner mechanism up. This was no ordinary lighter. Along with the fuel tube, it contained an even smaller glass case that held a second greenish disc, identical to the Russian's.

"Goddam it, Billy Dean." Tudberry slapped his thigh. "You had the damn thing with you. They coulda corralled you anytime."

The weatherman's look curtailed any laughter. "Open it," he ordered.

I pulled the lighter case from its housing and held it out. Struggling with his injured hand, Billy Dean popped one end off of Barsukov's glass case, pried out that little moon with a nail clipper, then shoved the bud into the opening of his lighter's case. It dropped into a tiny slot that had obviously been made for it, reunited with the one Billy Dean had carried all this time. The two discs, close together, resembled a glowing sign for infinity. Billy Dean snapped the lighter back together, and the Mexicans cheered.

A voice rose, and the celebration stopped. The GI was hanging out of the car, standing half on the ground, half in the car seat. His pistol was drawn, pointed right at Billy Dean.

"For Christ's sake, General," the soldier yelled, face red. "You've got him now. I say we shoot him."

Raven tensed. The Russians tensed, but Billy Dean looked skyward, and snapped his fingers.

The cloud above us immediately spouted lightning. A flurry of bolts slammed the ground all around us. I pulled Marilyn down, covering her. The refugees of Landview cowered, too. The Russians were on their knees. Only Cadwallader remained upright, leaning up against Raven's car.

The general recovered his feet, and the crowd and I looked at the driver at the same moment. He was slumped unnaturally back over his seat, smoke rising from a gash in his belly. All around us, in a jagged circle, plumes of smoke rose from where the electric charges had hit the wet grass.

Raven licked his lips. "Let him go," he said.

The exodus line re-formed, and moved again. Billy Dean dropped the precious Aachen lighter back into his pocket, and I moved closer to him.

"That's all this was about?" I asked. "No suitcase bomb? What can you do with a battery that small?"

"My Nazi colonel told me what a guy could do with it. As long as I have some wire, or organic matter that conducts, this battery can give me power for almost anything. Lots of it. Pretty handy for a guy who's going exploring through Time." My stomach fell away. Even with the prize in his hands, he was sticking with his ridiculous story. Marilyn gazed at the ground.

I whispered to her. "Don't you move."

Then to Billy Dean: "But you're not telling me anything. The Thors —how did you get to know them? It couldn't have been that colonel, could it? Rebecca?"

"You're gettin' warmer, Sport. A nice man who is very close to Miss Flock-of-Birds taught me that there are other worlds. How the hell else did I get the crazy idea to go travelin'?"

"What man?"

"Aw, quit actin' so dense, College Boy. You've met the bastard."

"Do you mean Victor?"

He smiled, but voices called from the depot platform, yells in Spanish and English, fingers pointing. I looked up to see a phalanx of army vehicles approaching on the road from the west.

Billy Dean gestured. "Hurry it up." A gust of wind seemed to answer him, and he extended a hand to Cadwallader. Shakily, the old man took it. "You gents better stay up here," Billy Dean said. "I don't want to bring unexpected passengers, like last time."

Ashen-faced, Marilyn took a step, but I pulled her close. Billy Dean took her other hand at the same time. "Let go, Hot Shot. I've taken a shine to you, but you're gonna be in a world of hurt if you insist on being stubborn."

This time, he wasn't ready. I hopped sideways, and put a fist into his forehead. He went down like a sack of potatoes, bounced back onto his feet in spite of his injured arm, but I was laying for him, and sent him back to the ground with a right to the belly. Then an explosion threw me skidding across the grass. My face dug into the mud, and I thought he had hit me with lightning until I looked up to see Guillermo pinning me down.

"Mr. Gringo College Scientist, don't you know anything?" he asked. "To go back through Time, the Thors require you have the same number of bodies as you did when you went forward."

Raven bellered into a radio. Someone argued with him. Tudberry un-holstered his silver forty-five, and the big Mexican let me up and rushed over to tend to Billy Dean. Pandemonium was breaking out because the jeeps were forming a large semi-circle in the field below.

"It's not Geary, is it?" I cried. "He has to be dead."

"Somebody in Washington's getting' cold feet," Tudberry answered. Raven was still cursing.

"I said to stand down, dammit," he screamed into the radio.

I put my arms around Marilyn. "We should surrender, Darling," I said, but she slipped from my grasp and stumbled full-force into Cadwallader. He reached for her hand and planted a hard kiss on her fingers. The act consumed him totally, and when it was over, the old man broke down in tears, and fell back against the car.

When I recovered her I saw that she, too, was weeping. Billy Dean approached, and I took another stance.

"Goddam it, Hot Shot."

"Don't," she said, hugging me fiercely. "Just come get me, Prince Charming. Go back to the Thors – they'll know how to find me."

Billy Dean shoved a finger into my forehead. "After I run my errands, remind me to come back here and kick your ass."

Guillermo herded the stragglers. "Patron, we're out of time."

Billy Dean glanced at the sky, then grabbed my collar. "Which reminds me," he said. "I dropped my Thor's blood when he shot me. Can you spare some?"

I rummaged in my bag and extracted a meager handful of the clay residue. I still had Marilyn's sleeve.

"You're not going anywhere, Billy Dean. There's no fucking train track, and those army guys are setting up to attack. What about Mr. Cadwallader's mother? Did she die in the shelling?"

The weatherman's eyebrows went up and we both glanced toward the old tycoon at the same time. He sat slumped on the fender of the car they had come in, looking a hundred years old. "You're stalling, Hot Shot. You've known Mr. Cadwallader's mom for a while, now." He laughed like it was the funniest joke in the world.

"You're full of --" I ran out of steam.

Marilyn colored and pulled my face close to hers. "Emil was born in eighteen ninety-six, George. That's why I have to go back. I've got less than nine months. You know what you've done to me."

"That's what this whole thing's about? You – you and he are the time loop? I don't believe it. Marilyn, stop this insanity. I love you."

She let me kiss her, then pulled away. "I'll try to wait for you, but you must hurry."

The world turned fuzzy. I felt her fingers drop, and my eyes filled with the bright Mexican colors of the costumes amassed on the depot platform. Billy Dean led her, and halfway down, he turned, looking snide. "You don't fool me, Hot Shot. You've already figured out that that old man over there is your first-born son." A wave. "Go console him. State lost to SMU yesterday. Good-bye number one ranking. Hell, maybe he'll even let you change his diaper."

A cavernous laugh. Guillermo helped the pair of them up the depot steps, and I could neither move nor argue with him, because I was paralyzed. My body was on autopilot, and I had to look at Cadwallader, as if he might confirm it was all insanity – but he only stared at the ground, tears streaming down his face.

Raven's voice broke the spell. "They're setting up mortars," he yelled. The infantry men were down, prone in the grass, their guns pointed up the hill at us and the depot. A lead vehicle gunned its engine and rushed pell-mell toward us. Tudberry stepped out into the middle of the road and fired his pistol gun as a warning.

"Stop there," he cried. As the jeep halted, a light mist started falling. I looked up. No more blue sky.

My gun was in my hand, too, but the soldiers fired two warning shots above the heads of the townspeople, hitting one window of the depot and splintering glass over the crowd. Screams, cries, and the citizens collapsed as a group, just as a bolt of lightning crossed the sky. Ninepins collapsed. A soldier below yelled something, then another volley, and then I saw Billy Dean stand up on the depot's wide lip, bring out his good hand, and heave a quartz rod into the air. In the next instant, the rain became a tropical downpour.

Chapter 48
Passenger Train

I knew this was it – surely the next volley from below would massacre the townspeople. Bodies moved quickly, and the marshal waved from the road. "George, take cover. There's too many for us to fight with these little popguns. Help me get your son into the hotel."

More yelling from below, and the dismayed Russians started down the hill in the downpour, hands raised in surrender. I trotted toward the man I had trusted in error all these years. "She's not – Marilyn can't be his mother. She's not pregnant, Rebecca's the one who's pregnant," I said.

"I know, son. You've been fornicating like a spring ram. Suck it up." Water poured off the brim of his Stetson. He waved his gun at Raven. "Dammit, General. Won't those boys down there do what you tell 'em?"

Raven's harsh, pinched face wore a look of total helplessness. "They're fighting for the American army now, Dumb Ass," he answered.

Another cry, and a bullet whizzed over our heads. Automatic fire started, splintering wood and glass all around us. Tudberry lowered his weapon, and grappled Cadwallader, pushing him toward the hotel. A couple of the soldiers crouched, advancing up the rise, but I had the drop on them, and fired my own shot over their heads.

"Throw those guns down, or I blow your brains out," I yelled. Then, over my shoulder -- "Billy Dean, what the hell are you gonna do?"

A string of bullets kicked up grass and mud at my feet. They had a bead on me, and rather than shoot the two soldiers in cold blood, I ran toward the depot, slipped and fell in the water-laden grass. I fired again – those two boys were picking up their weapons, but they dropped them again. It didn't matter. I was exposed, my only cover the sheer intensity of the rain. I glanced up to see the weatherman open his multi-colored purse and toss red pieces into the air. Sparks flew.

An officer below was hollering at us. "Cease and desist. Everyone put your hands up." Someone handed him a bullhorn. "Billy Dean Brown, surrender or die."

Billy Dean shrugged, laughed and answered, but his words were drowned by the raging torrents of rain and unceasing growling of the thunder. The townspeople huddled in clumps on the platform. Too many troops lay down there, and they wouldn't wait any longer -- When the order to fire was given, none of us stood a chance.

Then I heard it. From nowhere, from everywhere, a freight train was coming into the station. Even though I knew better, I looked to see if there really was a train track – and I swear I heard the engine's bell – the depot was surrounded only by lush grass. I rose slowly, dropping my pistol in the same instant the troops below began standing up, too, abandoning their own weapons. One started running, and their line broke. Now it was a mob, hustling toward the vehicles they had parked down in the trees. Then screams. A tightly wound tornado descended right behind them and began skimming the tops of the grass, sucking up their dropped rifles like a vacuum cleaner.

The funnel cloud's snout drifted down the hill first, flushing out any soldiers too scared or dumb to move. A single GI pointed his weapon at the swirl. Before he could fire, the rifle leaped from his hands and into the cyclone's point.

The massive whorl drowned troops' screams with its own howling. It turned toward the depot, blasting like a locomotive, and its wind knocked me down and pinned me in the wet grass. I squinted up into the torrent, and thought I saw the sun rising inside. The funnel's mouth gaped wider, and settled down over the depot's loading dock for but a second, then it lifted off and its circular cone opening closed again. Then, bucking and humping like Cadwallader's bullwhip, the whirlwind shrank in diameter, and retreated into the black-green thickness up in the sky, leaving the depot platform empty, pristine, except for sparkles of splintered glass.

Chapter 49
Gray Walls

I spent four months in a maximum security holding cell in Huntsville awaiting trial. Once in a while a merciful guard dispensed bits of news from the outside. The government had apparently been successful in keeping the whole revolution hushed up. To the public, brave President Kennedy had faced down that scoundrel, Khruschev. No admission that they had both cowered before the likes of a scrawny pool shark from Sironia, Texas. I thought back to what everyone said about television when it first came in: its roving, all-seeing eye was immune to deception; it would always reveal the truth. What a crock.

One morning, they took me into a stark room and chained me to a table. Word was that Marshal Tudberry's wounds were bad, requiring a long, tough convalescence. I expected him to drag in, full of apologies and a fatherly speech about how someone had to take the fall. Instead, the lanky form of Emil Cadwallader filled the door, followed by a buzz-saw: Andrea.

"Oh, George, you poor dear. Have you lost weight?" She hugged me. I couldn't return the favor, because the chains let my hands rise only so high. "Good lawdy, if you don't look better with a few pounds off. Doesn't he look good, Emil?" They took chairs on the other side.

"Hi, George." Cadwallader sat straight as a board. "Do they treat you right? If there's any brutality, I still know people --"

"I'm fine, sir." Strangely, after weeks in solitary, one might expect I would have been hungry for human companionship. As it was, I felt nothing for either of them. Even so, I found myself staring, watching every little movement, every grimace or gesture my son made.

"George, you would be proud of Emil. Oh, first, let me show you." Out came her hand and the reason for her bubbly excitement: a diamond ring the size of Oklahoma.

"When's the big day?" I asked.

"As soon as Emil's divorce is final. That'll be what, Dear? May? June?"

"I don't know." He spoke quietly, his eyes distant.

"Well, whenever it is, you're invited, George. You can even be an usher, if you want. As I was saying, Emil is sparing no expense on lawyers. We have the best in Texas, even a couple of New Yorkers on the team. They'll git you out of here in no time."

I looked away, a tactic that didn't usually shut her up, but this time it worked. "I appreciate it, Mr. Cadwallader, but why can't they get me out on bail now? Are there charges against me that I don't know about?"

Andrea turned on him. "Yes, Dear, are there?"

Cadwallader cleared his throat. "The charge is sedition, George. Aiding a group in trying to overthrow the government or secede, or both. Certain legalities about sedition make it easier to hold a prisoner without bail. The FBI is still fighting with the military over jurisdiction.

"I've been spreading money around, but the upshot is this: the feds will take their sweet time making sure that everybody who was involved will keep his mouth shut."

I didn't have to ask how he was still free. He had more money and connections than God and, given the circumstances, there was no reason he should ever tell anyone what really happened.

Andrea watched him like a supplicant watches the Pope. "See there, George? They'll get around to you pretty soon. And you won't tell. I, personally, assured the FBI you're the type who can keep a secret."

"Thanks."

A knock on the door brought them automatically to their feet. Andrea sighed. "They wouldn't let me bring a cake, George, but I will next time, even if Emil has to bribe somebody." She kissed my forehead. "Have faith, George. Go to chapel on Sundays. They do have chapel, don't they, Emil?"

Cadwallader shrugged. "I need to talk to him privately for a moment," he said.

Her eyes flared, and she pointed. "Now be nice, George. I don't want you boys comparing any love secrets."

"Of course, not, Dear." Cadwallader replied for me. When the door closed behind her, he leaned against the wall. "You know now why I took her away from you, George, don't you? I had to free you up to go after Marilyn. Not just for me. Surely you understand that. All those army scientists were claiming it would play hell with the cosmos if we didn't get you together with both women."

Long, silent seconds, and I didn't know what to say. Other than the obvious, logical thing. "Why didn't you just pay me to have sex with them?"

He grimaced and nodded toward the door, where Andrea's voice seeped through, scolding some guard for something or other. "You think that woman out there would have let that happen?" Then a deep breath, fingering his Stetson. "Besides, you're not that sort of man, George. It had to happen just the way they told me in childhood, or else Time would have come unraveled. I guess."

"So you were raised by Marilyn and Rebecca? And Rebecca had a child, too?"

"A boy. Name's Victor. Like a twin to me." The old, sad eyes bore into me. "As for who raised me, go talk to Anna. She'll explain it."

"Anna? Your wife?"

"For a couple more months." He sighed, and the sight of that long face would have inspired pity in most humans, but I felt only anger.

I pounded the table. "This whole thing defies science. I don't believe any of it. I can't, Mr. Cadwallader."

"Please don't call me that."

All that time in solitary, I had trained myself to stay calm, but I couldn't help thrashing. The chains were too strong to break, though. "There has to be another explanation. Some goddam logical explanation for all this."

He took a deep, wheezing breath, and closed his eyes. "You performed remarkably, George. I admire you. Just wanted you to know. I wish I could have grown up more like my father."

"That's enough," I said. I couldn't stomach that raspy old voice another moment. And the tears in those gray eyes – I couldn't watch them start falling. I put my forehead on the desk, and stared at the floor.

I heard him pause in the doorway. "Goodbye, Dad."

Chapter 50
Powers That Be

When you sit for long months in solitary, you invent imaginary friends to talk to. Billy Dean became my invisible foil, and I spent the nights lying on hard cement, lecturing him on all the things he could have done differently.

But he never answered, until a booming started in the sky late one afternoon, and the hints of a great lightning show flashed through the high barred window at the top of the wall. I remembered the Thors, and prayed that Billy Dean was finally taking pity on me, returning to escort me to my beloved Marilyn.

Even with that fantasy in my head, I couldn't believe it when the building shook like an earthquake, heavy debris clattered on the wall outside, then the roar of a freight train drove me down into the corner of my cell,

I embraced the toilet, in hopes that the plumbing would anchor me, but when I glanced up, the roof flew off, leaving me staring at a small tornado – the kind Billy Dean used to call a "tropical cell."My gripped loosened, and the sucking finger of roaring cloud pulled me right out of that dungeon, and in the next instant, I was wiping rain out of my eyes, glimpsing down at East Texas pines a mile below me,

until the raging wind grew gentle, and set me politely down
into rain-swollen grass a few miles away.

An old gray Packard waited at the edge of that
hayfield. Marshal Tudberry stood beside it in the downpour,
protecting his cigarette under the bill of his Stetson. He smiled
when I crossed the soggy field, then he opened the vehicle's
back door and gave me a change of clothes and a new identity.

"George," he said, "not everyone in the government
would say this, because not everyone knows. What you did
for this country and the world is beyond estimation."

"You move to Lake Texoma, yet?"

A sheepish smile. "Hell, if I didn't. They gave me a
two-story house. Want you to come fishin' with me sometime.
But we gotta be careful. Give Stubbins a call before you show
up. He'll know whether the coast is clear."

He had lost weight. Too much weight, maybe. "So
what am I supposed to do with this new name?"

"Do?" He chuckled and turned onto the new interstate.
"I won't pretend to tell this new man, Ken Marable, what to
do, 'cause he's bound to be as stubborn as George Blair ever
was. Keep your head down. Get yourself a wife. Have some
kids. I hear Santa Fe is nice. Somewhere out of the way."

"So I'll be on the run forever? Why me?"

A shrug. "Well, they can't find Billy Dean, so they've
given up on him. Damned if someone in the bowels of the
Justice Department didn't come up with the notion that you
helped plan the whole thing. They're desperate, Geor – I
mean, Ken."

He took a thoughtful drag, and blew the smoke out
into the drizzle. "So, sure, there's always a chance some hot
young G-man will try to track you down, but I think the U.S.
Marshal's office will stick to the playbook and head them off.
You'd better pray that enough insiders put off retirement to
keep you protected for a while. If anyone ever hauls you in,

even on a busted headlight charge, tell the officer, 'Code black-and-blue.' Remember that."

He took me to a car lot in Bryan. The salesman walked over and gave me the pink slip, filled out with my new name. "There'll be a small pension, too," Tudberry said. "Call the number on that card if you have to, and always give the code."

I leaned into the old Packard's window before I took my leave. "I've been wondering. How did Billy Dean get hooked up with Victor in the first place? He beat him in a game of billiards?"

The marshal chuckled. "Hell, no, George – damn. I gotta remember – Kenneth. Victor sought him out before the war, gave him his marching orders. Hell, somebody had to set all this right."

When Anna Cadwallader invited me into her city mansion, I marveled that I had finally found someone who could look more pensive than Marilyn.

"So you're the man all this fuss was about?" she asked as she served me tea.

"Yes, ma'am. Your – uh, Mr. Cadwallader said you could tell me who it was that raised him. You know, during his childhood."

"Well, it wasn't his father, now, was it?"

That was a challenge, her eyes suddenly unwelcoming. I had come through hell, but this classic lady had obviously been around the block, too. I decided I was no match for her, and kept my mouth shut.

We sat for a while, sipping tea, listening to a late spring fire crackle in the fireplace. At last, she rose, and was gone, then returned with a picture in a frame. The center of the photograph contained the vision of a strapping lad, shirtless, smiling. Ten years old, maybe twelve, in a haze of beige tintype. Emil Cadwallader as a handsome young boy. Behind him stood a vision of loveliness, angular jaws, smooth, broad Indian face. A mature Rebecca Flock-of-Birds.

For long seconds, I couldn't take my eyes off of her. I had forgotten how utterly beautiful she was. Then, frustration, for the other woman in the picture stood on the right side, back to the camera, her face hidden. If all of this bizarre insanity were really true, if that were she standing almost in front of the young Emil Cadwallader, then Marilyn had grown her hair longer after she left me, and let it go brown again. Perhaps hair dye was inferior back in the Nineties, enough so that she just gave up.

I looked closer. The woman's waist-long hair could not conceal the curves of her hips.

This wasn't Marilyn. But I knew who it was.

Finally, I knew what to do.

By the time I found Landview again, the last hotel had been demolished, Rebecca's tree cut down. The smooth dirt that used to host market tables under a roof that looked like an ocean was being reclaimed by grass. Only the deserted depot remained, and vandals had had their way with it. In the dry creek beds, though, I found the quartz as plentiful as ever.

I kept my distance from Emil Cadwallader until it was too late. A year passed before I finally swallowed my pride, and worked up the gumption to go and see my son. I pulled into the Channel Three parking lot at the same moment an ambulance did. Emil Cadwallader lay in his office on the flowery couch Andrea had picked out, dead of a heart attack.

I stood in the lobby, watching emergency attendants come and go, nodding to cops who covered the scene. I thought I recognized a couple of them, but no one gave me a second look. The newsroom had undergone one hundred percent turnover, so none of the reporters knew me, either. I thought I saw Paco's face in the window of the studio door, but couldn't be sure.

Sharon sat in her chair, face pale, officiating the sad hour. Of everyone, she was the most loyal. She had seen it all.

"You doing all right?" I asked. "I mean, until now?"

"Yeah," she said, and brushed her brown, highlighted hair out of her face. "He went peacefully. I'm sorry you weren't here a little earlier. He always had kind words about you."

"Story of my life." There was little else to say. I wanted to thank her, tell her about my year of self-doubt, stall until I had the nerve to ask her the question. It froze in my throat, but she looked steadily at me, and answered it on her own.

"Maybe you'd better go, George," she said. That sounded weird, because by then I was used to my new name. "I called Mrs. Cadwallader – uh, Andrea – when it happened. She'll be here any minute." My ex-girl finally had her fortune.

"Of course." I opened the glass door, and paused for one more moment, drinking in the curves of her young body.

"I loved him, George. When he first hired me, I guess I had fantasies about marrying him, taking his money, and waiting until he died. But that was before I got to know him – he wasn't what you might think --" She laid her hands on her ink-blotched desk calendar, eyes swollen and dreamy.

"That Andrea never saw through the money." She sighed. "He was so cute, like a busy little church mouse, but older. After my boyfriend and I broke up, all my affection just transferred to him. He was stronger and smarter than any other man I ever met. But helpless, too. He never made me feel like just an assistant. Sometimes, I wanted to be his mother."

"Sharon?"

"Yes?"

"You're going to think I'm weird, but I want you to get in my car. Now. It's not too late to have your wish."

And so I took Sharon to West Texas, and rented a ranch house with a trapdoor in the roof. We lived there until I collected enough Thor's blood. I learned how to bare my soul to those great beings, and how to enlist their aid in finding my lost love. Then I took Sharon back in Time, to 1897, and left her there to help raise my two sons from different mothers in Juarez, Mexico. She liked Victor a lot, but she and Emil were inseparable. When I again asked Marilyn to become my wife, Rebecca gave her blessing.

The winds returned my bride and me to nineteen sixty-four. The "grandfathers" let me bring Marilyn back, because I traded Sharon for her – the laws of space and time allow such a trade, though I had to discover that for myself. God knows Billy Dean never told me. I guess I just did what he would have done: played a hunch. All I had to go on was Anna's photo of Sharon with the ten-year-old Emil Cadwallader.

But it worked.

The love of my life has been living with me in the present ever since. We visit Victor in El Paso every Christmas. The true architect of the rebellion is ancient now. He laughs when I call him "Mr. Big." I learn a great deal from him. Everyone does.

Life with Marilyn is often sublime. It's true, that demon that I awoke in her does surface occasionally. Unlike Andrea, however, Marilyn never sleeps with plumbers or postmen or policemen. But I built a house near Santa Fe, and sometimes in the middle of the night, I will pretend I'm asleep, and watch her climb out of bed, pull on her jeans or a denim dress, and I listen to the freight train sound come roaring out of the sky above, and the wind chimes go into conniptions, and she climbs the ladder to the trapdoor I installed in the roof.

Sometimes, she is home by dawn, sometimes it might be a week or more before I see her pretty face again.

Somehow, her journeys have kept her young, even while I grow old. But I forgive her, because she always comes back with that guilty puppy look in her eyes, as well as a breathtaking, fresh sparkle that tells me she newly appreciates her love for me. Yes, I believe it that. I was her first lover, wasn't I? Wherever he is, I'm sure Billy Dean looks down on me occasionally and laughs his ass off.

And, no, I have yet to discover how Billy Dean actually discovered the art of traveling in tornados through time. He once called himself Prometheus – so sometimes I wonder if he wasn't, indeed, sent here by the gods. Or maybe he learned it the way I did. On trips through the clouds, after I had collected Thors blood from the great beasts a few times, I simply asked them to take me back to the eighteen nineties. The heart of a tornado is a portal of sorts, and to those massive, graceful creatures, Time is just another ocean to sail.

So my scientific mind can't really prove that Billy Dean came from the gods. He was probably just a yokel, like most of us, who stumbled into the right person, the right thing, at the right time – yet he was smart enough to recognize an opportunity when it stared him in the face, and take it. He met that German officer, then he met Victor after the war, or before the war – it all runs together in my head, and my second son only laughs when I quiz him about it. The finer aspects of a time loop will drive you crazy if you think about it too much.

I know it sounds fantastical – but that is the true story of what really transpired in those frightening October days a half-century ago. Kennedy and Khruschev played their parts flawlessly – maybe that's what we elect our presidents and premiers to do, anyway – to act. Like I did in school. Hell, if I had listened closer to Tudberry back then, maybe I could have wound up as president, myself.

Perhaps the day will finally come when governments let their subjects in on the secrets of the Universe, but I won't live to see it. I am one of the few players left who witnessed the Balcones revolution, and the frantic actions that patched up a potential hole in space and time that would have ended whatever it is that God has wrought.

Sometimes I catch a whiff of a G-man on my trail – but their little campaigns to recapture me and my secrets seem half-hearted.

Marilyn's travels have kept her as beautiful as the day I met her. But she always returns to me, and when she does, she is mine. For a while.

The mountains above Santa Fe are beautiful, too. There aren't as many storms here as in Sironia. Just enough to take an occasional trip on a booming cloud ship through electric skies, where ninepins are the game of choice.

The End

About the Author...

Bull Marquette is the penname for a Texas native who published his first novel, THE FIFTH PLANE, with Brave New Genre Books in 2008. This was followed in 2009 by his collection of short stories, GOT 8 IF YOU WANT 'EM.

Bull began his writing career as an ad and book jacket writer for Word Books, a religious book publisher, where he was privileged to interview notables like Jeb Magruder – refugee from President Nixon's Watergate scandal, and 1960s hoodlum-turned-civil rights activist Eldridge Cleaver, as well as authors who had come back from the dead.

He worked as an ad agency copywriter, convenience store clerk, high school teacher, construction worker, TV weatherman, radio announcer, apprentice cook under a world-class chef, waiter, bread delivery man, speech writer for a state legislator, branch manager for a national stock brokerage firm and financial advisor. Bull moved to California in 1982 to study parapsychology in the unique masters program at JFK University.

Bull was business editor and columnist for the FRESNO WEEKLY newspaper, and he co-hosted the nationally syndicated WEBMASTER RADIO SHOW, an interview show that featured the giants of the high tech world during the climax of the Dot-Com bubble, from February 2000 to November 2001. He is currently a financial advisor, a columnist for THE FRESNO BEE, and a sometimes announcer for KVPR – national public radio in Fresno.

A paranormal and "alternate history" buff, Bull is working on more short stories and novels, as well as a non-fiction work on the Unified Field Theory.